CARRYING THE GREEK TYCOON'S BABY

JENNIFER FAYE

TEXAN SEEKS FORTUNE

MARIE FERRARELLA

MILLS & BOON

First Published in Great Britain 2019
by Mills & Boon, an imprint of HarperCollinsPublishers,
1 London Bridge Street, London, SE1 9GF

Carrying The Greek Tycoon's Baby © 2019 Jennifer F. Stroka
Texan Seeks Fortune © 2019 Harlequin Books S.A.

Special thanks and acknowledgement are given to Marie Ferrarella for her contribution to the Fortunes of Texas: The Lost Fortunes series.

ISBN: 978-0-263-27219-2

0319

MIX
Paper from
responsible sources
FSC™ C007454

This book is produced from independently certified FSC™ paper to ensure responsible forest management.

For more information visit: www.harpercollins.co.uk/green

Printed and bound in Spain
by CPI, Barcelona

Award-winning author Marie Ferrarella writes fun, heart-warming, contemporary romances, filled with rugged cowboys, sexy billionaires and enchanting royalty. Internationally published, with books translated into nine languages, she is a multiple winner of the *RT Book Reviews* Reviewers' Choice Award. She has also won the CataRomance Reviewers' Choice Award, been named a TOP PICK author, and has been nominated for numerous other awards.

USA TODAY bestselling and RITA® Award-winning author **Marie Ferrarella** has written more than two hundred and fifty books for Mills & Boon, some under the name Marie Nicole. Her romances are beloved by fans worldwide. Visit her website, marieferrarella.com.

Also by Jennifer Faye

Heiress's Royal Baby Bombshell

Once Upon a Fairytale miniseries
Beauty and Her Boss
Miss White and the Seventh Heir

Also by Marie Ferrarella

The Cowboy's Lesson in Love
Diamond in the Ruff
Her Red-Carpet Romance
Coming Home for Christmas
Dr. Forget-Me-Not
Twice a Hero, Always Her Man
Meant to Be Mine
A Second Chance for the Single Dad
Christmastime Courtship
Engagement for Two
Adding Up to Family
Fortune's Second-Chance Cowboy
The Maverick's Return
The Fortune Most Likely To...

Discover more at millsandboon.co.uk

CARRYING
THE GREEK TYCOON'S
BABY

JENNIFER FAYE

PROLOGUE

March, Infinity Island, Greece

THINGS WOULD GET better.

They had to.

Lea Romes refused to accept any other alternative.

She pushed her chair back from the desk with its insurmountable pile of paperwork. In this modern age of technology, she thought paperwork would be a thing of the past. But alas, it seemed as though dealing with written documents would be a constant while the digital correspondence and spreadsheets just added to the burden.

At least she got to work in paradise as a wedding planner. She picked up her oversized coffee mug and moved to the French doors overlooking the private cove. She stepped out onto the spacious balcony, letting the vibrant sun warm her face. Since she'd inherited the island some thirteen months ago, her life had changed dramatically.

Her move from Seattle, Washington, to Greece had happened not in a matter of months or even weeks but days. Of course, it hadn't helped that she'd learned she had extended family in Greece from an attorney instead of her own parents—parents who had deprived her of that part of her life. It was a betrayal she'd never seen coming. She'd felt utterly blindsided and hurt beyond belief.

With nothing more than two suitcases and a disillusioned view of life, she'd set out on her journey to Greece. She hadn't known what to expect when she arrived on this small, lush Greek island. The attorney had informed her that Infinity Island had been in the family for generations. It wasn't until she browsed through all of the photos in the family home that she realized her own mother had been born and raised on this very island. It was like an arrow to the heart. How could her mother have kept this place and her family from her?

Lea hadn't spoken to her parents since their heated argument right before she left Seattle. But it wasn't like they'd reached out to her, either. Her parents were stubborn and so certain they'd done the right thing by omitting certain details of Lea's life. But right now Lea had bigger problems, starting with the fact that this wedding/honeymoon destination spot was in deep financial trouble—

Knock. Knock.

Lea stepped back inside the office. "Come in."

Popi Costas, her best friend and the other wedding planner on the island, stuck her head inside the office. Her dark brown ponytail swung over her shoulder. "Your guest has arrived."

"Already?" That couldn't be right. He wasn't due to arrive for another hour. Her gaze sought out the little smiling emoji clock on her desk. It was in fact 10 a.m. Not 9 a.m. Time had gotten away from her.

She'd wanted to touch up her makeup and hair before greeting this man—this very important man. She'd seen his photos on the internet. He was strikingly handsome in that tall, dark and mysterious sort of way. But she assured herself that wanting to fix herself up and put on a good—no, a great—first impression had more to do with business than anything else. He might just be the person to change everything for her and this island.

"Quit frowning," Popi said. They'd become fast friends when Lea had arrived on the island. It helped that they were of similar age and Popi was easy to be around. She could make Lea smile, even when she didn't want to. "You look amazing. As always." Popi gestured with her hand. "Come on. You don't want to keep him waiting."

She was right. The last thing Lea wanted to do was

give this man a bad impression right from the start. She dashed out the door, wishing she'd taken more time that morning in front of the mirror. She sighed. There wasn't time to do anything about it now.

Outside, the sun was shining brightly in the clear blue sky. One thing about living on a Greek island versus Seattle was there was sunshine almost every day of the year. And Lea loved it. Arriving on Infinity Island had felt, strangely enough, like coming home.

She climbed on the golf cart that she used to get around the small island. They had a whole fleet of golf carts for their guests as well as paved paths. She quickly maneuvered her way down to the marina. Most of their guests arrived from the mainland via a ferry or flew in via a chartered seaplane. In rare cases, a helicopter was used—but generally that was saved for emergencies or the occasional guest who could afford such extravagances.

When she'd first arrived on the island, she'd spent all her spare moments of that first month venturing down every meandering path littered with wild flowers and blazing some paths of her own. She'd met every human and every goat, of which there were many, that resided on the island. Most people there worked for the wedding business in one manner or another. They were like one big family and they'd welcomed her with open arms. Lea couldn't imagine a friendlier place.

Just then she noticed a seaplane preparing to take off over the calm blue sea. But it was the man in the dark suit standing on the wooden dock, with his back to her, that caught her attention. She took in his immense height and broad, muscled shoulders accentuated by his suit jacket— a very fine set of threads. It probably cost more than she made in a month. Definitely.

His dark hair was trimmed in a short neat cut just like in his online photos. Not a strand was out of place. She wondered if he liked his life to be just as neat and orderly. As she continued to stare, she imagined what it'd be like to comb her fingertips through his hair. Her fingers tingled with temptation. She tightened her hold on the steering wheel.

Lea tramped the brakes, causing the cart to skid to a halt. She quickly alighted and moved across the dock toward the man. His attire continued to draw her curiosity. Did he not realize he was coming to an island? Around here swim trunks were more common than a suit jacket. When the man turned to her, she realized he was also wearing a tie. She inwardly groaned. If he was as uptight as his appearance, she was in big trouble.

As the departing plane flew overhead, she leveled her shoulders and stepped forward. She held out her hand. "Hello. I'm Lea Romes."

The man's dark brows rose in surprise. "You are in charge?"

When she nodded, he took her hand in his. His grip was firm. She could tell just from his touch that he was quite strong. So, there was more to this man than just a designer suit.

Her gaze rose to his clean-shaven jaw and his mouth that was pressed into a firm line, not giving away what he was thinking. She'd caught him off guard at first but he seemed to have regained his composure.

When her gaze met his, she couldn't read anything in his dark eyes. So she decided to smile, hoping to lighten the mood. "Welcome to Infinity Island."

"Do you have many guests?" He withdrew his hand and glanced around at the quiet morning.

So much for the pleasantries.

She schooled her expression so as not to frown at his obvious lack of social niceties. "Not at the moment. We're expecting guests to begin arriving tomorrow for an upcoming wedding."

"So right now, the island is deserted, other than staff?"

She shook her head. "Not exactly. We have some honeymooners as well as some couples who have returned for a renewal of their vows and a second honeymoon."

He frowned. Apparently that was the wrong answer.

"If you'd like to come this way—" she gestured toward the golf cart "—I can give you the grand tour."

"Is there much to see?"

Was he being serious? Or was he being sarcastic? It was impossible for her to tell as neither his tone nor his expression changed much. His gaze continued to scan the area. And so she did the same, trying to see Infinity through his eyes. There was lots of green foliage interspersed with red, yellow, pink, purple and blue blooms. Wild orchids grew everywhere. A few of the buildings overlooked the cove. Her office happened to be one of them. And then she realized the problem.

She swallowed hard and turned to him. "You can't see much of the resort from here as the island has been strategically planned. The buildings have been placed in various locations over the island instead of concentrated in one spot." She should have grabbed a map of the island for him. It was something that was distributed to all the guests with their welcome basket. "Trust me. There's a lot to the island including acres of vegetable gardens. We grow most of our own food."

His gaze met hers, but she couldn't read his thoughts. "Let's proceed."

He bent over and it was only then that she noticed he had an overnight bag. She hadn't expected him to want to stay. Most business people who had flown in to meet with her had also flown out the same day. This was a situation that she hadn't quite anticipated.

She stepped forward and held out her hand to take his bag, but he resisted. She didn't know if he was being gentlemanly or if he was afraid that she might drop it. *Whatever.*

Once he placed the bag in the back of the cart, he joined

her up front. His bicep brushed against her shoulder. It was as though static electricity flowed through her body. And suddenly the cart felt as though it had shrunk to half its size. Her mouth grew dry as her palms grew damp.

She refused to turn to him. Their faces would be far too close together. And there was something about his mouth that made her wonder if he had to be in control even when he was kissing someone. And then realizing how out of hand her thoughts had gotten, she gave herself a mental shake as she started the engine and then pressed on the accelerator.

She had to keep it together. She had to be a professional instead of letting the lack of a love life get the best of her. After all, the future of Infinity Island rested on her making this deal. And so they set off.

It was late afternoon by the time she'd given him the full tour. He was the first potential investor who had stuck around this long. Lea's hopes soared. He had many questions about the island and she did her best to answer them. She was proud of her little island. As she'd spoken of the various aspects of the island, Mr. Marinakos made notes on his digital tablet.

This is going to work. This is going to work.

She struggled not to grin. After all, nothing was final yet—

"Miss Romes, I'd like to make you an offer."

Yes! Yes! Yes!

She stifled the giddy happiness bubbling up inside her. She had to maintain her cool just a little longer. Later she could celebrate her success with Popi.

"Please call me Lea." When he sent her a puzzled look, she added, "If we're going to do business together, there's no need to stand on formality."

He hesitated. "Agreed. Call me Xander."

"Okay, Xander." She sent him her brightest smile. "What do you have in mind?"

And then he stated the most amazing number. She never ever imagined that anyone would want to invest such an incredible amount of money in the island. She wasn't even sure what to do with that much money. Sure the place needed work, but none that would amount to that sum.

"Thank you. That is a very generous investment—"

"Wait. I think you misunderstood me. I'm not investing in your island. I'm buying it."

He wanted to buy her island? Her heritage? Her heart sank clear down to her white sandals. This partnership was over before it even had a chance to begin.

Lea shook her head. This couldn't be happening. She'd only just found this link to her past, and she wasn't about to give it up. No way.

Xander Marinakos could feel this deal slipping through his fingers.

That was a very foreign position for him to be in.

The stubborn look on Lea's face said she wasn't giving up this island. And part of him applauded her while the rest of him thought it was a foolish endeavor. But he wasn't a man used to walking away empty-handed.

"If you're holding out for a better deal, you won't get one from me or anyone else. That's my one and only offer." He wasn't one to be trifled with—no matter how gorgeous he found this woman. Business was business.

"I'm afraid you came here under a false assumption. The island never was and never will be for sale."

His lips pressed into a firm line. He wondered if she even considered what she could do with the money he was offering her.

This island could be the jewel in his real estate empire. It was beautiful and so private. And yet, it wasn't that far off the mainland. Talk about a perfect location. He could build the most opulent estates that would sell for outrageous fortunes. He might even build a vacation home for himself. Not that he ever took vacations. But maybe someday he'd start.

"Is there anything I can say to change your mind?" If it was within reason, he'd consider it.

She didn't even hesitate when she gave another firm shake of her head. "This island has been in my family for generations and I intend to keep it that way."

He sighed. He was smart enough to know when to walk away. "Do me a favor?"

"What would that be?"

"If you ever change your mind about selling, let me know. This place would make a wonderful locale for exclusive estates."

She didn't look impressed. "It's already a noted wedding and honeymoon destination."

He didn't want to argue with her. He'd never heard of the island before it was brought to his attention as a potential building site, but then again, he avoided anything to do with happily-ever-afters. However, he refrained from mentioning it to Lea. He liked it better when she smiled. "So it is."

Though the grounds were well maintained, the place needed to be moved out of the last century and into the current one as far as technology and decorating went. He just didn't see anyone coming in here and wanting to invest in the place to develop it as a venue for weddings— not when there were so many other more lucrative uses for the island.

He stared into her blue-green eyes, seeing the depths of her desperation. But no one could truly help her until she realized that fixing this wedding island was a waste of money. And as a respectable businessman with his thumb on the heartbeat of development, he couldn't in good conscience throw good money after bad. It wasn't like love lasted. If it existed, it was fleeting at best.

"I suppose you won't be staying for the night." Lea's voice held a disappointed tone.

"Actually, you made the island sound so appealing that I'd like to stay for the night." He had made no plans for the evening or the next morning as he'd thought that he'd be hammering out a formative agreement.

"Not a problem at all." She turned from her position by the rail overlooking the cove, where the sun was starting its descent toward the horizon. "I can show you to your bungalow."

He liked Lea. She was pleasant, and when she smiled, her whole face lit up. And it had been a long time since he'd taken time for a social life. He'd prided himself on being able to amass his fortune before the age of thirty-five. But it had come at a price—his work schedule meant he hardly had a normal life.

There was something about this island—something so relaxing. Or perhaps it was the company. His gaze met hers. "I hope that even though we couldn't do business together we can still be friends."

Surprise lit up her eyes, but in a blink it was gone. "Um…sure. No hard feelings."

"Good. Would you care to join me for an early dinner?" When she hesitated, he added, "I'd love to hear more stories of the island and tales of your most outlandish weddings."

Her beautiful eyes widened. Was sharing a meal really that unusual for her? Or was she surprised by his interest in the goings-on of this eventful island? But with their business concluded, this meal would be…well, it would be between friends. He liked Lea, and the way she told stories was genuinely entertaining.

"Unless, of course, you have other plans." He hadn't considered that. "Perhaps with your husband or boyfriend?"

She shook her head. "I'm single."

"Good." And then realizing how that might sound, he added, "I mean that you're available for dinner."

"You don't have to pretend that you're interested in my stories—"

"There's no pretending. It's been a long time since I've been so amused. And by stories of goats, no less." He gestured for her to lead the way. "Shall we go?"

"Um…yes. The Hideaway Café is right this way."

In less than two minutes, they were at the restaurant. There was a thatched roof, ceiling fans and lots of colorful art on the walls. The aroma of coffee wafted through the air.

Xander loosened his tie. Then on second thought, he slipped it off and undid the top buttons on his dress shirt. It'd been a long time since he let himself enjoy a woman's company.

To his enjoyment, they were escorted to a patio table. It was just too nice a day to be stuck inside. Most of his life was spent in offices. This was different. And when his gaze came to rest on Lea, he decided that it was very nice indeed.

Once they'd ordered the food, he leaned back in his chair to take in the scenery. The very beautiful—very tempting—scenery. He couldn't take his eyes off her. Lea was someone he longed to know so much better.

"I never expected to find someone so—" He stopped himself from saying "beautiful" and instead said, "…so young running the island. By your accent, I'm guessing you're not from Greece."

"I'm not. I grew up in Seattle."

"That's a long way from here. So why move here? Why give up everything to run a wedding island?"

She fidgeted with a spoon on the table. "Because I wanted to learn more about my heritage. Do you know why they call this Infinity Island?"

He shook his head.

"Because when two hearts are joined here, they are joined for infinity. Not for a year or two or ten. It's forever. That's why we're selective with our clientele. The happy couples that marry here come from all around the world."

"And if you weren't so choosy, you might not be in such a dire situation. You could have more than one wedding a week. There wouldn't be any downtime like now."

She frowned at him. "We aren't in it for the money. This island is special and I won't part with it for you to build some expensive homes for people that don't understand the significance of the island and its history."

"You speak like you've lived here your entire life."

"Sometimes it feels that way." She never made any secret about her past. "My mother left Greece when she fell in love with an American soldier. She followed him to the States, where I came to be."

"So how did you end up back here?"

"My aunt never had any children of her own. I was her sole heir and she entrusted me with the island."

"What about your mother?"

"She and my father still live in the States on a little island off the Pacific coast. My mother, well, she had a falling-out with her family."

"I probably shouldn't do this since I'd really like it if you would call me in the near future and sell me the island, but I have some advice to keep your business afloat."

Her eyes lit up with interest. "What would that be?"

"This place is practically empty." He waved around at the plethora of empty tables. "Open the island up to vacationers as well as wedding guests. It would keep a steady flow of people and increase the flow of revenue."

"I'll keep that in mind."

But he could tell she'd already considered the option and dismissed it. Apparently traditions ran deep where this island was concerned. Xander couldn't help but wonder if it was really the love of the island or if there was something else keeping her here away from her family—away from society.

But he kept those questions to himself as they savored a delightful array of fresh vegetables, seafood and cheeses produced on the island. The meal was leisurely and the food was out of this world. He was quite tempted to lure the chef away and put him on staff at the Skyrise Restaurant atop his headquarters in Athens.

Even though the sun had slipped below the horizon, leaving a pink hue in its wake, Xander wasn't ready to end his time with Lea.

They strolled down to the beach. No one was around, and they enjoyed the surf and sand alone.

"I really should get back to work," Lea said, but her voice lacked desire.

"I should, too. But why don't we play hooky this evening?"

She glanced at him as they ambled along the shore. "Do you usually play hooky?"

"No."

"Then why this evening?"

He stopped and turned to her. "Because you reminded me that there is so much more to life than business. I haven't laughed this much…ever. It has been a truly wonderful evening." He stared deep into her eyes. "I don't want it to end."

"You don't?"

"I don't." His gaze lowered to her lips. They were so inviting. He'd been glancing at them off and on all through dinner. They were rosy and glossy. Nothing about her appearance was overly done. She was more down-to-earth and much more appealing than any of the women he'd dated in the past.

He had a policy of not mixing business and pleasure. Tonight, he might have been tempted to break that long-standing rule, but he knew Lea wasn't going to change her mind about his offer. And so there was no reason to hold back. They could find out where the evening would take them.

He stepped closer, watching and waiting to see if she would pull away. She didn't. He glanced down, catching the slight pulse in her neck. She was as intrigued by him as he was by her. The most captivating thing about her wasn't her gorgeous face or luscious lips, but the beauty inside that glowed outward.

He reached out to her. His movements were slow so as not to startle her. And then his fingers caressed her smooth, soft cheek. "You are the most incredible woman I've met."

There was an audible hiss as she sucked her breath in through her teeth. Her eyes widened and then took on an inviting look. He had no intention of missing out on such a tempting invitation.

He lowered his head, but before he got very far, she was there—meeting him in the middle. Her tender lips pressed to his. The breath caught in the back of his throat. Her touch was like a static charge—sending a current through his body, making every cell vibrate with desire.

His hand lowered to her waist. He drew her to him. Her hands came to rest on his chest as their kiss deepened. He hadn't ventured to Infinity Island with a thought of having a romantic tryst—not at all. He'd been disappointed that he hadn't been able to purchase the island, but this wasn't so bad as a consolation prize. And though he'd deny it to anyone, he'd ended up with the better of the two options.

The more he tasted Lea, the more he wanted her. She snuggled up against him. Her soft, voluptuous curves fit perfectly against him. He had a feeling this evening was only going to get better and better.

CHAPTER ONE

Late June...

TWO PINK LINES…

Three separate results…

Diagnosis: Pregnant.

Every time Lea thought about it, which was quite often, she started to hyperventilate. This couldn't be happening. Not now. Not when her life was in such an uproar.

But she'd had all of the early symptoms, from her missed cycle to tender breasts. As much as she wanted to live in the land of denial, she couldn't. There was now a baby to take into consideration. And a man who didn't have a clue he was about to become a father. Well, he would if he'd answer his phone.

After a trip to the doctor for official confirmation, Lea had tried repeatedly to reach Xander and let him know she was pregnant, not because she wanted anything from him but because it was the right thing to do. But each time she called, it went straight to voice mail. It wasn't until she tracked down the number to his office in Athens that she learned he was out of the country on business.

So once again, she called him. Once again, her call was forwarded to voice mail. "Xander, this is Lea. Um…" Her stomach churned with nerves even though he wasn't on the other end of the line. "I need to talk to you. Could you give me a call when you get a chance?"

She pressed the end button on her phone and took her first full breath. And then she realized that "when you get a chance" probably didn't convey the urgency that she felt or the importance of the news she had to tell him. Still, it was better than nothing. He would get back to her soon. Until then she had an island to save and a baby to prepare for. Plenty of things to keep her mind off Xander...as if that was possible.

He listened to the voice mail.

And then he listened to it again.

Xander could tell there was something off in Lea's voice, but he couldn't quite narrow down the problem or determined if there even was one. And then he realized what it must be—she was disappointed that he hadn't phoned her. Not that the thought hadn't crossed his mind more than a few times.

In fact, he hadn't been able to get Lea off of his mind since their lost weekend in paradise. Random memories of her distracted him from his work and filled his dreams at night. She was an amazing woman, not only in looks but in everything about her. It was so tempting to pick up the phone and call her back. If it were possible, he'd drop everything and return to Infinity Island. But his busy life didn't allow for such indulgences.

At first, he hadn't believed it, but by the time he departed Infinity Island, he knew there was something extra special about it—about Lea. Maybe he'd let himself get caught up in the most amazing views of the sea or the tranquil cove or even the colorful vegetation. Or more likely it was letting his guard down with Lea and enjoying the moment that had him so distracted from his work.

But right now, he was fully involved in a resort deal with his younger sister, Stasia. It was their first business deal together. And with his sister at loose ends after losing her husband, Xander was willing to do whatever he could for her.

And his sister, against his recommendation, had risked her entire life's savings on this project being a success. That was a responsibility he didn't want, but being stubborn and insistent, Stasia had put him in that very unwelcome position.

As much as he would like to see Lea again, it would have to wait for quite a while. Business came first. It always had. And it always would. Except when family shoved their way to the front of his priorities. Of course, his sister knew how much he adored her. He would do anything for her. And the feeling was mutual.

He set aside his phone and loosened his tie. His trip to the interior of Asia had not been fruitful. He'd known that it would be a long shot from the start, but long shots were what had catapulted him to the top of his field. Sometimes leads panned out and other times, well, they were a waste of time. But it never stopped him from seeking out the next big deal, in some of the most unlikely places.

He'd just hung up his tie in his walk-in closet that was the size of a second bedroom when he heard his phone buzz. He was really quite tempted to let it go to voice mail. He'd been traveling all day and what he longed for was a hot shower to ease the tension in his neck. But he had been out of contact for an extensive amount of time… and this could be important.

With a deep sigh, Xander headed back into the bedroom. On the way, he loosened the top buttons on his white dress shirt. He glanced down at the phone and was surprised to find Lea's name on the caller ID. She was calling again? That struck him as odd.

Sure, he hadn't known her that long, but she didn't strike him as the pushy type. In fact, she seemed quite the opposite. And she was more than willing to stand on her own two feet. Was it possible that he'd incorrectly interpreted her earlier voice mail?

Not giving himself time to think about it further, he answered the call. "Lea, how are you?"

"Xander, finally. I've been trying to reach you for a

while now. I was beginning to think that you were avoiding my calls—"

"Whoa. Slow down." Something really had her worked up. "I just got home a few minutes ago. What's wrong?"

"I… I don't know if you'd say it's wrong or not."

"Just tell me what it is and we'll go from there."

There was an extended pause. He could imagine her worrying her bottom lip, like she did when she was unsure of something. While he'd been on Infinity Island, he'd picked up on her mannerisms. He found her quite captivating. It was one of the reasons he'd avoided calling her. He knew if she asked him to return to the island, it would be too great a temptation.

As the silence dragged on, Xander said, "Lea, I can't help until you tell me what's the matter."

"I'm pregnant."

Xander stumbled back as though her words had physically slugged him in the chest. The back of his knees hit the edge of the bed. He slumped down onto the mattress. Maybe he'd heard her incorrectly.

"Could you say that again?"

"Xander, I'm pregnant. And you're the father."

That was what he thought she'd said.

But this can't be true. Could it?

Xander knew all too well that it was quite possible. They'd spent that not-so-long-ago weekend in bed…and there was the time on the floor…in the living room—

He halted his rambling memories. He didn't normally let loose like that. In fact, he'd never had a weekend like that one. It was unforgettable. And apparently in more than one way.

But he had to be absolutely sure of what he heard. "Could you say that again?"

"I'm pregnant."

His heart pounded so loud that it echoed in his ears. As

though all the energy had been drained from his body, he fell back on the bed. His fingers combed through his hair as his palm rubbed against his forehead, where a throbbing headache was starting.

The silence grew heavy. He should say something. Anything. But what? He'd never been in this position before.

He needed time to think because right now all that was going around in his mind was that he was going to be a father. He wondered if this was what shock felt like.

"I… I need a little time to absorb this," he said. "We'll talk soon."

He wasn't even sure if he said goodbye before disconnecting the call. He had no idea how long he lay there staring into space before the buzz of an incoming text jarred him back to reality.

I'm going to be a father.

The profound words echoed in his mind.

How could this be? Well, of course he knew how it happened. It was a weekend that he would never forget, much as he had tried. Lea's stunning image was imprinted upon his mind.

Still, he'd never thought he'd hear that he was going to be a father.

A father.

Those two little words sent his heart racing as his palms grew damp. His mind slipped back to the time he'd spent on Infinity Island. He'd never expected it to change his life. But it had. And now he had to figure out a plan. He was known for thinking on his toes, but this was different. This was a baby. His baby.

And he had to do whatever was best for the child.

But what was that?

CHAPTER TWO

Had he been stunned?

Was that why he'd ended the phone call so quickly?

Maybe he'd been in shock. He had said that they'd talk soon. What exactly did *soon* mean?

The next day Lea was still playing over her conversation with Xander. It had ended so abruptly that it startled her. She didn't know what she'd been expecting, but it hadn't been for him to become so quiet. Perhaps she'd been waiting for him to lob questions and accusations but none of that had come.

Did he outright not believe her? She knew that was always a possibility, but she just wanted to believe that Xander was more of a man than to shirk his responsibilities. Granted she didn't know him that well, but she sensed he was a good guy—a man who cared for those closest to him—even if to the world he portrayed himself as a ruthless businessman. In private, he was a very different man. That much she was certain about.

Or the other possibility—the one that she was going with—was that she had absolutely blindsided him with the news of the baby. How could he not be shocked? She certainly had been. A baby was the last thing she'd had on her mind at the moment. Her priority had been trying to keep a roof over her head in the upcoming year.

She sighed, not about the baby but about the state of the island. She straightened up the papers on her office desk. She felt as though she were letting down her family, which was silly when you thought of it, because she didn't know any of the people who had run the island before her. And her parents, well, they wanted nothing to do with the island. So perhaps she felt as though she were letting down herself.

When she first learned that she'd inherited this gorgeous island, she'd imagined swooping in here and making it the best—the most shiny, sought-after wedding destination. Instead she was patching holes, painting walls and duct-taping hoses. Half of the guest rooms were shut down due to one reason or another.

In addition, she'd had to reduce the staff. As a result, she'd had to take on additional responsibilities that took up any free time and had her falling into bed at night utterly exhausted.

She stood and moved out from behind her desk that still had a slew of unfinished tasks. A more urgent problem needed her attention. A leaking faucet. Thankfully her parents had had no gender bias when raising her. She used to assist her father with all sorts of tasks around the house—including plumbing.

Lea moved to the closet, opened the door and retrieved a red toolbox. She almost felt as though she needed a tool belt to sling around her waist—to give her that authentic fixer-lady look. She wondered what Xander would make of the look. A giggle rose in her throat as she imagined a horrified look on his handsome face.

Dressed in a loose T-shirt and a pair of old jean shorts that had the top button loosened to make room for her expanding midsection, she set off for the bungalow midway across the island. She hoped it was just a worn-out washer and nothing more serious. She had a big wedding this weekend. She couldn't afford to lose yet another accommodation because there was nowhere else to house people unless she gave up her bungalow.

She'd just placed the toolbox in the golf cart when she heard the whoop-whoop of a helicopter. This couldn't be good. They weren't expecting any new guests today.

The people on the island either lived and worked there

or were lingering guests from the past weekend's wedding. There was also a couple celebrating their fiftieth anniversary. Some of their guests liked to return every year for their anniversary, sort of as a reminder of how it felt when their love had been so new, fresh and exciting.

She worried her bottom lip. Could it be a medical emergency? No. She would have been informed.

But as the warm breeze caressed her skin, she put a hand to her forehead, blocking the bright sunshine. She tilted her chin upward to watch the helicopter descend to the helipad not far from her office. Whoever this was, they weren't a guest.

Her body tensed as the long seconds dragged out. She never knew it could take so long for a chopper to land. But she knew that in reality not much time had passed at all. It was just her anxiety that seemed to have slowed the world down as she waited to see what new problem awaited her.

And then the door to the helicopter opened. And…

The breath of anticipation hitched in her throat. And…

A man emerged from inside. His head was ducked, but he had dark hair. And his clothes appeared to be a business suit. Her heart plummeted to her tennis shoes. Could this be an attorney putting some sort of lien against the island as she wasn't quite on top of all of her bills. She tried. But some months she had to pay some accounts and then the next month she paid others.

But as the man rushed away from the helipad, there was something familiar about him. She couldn't put her finger on what exactly it was, but she sensed she knew him. And then as the man reached the steps leading away from the helipad, he lifted his head.

A breath hissed past Lea's teeth. *Xander.* She blinked. He was still there and he was staring directly at her.

She sucked in a deep breath, pulling in her baby bump, but that only succeeded in making her ever-expanding breasts stick out even further. She immediately released the pent-up breath. There was no hiding that her body was changing.

What was he doing here? And then she realized that in her shock, she'd asked the most ridiculous question. He wasn't here to see her—not like she'd dreamed about at night where they'd rushed into each other's arms. No, he was here about her baby—their baby.

She'd only told him the news yesterday. She couldn't believe he was standing in front of her. But he was looking a little out of sorts. His necktie was missing. His collar was loosened. He hadn't shaved, leaving a dark shadow of stubble to highlight his squared jaw.

It was then that she noticed he wasn't smiling as he made his way to her. If he wasn't happy about the baby, why bother coming? It wasn't like she'd placed any demands upon him. She wasn't poor, even if the state of the island said otherwise. This land was worth a lot of money—he'd pointed that out to her. If the absolute worst happened, she could sell the island and live comfortably the rest of her life. But she would have to be desperate to sell her heritage. At this point, she wasn't desperate. At least that was what she kept telling herself.

Hang in there. This is all going to work out.

She wondered if the pep speech was about the dire state of the island or about her impending meeting with Xander. She hadn't moved since she'd watched him arrive. Normally she would have met a guest halfway, but not today—not with Xander frowning. She had to be strong and stand her ground. He could come to her.

When Xander finally stopped in front of her, she stood silently. Her stomach churned nervously. She hadn't invited him here. It was up to him to decide how this conversation should go.

"I'm here." He stared at her with tired eyes.

That's it? That's all he has to say?

She leveled her shoulders and tilted her chin upward.

"I didn't ask you to come. We could have handled this over the phone."

"This is too serious for a phone call."

But with a phone call, she would have been able to concentrate on the conversation instead of how he looked even sexier than she recalled. She fidgeted with the gemstone bracelet on her wrist before forcing her hands to remain still at her sides.

This conversation definitely would have gone smoother over the phone. As soon as she would have assured him that she wasn't plotting a messy paternity or support lawsuit, they could have gotten back to their lives. Because she could do this parenting thing on her own. In fact, she was looking forward to being a mother.

When Lea noticed him staring expectantly at her, she said, "I thought you'd be busy with work."

A definite note of incredulity clung to his voice. "You can't just deliver a bombshell, over the phone no less, and expect me to do nothing."

"What do you want to know?"

"How about for starters, are you sure the baby is mine?" His gaze narrowed as he stared at her as though by look alone he could ferret out the truth.

The fact that he would question her about something so important hurt—it hurt deeply. Apparently they didn't know each other at all. The weekend they'd spent in each other's company for every exquisite moment had meant more to her than him. So be it.

"Yes. I'm sure." If he thought she was going to stand here in public to be interrogated, he was mistaken. "I have to go. I have an emergency."

Without giving him a chance to respond, she turned back to the golf cart. She climbed inside and started it. She glanced up and was about to put her foot on the accelerator when she found him standing directly in her path, with his arms crossed over his broad chest and a definite frown on his face.

She sighed. "I don't want to fight with you. In fact, I don't want anything from you."

"Then why call?"

Seriously? He had to ask that?

And then one of the staff started in their direction. The man was giving them a strange look as though trying to decide whether he should step in or not. She made a point of painting a friendly smile on her face and waving at her employee. The man smiled, nodded and kept moving.

Lea turned back to Xander. "Would you stop standing there like some Greek statue and get in?" When he didn't move, she said, "Xander, don't make a scene."

Without a word, he climbed in beside her. His shoulder brushed up against hers, sending a wave of nervous energy racing through her body. It settled in her chest. As she breathed in his spicy aftershave, the heat in her chest gravitated southward to her core. Her back teeth ground together, refusing to give in to her body's desires. That boat had sailed. It was out of the docks, out of the harbor, and was headed into open seas.

CHAPTER THREE

HIS QUIETNESS WAS UNNERVING.

Lea sent Xander a sideways glance. The set of his jaw and the twitch in his cheek let her know that he was angry. Sitting so close to him, she could feel the agitation radiating off him.

She didn't know what gave him the right to be so upset. It wasn't like she'd ended up in this condition by herself. It definitely took two to tango. If she'd hidden the baby from him, it would be different. But that hadn't happened. And lastly, she didn't expect or request a thing from him. So if he wanted to be mad at her, he could just sit there and stew. She had work to do.

Lea slowed the golf cart to a stop outside the honeymoon bungalow. Without a word, she got out. She grabbed her toolbox with a replacement rubber washer in it and headed up the four wooden steps to the front door.

The guests were supposed to have checked out by now, but as was standard procedure on the island, Lea rapped her knuckles soundly on the door. "Hello. Maintenance."

A moment passed with no response.

She lifted her hand to insert her passkey but missed. If only Xander would go away, the slight tremble in her hands would stop. Lea inhaled a deep breath and tried again. This time she got it.

Footsteps sounded behind her. She didn't have to turn to know it was Xander. She could smell the faint whiff of his cologne mingled with his male scent. It was an intoxicating combination.

Ignoring Xander, Lea opened the door slowly so as not to startle anyone that may be lingering on the inside.

"Hello. Anyone here?" She glanced around for any sign of guests. "Maintenance coming in."

With the door wide open, she stepped inside. No people. No luggage. No discarded dishes or drinks in the living room area or the kitchenette. They were alone—

Alone with Xander in a honeymoon bungalow. What made her think bringing him along was a good idea? Oh, yeah, he hadn't given her a choice.

Then the door snicked shut behind her. She glanced over her shoulder, her gaze verifying that the door was indeed closed and then registering that Xander was standing very close to her. So close she could reach back and place her hand upon his chest. She swallowed hard and resisted the temptation.

So as not to give into her impulse, she faced forward, as though by turning away she'd be able to forget just how sexy he looked. In her mind, she pictured him clearly in that navy blue suit, sans tie and with the top buttons of his light blue dress shirt undone, giving a hint of the few dark curls on his chest. Lea stifled a moan.

On stilted legs, she headed toward the master suite. Her heart was racing. Her palms were damp. How was she ever going to be able to work with him lurking over her shoulder?

She stopped before reaching the bedroom. "You can take the golf cart and head back to the offices." She was getting desperate for some space—a chance to think clearly. "I can walk. It'll be good for the baby."

"Why would I do that?"

Because you're making me a nervous wreck.

Lea moistened her dry lips. "I didn't think you'd want to stick around and watch me fix a leaky faucet."

"Why are you doing maintenance work? Don't you have people to do those sorts of things? I mean in your condition, should you be doing manual labor?"

She turned a narrow gaze on him. "I'm pregnant, not

dying. And now that the morning sickness has passed, I have a lot of energy." She tilted up her chin. "Trust me, I won't do anything that would endanger the baby."

He nodded in understanding. "I still don't understand why you're doing this."

She didn't want to tell him just how bad off the island was these days. With more and more accommodations shut down because of needed repairs, the fewer weddings she could book. The fewer weddings booked, the less income for repairs. It was one big downward spiral and she had yet to find a way to stop it. If only she could find an investor who didn't want to change the island or the way the business was run. But so far, she hadn't found that right person. And it certainly wasn't Xander, who wanted to rip down everything her ancestors had built and loved.

"That's not the kind of owner I am. I like to be a part of everything. Make sure things are functioning properly."

He arched a brow. "And you can tell all of that by fixing a faucet?"

His tone let her know he didn't believe her. But that was his problem. She didn't have time to alleviate his curiosity. She had work to do. And this was her best unit on the island.

When she reached the master bedroom, she immediately stepped in water. It seeped up over her sandals. The breath hitched in her throat, smothering a scream.

A little leak? A drippy faucet?

Lea muttered under her breath as she rushed toward the bathroom. Her foot slipped on the wet floor. The next thing she knew, she was falling back. Strong hands reached out and caught her. She didn't have time to thank him, she had to shut off the water.

Inside the bathroom, oblivious to the water, she knelt down and leaned under the countertop. She tried the shut-off valve under the sink but it wouldn't budge. Using her whole-body strength, she groaned, but the valve didn't move at all.

"Here. Let me try," Xander said from behind her.

She turned to him and was about to tell him that this wasn't his problem, when she noticed he'd divested himself of his suit coat. It now hung over the towel rack and his shirtsleeves were rolled up.

He held a hand out to her. "Hurry up. The water is still pouring in."

He was right. This was not the time to stand on pride. If she lost this unit, the island would go out of business and her heritage would be lost. She couldn't let that happen. It was her job to protect her family's legacy—something her mother refused to do.

Lea watched as he clenched the wrench. The corded muscles of his forearms strained. His neck grew taut as his lips pressed together in a firm line. A deep groan filled the room as he gave it everything to move the valve.

After a few failed attempts, he turned to her. "Where's the main water shutoff for the whole unit?"

"Outside. In the back, I think." Up until this point, she hadn't had any need to turn off the water main, but she knew the bulk of the units had the utility hookup in the back, out of view from the guests.

Xander stood. The water dripped off him—his suit was going to be ruined. And then she noticed his black leather dress shoes. They were partially submerged in water. Lea inwardly groaned as she thought of how many hundreds or more likely thousands of dollars his attire cost—something she didn't have the extra cash to replace. She would have to deal with that later.

She took off for the door with Xander hot on her heels. The water shutoff thankfully was easy to find. And unlike the valve inside, it turned pretty easily.

Turning the water off was only the first step in fixing this huge mess. They rushed back inside, using everything available to mop up the water from the floor. Xander opened all of the windows. They continued to work together in peaceful harmony.

When the last of the water had been mopped up, Lea stood and inspected the damage. Thankfully the wood floor wasn't discolored. It didn't look like the water had been there long. Lea thanked her lucky stars.

As she placed the last wet towel in a laundry bag, she turned to Xander, who had just gotten to his feet after checking the plumbing joint under the sink. "Thank you."

"No problem."

Her gaze took in his wet, wrinkled suit. "I think your clothes are ruined."

He glanced down as though he'd forgotten he was wearing dress clothes. "I've got more."

"I didn't see any luggage."

"True. Everything is back in Athens. I was in a bit of a hurry."

"Obviously." She gave it a little thought. "Let's drop off these wet linens and then we'll get you something dry to wear."

He gave her a strange look. "I don't think you'll have anything that will fit me."

His words inspired an image of him in women's clothes and a smile pulled at her lips. As they climbed in the golf cart, the image of Xander wearing her clothes wouldn't leave her. She pressed on the accelerator.

"You're picturing me in your clothes, aren't you?"

"I…uh…no, I'm not." But she couldn't subdue her amusement.

"You are. I know it. But trust me, nothing you have would fit me."

The frown on his face only added to her amusement. She knew that after the disaster at the bungalow she shouldn't be smiling, much less laughing, but she couldn't help herself. The laughter bubbled out of her.

Maybe it was some strange reaction to stress. Or perhaps it was her pregnancy hormones. Whatever it was, she couldn't stop laughing. And looking in Xander's direction only made it worse.

"What?" he asked as his frown deepened. "Do I have something on me?" He then started to wipe his face off. "Would you stop that?"

"I'm trying." Lea did her best to subdue her unexpected amusement. "It's not you."

He arched a dark brow. "Then why are you laughing at me?"

She shook her head. "I'm not."

"Sure seems like it to me."

"I've just never seen someone in expensive clothes crawling around on a flooded floor." She dabbed at her damp eyes. "You're a mess."

"And that's funny?"

"No. Not really." The grumpier he became the cuter he got. That acknowledgment sobered Lea. Being attracted to him was what had gotten them in this situation in the first place. "Anyway. What are you doing here?"

"You need to ask?"

"Apparently I do or I wouldn't have asked you."

She pulled the golf cart to a stop in front of her bungalow—the same place that their baby was conceived. It was as though they'd come full circle and were now back at the beginning. She got out and headed for the door.

She glanced over her shoulder, finding Xander still sitting in the cart. "Come on. You can't go around looking like that all day."

She let herself inside the small but airy bungalow, lit abundantly from the floor-to-ceiling windows. She wasn't quite sure how to act around Xander. It wasn't as though they were strangers, but there was definitely a thick layer of awkwardness between them.

"The shower is through there." She pointed to the guest bathroom.

He looked at her. "Are you sure you don't want to get one first?"

She glanced down at herself. She was as wet as him, with some black grease marks here and there.

Her hand moved to her hair. It was still damp on the ends and the rest of it was growing frizzy. She must look a sight. No one would desire her in this state. And that was for the best. She tried to tell herself that she was relieved but what she was really feeling was disappointment.

Not wanting to dwell on her disheveled appearance, she grabbed her purse from the side of the couch and headed for the front door. "I'll be back shortly."

"Where are you going?"

"To get you something to wear." Not waiting for his response, she strode outside, pulling the door shut behind her.

There was only a limited number of retail shops on the island. Most people who visited weren't interested in shopping, except for the occasional necessity. But they did have a boutique and that was where Lea headed.

The only problem was that everything in the island boutique was geared to leisurely, fun-in-the-sun clothes. There were no suits, not even jeans because it was hot outside with only the sea breeze to cool you off. There was actually a pair of gray sweats lurking on the back shelf, but Lea dismissed them. Xander would melt in them.

She moved on to a pair of navy shorts with a white anchor pattern. This was more like it. Her mind filled with an image of Xander in them, showing off his well-defined calf muscles. The man was a walking advertisement for the benefit of working out daily.

She picked up a white T-shirt with *Infinity Island* emblazoned across the front of it. Her gaze moved to the section of the shop with the more intimate items, but there was no way she was buying him underwear. Not a chance. She had to draw the line somewhere.

She started for the checkout but realized she was being silly. If she could have his baby, she could pick out some boxers. Still, it felt like something a girlfriend or, dare she say it, a wife would do. As she scanned over the various colors and styles, her mind conjured up images of Xander wearing them.

She resisted the urge to fan herself. Boy, was it getting warm in here. Eager to get this over with, she grabbed a few pairs of extra-large boxers. If he wanted something else, he could come here and shop for himself. With her face still warm, she started for the front of the store, passing by the rack of flip-flops. She grabbed a pair. He would be all set to go—to go home to Athens.

With her purchase made, Lea headed back to her place. Soon Xander would be gone and then she could relax. She glanced at the time. The once-a-day ferry would be arriving at lunchtime and he could hitch a ride back to the mainland. Whatever he'd hoped to accomplish by coming here wasn't going to happen.

He had his life.

And she had hers.

Could they stay in contact for their child? If he wanted. She didn't have any qualms about updating him on the progress of the pregnancy.

And that was exactly what she planned to tell him when she entered the bungalow. She dropped her purse on the living room couch and moved to the guest room. She knocked on the open door but got no response. It was then that she noticed the sound of running water. She moved to the bed, hoping to leave the clothes there and get out before he came out of the shower. She'd just placed the bag from the boutique on the bed when Xander emerged from the bathroom.

A billow of steam surrounded him like he was some

Greek god. His hair was still wet and spiky. His face and shoulders were damp. And beads of water trailed down over his muscled chest before being absorbed by the fluffy pink towel slung low over his trim hips.

Lea swallowed hard. It was like having her very own hot-guys calendar come to life—not that she had such a calendar. But after seeing Xander, the idea was tempting. So long as he was in it. But then she knew she'd never switch the month. It'd always be Xander's month.

He cleared his throat, drawing her gaze upward. "Is that for me?"

Heat rushed from her chest to her face, scorching her cheeks. With great reluctance, she glanced away. "Yes, there are some, uh, clothes. They should fit." And then realizing she shouldn't be here at this particularly awkward moment, she said, "I'll, um, wait for you in the living room."

"There's no need for you to run off." A knowing smile lit up his face.

But Lea didn't look back and didn't pause until she'd reached the kitchen sink. Noticing that her mouth was parched, she grabbed a drinking glass from the cabinet and filled it with some ice-cold water from the fridge. She downed the entire thing in one long gulp, but it did nothing to cool her down. Thankfully he would soon be on that boat and out of her space. Not much longer now.

"Thanks for the clothes." Xander's voice came from behind her. "But you didn't have to."

"It's the least I could do—" The words died in her throat as she turned to him. On second thought, she should have gone with the sweat suit. Then he'd be just as uncomfortably warm as her.

The T-shirt barely fit him as it was pulled tight over his broad shoulders and chest. The man could probably lift one of her in each hand without breaking a sweat. His waist was narrow. And the shorts didn't hang as low as she'd have thought. She definitely had a view of his legs—legs that weren't tanned. Her gaze moved to his arms. They weren't tanned, either. The man definitely spent too much time in a suit.

She could ask him to stay. He obviously needed some downtime in the sun. But that was not a good idea. She did not need any more complications.

He moved to the couch and sat down. "No more distractions. We need to talk."

He was right. It was time to get it all out there in the open. "I don't expect anything from you if that's what you're worried about. I can take care of the baby."

He patted the couch cushion next to him. "Come over here."

She didn't trust herself being so close to that sexy hunk of a man, but she refused to let on that he still got under her skin. She forced her feet one in front of the other. She perched on the edge of the couch, leaving as much space between them as possible.

She could still remember how good his kisses were and how his hands created the most arousing sensations wherever he touched. The mere memories sent her heart racing. When her gaze met his, there was a challenge reflected in his eyes.

She glanced at the clock on the stove. "If you don't hurry, you'll miss the ferry. It's the only one today."

"Is this the way it's going to be?"

She turned her full attention to him. "How *what* is going to be?"

"You and me. How do I even know the baby is mine?"

"I'd like to think that no one would lie about such an important thing. But you obviously don't trust me. So after the baby is born, a test can be done. But there's no way I'm having one of those great big foot-long needles stabbed into my stomach." She visibly flinched at the memory of what she'd seen on the internet. She didn't like needles. They all looked huge to her.

"I want to trust you, but I've had people lie to me in the past about much smaller matters." Pain reflected in his eyes.

"It's understandable that you would want confirmation. It isn't like we've been in a loving, committed relationship."

His eyes widened. "Is that what you want? For us to marry for the sake of the child?"

"No." It was a short, straight-to-the-point answer.

His gaze narrowed. "Are you sure?"

Why was he pushing this so much? Surely he didn't think marriage was a good idea, did he? It was not even like they were in love. They were, well, they were friends at best. And not very good friends at that.

"I'm sure." Her tone was firm. "Besides, you don't have time for a family. You're always working."

"I can make time for everything—" Just then his phone buzzed and he retrieved it from his pocket.

"Point proven."

After nothing more than a glance, he returned the phone to his pocket. "So you're planning to do this all on your own?"

"If you mean raising the baby, then yes, I plan to be a single parent. It's not like there are a lot of single guys on the island. Most are bridegrooms or a guest of a wedding party. They generally bring a date and don't flirt with the island staff."

"You're going to stay here on the island and raise the baby?"

"This is where my ancestors were born and raised. It's where my mother grew up. If it's good enough for them, it's good enough for me and the baby."

"And what about what happened today with the honeymoon bungalow?" he asked.

"What about it? Things break." She tried to brush off

the incident as nothing out of the ordinary, but she knew it was a very big deal indeed.

He leaned forward, resting his elbows on his knees. "Don't act so blasé. I saw you earlier. You were practically in a panic. This island needs a lot of work—work that you don't have the money to do."

Her mouth gaped. *How dare he?* "Since when do you know about my finances?"

"Since I did some digging when I wanted to buy the island. I needed to know just what I was getting myself into."

She wanted to ask what he'd learned, but she didn't. Nothing good would come of it. Where finances were concerned Infinity Island was in disastrous straits.

Xander gazed into her eyes, making her heart race. "You need to rethink this—"

"Rethink what? Giving up my home? My past? My future?" She shook her head. "If you think you're going to talk me into selling you the island, it isn't going to happen. Remember? We already had this conversation."

"You don't have to stay here. I can set you up in Athens. Anywhere in the city. You name it."

She crossed her arms. "I'm not leaving the island."

"Stop being so stubborn and see what's right in front of you."

Her voice started to rise. "I do see it. And just because this place isn't perfect doesn't mean I should turn my back and walk away."

He sighed and got to his feet. Without another word, he started for the door.

"Where are you going?" she asked.

"Out." And with that he stepped onto the covered deck.

She should be relieved, but she wasn't. She felt like they'd talked about everything except what he really had on his mind. And then there was the whistle of the approaching ferry.

She rushed to the doorway. "You're going to miss your ride back to the mainland."

"I'm not leaving." He kept walking.

Not leaving? He made it sound like it would be indefinitely, but she knew that couldn't be the case. He had a business empire to run.

She assured herself that he'd just be here for a day or two. Just long enough to figure out how this pregnancy would affect their lives. Then he'd go back to his life in Athens. And she would remain here on the island.

CHAPTER FOUR

WHAT EXACTLY WAS he supposed to do now?

Xander raked his fingers through his hair, not caring what it looked like. For once, his appearance would make no difference in the negotiation. Usually he made a point of looking on top of his game, with the finest suit, the best haircut and a clean shave. He liked to let his competitors know that he was used to winning—that he didn't accept being second best.

But dealing with Lea was totally different. Money didn't impress her. She understood its necessity to survive, but it wasn't her driving force. And that was something foreign to him. Since he'd been a teenager, he'd been focused on amassing a fortune. And now at the age of thirty-one, he had more money than he could possibly spend in this lifetime, but he still wasn't satisfied. He was still looking to make the next deal—something to fill the emptiness inside.

His gaze moved over the island. This time he wasn't taking in his surroundings the same way as he had during his prior visit. Before, his interest was in the landscape and the eventual demolition followed by its rebirth. This time he was looking to see what it would take to make this island viable as a wedding destination for the foreseeable future.

He'd noticed the determined glint in Lea's eyes when he'd mentioned selling the island. It was the same look he imagined he had when he bought his first piece of property that had been uneven and heavily vegetated. His father had told him that he'd thrown away his money. Xander had secretly been having his own doubts, but his father's words had been like a challenge. Xander had done everything to clear and level that plot of land. In the end, he'd tripled his money. With the proceeds he'd bought more property.

Lea would stay here on Infinity Island and do whatever it took to keep the family business going—even if it took the last bit of money she possessed. And it would. Most of the structures needed new roofs. The landscaping needed to be reworked in places. The bungalows needed new windows and paint, and that was just scratching the surface.

He didn't know how long he'd walked—wearing off his frustration. In the process, he'd been trying to wrap his mind around the fact that he was going to be a father. He'd always thought fatherhood was something he didn't want, but now it was no longer a choice. He refused to turn his back on his baby like his biological parents had done to him when they'd left him on the steps in front of the hospital.

And though his adoptive parents had loved him, it just hadn't been the same as what they felt for his sister—their flesh and blood. Growing up, he'd blamed himself—telling himself that he wasn't good enough. If he'd have just tried harder, they'd have loved him the same as they loved his sister. He'd never allowed any of them that chance.

Now he had a baby of his own. He would do whatever it took to see that Lea and the baby were taken care of. Money wouldn't be an issue.

If Lea insisted on remaining on the island, he could have the island all fixed up. And he would contact his financial planner to set up a trust fund for his son...or daughter. He liked the idea. At last, he had the beginnings of a plan.

As for being an involved father, he was less certain about it. With his past, he doubted he could be a loving parent. They'd all be better off if he remained in the shadows.

Xander pulled his phone out of his pocket and pressed the speed dial. The phone was answered on the first ring as though Roberto, his second-in-charge, was sitting there waiting for him to call. But of course, he wouldn't be because he had too many other things he should be doing.

Xander dispensed with the pleasantries and went straight for the important stuff. "Roberto, I need you to drop everything and pull what you have on the resort deal."

"Isn't that something your assistant could do?"

Since when did his employees second-guess him? Even if Roberto was right. Xander's back teeth ground together. He got Roberto's veiled message: Xander wasn't giving him tasks worthy of his position.

Xander's grip on the phone tightened. "Amara won't know what all needs pulled. Once you have the information gathered, give it to Amara. She'll see that I get it."

"Yes, sir."

"Thanks. I don't know when I'll be back. You can reach me on my cell if anything comes up."

"In the meantime, is there anything I can do?"

Xander had always been on top of everything. He didn't see a reason to change that now. Still, it wouldn't hurt to give Roberto a little more responsibility. After all, Roberto was a good man and quite capable. "Yes. Make sure nothing goes awry while I'm out of the office. We have a number of deals in the works. Are you up for the task?"

"I am." There was absolutely no hesitation in his voice.

"Keep me in the loop."

"Yes, sir."

They went over a couple of other open items and then he was transferred to his assistant. In addition to other tasks, he requested she send him clothes—casual clothes. He had no idea how long he'd remain on Infinity Island.

For the moment, Xander was free to focus solely on Lea and the baby. And his first order of business was to tell Lea that he would invest in her island, even though he didn't believe in what it stood for—infinite love. That kind of love didn't exist. But he'd keep that last part to himself.

* * *

"What do you mean Xander's here?"

Lea really didn't want to talk about this latest development in her personal life, but Popi wasn't about to let it go. Lea looked over the top of her computer monitor and took in her friend's pink top that said, "Precious Cargo Onboard." Popi had volunteered to be a surrogate for her sister and brother-in-law.

Before Lea answered her best friend's question, which inevitably would lead to another one, Lea had a question of her own. "Where did you get that top?"

Popi sent her a puzzled look before glancing down. "I ordered it online. And their stuff is so comfy I've ordered more."

"Do they have anything more professional? I hardly fit in any of my clothes." The truth was she didn't fit in them, at least not the way they were supposed to be worn.

Popi nodded and then gave her the web address. "Now, stop changing the subject."

"What were we discussing?" Lea knew perfectly well the topic of conversation, but she was amused when Popi became frustrated and pinched her lips together like she was doing right now.

"You were about to tell me what Xander's doing here?"

Lea sighed. "I told him about the baby. I had to. I couldn't live with myself if I kept it from him."

"You did the right thing. But I thought you said he wasn't a family man. You said he was all about the business and had no room in his life for kids."

"That's what he told me when he was here last time."

"So once he found out he was going to be a father, he changed his mind?"

Lea shrugged. "I don't know. I told him about the baby last night and today he's here. I don't know what he wants from me. Your guess is as good as mine. But he is acting rather strange."

"Strange how? He wants to marry you? He wants to take the baby away from you? He's moving in?"

"I told you I don't know." She seemed to be saying that a lot lately. "The only thing he has told me is that the island is slowly falling apart and I don't have the funds to fix it."

"Ah… So he's still after the land. He thinks he can force you into selling it to him now that you're pregnant."

Lea wanted to disagree with her—to tell her that Xander wouldn't stoop so low. But could she really argue the point? It wasn't like he'd talked about much else, other than how the island wouldn't be able to sustain them.

Popi was about to say something else when the office door swung open. There stood Xander, looking more casual than she was used to seeing him. Though Lea's attention was zeroed in on Xander, she could feel Popi's gaze moving back and forth between the two of them.

"I've got something I need to do," Popi said hesitantly. "I'll, uh, just catch up with you later."

"Sounds good." Lea continued to stare at Xander as he stared right back at her, making her heart race.

She wondered if she should have introduced Popi and Xander, but it was already too late as her friend had rushed out the door as though the office was on fire. Besides, it didn't matter. It wasn't like Xander was on the island for a social call. Was Popi right? Had he come here because he thought he had a real chance to buy the island out from under her now that she was in a difficult position?

"You missed the ferry." She forced her gaze away from him and stared blindly down at her monitor. "The next one won't be here until tomorrow. But I can request a seaplane to pick you up."

"I won't be needing it."

That got her to lift her head. "You can't just stay here

indefinitely. Whatever needs said can be done via the phone."

"It's better face to face."

She didn't agree. Being so close to him distracted her. "There's no room available. And…" Her rapid thoughts tripped over each other. "And there's a wedding this weekend. And we're booked solid."

He stepped forward and made himself comfortable in one of the two chairs facing her desk. "I'll guess we'll be bunking together. Again."

Immediately her thoughts went back to the time when they had in fact bunked together, but there had been no sleeping done that night—no sleeping whatsoever. And not much the following night. Heat swirled in her chest and rushed up to her face. She immediately squelched the very steamy memories.

Stay focused. Don't let him rattle you.

"That isn't going to happen again." She maintained as firm a tone as she could muster.

A smile lifted the corners of his mouth. "That's a shame because it was quite an unforgettable night."

He's definitely right about that.

She gave herself a mental jerk. *Stay focused.*

She tilted her chin upward. "So, you see that leaving is the only option."

"Actually," he said, leaning back in the chair, resting his elbows on the arms and steepling his fingers, "you have an empty guest room. I'll just stay there. And then we can talk."

"There's nothing to talk about." *Liar. Liar.*

The look on his face said he didn't believe her. "Even you don't believe that."

She leaned back in her chair and crossed her arms. "Fine. We can talk now. You start."

"I've had a look around the island and it needs numerous repairs and updates to bring it back to its former glory, as I'm sure you know." He sighed. "I don't want to make this sound harsh, but if you're already struggling, how are you going to handle things when the baby comes?"

She lifted her chin ever so slightly. "I have a plan."

His eyes filled with interest. "Mind sharing the details?"

"Actually, I do mind." Anxious to wrap this up, she said, "Now if there's nothing else—"

"There is something else." He leaned forward. "I'm willing to invest in the island." She shook her head but he continued. "You can't afford to turn me down." And then he named a staggering sum of money.

She didn't know anyone that had that sort of wealth. The things she could do with it. The island would once again glow like a rare Mediterranean jewel. They'd be able to take on twice the number of weddings.

But in the end, she knew what her answer must be. "No. This is my problem. I'll fix it on my own." She stood. "I really do need to get back to work."

A distinct frown settled on his face. "Why are you refusing my help?"

"Do you really need to ask?"

"Apparently I do."

It boiled down to one simple fact. "If it's your money, you'll want to call the shots."

"And if I said the money came without strings—"

"I wouldn't believe you. We aren't talking about a small sum of money." She noticed how he didn't argue that point.

"And that's it? There's nothing I can do to change your mind?"

"No." She opened an email and started to respond to it.

He turned and started for the door. His hand rested on the handle when he turned back to her. "This isn't over."

"I didn't think it was."

"I'll see you later at the bungalow."

When he was finally gone and the door was closed, she took her first easy breath. Why was he sticking around? She wanted to believe that it was because of the chemistry arcing between them. But she refused to let herself go there.

CHAPTER FIVE

THIS IS GOING to work.

Lea had told herself that all the next day. An older couple, Mr. and Mrs. Kostopoulos, flew in that morning. To Lea's surprise, they'd decided against being silent investors. Instead, they were entertaining the notion of buying the island to run as Lea's family had done for decades—bringing two hearts together for infinity.

Selling the island wasn't what Lea ultimately wanted. But she was running out of time and funds. If she could find a buyer that wanted the island as it was, it would be better than selling to a developer like Xander, who was only interested in making money and cared nothing about preserving her family's legacy.

After a comprehensive tour of the island, they stopped at the Hideaway Café to get refreshments. Lea was so nervous about this working out that her hands trembled ever so slightly as she held her iced decaf caramel latte, a Lea-suggested addition to the menu.

The three took their refreshments outside to sit at one of the tables shaded by umbrellas. She couldn't tell if the couple was still interested in purchasing the island or not. Their comments throughout the lengthy tour were mixed. Her impression was that they liked much of the island, but she noticed how they were quite hesitant about the amount of work that needed to be done to bring the island back to its glory days.

"I hope you enjoyed your tour," Lea said to get the conversation started.

"We did," Mrs. Kostopoulos said. "It's so beautiful here. You're lucky to have such an amazing home."

"Thank you." Lea turned her coffee cup around. "I think this is the most beautiful place on earth. That's why I want someone who loves it as much as I do to take it over."

"I understand." Mrs. Kostopoulos smiled. "If this were my home, I would want the same."

Was that a gentle way of letting her down? Lea's stomach twisted in a knot. She glanced at her coffee, but she had no desire to drink it.

"What my wife is trying to say is that we love the island, but with us nearing retirement age, there's more work here than we are up to doing. I know that's not what you want to hear, but I'm sure you'll find the right person for this place." Mr. Kostopoulos paused. "Unless you already have—"

"Hello, everyone." Xander's voice came from behind her.

What was he doing here? Lea stifled a sigh. Why should she worry? It wasn't like he could do any damage now. The Kostopouloses had already turned her down. But Xander didn't know that and she wasn't in the mood to enlighten him.

Everyone looked pleased.

Was this it? Had Lea found people to run the island just as she wanted?

Xander's chest tightened. If she had, then his chance of being close to her and the baby was slipping through his fingers. She wouldn't need anything from him and she could go anywhere in the world.

The thought of her moving far away didn't sit easy with him. It didn't sit well at all. He could only think of one desperate move to make—marry her.

As quickly as the thought came to him, he dismissed it. There had to be something he could do that was less drastic. He just couldn't think of what that might be at the moment. But he wasn't giving up. He wasn't a quitter—especially when the stakes were this high.

Xander shook hands with the Kostopouloses as introductions were made. And then as quickly as possible, he drew Lea aside.

"Why would you sell the island to them and not me?" he asked. "If it's the money, I will top what they're offering you."

Lea's expression didn't reveal her reaction. In a calm voice, she said, "It isn't about the money. What the baby and I need can't be bought and paid for."

He studied her for a moment. Was she saying that she wanted a family? With him? Impossible. She'd already made it clear that she could get by on her own.

Still, he thought she was being foolish for clinging to her pride instead of taking the money. In his business, he hadn't met many people who didn't value money above most everything. But the better he got to know Lea, the more he realized she was unlike anyone else he'd ever known.

"I need to get back to my guests," she said.

As she began to turn away, he instinctively reached out to her. His hand skimmed down her forearm and caught hold of her hand. She turned back with a surprised look in her eyes that were more green than blue today.

And then her gaze lowered to their clasped hands. He reluctantly let go of her. He was surprised by how much he missed her touch.

"Lea, please reconsider."

"I don't want to be indebted to you." She shook her head. "It wouldn't work."

She walked away before he could figure out his next words.

He remained at the café and purchased a black coffee while Lea escorted the couple to the seaplane waiting in the marina. He wondered if she'd made the deal. He couldn't tell. From where he stood by the railing of the café that looked out over the cove, he was able to see them on the dock. Lea shook hands with the man and the woman gave her a hug. It was a very friendly exchange.

Xander's jaw tightened. He had to make some big decisions and quickly. The first being, how far was he willing to go for Lea and the baby? To his surprise, he didn't have to think very long. The truth was he'd known the answer all along. He'd do whatever it took to keep them in his life.

Trying to invest in the island wasn't working. It seemed like Lea would rather let it fall into complete and utter ruin rather than take his money. He supposed it was because she felt a protectiveness toward this place. He'd never felt that sort of connection to any place. His lack of connection was what had made it easy for him to buy properties and sell them without any hesitation. Even his parents' home hadn't been hard for him to sell after their deaths. His sister, on the other hand, had an awful time parting with it. And for her sake, he had let his sister set the pace of the sale.

But Lea hadn't grown up on the island. It wasn't steeped in childhood memories for her. And yet she seemed to have automatically bonded with the island.

However, the more time he spent here, the more solace he found in its peacefulness. There was no rush-rush, no aggressive traffic with the angry horn blasts, and everyone was so friendly and helpful.

He needed a Plan B. That was how he'd gotten to the top of his professional world. So if he came at this from a business view, the first thing he needed to do was more research. He needed to learn how this island and Lea's business worked. It might just give him the insight he needed.

CHAPTER SIX

HIS GAZE FOLLOWED HER.

She could sense it.

It was late in the afternoon when Lea had finished with her guests. As she saw them off on a seaplane, she was aware Xander stood at the café, looking directly at her, but she turned her back and walked in the opposite direction.

She resisted the urge to glance over her shoulder. She'd made her decision and she wasn't going to change her mind now. It wouldn't work having Xander overseeing her every move and second-guessing her plans. He was used to being the one calling the shots and eventually he'd take over the operation of Infinity Island—just like Charles had attempted to take over her life.

Charles had been her boyfriend in college. At first, she'd thought it was cute how he would order for both of them at the restaurant. But then his opinion started to override hers in other areas of her life, from what movie to watch to what vehicle to buy. Eventually her voice was drowned out.

It took her roommate pointing this out for Lea to see what she'd let happen. And then she'd dumped him. He hadn't taken it well, telling her that she didn't know what she wanted—that she was allowing her friends to influence her. That last part would have made her laugh if he hadn't just done that very thing to her.

When Charles had pleaded with her to take him back, she'd given him the short answer. No. Unable to accept rejection, he'd persisted. She'd firmly held her ground. Eventually he'd gotten the message.

She had a voice and she wanted it to be heard. She had

opinions and she wanted them to matter. She could make choices and she wanted people to respect them.

"Is this how it's going to be between us?" Xander's voice came from behind her.

She straightened her shoulders and turned. "I don't know what you mean. I'm simply doing my job."

He nodded toward the plane that was just beginning to lift into the air. "Did you have a good meeting?"

Lea hesitated, trying to decide how much to tell him. She finally sighed in resignation. "You might as well know that they didn't make an offer for the island."

"Really?" Genuine surprise echoed in his voice. "May I ask why?"

She turned to walk back to her office. She gave the hem of her blouse a firm tug, wishing it was a little larger. She'd placed an order from that online boutique that Popi had recommended and even with expedited shipping, it wouldn't get to the island fast enough. Sometimes living remotely had its disadvantages—but thankfully not many.

As Xander fell in step next to her, she said, "The island needs more work than they are willing to invest at their age."

"So they were planning to keep running the island as a wedding destination?"

Lea nodded. "That's the only way I would even consider selling the island."

"And so if I were to promise to keep the wedding business going just as you have it, you would sell to me?"

Lea stopped just outside her office and looked at him. "Do you even know what goes into running Infinity Island?"

"I guess not."

"That's what I figured." She opened the door and stepped inside.

Xander was right behind her. She could see why he was

so successful as a businessman. He never gave up when he wanted something. But this time he wasn't going to get his way—no matter how much money he threw at her.

The breath hitched in her throat. Had she really thought that? Was she really that dedicated to her family's tradition that she would pass up a fortune in order to keep this island?

And the answer was a resounding yes. She loved the island. She loved the people that worked here. And she loved bringing two hearts together for all of infinity. The fact that there was no record of a couple married on the island ever getting a divorce was the most amazing thing about the place.

With so much chaos and hate in this world, finding a place full of love was rare. There was something magical about this island. It was worth fighting for.

"What are you thinking?" Xander's voice interrupted her thoughts.

"I was thinking how special this island is."

"Tell me about it."

She turned to him. "Like you want to learn about the wedding business."

"I do."

She shook her head. "You just want to figure out a way to level it and build your mansions."

"Lea—" he stepped closer until they were just inches apart "—I'm being serious. I realize that you're never going to allow me or anyone to develop this island. I've made peace with that. But I can't just walk away without understanding what goes on here—what makes it so special."

She studied him for a moment. "You're being on the level?"

"I am."

"You want to learn what? How I decide who gets married here? And how we have a hundred percent success rate of picking the couples that will make it through all of infinity?"

He shrugged. "Yes. You have to realize that it sounds totally impossible. Couples just don't stay together for long these days. Divorce, well, it's the norm."

"Not in my world." If she got married, it would be forever. "If a couple is married here on the island, they stay married."

"Show me."

Lea moved behind her desk. "Show you what?"

"How it all works? I want to see this in action."

"But I can't. I don't have anyone right now applying to marry on the island. I've had to cut back on how many couples we can take."

He dropped down in a chair. "How does it start?"

He really was curious. She couldn't help but be a bit proud of her work on the island. And most people never bothered to find out more about what she actually did. What would it hurt to give him a little insight into the process? It wasn't like he was going to start his own wedding venue. The thought made her smile.

"What's so funny?" he asked.

"I was just thinking of you as a matchmaker."

He gave a firm shake of his head. "It's not going to happen. But that doesn't mean I'm not curious about your work."

"Come here." And then she typed the island's website address into her computer. "This is where everything begins."

"A website? Interesting. But I'm guessing your grandparents didn't have it so easy."

"No, they didn't. They would advertise in newspapers and magazines. Then they would send out questionnaires.

It was a very long process. And it was still done that way until I took over."

"Really?" He rubbed his palm over his jaw. "I take it you've done a lot to speed up the process."

"I did…on my end. But it is still the same process for the prospective bride and groom. Digital or not, it still yields the same results."

"Mind if I try this process?"

He was joking, right? Why would he be interested in a matchmaking program? But he was the first man to show a genuine interest in her work. And it felt good to be taken seriously. Her parents had told her coming to the island was a waste of her time—a waste of her education. The echo of their words still hurt.

And so Lea turned to her computer. "Here it is."

"Do you mind?" Xander indicated that he'd like to sit in her chair for a closer look.

"Not at all." She stood and moved aside, careful that they didn't bump into each other. It wasn't until now that she realized how little space there was behind her desk.

He took a seat and perused the home page. "I like the setup. For some reason, I was expecting a bunch of red and pink hearts everywhere and maybe a cupid or two."

Lea gazed over his shoulder at the computer monitor that displayed a photo of the cove at sunset. She'd always thought it was so romantic. If she were ever to get married, she would love for it to be on the patio of the café that overlooked the cove. She couldn't think of any better backdrop for a wedding. Surprisingly, none of her guests had requested such a wedding. Not that Lea was planning on getting married any time soon. She had other more pressing matters—like her baby. And saving her home.

"I don't run a cheesy business." And then realizing that she'd misspoken, she said, "Well, I do have a cheese business, thanks to the goats. What I mean is—"

"I know what you mean. I like what I've seen so far." He flipped to the next page. "The website is well laid out and contains some stunning photos of the island."

The web page also spoke of its history and how successful the marriages on the island had been. It also spoke of Lea's grandparents who ran the island before her. She'd come across photo albums with black-and-white photos. She was able to digitize some of them and include them on the website.

The next page contained testimonials of happily married couples, from people who were married just a few years to others who had been married fifty or more years. Talking to those couples and reading their testimonials of what Infinity Island meant to them was what drove Lea to fight the good fight. This would work out somehow. Infinity Island would go on being the stepping stone to happily-ever-afters.

The following web page was where engaged couples began their journey. Many applied to be married on the island but only a few made it through the process and were chosen.

Xander studied the page. "So this is it? They just fill out this form and you know whether they are lifelong partners or not?"

"Something like that." She wasn't about to give away her family's secret. There was a certain, some might call it, magic to it all.

"I don't know." Xander rubbed the back of his neck. "I just don't see how this survey or whatever you call it can pick out true love. I'm not even sure there is such a thing."

"Trust me, there is. I know. I've seen it." And though she was still upset with her parents, she knew they had found true love—even if they hadn't been married on the island.

"What's the matter?" Xander's voice drew her out of her thoughts.

"What?"

"You were frowning. Was it something I said?"

She shook her head. "It wasn't you."

"Then what's the matter? If it's something I can help with, I will."

Really? He wanted to help her? The thought of not being in this game called life all alone sounded nice. Sure, she had Popi, but right now her best friend was very distracted with the baby she was carrying for her sister and brother-in-law.

She shook her head. "It's nothing."

Xander sent her a look that said he didn't believe her, but he thankfully let the subject drop. "Can I take one of your surveys?"

"Why would you want to do that?" She arched a brow. "Are you planning to get married soon?"

"I'd like to learn more about your process."

She noticed how he ignored her question about him getting married soon. She wondered if she should read something into that…or not. Still, the thought of him being involved with someone sent a burning sensation in her stomach. She refused to let herself accept the reason for such a reaction.

"I don't know—"

"I just can't believe such innocent questions can predict a lifetime of happiness." He turned the chair around to face her, causing her to jump back. "Have you ever taken the survey?"

She shook her head. "I've never had a reason to."

"Not even out of curiosity to see how exactly it works?"

"Not even then."

"Well then, I want to take the survey. I'm curious to see what sort of results this mysterious and accurate system produces."

"But you can't." When frown lines bracketed his lips

and eyes, she added, "I mean the system is geared for two people to take it. One person can't do it alone."

"Then you can take it with me."

She shook her head. "I don't think so."

"Is that because you know all of the right answers?"

"There are no right answers. It's a compatibility test."

"Then take it with me."

"But we already know that we're not compatible." And then her mind flashed back to that amazing weekend they'd spent together. For those few days, they'd been quite compatible.

"I'm not so sure about that. Why don't we take the test and see?"

He knew as well as she did that their weekend together was just a fluke. A momentary suspension of reality. There was no way they would ever get along that amazingly in real life. It had been an illusion—a moment of deep infatuation.

"I don't think so," she said, turning to the pile of mail on the side of her desk. "I still have a lot of work to do."

"I think you're afraid to take the survey with me." His eyes challenged her. "I think you're afraid of what the results will say."

She pressed her hands to her hips and stared at him. "I'm not afraid." When he continued to stare at her with a look of disbelief in his eyes, she said, "I'm not." And then with a dramatic sigh, for his sake, she said, "Fine. Let's get this over with. I really do have work to do."

A small smile of victory pulled at the corners of his mouth. Happiness was a good look on him. It eased his frown lines and made him look more handsome than any man had a right to.

She walked over to a cabinet where she kept some digital tablets that she used when working with the bride and groom as well as the wedding party. It was always so much easier to show people what she meant rather than explain everything.

She pulled up the website and then handed Xander one of the tablets. She kept the other one. She moved to one of the chairs opposite the desk. The added space between them made it easier for her to think clearly.

"I thought we were supposed to do this together," he said.

"We are." She stared at her tablet because every time she stared into his eyes, it felt like a swarm of butterflies was set loose in her stomach. "I have both tablets set up so that we are on the same survey. Just follow the questions."

"Seriously?"

She glanced up to find him frowning at the tablet. "What's wrong now?"

"It wants to know my favorite color."

"And?"

"Well, that doesn't seem like a very definitive question. How is it going to decide if we're compatible by the color I choose?"

"That's the mystery of the survey. Don't think you're the first to try to figure out the inner workings of the system."

"Really? Others have tried to copy you?"

She nodded. "And not just since I took over the business but when my aunt was running it. I even found correspondence of people and companies trying to buy the information from my grandparents."

"And they always turned them down?"

She nodded. "Some things are worth more than money. And it's not just the survey. There's something special about Infinity Island. A number of the couples married here come back year after year for their anniversary."

"I must admit that I just don't get it, but I can't argue

with the results you've been getting year after year, decade after decade."

"So what is it?" He looked confused, so she clarified. "What is your favorite color?"

"Isn't that cheating?"

"No. I don't have that question."

He shook his head as though he were utterly flummoxed. "It's red."

"Sounds about right." Red was a color of power—something Xander exuded.

"What does that mean?"

"Nothing. Do your survey. Remember this is your idea."

And so for the next half hour, they sat there in silence answering question after question about their likes, dislikes, personality and general topics. Lea had to admit that this was rather fun—even though she knew their results would turn out as incompatible.

"Finished," Xander said as though this had been a race.

Lea had one more question to answer. And boy, was it a tough one.

What do you like most about your partner?

Since all of the answers were multiple choice, she started going down through the answers. Eyes? Smile? Sense of humor? Voice? Kindness? Thoughtfulness? And the list went on.

Well, she did like his eyes. In fact, she could stare into them all night long.

And as she recalled, he did have a good sense of humor. He could even laugh at himself.

And there was his voice—his voice was so rich, like a fine dark chocolate.

How in the world was she supposed to settle on just one thing?

"Is there a problem?" Xander's voice cut through the debate in her head.

She clicked on the first option. His eyes. After all, weren't they the mirrors to one's soul? If so, there was a lot more to this man than she knew so far. And maybe it wasn't the wisest thing, but she was curious to know more about him. She tried to tell herself it was for the baby. When their child grew up, if Xander backed out of their lives, she'd be able to tell their son or daughter about their father. But she had a hard time swallowing that excuse. Her need to know came from a much deeper place.

"Finished." She looked up and found herself gazing into those eyes—the eyes that felt as though he could see through her thinly veiled excuses and the wall around her heart.

She glanced away. He couldn't see that much. She wouldn't let him.

Something was up.

Xander had noticed a difference in Lea since they started the survey. The questions of which he found unusual and sometimes quite probative. Like the one about what he liked best about Lea. That had been one of the easiest questions. He was drawn to her kindness.

Sure, she gave him a hard time, but that was because she perceived him as a threat—to her home, her independence and her ancestry. But he remembered the weekend they'd spent together. Once the business portion had concluded, she'd been sweet, kind and totally irresistible.

And he'd seen her with her employees. She was compassionate. She never asked them to do anything that she wasn't willing to do. He recalled her sopping up water in the honeymoon bungalow. She hadn't hesitated, not for a moment. She'd dived right in and gotten the messy job done.

Now if only he could get her to see him as someone other than the enemy. As much as he wanted to back away from this complicated situation, he couldn't. He believed her about the baby. Things had gotten a little out of hand that weekend and obviously mistakes had been made.

And now they had to come to an understanding that gave him peace of mind when he returned to Athens. He had no idea what the future would be like for any of them. It would help if Lea would tell him what she expected of him instead of being so stubbornly independent and insisting she could do everything on her own. They'd gotten into the awkward position together, and now they should both take part in an amicable solution.

"When will we get the results?" He had to admit he was rather curious to see what this survey would say about their prospects as a couple. He had a feeling it wouldn't be good. But that wouldn't stop him from attempting to keep his family together.

"Are you really that curious?" Lea asked.

He shrugged. He didn't want to reveal the extent of his interest. "I'm a businessman. I like to know how everything works—from a bystander aspect."

There was a part of him that wondered if Lea would accept it if this system—this reliable system—this age-old system—said that they were a good match. Would he?

Lea sighed as though in resignation. She got to her feet and moved around the desk, stopping next to him. "Do you mind?"

It took him a second, because he was so used to being the one behind the desk, to realize that he'd taken over her spot. He got to his feet and moved to the other side of the desk.

Lea took a seat and started typing on her keyboard. "Since I have automated the entire process, the results are basically instantaneous." She hesitated. Then glancing at him, she asked, "Are you sure you want the results?"

He got the feeling she didn't want them. Was that because she thought they'd make a good match? Or because she knew they were ill-suited for each other?

Since he wasn't good with personal relationships, he didn't have a clue how this would pan out. And so he wanted the answers. He wasn't sure he would believe them, as he'd spent his life breaking through other people's expectations of him.

"Yes. I want the results."

"Okay." Lea paused and then pressed one button.

She gasped.

In a heartbeat he was in motion, rounding the desk to find out what was the matter. He stopped next to Lea's chair and hunched over to get a good look at the monitor. His gaze searched through the words, looking for what had shocked Lea.

Had it totally rejected them?

Was she worried about them not being suited to co-parent their child?

And then two-thirds of the way down the screen, he read: *Perfect Life Partners.*

"Really?" He just couldn't believe those were the results. Had Lea pressed the wrong button? Were these the results for some other couple?

Lea swung her chair around to face him, causing him to jump back out of the way. "You cheated."

"What?" Surely he hadn't heard her correctly. "I did not."

Her fine brows drew together in a formidable line. "You had to because these results aren't right."

He crossed his arms and stared directly at her. "And how would I have cheated? I still don't understand exactly how this all works."

She paused as though taking his words into consideration. "This can't be right." She turned back to her computer and started pressing buttons.

Xander would concede that they were perfect together when it came to chemistry. In fact, he would say their sexual compatibility was off the charts, but as far as being perfectly suited as lifelong partners—no way. Lea's system must have a bug. Because he was all about facts, balance spreadsheets and boardroom meetings. She was all about warmth, adorable animals and greeting card verses. Those two didn't sound like they were meant to intertwine.

"Well," he said, growing impatient, "did you fix it?"

Lea didn't move. She just sat there staring at the monitor. The same results were still on display: *Perfect Life Partners*. "There's nothing to fix."

He tried to process this. "So you're saying you and me—two very different people—are meant to be together?"

She didn't turn to face him this time. "No."

He breathed a little easier now. *Thank goodness.*

"It means that if we wanted to be together it would work—we would work." She swung around. Her gaze met his. "But neither of us wants that."

"Right." He didn't know if her last statement was a question or not, but he was agreeing with her. He didn't want there to be any miscommunication.

He may want Lea and the baby in his life, but it wasn't going to be some sweeping love story. It was going to be much more basic than that.

CHAPTER SEVEN

SHE WOULD NOT give up.

She refused.

Lea curled up on the couch that evening with her laptop. Since her attempt to find investors in the island had failed, she was continuing her search for someone already in the wedding business who was interested in spreading their wings. It needed to be someone that believed in love and happily-ever-after. They had to have money available to invest in something proven to work, that guaranteed one successful marriage after another.

Then Lea's thoughts turned to the results for her and Xander. Was this place and its methods so reliable? Or had they just gotten lucky so far?

She didn't understand their compatibility results. Someone just had to look at them to see they weren't meant for each other—not that either of them was even considering it.

Was it possible her family's long-standing system for sorting out the perfect couples was flawed? Had she made a mistake when she'd meticulously automated the process?

Yes, that was it. She must have made a mistake. She would have to painstakingly audit the entire process to find the glitch.

A fluttering sensation in her midsection distracted her. Was that the baby? She sat up straight, waiting for the sensation to return.

"Is something wrong?" Xander asked from where he was working on his laptop at the dining room table.

"I don't think so. Wait. There it is again."

"There's what?" A frown of concern pulled at his handsome face.

"I think it's the baby kicking." It was the most marvelous butterfly sort of sensation.

He knelt down beside her. "Does it hurt?"

"Not at all." She took his hands and placed them on her baby bump. "Feel it?"

He was quiet for a moment, as though concentrating. And then he shook his head.

She felt bad for him. "I'm sorry. As the baby grows, it'll get stronger and then you'll be able to feel it."

His hands were still touching her when their gazes locked. Her heart began pounding. It would be so easy to forget that they were only co-parents and not so much more.

Was that what she wanted from Xander? More than this one fleeting moment? If she leaned over and kissed him, would it be a mistake? Until she had the answer to those questions, it was best not to further complicate things—for both their sakes.

She leaned back on the couch. "I better get back to work."

"Don't you ever take time off?" He took a seat in the armchair just a few feet away.

"What kind of question is that?" She frowned at him. "You're a workaholic. I doubt you ever take time off. Your time on the island must be your first vacation in forever. Your work is the most important thing to you—above family—"

"Whoa." His eyebrows rose high on his forehead. "Since when have you become an expert on me?"

"I... I'm not." She inwardly groaned. She hadn't meant to let it slip that she'd read one, okay, maybe two or three press releases about him. "But don't all successful businessmen work all of the time?"

His eyes said that he didn't believe her flimsy excuse.

"You've painted me to be some sort of villain, but you don't even know me. Not really."

The truth was she'd sought out every article she could find about him online. How could she not? He was the father of her baby. And so far, he'd been reluctant to share much about himself.

She crossed her arms. "Are you saying I'm wrong about you?"

He hesitated. "I'm saying you should give me a chance. Maybe I'll surprise you."

"You won't be here long enough to surprise me."

"Actually, I've decided to stay on for a few days, maybe a week."

"You *what*?" Surely she hadn't heard him correctly.

"I'm taking some time off from my business. You and I have lots to figure out."

Her lips pressed together in a firm line, holding back all of the reasons why his staying here with her was such a bad idea. And then she took in the resolute expression on his face. He was serious? He was staying? Here with her?

Unable to hold back any longer, Lea said, "This isn't going to work."

He sent her a reassuring smile. "Sure it is."

She shook her head. "No, it isn't. I have work to do. I can't just sit around and entertain you." She waved her hands around. "If you hadn't noticed, I have big problems here."

"If you'd let me, I could fix those problems."

If only she could trust him, she might entertain the idea. But she knew how much he wanted the island to add to his prestigious list of stunning properties. Besides, this was her problem, not his. She would figure a way out of it.

"I've got this." She hoped she sounded more confident than she felt.

Xander raised a questioning brow. "While you deal

with those problems, I'm going to see about making the honeymoon bungalow usable again."

She couldn't believe her ears. He was volunteering to do manual labor…for her…for free. Impossible. "Thank you. But you don't have to—"

"I know I don't. I want to. My grandfather always said it was good to get back to your roots now and then, otherwise you're likely to lose your path in life."

This was a different side of Xander—much different than she'd known to this point.

Lea closed her laptop. "I do have someone who can do the work."

"And I also know you're understaffed. So let me take this off your plate."

It was silly to argue with him. She already knew he was going to do as he pleased, no matter what she said. And if he was busy, it would keep him out of her way while she continued her search for the perfect buyer.

What was it going to be like being Xander's roommate? Her gaze moved to his face and then lowered to his lips. She remembered just how good they felt against hers. She knew it was a one-time thing—not to be repeated. But that didn't stop part of her from wanting more.

It would take time.

But the important things were worth the wait.

Late the next afternoon, Xander slung a wrench back in the borrowed toolbox. While he'd done manual labor that day, his mind had wandered to Lea and the baby growing in her belly. He was drawn to them in a way that he'd never experienced before. It was like they all belonged together—though he had yet to figure out what that family dynamic would look like. There were so many details to take into consideration.

He picked up a few more tools that he'd used to replace the pipes under the bathroom sink. There shouldn't be any other leaks. He remembered how his father had taught him to work with his hands as a kid. His father believed in doing things around the house himself instead of calling for a handyman. However, try as Xander might, he never did things the way his father had wanted them done.

At the time, Xander didn't think he'd ever use what his father had taught him. As he'd disappointed his father time after time, Xander promised himself that one day he would amass a fortune and when he did, he wouldn't have time for such menial tasks. Xander knew that if he wanted his parents' approval, he would have to be extraordinary—

"Is something wrong?" Lea's voice drew him from his thoughts.

He turned to her. "Sorry. I didn't hear you."

"I didn't mean to sneak up on you. I knocked but you must not have heard me. What has you so distracted? Is it the plumbing? If so, I can figure out some way to get a professional in here—"

"Slow down." He saw the worry reflected in her eyes and rushed to alleviate her concern. "The faucet is all fixed and shouldn't leak again."

"Really?"

He nodded. "I replaced everything as the parts were pretty old."

He had a feeling the plumbing he'd just replaced was indicative of most of the things on the island. And if that was the case, Lea was in bigger trouble here than she knew. As his gaze moved to her slightly rounded midsection, he decided not to enlighten her about how extensive the repairs could be. She already had more than enough on her mind.

"Oh." She looked a bit flustered as though she didn't know what she should say next. "Thank you. You really didn't have to do all of that."

"I didn't mind. I told you I want to help you succeed."

Just then there was a flash of lightning quickly followed by a loud crack of thunder. Lea jumped when the bungalow shook. Xander's gaze moved to the window, noticing that it was dark as night outside.

With a hand pressed to her chest, Lea said, "That's why I stopped by. I wanted to warn you about the approaching storm. But it was moving faster than I thought."

Xander closed the toolbox and stood. He moved to the front door and stared out as big fat drops of rain started to pelt the ground. "Looks like we're stuck here for a bit."

When Lea didn't say anything, he turned to check on her. Her gaze didn't quite meet his. Ever since he'd surprised her by showing up on the island after learning he was going to be a father, there had been a wall between them. And he really wanted to get past it.

Another strike of lightning lit up the sky followed by a crack of thunder. At the same time, the power flickered and went out. A few seconds later, the lights came back on.

"It's been a while since we've had a bad storm," Lea said. She moved to sit on the couch. "With all of the lightning, we should wait out the storm in here. Normally I'd sit on the porch and listen to the rain. It's just so relaxing and I love the smell of rain."

"The smell of rain?"

She nodded. "It's a fresh scent, unlike any other."

Not wanting this peaceful moment to end, he moved to the couch, leaving a respectable distance between them. When the thunder once again rumbled through the room, Lea jumped. He wanted to reach out to her, but he resisted the urge.

"I take it you don't like storms," he said, struggling to make light conversation.

"Rain, yes. Storms, not so much."

He had a feeling there was more to her discomfort than she was saying. He wasn't sure if he should ask about it or not. But if they were ever going to break through this wall standing between them, they had to start taking some risks instead of politely dancing around each other.

"Did you have a bad experience with storms?"

She nodded as the sky lit up again. Rain beat off the roof and echoed through the bungalow. "It was a long time ago. I'm not sure why it still gets to me."

Bit by bit, he could feel the wall starting to come down. He had to keep the line of communication open. "What happened?"

She glanced at him. "You don't want to hear this."

"Sure, I do. If you're willing to tell me." He realized in that moment that he wanted to know anything and everything about Lea. She intrigued him more than anyone else in his life ever had. Right now, she could tell him the story of her life and he'd hang on every word.

She turned her gaze to the front door that stood open. Only a screen door stood between them and the outside. A cool breeze rushed in, sweeping over them. But neither of them made any motion to close the door.

She stared outside. "I was only nine at the time, but I recall it so clearly. My family, we lived just outside of Seattle. It was late at night and I was asleep in my bed until a loud crack of thunder woke me. Until that point, I'd always been drawn in by storms. I thought they were so amazing, so powerful and so beautiful with the way the lightning would slice through the dark sky."

"I have to admit that I like stormy nights."

"After I was awakened that night, I couldn't go back to sleep. I moved to my bedroom window and while sitting there I saw the brightest light I've ever seen. It lit up the entire yard just like it was daylight out. Lightning struck the huge tree near our house."

He hadn't been expecting that. No wonder storms put her on edge. But he remained quiet, letting her finish.

"The tree burst into flames. I didn't know what to do. I think I tried to scream but nothing came out. The boom of thunder woke my parents. Just as they got to my room, the tree split down the middle. And then one half fell into the house."

He couldn't even imagine what that must have been like for a scared little girl. He didn't move as he waited for her to finish her story.

Lea's voice grew soft. "The limbs broke through my windows, sending glass flying through the room. After that the memories are a bit of a blur. I know my parents rushed me outside and a neighbor called the fire department. Luckily they were able to put the fire out before the whole house was damaged."

"And what about you? Were you hurt?"

"I had some cuts from the glass, but it could have been much worse. It's not like…"

And then she stopped. She was leaving something important out. They were finally getting somewhere. He willed her not to shut down now.

"It's not like what?" His tone was soft and coaxing.

"It's not like…like I was burned like my father." She glanced down at her hands that were clenched in her lap. "He was burned by a falling branch while he was trying to use the garden hose to put out the flames."

"That must have been horrible for all of you."

She nodded. "It was. My father's scars are a constant reminder of that night and how close we came to losing him. Every time I see his scars, I'm hit with a fresh wave of guilt."

"Why should you feel guilty?" Xander didn't understand. It was all due to Mother Nature and that was something no one could control.

"Because I was enthralled with the storm. I wished for more lightning. I'd willed it closer to my house so I could see it better."

At last he saw where she was going with this. "And so you feel like you wished the harm on your father."

"In a way. And I guess that's why I let my parents manipulate me for so long." Her gaze didn't quite meet his. "But learning the depth of the secrets they'd kept from me ended all of that. You probably think I'm silly for letting it go on for so long."

"I don't think you're silly." He reached out to her, placing a finger beneath her chin. He guided her face around until their eyes met. "I think you're a very caring person, who loves her father very much. I'm sure he never would have blamed you, so you should stop blaming yourself for something you had no control over. If wishes could control the weather, I guarantee you that it wouldn't be storming on Infinity Island right now."

"I don't know why I told you all of that."

Their gazes connected. He noticed how her eyes were more green than blue. It didn't seem to matter what color they were. He found them captivating.

And then his gaze lowered to her lips. There was no lipstick on them. No gloss or any other makeup. It was just her pink flesh and he was taunted by the memory of her sweet kisses.

He swallowed hard. "Do you know how much I want to kiss you?"

When she didn't say a word nor did she pull away, he took that to mean she wanted the same thing. He wondered if it could be as good as he remembered. He'd heard it said that you could make of your memories what you wanted. He'd been telling himself that he'd exaggerated the sweetness of her kiss because no kiss could be that good.

But when his lips pressed to hers, his heart pounded so loudly that it echoed in his ears. He'd never wanted something so much in his life. Her lips were soft and smooth. And in that moment, he regretted that they were seated on the couch. He wanted to pull her closer—much closer. He wanted every soft, curvy portion of her body pressed to his hard planes.

He slid closer until the length of his thigh was pressed

to hers. The softest moan reached his ears as she opened her mouth to him. Their tongues danced together in the most provocative way. His hand moved until his fingers were combing through her silky hair.

His memory of their time together hadn't been an exaggeration. In fact, it wasn't as good as the real thing. Not even close.

And then there was the sound of a motor. He was certain it was someone passing by on the beach. He dismissed the distraction and turned his full attention to treasuring this moment with Lea. If anything was going to convince her that there were still unresolved issues between them, it was this—their undeniable chemistry. She had to feel it—

Thump. Thump.

Footsteps?

"Hello," a female voice called out.

Lea flew out of his arms as though the lightning had struck them. He regretted that their moment had ended so quickly. For just a second, he considered reaching out and pulling Lea back to him, but he knew by the serious look on her face that she would resist his attempt.

Knock. Knock.

"Lea, are you here?"

Lea smoothed her fingers over her hair before tracing her fingertips over her lips as though to hide any evidence of what had just transpired between them. But she was wasting her time. Her lips were now berry-red and her cheeks were flushed. She'd been well kissed and it showed.

He wasn't sure how he felt about her attempts to hide their kiss. He'd never been erased before. It didn't feel good. He wanted Lea to be proud to be with him. Not hiding this—whatever you wanted to call their relationship—from the people in her life.

"Popi, I'm right here." Lea started for the door.

Popi responded but Xander wasn't able to make out the words.

When his gaze turned toward the door, he realized the storm had quickly passed over. The sun was once again shining, but in the wake of the storm the breeze had cooled—unlike him. But the kiss would have to be put on the back burner for now.

Lea rushed out onto the porch. "I got caught in the storm and thought this would be a good place to ride it out."

Popi glanced inside. Xander remained on the couch. He waved at her. She raised a questioning brow before turning back to Lea.

"I see you had company."

'Um, yeah. Xander was working on the plumbing issue."

Lea moved the conversation to business. As she spoke of the upcoming wedding that weekend, he wondered if she had so easily dismissed that stirring kiss, because he hadn't been able to do that. Not even close.

But sitting here hoping she would return to him was pointless. He knew the moment had passed. And so he got to his feet and walked to the bathroom to gather his tools.

This thing between them wasn't finished. In fact, he was certain that it was just getting started.

CHAPTER EIGHT

EARLY THE NEXT morning, Lea decided not to rush to the office. After all, what was the point of being the boss if you couldn't give yourself permission to work from home. And so she quietly moved through the bungalow, trying not to wake up her houseguest.

She'd thought about having him stay elsewhere, but try as she might, the number of bungalows in good condition was quite limited and they had to be reserved for the incoming guests. She told herself that was the reason she kept Xander close by. She refused to acknowledge that she liked seeing him all the time.

As she settled at the kitchen island with her laptop, her thoughts strayed back to their time in the honeymoon bungalow. That kiss, it had stirred her to her very core. Her face warmed at the memory, even though she'd replayed that scene a million times by now.

She couldn't believe she'd opened up to him about her childhood. She'd never told anyone that story—not even Popi. It wasn't that it was a secret or anything, but rather she didn't like recalling that level of fear—so scared that no sound had come from her mouth.

By reliving that memory, she'd reminded herself of one other thing—she missed her parents. This long silence between them was taking its toll on her. She'd always been close to her parents until she learned that they'd lied to her about her extended family.

To this day, she still didn't understand their reason for keeping her from knowing her mother's side of the family. From everything she'd unearthed while here on the island and from talking to the couples that routinely returned to the island to celebrate their anniversaries, she'd learned her aunt and grandparents were amazing people. She really wished she'd been given a chance to get to know them.

"What has you so deep in thought?"

She turned her head to find Xander standing a few feet away, wearing low-slung navy boxers and a bare chest. It was all she could do to keep her mouth from hitting the floor. His ripped abs were better than the ones splashed across the sizzling romances she liked to indulge in late at night.

Then realizing she was ogling him, she lifted her gaze. When their eyes met, she found a big grin on his face. The heat in her chest rushed up her neck and settled in her cheeks.

"Find something you like?" he asked with amusement dancing in his dark eyes.

She immediately turned her attention back to her laptop. She had absolutely no idea what she was about to type so she opened her email. She didn't care what she did right now so long as she didn't let her gaze stray back to his bare chest and those oh-so-tempting washboard abs. She stifled a groan.

"I thought I'd work at home this morning." The truth was her stomach was feeling a bit iffy. Her morning sickness hadn't been bad and had passed a few weeks ago. Could it be back? Or was it her nerves—between having Xander under the same roof and the dire straits of the island to worry about?

Regardless, she didn't want to go to the office only to make a spectacle of herself by running to the bathroom. But perhaps staying home wasn't her best move. "I'll just gather my things and get out of your way."

"No. Stay." His voice was so close.

He sat down next to her. She swallowed hard. She willed her body to move, but she remained there next to Xander as though he had some sort of magnetic force.

He glanced over at her computer. "Already working?"

"I have a lot to do."

"I see you have some emails about the island. I take it there's lots of interest in buying it."

Lea closed her laptop. "I'm still working on finding the right person to replace me."

"Replace you?" Xander was wide awake now. "I don't think that's possible. Besides, when we met you said you'd never walk away from the island."

"That was before."

"Before what?" He paused. "You mean before me?"

She shrugged. "A lot has changed since I met you. For one, I'm pregnant. For another, I've experienced just how much work this island needs and as you're quickly proving, it's more than I can do on my own."

"So you're just giving up? Walking away?"

"That's not what I said." But it felt like that was what she was doing. Her aunt had trusted her with their family's legacy and she'd failed.

"You can say it in some other words, if it makes you feel better, but it amounts to the same thing in my book. This is your dream. You shouldn't have to give up. There has to be another way."

"Sometimes dreams change." She thought of the baby. It was her priority now. Right or wrong, she had to do what she thought was best for the baby.

"I don't think you're going to be able to find anyone to take over the island and run it the way you do. You're so passionate about it—about bringing two hearts together. And from what I've heard, you're a terrific boss. Everyone on the island sings your praises."

They did? Her cheeks warmed. She was immensely touched. "I try my best. Sometimes I wing it. It isn't like this job comes with an instruction manual. But I'm sure there's someone who can do it better than me. After all, look around. This place needs some help—if I was so great, it would be all upgraded and fully maintained."

"You can't blame yourself for the problems that you inherited. These problems have been building over time. Some were covered up and hidden. But that can only be done for so long."

"It's just—" She was just about to say *too much*, but she stopped herself in time. "It's just time for me to move on."

"And what do you plan to do next?"

In that moment, she knew what she needed to do. Take a step back and reevaluate her life. "I'm moving to…" She wasn't sure where she wanted to move. "You know it really doesn't matter."

"Of course it matters. You and I, we're family now."

He stared at her for a moment. And she wondered what was going through his mind. Was he really worried that she'd disappear into the night? Or would he be relieved that she'd be gone—that he wouldn't have to deal with an unplanned family?

She looked into his eyes. Her heart started to beat faster. There was something special about him. When he looked at her, it was as though he could see straight through her— read her every thought—know the way he could make her body respond without even touching her.

She wanted to glance away—to keep him from knowing too much. But her pride kept her sitting there—staring at him. She swallowed hard. "Don't worry. I'll make sure you know where we end up." And then she decided to err on the side of caution. "If that's what you want."

"Of course, it's what I want. You and I, we have to learn to trust each other. How else are we going to raise a baby together?"

He had a point. But the "raise a baby together" part sent alarm bells ringing in her head. "How together are you planning for this co-parenting to be?"

This time it was Xander who looked uncomfortable

with the direction of the conversation. At last, he said, "That's what we're trying to sort out, isn't it?"

Suddenly she felt as though she were on display—as though he was here to see if she was good enough to fit into his world. That didn't sit well with her. She didn't do casting calls and she didn't shrink herself to fit into someone else's mold. If she did, she would still be on speaking terms with her parents. The thought made the breath hitch in her throat.

Her parents, they didn't even know they were about to become grandparents. The thought of having a baby and not being able to share it with them made her sad. But how was she ever supposed to trust them again after they'd lied to her about something so monumental?

"How have your parents taken the news about the baby?" Xander's voice stirred her from her thoughts.

She gave him a searching look. How had he known that she was thinking of her parents? Could he really read her mind? Then realizing how ridiculous the thought was, she dismissed it as quickly as it had come to her.

"Why do you ask?"

"Because if you're leaving here, it seems likely that you'll move close to your family."

Perhaps she should have given her words more consideration before she dove into the subject of her moving. The memory of the angry words passed between her and her parents came flooding back. And so did the pain of loss when they'd told her she had to choose, them or the island.

Most people would think she was strange for feeling like she'd lost two of the most important people in her life even though they were still alive. But the people who had raised her—had loved her—had taught her to reach for the stars—well, they had disappeared somewhere along the way.

The parents she had now, she didn't know them. She didn't know these people that would lie to her time and time again. These people who stole her chance to get to know her extended family—her grandparents and aunt—they weren't the parents she'd loved. They were strangers to her.

And the people who had given her an ultimatum between choosing them or choosing Infinity Island—her birthright—had left her no choice. She wasn't going to choke down whatever lies they chose to tell her. She was going to learn about her family herself—

"Lea?" There was a note of concern in Xander's voice. "What's wrong?"

The backs of her eyes stung as the thought of all she'd lost came roaring back to her. She blinked away the tears. The last thing she wanted was for Xander to think she was weak.

She was strong—strong enough to raise this baby as a single mother. If he had any doubts about that, she would make sure to put them to rest before he left the island, which she hoped was soon.

She swallowed down her emotions. When she spoke, she hoped her voice didn't betray her emotional state. "My parents don't know about the baby."

His brows rose. "Why didn't you tell them?"

She glanced away. "Does it matter?"

His gaze narrowed. "What aren't you telling me?"

"Nothing."

"Oh, it's something. Talk to me. Maybe I can help."

She glanced at him. "Why would you want to do that?"

"Because whether you want to believe it or not, I want to be your friend."

"And not steal the island out from under me?" The hurt expression on his face made her regret her words. "I'm sorry. I didn't mean that." Not really. "It's just that everything in my life is changing at once and it has me uptight."

He didn't say anything for a moment as though considering her words. At last, he stuck out his hand. "How about we call a truce?"

She glanced down at his hand. The last thing she wanted to do in that moment was touch him. Every time their bodies connected, it was like her mind short-circuited. Still, he was trying to do the right thing. The least she could do was meet him halfway.

She reached out her hand and as their fingers and palms touched, a shiver of excitement coursed up her arm, settling in her chest. Was it just her imagination or did his fingers move ever so slowly over her palm? And there was this look in his eyes—the kind of look men gave her when she went onto the main island with Popi and they stopped in a *taverna*.

But then in a blink the look was gone, and after a quick shake, he withdrew his hand. Lea was left wondering if she was just seeing what she wanted to see or if Xander was actually still interested in her.

"There." He smiled. "Now can we act like friends instead of adversaries?"

"I didn't think I was being adversarial."

He sighed. "You're doing it again."

"Doing what?"

He smiled and shook his head. "So now that we're officially friends, talk to me. Why haven't you told your parents about the baby? Are they old-fashioned? Will they insist we get married?"

She leveled a serious stare at him. "You aren't going to leave this alone, are you?"

He shook his head. "Not a chance. I told you I'm your friend. I'm here to help."

Lea was surprised by how much she wanted to believe him. She'd been going it alone since she'd moved to Greece. She did have Popi, but ever since her friend had agreed to be a surrogate for her sister, Lea hadn't felt right about sharing too much of her problems. Popi had a lot to deal with.

Lea was so proud of her friend for doing something so selfless. Lea knew what it was to have a baby grow inside her and she didn't know if she could go through that very special relationship and then hand off the baby—even to a sibling. It took someone very strong, very loving and very special to be a surrogate.

Lea's gaze met Xander's. Sincerity and kindness reflected in his eyes. Maybe it was time she let go of the past and gave him a chance—a real chance. "My parents aren't particularly old-fashioned. I think they'd be okay with me being a single parent."

"Then what's stopping you?" He rubbed the back of his neck. "I don't know much, let me rephrase, I don't know anything about pregnant women, but I would think it's a time when a woman would want her mother."

She did want to talk to her mother and get her advice on different aspects of her pregnancy. Most of all she just wanted to share the joy.

"Under normal circumstances that would be the case," Lea said.

"But these aren't normal circumstances?"

Lea shook her head. She took a deep breath. If she was going to trust him, she had to continue opening up to him. "When I left Seattle and moved to Greece, there was a big blowup with my parents." She paused. How much should she say? After all, he was just being nice. He wouldn't want to hear the whole sordid story. "We haven't spoken since."

"I see." His expression changed as though he were troubleshooting the situation. "Maybe the baby could be the bridge to bring you back together."

Lea shook her head and placed a protective hand over her abdomen. "I won't use my baby that way. If my parents and I work this out, it'll be because they want to—not because it's the only way for them to get access to their only grandchild."

"You say if they want to, but what about you? Do you want to work things out?"

That wasn't an easy question to answer. "Yes. And no."

His brows rose. "Care to elaborate?"

She sighed. "My parents lied to me, both by omission and with flat-out lies. They didn't tell me about this island—about my grandparents and aunt. They knew if they told me I'd insist on coming here—on meeting and knowing my extended family." Just mentioning it made her body tense. "And now they are all dead and all I have are the pictures and notes that are here on the island to give me a clue what these people were like. It wasn't fair. My parents robbed me of a piece of my life—something I'll never get back."

"I had no idea. No wonder this island is so important to you. But surely your parents had a good reason to keep it all from you."

"According to them, my grandparents forbade them to marry and said if they did that they would disown my mother."

"Maybe that's why they didn't mention this part of the family. They had written your grandparents out of their lives."

"But what about my aunt? She didn't disown anyone. In the end, after my grandparents died, she was left on this island without any family. She was alone when she died. It wasn't how she wanted it."

"How do you know?"

"Because there was a letter to me in her will. She told me that over the years she'd tried to reach out to her sister, but the letters were always returned unopened. When the internet became a thing, she found out about me, but before she could contact me, the attorney told me that she died of cancer. Can you imagine dying all alone with no family?"

Xander reached out and pulled Lea close until her head rested on his strong shoulder. He didn't say anything. Instead he just sat there for a bit holding her until she had her emotions under control.

When Lea pulled back, she did so reluctantly. She hadn't allowed herself to remember how good it felt to be held in Xander's arms. And now as she leaned back on the barstool, she missed his warm and comforting touch.

"I should get to the office. I have a lot to do."

He nodded in understanding. "And I told Joseph that I would help him today with a bungalow on the other side of the island."

Joseph was a very loyal employee. He'd been working on the island for more than twenty years and he was a very talented man—a jack of all trades. But he wasn't a people person. He would rather keep to himself unless he knew you well.

"So you and Joseph hit it off?"

Xander nodded. "Is that a problem?"

"No. Not at all." She was just surprised. She wondered what Joseph saw in Xander to take him under his wing so quickly. "I'll see you this evening."

"We still have more to discuss."

As Lea let herself out the door, she reminded herself that the tender moment hadn't meant anything other than that Xander was a caring friend. She couldn't allow herself to read more into the moment—it'd only lead to more heartache for her. She knew that sooner or later the people closest to her would let her down.

If she allowed Xander into her life, she had to make sure to keep him at arm's length. That would prevent hurt feelings and misunderstandings. She told herself it was best for their baby. Two parents who could coexist in peace was worth the sacrifice of not finding out if there could be more with the man who made her heart race with just a look.

CHAPTER NINE

HE COULDN'T JUST let her walk out of his life.

Move to the other side of the world.

The following afternoon, Xander frowned as he entered Lea's empty office. Sure, he was rich and could travel, but he couldn't relocate his real estate conglomerate to the States. Nor could he afford to be gone for long stretches of time. And then what would happen? He'd have to choose between the empire he'd built and his child?

Could he do that? Could he choose between the two things that meant the world to him? His child? And his life's work?

It seemed as if it didn't matter which he chose. He would be losing a piece of himself. But he refused to give up. There had to another solution—something he wasn't seeing—something within his power to resolve. Because he couldn't stand the thought of another man raising his child.

As the thought of someone else taking his place in his child's life took root, he realized that would mean another man would also play a significant role in Lea's life. Suddenly the image of a man holding and kissing Lea's tempting lips filled Xander's imagination. His body tensed as his hands balled up. That couldn't happen.

Maybe if he stuck around and showed her how good they could be together as friends—as business partners— she would change her mind about leaving. It would mean spending even more time here on Infinity Island. And that would mean complications with his business and his sister. Still, he had to make Lea and the baby his priority.

And with that thought in mind, he removed his phone

from his pocket. His fingers moved rapidly over the screen as he wrote a message to his sister.

Unavoidably detained. The plans for the Italian resort will have to be put on hold. Sorry. Will make this up to you.

As though Stasia had been sitting there with her phone in her hands, waiting for him to send a text, his phone rang. Caller ID let him know that it was in fact his sister. He knew if he answered it wouldn't be a short conversation. Not by a long shot. So he let it go to voice mail.

The truth was he felt guilty and that was not something he felt often. He was used to making the tough decisions—the decisions others didn't agree with. But this time his decision was affecting someone he loved. It was a tough thing to swallow.

They both knew if he didn't fly to Italy the following week to close the important deal they would lose their initial investment and any future chance to take part in such a promising venture. But he would make sure his sister wasn't out any money—even if his own company took a significant financial hit.

It was only then that Xander realized he was gambling with his future for a woman who didn't even seem to want him around. That had never happened to him before. He was venturing into uncharted water without a life vest. And he was very likely to sink—

"Something on your mind?" Lea's voice interrupted his troubling thoughts.

He turned to her as she crossed her office to take a seat behind her desk. "Yes. I wanted to let you know that we've hit a bigger problem than was first suspected with the Seashell Bungalow. In this case there actually wasn't a leak with the plumbing."

"But the wall had all of that water damage."

"It's actually a leak in the roof."

"But the ceiling looked fine."

"The water bypassed the ceiling and made its way down the wall, causing problems with the wall and floor."

A frown pulled at Lea's face. "That sounds like an expensive problem to fix."

"Don't worry. I have this all under control."

She arched a brow. "You do roofing work, too?"

"No. But I know people that do and I've called in a few favors."

"Xander, no." She got to her feet. "You can't be doing that. This isn't your problem. And…"

"And what?"

She averted her gaze. "Nothing."

"It was definitely something. And what?"

Her gaze met his. "And I don't want to be indebted to you."

He could feel himself begin to sink and there wasn't a life vest anywhere in sight. She didn't want to be indebted to him, meaning she didn't want to be involved with him. The knowledge hit him with a sharp jab that left a piercing pain in his chest. If Lea let him into her life, it would be because she wanted to…not because she had to.

His parents had let him remain in their lives after his sister was born because they had to—because they were already obligated. Not because they loved him—not like they loved his sister. Growing up, he'd seen it was all about his sister this and his sister that. Even now the memories hurt, but he shoved aside those thoughts, refusing to get caught up in something that he couldn't change.

"You won't be." He said it with certainty.

She looked at him with skepticism reflected in her beautiful eyes. "Then why would you do it? Why put off getting back to your business?"

"Because you need help and I can help you." He sighed. "Lea, I know our relationship is complicated, but I'm not the enemy. I'm not here to pull off some elaborate scheme and steal your island away from you. I promise."

She didn't say anything for a moment, as though digesting his words—weighing them. He willed her with his eyes to believe him. He'd never had a problem getting a woman to believe him before—but Lea wasn't just any woman.

"If I was smart, I'd turn you down." She no longer looked upset. "But as my mother used to say, a beggar can't be choosy. And if you mean it about lending a hand, it just might help me land a buyer."

That wasn't exactly what he had in mind, but he could only deal with one problem at a time. For the moment, he had Lea's blessing to remain in her life. He didn't miss the enormity of the event. But he also realized that in order to keep Lea in his life, it was going to take more of a commitment from him than he'd originally planned on.

So he'd have to move this thing with Lea along—his plan would now have two parts. First, he would find a way to pay off her debts, as this island was special. It truly was starting to grow on him. And second, he needed to do something for the baby—something more than providing financial support. The thought churned in the back of his mind.

But he had to know exactly what he was up against. "How is the search for a buyer going?"

"I've actually had a number of inquiries. But none have panned out."

"Have you given more thought to contacting your parents?" Xander didn't want her to leave Greece—with each passing day he was certain it was a big possibility. It might be the only thing he was certain of at this moment.

"I... I haven't had a chance to speak with them. I've been so busy with the sale of the island."

"I see." But he didn't. Not really.

"What?"

He sent her an innocent look. "I didn't say anything."

"You didn't have to. You have that look on your face."

"What look?" He was a master at the poker face. It had played a large role in getting him to the top of his profession.

"The look that says you don't believe me."

"Why wouldn't I believe you? Or maybe I should ask why I shouldn't believe you?"

Lea turned to the window, keeping him from reading the emotions reflected in her expressive eyes. "I've been busy. I haven't had time to think about it."

So she was procrastinating. As much as he wanted to keep Lea in his life, he wanted her to have the support of a loving family—something he'd had a glimpse of when he was very young.

"You should call."

She turned to him with her arms crossed over her chest. "Aren't you being a bit bossy?"

He wasn't going to be distracted. "I mean it, Lea. Life is unpredictable. And it's short. Don't waste this time."

Her gaze changed. "You aren't talking about me anymore, are you?"

"Of course I am."

"I'm pretty certain you're not." She approached him and stared deep into his eyes. "What aren't you telling me?"

Xander rubbed the back of his neck. He hadn't wanted to get into this. For many years he'd pretended that his parents didn't exist. Which was a reason he'd avoided his sister for much of that time. She loved the memory of their parents and was forever touting their parents' merits. He never corrected his sister when she said how much their father loved him. It wouldn't have done a thing to make either of them feel better.

As such, he'd kept his distance from his sister until she lost her husband. Xander would have done anything to make her happy—even when she came up with this plan for them to go into business together. When Stasia threatened to go into the real estate market with or without him, he couldn't let her venture into uncharted water without him. He wouldn't let her lose her entire savings.

"Xander, talk to me." Lea's coaxing voice dragged him from his thoughts.

He shook his head, chasing away the memories. "You don't want to hear this."

"I do. If you'll tell me."

He glanced around the office, suddenly feeling boxed in. "Not here."

Without waiting to hear if she was going to accompany him, he headed for the door. The memories of his childhood came rushing back to him. He needed to get outside. He recalled how he'd constantly done things to get his parents' attention, especially his father's. When good things didn't garner words of praise, he'd turned to the bad things. Xander squeezed his eyes shut, trying to block the flashes of memories. Still, they kept coming. The good ones. And the bad ones.

He kept putting one foot in front of the other. He couldn't take a full breath. It wasn't until he was outside in the bright sunlight with the fresh sea air blowing in his face that his footsteps slowed. At last he could breathe easily.

And then there was a hand on his shoulder. "Xander, what's wrong?"

He shook his head. How did he allow this conversation to get turned around on him? "This conversation isn't about me. It's about you and your family."

"Talk to me about your family."

Why did she have to keep pushing this? He never talked about his family with anyone. *Not ever.* Unable to stand around while having his past dredged up, he continued walking until he reached the beach.

"You can keep walking, but you aren't going to lose me."

She rushed to catch up with him. "You can't expect me to trust you—to open up to you—and you not do the same."

She was right, but that didn't make him feel better. He kept moving but his thoughts were light-years away, racing through the past. Lea wasn't going to understand. She was going to think, just like his sister, that he was making too much of things. His sister had never noticed how their parents treated their adopted child differently than their biological child. He didn't care what happened, but he would never make his son or daughter not feel good enough.

Suddenly there was a hand gripping his arm, pulling him to a stop. "Xander, are you serious about us becoming good friends?"

He stopped. He wanted them to be more than friends—he wanted the family that he'd been robbed of his whole life, the family he'd lost when his biological parents had left him on the hospital steps and his adopted parents had found he couldn't match up to their biological child.

But he couldn't rush things. He couldn't blink his eyes and create the perfect family. And he was beginning to realize this endeavor was going to require so much more of him than he'd ever considered investing. It would mean laying his tattered heart on the line.

He turned to Lea, catching the concern reflected in her eyes. "Yes, I want us to be closer."

She took his hand in his, surprising him. She drew him over to a large rock where they could sit and stare out at the sea.

When Lea spoke, her voice was soft and coaxing. "Tell me about your family."

His immediate reaction was to change the subject, but he knew this was his chance to gain her trust—to take their relationship to a new level. And more than that, maybe his story would convince her of the importance of clearing things up with her parents sooner rather than later.

"I was adopted." The words just came spilling out.

"I… I didn't know."

"I don't talk about it—normally." He struggled to figure out where to start. "I didn't know my biological mother… or father. I was left on the hospital steps when I was a few months old."

Lea squeezed his hand, letting him know she was there for him. He took comfort in the simple gesture.

"My parents didn't think they could have children of their own and so they adopted me. For the early years, things were great. And then when I was four my mother got pregnant with my sister. Everyone was excited. Me included. But as my sister grew older, I noticed how they made time for her school programs but not mine. They gave my sister what she wanted but told me that I had to work for what I wanted."

"That must have been rough, but I'm sure they loved you, too."

"Really? Because I wasn't sure."

"Maybe it was just the difference of you being a boy and your sister being a girl."

He shook his head. "Don't go there. I've already tried to explain it to myself. But I know different."

"You know? You can't know."

"Oh, but I do. I had it directly from my father."

The painful words came rushing back to him. He hadn't thought of them in a very long time. In fact, he had told himself that if he didn't recall the memories for long enough they would disappear just like a nightmare eventually faded away. But as he recalled the incident, the exact words came rushing back to him.

Lea didn't say anything as though she was sitting there waiting for him to find the words to explain it to her. Why did he keep opening up more and more to her?

Xander swallowed past the lump in his throat. The best thing was to get this over with as quickly as possible. "I was sixteen at the time. I'd been getting into a lot of trouble at school and at home, while my sister could do no wrong. Now, don't get me wrong, I love my sister. She's great. But we are as different as night and day. She didn't have to fight for my parents' attention."

He searched his memory for that one poignant day that altered the course of his life. "I had just gotten my driver's license and I wanted my own motorcycle, but my father said if I wanted one, I had to earn it. I also had to pay my own insurance."

"Dare I say it sounds reasonable? You know, teaching a child responsibility."

"It would have been if the conversation had stopped there." He took comfort in having her fingers entangled with his. He rubbed his thumb over the back of her hand. Her skin was so smooth—so tempting.

"You don't have to tell me if it's too painful."

Those words were like a challenge to him. "I refused to accept my father's decision. I kept pushing."

"Didn't we all at that age?"

"It was during one of our arguments that my father reached his breaking point. He turned on me and said I wasn't his son." Xander had never admitted that to anyone, ever. Not even to his sister. "My father told me boarding school would put more structure in my life. That was when I told him that I hated him. I told him I never wanted to see him again. At which point he said unless I changed my attitude not to come home for the holidays." And then realizing he'd let the conversation get too serious, he said, "I bet you were the perfect daughter."

Lea was quiet for a moment. "Not exactly. There was this one bad boy in high school with a few tattoos and a big bad attitude that my parents wouldn't let me date. We did get into it about him, but looking back on it now and knowing the guy was picked up for breaking and entering, I'm glad I lost that argument."

Xander knew she was trying to make him feel better and he appreciated the effort. But there was more. He drew in an unsteady breath.

Xander raked his fingers through his hair. "Now that I'm older, I realize it wasn't all my parents' fault. I was stubborn and angry. Even though my mother tried to smooth things over at the holidays, I noticed my father never said a word. As such, I quit going home for the holidays. I either stayed at school or went on holiday with friends. During the summer, I would work for my grandfather—my mother's father. He was into real estate. He would give me odd jobs of mowing lawns, painting houses, and one summer he got me a job working with a contractor. I learned a lot that summer."

"What about your sister? She had to have missed you a lot."

"She did. She would call and beg me to come home. When I told her I couldn't because our father didn't want me around, she insisted on visiting my grandparents while I was there." Xander smiled as he remembered his sister's insistence that they not grow apart. "She was tenacious when she wanted something."

"And she loved her big brother."

He nodded. His sister's love was something that he never doubted. "She's great—even if she can be a bit pushy at times."

"You keep telling me that it's not too late to repair my relationship with my parents. Why don't you do the same?"

This was the part that hurt the most. The ache in his chest ebbed. "I can't do that—"

"Sure you can—"

"No, I can't. They died when I was in college. It was a car accident."

"I'm so sorry."

"My grandparents took in my sister. I pulled away—even from Stasia. I felt angry that I had been robbed of the chance to ever fix what had been broken between me and my parents. And I felt guilty that I'd ignored my mother's repeated pleadings for me to come home. I knew my father would be there and I didn't know what to say to him. And in the end, I don't think he knew what to say to me, either."

"I know I don't have to say this, but I'm going to anyways. Your parents loved you. Maybe they didn't always show you how they felt in the way you needed them to." She squeezed his hand. "But they did until the very end. And they knew you loved them, too."

He shook his head. He knew she meant well, but she didn't know the entire situation. She couldn't. She hadn't been there. But he wasn't going to argue with her. It wouldn't do either of them any good.

"Why did you tell me this?" she asked.

He pulled back a little in order to look directly at her. "You know why I told you."

"It was more than wanting to share. Were you trying to tell me how important it is for you to have a strong relationship with our child?"

How did she do it? How did she see through him so clearly?

"Yes, I suppose that was part of it. I can't—I won't let my child ever doubt my love for him or her."

A big smile lit up Lea's eyes and made her whole face glow. "You already love the baby?"

He hadn't thought about it before. Not in those terms. *Love* was a word that he avoided. Until now.

He lifted his gaze until he was staring into the greenish blue depths of Lea's eyes. It was there that he found caring and understanding instead of pity. He drew strength in her compassion.

He knew how risky it was to love someone. He knew they could betray him. They could cut him to the quick. And yet in that moment it was what he craved more than anything.

Xander continued to stare into Lea's eyes. "Yes, I do."

Lea's eyes shimmered with unshed tears. She blinked repeatedly. "I'm head over heels in love with the baby, too. I never knew I could love anyone this much."

"Enough to give up your dreams here?"

She nodded. "Yes, that much."

In that moment, he felt a tangible connection to Lea. It was such a strong feeling that he couldn't actually describe it, but it filled him with warmth.

With his free hand, he reached out to her and traced his finger down her silky-smooth cheek. "Do you know how amazing I find you?"

"You do?" Her voice was barely more than a whisper.

"I do." His gaze moved to her lips. They lacked any lipstick and yet they were still rosy pink and tempting. When his gaze lifted to meet hers, he caught the spark of interest in her eyes. It made him want her all the more.

"I'm going to kiss you," he said softly.

"And I'm wondering what's taking you so long."

He moved at the same time she did. Their lips met in the middle. He remembered when they'd kissed in the past. It had been full of discovery and curiosity. This time, though, his mouth moved over hers knowing what she liked.

They may have only spent a long weekend together a few months ago, but the memory of her kiss was tattooed upon his mind. Their kisses had gone on and on, partly from an unending desire and partly because he knew it would end soon and he wanted—no, he needed—to remember the way she felt in his arms and the way she tasted so sweet like ripe, red berries. But those memories were nothing compared to the real thing.

As his mouth moved over hers, coaxing her to open up to him, he realized just how much he'd missed this—missed her. He'd tried fighting it. He'd told himself it wasn't her but the human connection that he missed. He'd told himself that he'd worked too hard for too long. He needed to spend some time away from the office.

But now, as his fingers slid down over Lea's cheek to her neck, he knew he'd been lying to himself. He'd craved Lea all of these weeks and it had nothing to do with his workload or his lack of a social life. It had only to do with Lea and how much he'd missed her.

Her hands slipped up over his shoulders, up his neck. Her fingers combed through his hair as her nails scraped over his scalp, setting his nerve endings atingle. A moan swelled within the back of his throat. If they weren't here on the beach in the middle of the resort, he would definitely take things further.

Before things got totally out of control, he had to stop this madness. But he made no motion to pull away from her. He needed her more than he needed oxygen—

That thought jerked him out of the clouds and brought his feet back down to earth with a jolt. He pulled back from her. He couldn't lose his head. Because there was absolutely no way he was falling in love. None. He'd promised himself that he would never let himself become that vulnerable again.

"What's the matter?" Lea asked.

He shook his head and forced a smile to his lips. "Nothing. Nothing at all." And then his gaze met her confused look. "I... I need to get going. I have to get to the dock."

"What? But why?"

"Those men I have coming to work on the bungalow—" he checked the time "—should be here now."

"Oh. Okay." The look of disappointment on her face was unmistakable.

He longed to take her back in his arms and kiss away her unhappiness, but he stilled himself. To do that—to cave in to his desires—he'd give her the wrong idea. He'd give himself the wrong idea that this relationship was more than a convenience for co-parenting their child.

"I'll talk to you later." He turned and started to walk away. He should say something else, but what?

"I'll see you later," Lea called out.

He stopped and glanced back. "See you then."

Xander walked away feeling more confused than ever. And that was a state he wasn't familiar with. He was a planner, a decision maker. He didn't have time in his life for indecision—until Lea stepped into his life.

Ever since that first day when his gaze had settled on Lea, he'd known something was different about her. He hadn't been able to put it into words at the time. And even now, he couldn't describe the effect she had over him. And he wasn't eager to examine it too closely.

But he was even more determined to do something special for their baby. He worried about being there for the child emotionally with his own scarred past, but he could do something with his hands—something to show Lea that he cared.

CHAPTER TEN

WHAT IN THE world was that about?

It was the question Lea had been asking herself since she shared that kiss with Xander the previous afternoon. She kept telling herself she'd been trying to comfort him and it had just gone too far. But had it gone too far?

Wasn't that kiss what she'd been dreaming about night after night? Didn't she want him to hold her in his arms like he'd done not so long ago? The questions whirled round and round in her mind.

And then she'd waited around last evening hoping they'd have dinner together—a chance to straighten things out—but he hadn't shown up. She'd even resorted to texting him but he hadn't responded. When she'd gone to bed, he still hadn't returned.

And this morning when she'd awakened, she heard the front door banging shut. She glanced at the clock to see if she'd slept in, but she hadn't. He was up and gone with the sunrise. Was he avoiding her? Did he regret their kiss that much?

The thought of him not enjoying the kiss as much as she had sent an arrow of pain slicing into her chest. She assured herself that it was her pride being wounded and nothing more. It had to be: she knew to be careful with her emotions because people let her down—even if they didn't mean to.

The much-anticipated arrival of maternity clothes—professional and casual—wasn't enough to gain her full attention. Not even the little black dress she'd spent too much money on had nudged her out of her subdued mood. She told herself she'd indulged on the dress so she'd have something to wear to oversee the weddings, but she wasn't that good a liar—she wanted to look good for Xander most of all.

Refusing to dwell on a man who was now avoiding her, she closed the box of maternity clothes and turned her attention back to the computer monitor. She had a handful of new offers to buy the island.

As she scanned the offers, thoughts of Xander came back to her. She recalled how their encounter had started. He'd been trying to talk her into contacting her parents. A part of her knew he was right. But another part of her was still trying to deal with their betrayal. How could she ever trust them again? But she didn't want to end up like him, with no chance to right what had gone wrong.

She reached out for the phone on her desk. Her hand hovered over the receiver, but she hesitated. What would she say? Should she apologize for leaving in such a huff? But was she sorry? She loved Infinity Island and the people who lived here. If she had to do it again, she'd still make the same choice.

As her hand settled on the phone, it rang. The buzz startled her. Was it possible that it was her family? Maybe they were thinking of each other at the same time.

Knowing it was a silly notion, Lea checked the caller ID. It was Xander. For the briefest second, her heart dipped.

With an ache in her chest, she answered the phone. "Hey, we've been missing each other."

"Lea, I need you to come home now."

And then the line went dead.

What was up with that? She stared at the phone. Was something wrong? Had Xander gotten hurt? The thought sent her heart into overdrive.

She quickly dialed his number. The phone rang. And rang. But he didn't answer. What was going on?

She raced out the door, shouting to her assistant that

she'd be back later. Her assistant said something, but Lea didn't catch the words. She kept going. Her thoughts turned to Xander and his cryptic phone call. *Please let him be all right.*

Lea jumped in her golf cart and set off. For the first time, she realized that living halfway across the island was a problem when there was an emergency.

The more she thought of Xander and pictured him in trouble, the harder she pressed on the accelerator. Everything would be all right. But what if it wasn't. She floored the accelerator, wishing it would go faster.

When the cart skidded to a stop in front of the bungalow, she jumped out. She raced up the steps and swung the door open. "Xander? Xander, where are you?"

And then he stepped out from the kitchen with a dish in his hands. "I'm right here."

Her gaze swept over him, checking for any injuries or blood, but he looked perfectly fit. Noticing her white apron slung around his neck, she glanced at the stove to see if something had caught fire, but all looked to be fine.

"What's the emergency?" she asked.

"What emergency?" He moved to the dining room and placed the covered dish on the table where there was already a bottle of wine, fresh flowers and a candle.

She was so confused. "When you called, you said I had to rush home. I thought something was wrong. I thought…" She stopped herself, not wanting to admit how worried she'd been when she thought something had happened to him. "I didn't know what to think when you hung up on me. And then you didn't answer when I called back."

"Sorry about that. I was worried that lunch was going to burn."

She stepped closer to the table, taking in the perfectly made up table. "You did all of this for me?"

He turned to her. "Yes. I did."

She suspected he was up to something. But what? He'd

avoided her since their kiss and now he was cooking for her? And picking flowers?

Part of her wanted to go with the moment and just enjoy the gesture. But another part of her wanted to understand Xander's motives. Her mother had taught her that if something appeared to be too good to be true, then it most likely was.

Xander lifted the bottle of wine as though to open it and then paused. "What was I thinking? You can't have this." He started for the kitchen. "I'll get something else."

She followed him. "Xander, what are you up to?"

"Why do I have to be up to something?"

"Because…"

He removed some fruit punch and club soda from the fridge. "Because what?"

"Because after you kissed me yesterday, you've been avoiding me. And as sweet as lunch is, I have to wonder what changed your mind."

He approached her. "First, I haven't been avoiding you."

"It sure seems like it to me."

He shook his head. "Remember I brought in a crew to work on the bungalow?" When she nodded, he continued. "I'd heard there was a big wedding this weekend and you might not have enough space. So I worked with the crew late into the night and this morning we finished up."

"You did?" Wow! A big smile pulled at her lips. She recalled that there was a lot of work to be done on the bungalow.

He returned the smile. "I thought it would please you."

"It does." Her natural instinct was to hug him for being so awesome, but she refrained, unsure it was the right thing to do under the circumstances. "Thank you. But you shouldn't have gone to all that trouble."

"You're welcome. And since I can't help you carry the baby, I'm trying to help in other ways."

This thoughtful side of Xander was not something she

would have expected of the astute businessman she'd met a few months back. But during his stay on the island, she was getting to see a different side of him—a side she really liked.

And that made her wonder if he was also becoming more invested in the baby—if he was thinking of playing a more prominent role in its life. Lea hoped that was the case, but she knew a life-changing decision like that would take time to adjust to.

"Have you thought about the baby?" she asked. "You know, whether you're hoping for a boy? Or a girl?"

He shook his head. "Honestly, either is fine by me. But a little girl that looked just like her mother would be nice."

"Or a stubborn little boy with those amazing brown eyes like his father's would be so adorable."

A smile pulled at Xander's lips. "I'm not as stubborn as the baby's mother."

"I don't know about that."

"When will you know if it's a boy or girl?"

"I guess any time now, but I was thinking of waiting to find out the sex." She wondered how Xander would feel about her decision.

"Till when?"

"The birth. That probably sounds old-fashioned but I really enjoy the not knowing—the possibilities. Is that strange?"

He shook his head. "It'll be a nice surprise at the end of this adventure. But what will you do about buying things for the baby?"

She shrugged. She honestly hadn't thought that far ahead. "I guess I'll stick with neutral colors like…like pastel purple and green."

He paused as though giving it some thought. "Sounds like a plan. Now I better get us some lunch before you have to return to the office."

Once the bubbly fruit punch was poured into their respective wine glasses, he sat across the small table from her. He glanced around the table and frowned.

"What's wrong?" she asked.

"I'm forgetting something." He snapped his fingers. "I know what it is."

He jumped to his feet and rushed to the kitchen. She couldn't help smiling. She'd never seen him work so hard to make her happy. What in the world was he up to?

Xander returned and lit the candle in the middle of the table. "There. Now we can eat."

She glanced down at the food in front of her. A salad, pasta with a giant meatball atop it and fresh bread. It looked delicious. And she was hungry. Her appetite was in overdrive now that she was pregnant.

They ate their salads in a peaceful quietness. When they started to eat the pasta, she noticed that the sauce had a different taste.

"Did you make this from scratch?" she asked.

"That depends."

"On what?"

"If you like it, I made it. If you don't, I had nothing to do with it."

She couldn't help but smile. This side of Xander was like the man she'd fallen for when they first met. She was beginning to think she'd imagined his lighter side, but this proved that there was a part of Xander that he kept hidden from others.

She took another bite. It was definitely good—very good. All the while, she could feel his gaze upon her. When she glanced up, he was just sitting there staring at her.

"What? Do I have sauce on my chin or something?" She immediately reached for her napkin and dabbed around her mouth.

"Your face is fine. I'm just waiting to hear the verdict about the food."

"Oh." Heat rushed to her face. And then she had to decide if she wanted to tease him a little longer or whether she wanted to put him out of his misery.

The fact he wanted to know—that he appeared to care so much about her opinion—moved her. Her own parents didn't seem to care what she thought. And it wasn't just her extended family that they had decided she didn't need to know about. There were also colleges that had accepted her but the letters had gone missing. It wasn't until after she'd settled on an in-state university that she found out about the other schools. Her parents had told her that they were just trying to help her. Now she wondered what other parts of her life they had tried to manipulate.

Xander's phone buzzed. He went to reach for it and then hesitated.

"If you need to get that, go ahead," Lea said.

He looked torn. "Are you sure you won't mind? It won't take long."

She shook her head. "I'll be fine."

Xander slipped outside to take the call, most likely about business. Over the time he'd spent with her, he'd received countless phone calls and even more text messages. Business in his world obviously wasn't relegated to the usual office hours. The interruptions came at all hours of the day and night. He was a workaholic.

Not that she could point her finger at him unless she was willing to point it at herself also. It was more than a job, it was more like a calling. It was doing what she loved— making people happy by making their dreams come true. They filled out the surveys and then between her and Popi, they made their dreams a reality. Some weddings were classic while others were quite imaginative. Regardless, it was a privilege to be responsible for someone's dreams.

"I'm sorry about that." Xander's voice drew her back to the present and this lovely meal.

"It's okay." But she secretly wished she ranked as the priority in his life.

"It sure doesn't look okay. I wouldn't have answered but there's a multi-million-dollar deal on the line. And I just need to keep a close eye on things. But enough about work. Let's finish eating." He glanced at her plate with half the food still remaining. "Listen if the food tastes bad, you don't have to eat it."

She shook her head. "That's not it. The food is amazing."

"You don't have to say that just to make me feel better."

"Trust me, I'm not. If you didn't already have a career buying and selling real estate, I'd tell you to go into the restaurant business. This is amazing."

"If it's so amazing why'd you stop eating?"

She twirled the pasta around the tines of the fork. "See? I'm eating. I wouldn't let something this good go to waste."

He studied her for a moment as though he could gauge the truth just by staring into her eyes. The breath hitched in her throat. She didn't know how insightful it was, but she did know that every time he stared at her her heart accelerated.

When she broke the intense stare, she found her gaze dipping to his lips. What she wouldn't do for another kiss—another chance to be held in his very strong arms. A sigh attempted to escape her lips, but she stifled it. She didn't need Xander reading her every thought.

"You're being serious?" he asked.

"Of course. Why don't you believe me?"

He shrugged. "I just don't have much experience cooking for other people."

"Feel free to cook for me any time." And then she set to work finishing the delicious meal before it grew cold.

When she glanced over at him, she found his plate still had most of the food on it. It was as though he'd done nothing more than move the food around his plate throughout the meal. And now he was staring off in the distance.

"Xander?"

His gaze met hers. "What did you say?"

"Is everything all right? You've hardly eaten anything."

He glanced down at his plate. "I guess I was just a little distracted."

He set to work cleaning off his plate. But he remained unusually quiet as though he had a lot on his mind. But she wasn't going to push him. She didn't want to ruin the newfound peace. She liked it—perhaps more than was safe.

A few days had passed since Xander had come up with his idea of how to impress Lea. And he hadn't wasted a minute of that time. If this idea didn't win her over, he wasn't sure what to try next, but he wasn't giving up—

"How's it going?"

The male voice drew Xander from his thoughts. He paused from hand-sanding the cradle. He turned to his new friend on the island. "Joseph, thank you for letting me use your workshop."

The island handyman nodded. "Just make sure you clean up when you're done."

"I will. Don't worry."

The older man grunted, attempting to sound grouchy, but Xander knew the man may be crusty on the outside but inside he had a heart of gold. Joseph reminded him a bit of his own grandfather. Neither wanted to let on that they were both big softies when it mattered.

Xander had been working on the cradle for days—cutting, gluing and sanding. He turned his attention back to rounding out a corner. Maintaining steady pressure, he worked with the grain. He wanted this cradle to be as smooth as he could make it. No mistakes or blemishes were acceptable. He wanted everything to be perfect for the baby.

Xander paused to give the piece a quick once-over. Just a bit more sanding and it would be time to secure the rockers to the bottom of the cradle. The thought of his baby sleeping in it drove him to work harder—striving for perfection. And when his phone buzzed with yet another message from the office, he put off answering it until later.

Nothing less than his best effort would do for his child. And his gut told him that it would come in handy because Lea wouldn't want the newborn to be far from her side.

Once the cradle was fully assembled, Xander pressed down on the foot, making sure it rocked smoothly. There couldn't be any jolts that would jar the baby from its nap.

He stifled a sigh. He was tired of referring to the baby as it. Anxiousness consumed him to know if it was going to be a boy or girl. But what should the name be? He knew Lea wouldn't need his input, but that didn't stop him from going through names in his head.

Basil? Hercules? Kosmos? But it could be a girl. Hmm... Calla? Nara—

"Xander?" Joseph's voice drew Xander from his thoughts. The older man sent him a strange look. "Did you fill Miss Lea in on your plans about the cradle?"

Xander shook his head. "I decided to surprise her."

"You think it's a good idea?"

He had thought it was, but now he was second-guessing himself. "I take it you don't."

Joseph sorted through his collection of tools as though looking for something specific. "Don't ask me. I'm single for a reason. Can't figure out women."

Xander turned away as a smile pulled at his lips. "That makes two of us."

At last, Joseph grasped a tool and turned around. Xander couldn't help but wonder if the man truly had trouble locating a specific tool or if he'd used it as an excuse to linger…and chat.

"Hey, Joseph, you've been on this island for a while, haven't you?"

The man nodded. "Sure have. I was born here. Never saw any reason to leave."

"Do you believe what they say? You know, about the magic of the island bringing hearts together for infinity?"

Joseph glanced down at the long-handled screwdriver. "Don't have any firsthand experience, but I've never seen or heard of any marriage that didn't last. And it's been a lot of years."

Xander guessed the man's age was somewhere in his seventies, by the deep lines etched upon his face and his snow-white hair. But Joseph moved with the agility of someone half his age.

Joseph arched a bushy white brow. "You thinking of testing the island's magic?"

Xander took a step back. "Me? Get married?" He shook his head vehemently. "Not going to happen."

"Uh-huh." The man's eyes said that he didn't believe him. Without another word, he turned and headed out the door.

Xander stared after him, refraining from shouting that he was never getting married. It was true. He wasn't going to marry Lea, or anyone else, for that matter. He was not marriage material.

However, he and Lea were coexisting peacefully. In fact, they were doing better than peacefully. He looked forward to dinner these days. It was no longer a hurried take-out sandwich or Chinese in a paper box.

These meals with Lea weren't rushed. He actually sat down and noticed what he was eating. And best of all was the beautiful company. Perhaps he shouldn't dismiss the thought of marriage too quickly. There were possibilities.

But…if he did marry Lea, it would solve a lot of problems for both of them. And who said that marriage had to be based on love? Friendship, preferably with benefits, and the shared goal of raising their child would be a strong foundation. But was he dreaming of the impossible?

CHAPTER ELEVEN

AT LAST IT was done.

The cradle hadn't turned out too bad, if he did say so himself.

Four days later, Xander waited until Lea headed off to the office where he knew that she would be busy all-day meeting with various members of the staff as they prepared for one of the biggest weddings of the year. This time a member of royalty was saying "I do." A prince from some small country that Xander had to admit he hadn't heard of before.

Lea was all excited about the event. From what Xander could gather, the marriage had been frowned upon by the royal family and so the couple had decided to run off to get married and had settled upon Infinity Island for their nuptials.

When Xander had asked if Lea was nervous about going against the royal family and hosting the wedding, she hadn't hesitated a bit when she said no. The couple had passed their compatibility test. When he asked if she would have turned down the prince if he'd have failed the test, he noticed how Lea avoided answering by changing the subject. It left him wondering what she really would have done. Did people really say no to a prince?

But then he'd had the thought that if the royal family had rejected the union, would anyone come to such a wedding? Xander recalled the look of amazement that had come over Lea's face, like he'd asked the dumbest question ever. It would appear that everyone but the immediate royal family wanted to be in attendance, including an army of paparazzi. It showed how little he knew about these matters.

So while Lea was off dealing with the last-minute details for the big event, he had the bungalow to himself. He'd retrieved the now finished cradle from Joseph's workshop and carried it to the room he'd been staying in. However, when he placed it in the room, he found it didn't fit in with the decor.

The room was done up in yellow and teal. It was an okay room, but not for a baby. And then the next step of his plan to win over Lea came to him. He would create a nursery for the baby. It would be his gift to his son or daughter. Even if he couldn't be the loving, doting parent his child deserved, he could do this for the wee one.

He grabbed his laptop and set to work. There was paint to be ordered. Curtains. Furniture. And toys. Definitely lots of toys. And he needed all of it shipped to the island ASAP.

This was going to be the best nursery. It would have all of the latest techno gadgets to make Lea's life easier and the child's life safer. And it would be a fun room—someplace that his child would want to spend time.

And then he looked at the corner of the room and the image of him with the baby in his arms came to mind. It was such a foreign concept as he'd never held a baby. And yet excitement and longing filled him at the thought of sitting in a rocker and holding his daughter or son.

That was what he needed, a rocker. The perfect rocker.

His gaze returned to the computer monitor, straying across the date at the bottom of the screen. Somewhere along the way, June had become July. In the course of the two weeks that he'd been on the island, he'd gone from multi-million-dollar real estate deals to buying building blocks and teddy bears. Xander spent the afternoon researching baby products and ordering everything with expedited shipping. He hadn't been this excited in a very, very long time.

Now what color would Lea prefer? Hmm…

Life passed in a blur.

Lea had so much on her plate. It was taking both her and Popi to pull off this royal wedding. The budget was endless and the wants were continuous. To say the wedding was over the top was no exaggeration.

The theme colors were white and purple. The garden was resplendent with large white trees strategically placed throughout. Purple floodlights highlighted them. No area was left undecorated, including the brick walkway to the garden. Arches of twinkle lights and flowers adorned the guests' path.

Lea had to admit she liked the part the bride had insisted on: when the couple were pronounced husband and wife, an army of cannons would shoot white rose petals that would rain down upon the guests. For that reason, Lea had insisted the vows be separate from the reception. She didn't even want to think what it would be like cleaning up thousands of petals while guests were milling about.

No part of the wedding was ordinary. Every detail was extraordinary in one way or another. There were even white and purple orchids cascading from centerpieces suspended above the tables. And above the flowers was a network of white twinkle lights. The stars would get some help that evening.

And if that wasn't enough, the night would conclude with a spectacular fireworks display. The bride didn't know about it. This was a surprise that her groom had set up without her knowledge. Lea thought it was a wonderful way to wrap up such an amazing wedding.

"Have the pyrotechnics arrived?" Lea asked Popi as her gaze skimmed down over the extensive checklist for the wedding.

"They arrived this morning. I met the crew down at the dock. And you'll never guess who I saw there."

Lea glanced up from her checklist. "Please tell me the soon-to-be princess hasn't arrived. We're not ready for her. Nothing is in place and we all know how nervous brides can be."

"Don't worry. I didn't spot a nervous bride, but I did see a Greek mogul receiving a rather large crate."

"A crate?" Lea frowned. What would Xander need that was that big? "What did he say it was?"

"That's the thing. I didn't have a chance to speak with him. I was drawn away by the pyrotechnics guy. He had a lot of specifications for where the fireworks could be stored."

Lea frowned. She honestly knew nothing about these things. This was her first fireworks send-off. "Wasn't the warehouse good enough?"

"Yes, it was. But he wanted to make sure it was guarded. He didn't want any young kids or old fools to get near the stuff. He's the cautious type and frankly I couldn't blame him. The prince ordered enough aerial mortars to light up the entire Mediterranean Sea."

"That much, huh?"

Popi nodded. "I don't think the prince and his intended know how to do things in a small way. But anyway, I was just wondering if you and Xander had decided to make your arrangement more permanent."

"Not that I'm aware of." What was her roommate up to? He wasn't planning to stay forever or anything like that, was he? She would get to the bottom of it soon enough.

But as long as Xander was distracted she could immerse herself in the details of the wedding. Still there was a part of her that wanted to drop everything and rush home to see what he was planning. Surely he didn't think they could be roommates forever, did he?

* * *

It wasn't until hours later that Lea was able to head home. She was dragging her feet, by then. The ferry from the mainland that normally only made one trip daily had made three trips that day to accommodate the supplies needed for the royal wedding. Lea couldn't even imagine what the arrangements would entail if this wedding had the king and queen's blessing.

As it was, only a thousand guests—the prince and his intended's closest friends and family—would be attending the nuptials. The number was too large to accommodate on the island, and special arrangements were made to ferry the guests back to the mainland after the reception.

The plans kept circling around in Lea's mind as she took the golf cart back to her bungalow. Tomorrow the prince and his bride would arrive. Popi had opted to see to the royal couple's needs, which was fine with Lea. The couple wanted to be here in advance of the big day to "make sure" nothing went wrong. Somehow Lea couldn't help but think that they would be more of a hindrance to the preparations than a help, but who was she to argue when the prince was the one picking up the large tab for this elaborate affair, including a bonus for pulling it together on a moment's notice.

When Lea finally let herself through the door of the bungalow, it was dark inside. She frowned as she flipped on the light. Where was Xander?

And then she heard a muffled voice. She headed for his room. The door was closed but light shone at the bottom. He muttered something in a grouchy tone but she wasn't able to make out the words.

She raised her hand to knock but then hesitated, not sure she should disturb him. But then again, this was her home and he was her guest. She tightened her fist and rapped her knuckles on the door.

"Xander, is it all right if I come in?"

"Um…hang on."

Something crashed to the floor.

That was it. She was going to find out what was going on. She grasped the doorknob but found it locked. Really?

She knocked again. "Xander, is everything all right?"

There was a slight pause. "Yeah. It's fine."

It? What was the *it* he was referring to?

"Are you sure?"

"I'll be out in a minute. Just get comfortable. I have dinner warming in the oven."

Dinner? Her stomach rumbled its approval. It had been a very long time since lunch. As her stomach growled again, she realized that now, being pregnant, she couldn't let work be her main focus and neglect regular meals.

And that wasn't the only change this baby would bring to her life. She wondered just how big a role Xander would play in their lives. Would he want to have their child every other weekend? Or would he take a more distant role? The thought didn't please her. Their child deserved to have both an active mother and father. But would Xander agree?

Xander sighed.

Putting together baby furniture was more frustrating than he'd ever imagined. And the instructions might as well be written in a foreign language because he'd done what they'd said five times and he still didn't have the changing table fully assembled. If the furniture was this difficult, he didn't even want to imagine how daunting it must be to be a good parent.

It made him think of his parents. With distance and a better perspective, he was beginning to think that he'd been too hard on them. Sure, his father hadn't indulged him, but he knew his paternal grandfather hadn't been easy on his father. So his father had done what he knew.

So what did Xander know about being a father? Would

he repeat his father's mistakes? Could he do it different? Should he even try?

The questions came one after the other, but the answers didn't come as easily. However, he couldn't stand around in his room searching for those elusive answers. He glanced around at the ripped-open boxes and the furniture partially assembled. Maybe he should have waited to start this project when he was fully awake.

He turned his back on the mess. He'd deal with it later. His hand grasped the doorknob, releasing the lock. He opened it cautiously just in case Lea was lingering in the hallway, but she'd decided to move on.

In the kitchen, he found her staring in the fridge. "Are you hungry?"

She jumped and then pressed a hand to her chest. She closed the fridge and turned to him. "You have no idea."

He arched a brow. "You are eating enough, aren't you?"

She nodded but then hesitated. "I just missed dinner."

"I don't know much about pregnancy but I do know you have to eat regularly for you and the baby."

"I know. I just got wrapped up in things." The guilty look on her face stole his heart. "It won't happen again."

That was all he needed to hear. He moved past her and opened the oven. With pot holders, he pulled out a casserole dish. "I hope it's good."

"It smells delightful. What is it?"

"It's something my mother used to make. At least, it's supposed to be similar. I didn't have the recipe so I called my sister and she gave it to me. I don't know if it's good—"

"Xander, relax." She smiled at him for rambling on. "What do you call it?"

"I don't know the actual name but it's lemony rice pilaf with chicken. My mother used to make it when I didn't feel good."

Lea continued to smile but she didn't say anything.

At last his curiosity got the best of him. "Why are you smiling?"

"I'm just happy that you found a good memory."

She was right. For so long, he'd focused on all the things that had gone wrong instead of the things in his past that had been good. Perhaps he needed a different perspective on the past.

Xander dished up the food and then joined Lea on the couch. It was far too late in the evening to worry about proper etiquette. If he were alone in his condo in Athens, he'd be eating his food in front of the television, catching the end of a European football game.

"What were you doing when I got home?" Lea asked after demolishing half the food on her plate.

"I was just working on some stuff." He wasn't about to tell her about the nursery until it looked more like a baby's room than a junk room.

"Would that stuff be what you had shipped in?"

His fork hovered in the air. "You saw that?"

"I didn't, but Popi noticed you had a large shipment and she thought you were moving in here permanently." Lea eyed him up. "Are you shipping all of your stuff here?"

He laughed. This bungalow wasn't even half the size of his condo. His things wouldn't fit. If he were to relocate to Infinity Island, he'd have to build them a whole new home. Not that he was planning to move here.

"What's so amusing?" Lea asked.

It was only then that he realized his thoughts had translated into a smile. "I just found it amusing that Popi was jumping to conclusions. You don't have to worry. All my possessions are still back in Athens."

"Then what was in the big box?"

She wasn't going to let this drop until he gave her a reasonable answer. "It was some work stuff that I need to sort out."

Lea hesitated and then she turned back to her food. "Sounds like they shipped you the whole office."

"Not even close. But don't worry. I promise to keep it all contained in my room." He knew she liked to keep her bungalow spotless. Even the dishes were promptly rinsed and loaded in the dishwasher.

"Thank you. I appreciate it."

And then worried she might decide to start snooping, he added, "Just so you know, all of the stuff is confidential."

"Top secret, huh?" She sent him a teasing smile.

"Something like that."

"Don't worry. As long as you keep it out of sight, I won't bother anything. Not that I'll have any time, with the upcoming wedding."

And so he was safe for now. As Lea started to tell him about the latest developments with the royal wedding, he found himself interested in what she had to say. It wasn't the subject so much as the way she described things. She was an entertaining storyteller. He could listen to her for hours.

CHAPTER TWELVE

THINGS WERE GOING WELL.

Better than he'd ever imagined.

Xander surprised himself with how much he enjoyed spending time with Lea. He looked forward to their conversations. He even took pleasure in the companionable silence.

And for the first time, he realized his interest in Lea went deeper than co-parenting. There was something special about this woman that attracted him. Dare he admit that he could envision sharing his life with her—with their child?

It wouldn't be a marriage created out of greeting-card platitudes and Valentine's Day chocolates. It would be better. It would be based on mutual respect, friendship and attraction.

She wasn't as immune to him as she wanted both of them to believe. He noticed how she stared at him when she didn't think he was paying attention. And he saw how she trembled with desire when he held her in his arms.

But it was more than the undeniable passion they shared. It was something much deeper. It was her compassion when he told her about his parents. She hadn't looked at him with disbelief that after all this time he still cared about what his parents had thought of him. And she didn't look at him with sympathy that made him want to turn away.

She'd looked at him with warmth and understanding. And her touch had given him the comfort and strength to put words to the feelings that he'd been stifling inside him all this time.

The following evening, once the dinner dishes had been cleared, Xander turned to Lea. "Do you have any plans for the evening?"

"Just some computer work and answering some emails. Why?"

He stepped up to her and held out his hand. "Come with me."

She glanced at his outstretched hand and hesitated. Then her confused gaze rose to meet his gaze. "Where are we going?"

"I have a surprise planned."

"A surprise?"

He nodded. It was then that she placed her hand in his and they headed for the door. During his stay on the island, he'd made many friends. And one of those friends just happened to run the marina and had offered to lend him a boat.

Xander led her to the pier.

"What are we doing here?" Lea sent him a puzzled look.

"You'll see."

"Xander?"

"Trust me."

He climbed aboard the speedboat and then turned to her and held out his hand. She smiled. "How did you manage this?"

"I have friends."

"Friends, huh?" Without needing his assistance, she climbed aboard. "I think I'm going to have a staff meeting about not letting people sweet-talk them into doing things that are against the rules."

"You wouldn't get Caesar in trouble, would you? After all, he lent me the boat for the evening because he knew it was for you."

Her eyes widened. "So what you're saying is that you

took advantage of our relationship to coerce my employee to break the rules and lend you this boat?"

Xander saw the twinkle of mischief in her eyes. She was having fun with this. And who was he to ruin her enjoyment? "That sounds about right."

"Xander Marinakos, has anyone ever told you how bad you are?"

He grinned at her. "And you don't even know the half of it. But I'd be willing to show you."

Just then he took her in his arms. His intent was to kiss her until she couldn't think straight—until the word "no" was the very last thing on her mind. But he also saw the surprise in her widened eyes as her hands landed on his chest. He realized he was overstepping their newfound friendship. And as much as he wanted to kiss her, he couldn't risk losing the easiness that had grown between them.

With great reluctance, he released her. If they were to kiss again, she would have to make the first move. He just hoped she didn't wait too long.

He turned his attention to the controls of the boat. "I thought we'd take an evening ride around the island."

"It's been a while since I was out on a boat. I'm afraid I've become a workaholic and spend most of my time in my office or else putting out fires around the island."

"Sit down, then." He gestured to the white seat next to his. "And we'll have a relaxing evening ride. I'm really anxious to see all of the island."

She sat down beside him. "Well, since you went to the trouble to get this boat, let's make this happen."

"Your wish is my command."

As he maneuvered the boat out of the marina, he was surprised by how true those words were. He was anxious to make Lea happy. Because when she was happy, he found himself happy too. And that most definitely would be good for their baby.

* * *

The evening sun sank low in the sky, sending rays of sunshine dancing upon the gentle swells of water. And as beautiful as the setting was, Lea found the boat captain to be even more captivating. Xander looked at ease behind the controls of this expensive boat, normally reserved for the newlyweds. She was both surprised and impressed with the evening that Xander had planned. But a niggling thought kept intruding on her enjoyment—what was his end game?

"Something wrong?" Xander slowed the boat so they didn't have to yell over the roar of the engine.

"Um, no." She flashed him a bright smile as proof.

He gave her a hesitant look but then let the subject drop. "This island is amazing. It has so many different types of landscapes, from the smooth, white sandy beaches over by the marina to the high and jagged cliffs on this side of the island. This looks like a great area to hike."

"You're an outdoors man?" Somehow she didn't imagine him as one.

"I was when I was younger, but as the years have gone by and my business has grown, I've had less time for recreation."

"That's too bad. You know what they say—all work and no play makes Xander a dull boy."

He arched a brow as he glanced over at her. "So that's what you think of me? You think I'm dull and boring?"

Oops! Heat rushed to her face. "That's not what I meant. I… I just meant that you work too hard."

"And I'm boring."

"No, you're not." Her mind was racing to come up with something—anything—that would get her out of this awkward conversation. After this, she just might gag herself to keep from sticking her medium-sized flip-flop in her mouth. "Really. I mean it."

He flashed her a smile. "Relax. I was just teasing you."

She took her first easy breath. "That wasn't funny."

Xander stopped the boat. "Listen, I'm sorry. It's just that everything between us is so complicated. And I wanted to lighten the mood. I'm sorry it didn't come across that way."

She shook her head. If he was going to be open and honest with her, she owed it to him to do the same thing. "It's not you. I think I'm just a little touchy. I... I want..."

Xander moved closer to her. When he spoke, his voice came out deeper and softer than normal. "What do you want?"

She found herself staring deep into his eyes. Her heart pounded in her chest as the truth struggled to free itself. She wanted him. And that scared her more than when she'd left the only home she'd ever known to move half-way around the world to Greece. And it scared her more than the prospect of being a single parent.

"Lea?" His gaze searched hers.

Not trusting her voice or the words that might escape, she lifted up on her tiptoes and pressed her lips to his. She hadn't given it much thought. But he had asked what she wanted. And this was it...

Her lips moved over his. At first, he hesitated. It was as though he was surprised by her actions. This surely couldn't be that much of a jump for him. After all, he'd almost kissed her back at the dock.

And then his arms wrapped around her waist, pulling her to him. Her hands landed on his firm chest and then slid up over his broad shoulders. As he responded to her, a moan swelled in the back of her throat.

It didn't get any better than this. The setting sun in the background, the lapping of the water on the side of the boat and no one else around. Suddenly the reasons she'd been holding herself back from him didn't seem so important. Maybe she'd been trying too hard to keep him at arm's length. Because being in his arms was so much better.

Sputter. Sputter.

Silence.

Xander pulled back. "The engine died. I better check it."

With great reluctance, Lea loosened her hold on him. "What do you think it is?"

"It probably just stalled." He turned the key.

Sputter. Silence.

He tried again.

Silence.

"What is it? What's the matter?" Suddenly their perfect romantic spot seemed rather dark and desolate.

"Give me a second." He removed his phone from his pocket and turned on the flashlight function. He moved it around the control panel. "I checked the fuel before we left. It says there's still enough in there to get us back to the marina."

"I'll call for help." Lea dialed the marina office, hoping someone was still there. But the phone didn't ring. "There's no signal out here."

Xander glanced around. "It looks like I took too long circling the island. I don't think there's any civilization on this side."

"There isn't." Even though it was a small island, there were still parts that weren't developed. And this happened to be one of those areas.

"We aren't that far from shore. How are your swimming skills?"

Her mouth opened but nothing came out. By now, the sun had sunk below the horizon, sending long shadows over the land. And she had a choice to make. Staying here with Xander for the evening with the moon and stars overhead. The idea so appealed to her.

Or she could fess up about the emergency radio.

"Lea, it's okay if you can't swim. We can make do here on the boat."

"I... I can swim—"

In that moment, Xander yanked off his shirt, revealing his muscled chest. Any other words stuck in the back of her throat. My goodness, he was so sexy. Her mouth grew dry as she took in the spectacular view. She really was leaning toward forgetting about the emergency radio.

She kept staring at his defined chest and his sculpted abs. Her fingers tingled with the desire to reach out and trace the lines of his muscles. He was oh, so tempting.

"See something you like?" His teasing smile lit up his face.

Heat rushed up her neck and set her cheeks ablaze. The look in his eyes tempted her to start something—something that would most definitely spin out of control. But would she just get burned in the end?

The question had her hesitating. Why was she making such a big deal about this now? They'd already spent an amazing weekend together, wrapped in each other's arms. How could another romantic evening make things worse?

But things had changed dramatically since that unforgettable weekend. With a baby on the way, they would be in each other's lives forever and the thought of making that relationship even more complicated was the only thing holding Lea back from rushing into his arms.

"Or—" Xander's voice drew her attention "—I can go alone. I'll send help."

Evening had settled over them. But it wasn't that dark out, with the full moon reflecting off the water. She knew what she wanted, but did she have the courage to follow her heart?

As though Xander could sense her indecision, he stepped up to her. "Lea, it's okay. I'm sorry this happened. I swear I didn't plan it."

"It's not that." Her insides shivered with nervous energy. For so long, she had been enforcing the rules, walking the straight line, and now she was considering living on the edge and following her desires. "Let's go for it."

The look of surprise lit up Xander's eye. "Are you serious?"

She nodded. "I am."

This time she was the one to pull off her shirt and toss it on the white leather seat next to Xander's discarded shirt. When she glanced up, she caught him staring at her with his eyes rounded and his mouth gaping.

"What?" She refused to blush. They were both adults here. Consenting adults. "You surely didn't think I was going to swim with all of my clothes on, did you?"

And besides, her bra covered more than her itty-bitty bikini. She didn't tell him that. But she couldn't resist glancing up at him as she shimmied out of her capris and stood there in her lacey boy-shorts undies. She heard a distinct hiss of breath from him. Playing the seductress was new for her and she was finding that she liked it.

"Last one to shore has to collect the firewood." And with that she dove into the water. She didn't look back as she planned to win this race.

The water, though warm as far as large bodies of water went, was still cold against her heated skin. She kept moving quickly through the water. The faster she moved, the warmer she got. And before she knew it, the water grew shallow and she stood up.

She glanced back to find Xander hot on her heels. She ran out of the water and didn't stop until she was standing on dry sand.

She turned back to the water where Xander was getting to his feet. The moonlight caught upon a bag in Xander's hand. What was that man up to now?

Guilt niggled at her conscience. She should have told him about the emergency radio. Just then a breeze whished past her body, leaving a trail of goose bumps over her skin. She shivered. She was beginning to think she was never going to get warm again.

Xander turned and retrieved the bag from the sand. "I

don't know if this is still dry." He struggled with the knot in the bag. After a few seconds, he opened it.

He withdrew a large towel and draped it around her. "I thought you might want this."

"Thank you. But what about you?"

"Don't worry." Xander wrapped his arms around her. "I know how to stay warm. I'll just hold this very hot woman in my arms."

"I don't know about being hot. I feel more like a very cold fish."

He tightened his hold on her, rubbing his hands over her back. "Definitely not fishy. I'm beginning to think you're part mermaid."

She lifted her chin so that their gazes met. "I take it you have a thing for mermaids."

"I didn't before, but with a little encouragement, I might change my mind."

"Mm... And what sort of encouragement do you have in mind?" She snuggled closer to him, seeking the warmth of his body.

He lowered his head toward hers. "This kind."

She tilted her chin upward. And then Xander pressed his mouth against hers. His lips were smooth and gentle. His touch sent an arrow of arousal through her core. Her insides immediately heated, warming her from the inside out.

And then all too soon, he pulled back. "I better get a fire started. It might be a little while until they get here."

"Get here?"

"Yes, you surely didn't think we were stranded out here, did you?"

"So you found the emergency radio?"

With the moonlight highlighting Xander's handsome face, he arched a brow and smiled at her. "Were you holding out on me?"

"I, uh... Well, I uh..."

Xander laughed, a deep rich tone that wrapped around her and let her know everything was going to be all right.

He sobered up. "It's all right. I wanted to spend more time with you, too. But I didn't think you'd want to spend the whole night on the beach and so I used the radio to call the marina office. They're sending out a couple of boats."

"Well, aren't you my hero?"

"I'm just trying to watch out for a gorgeous mermaid."

A hint of a smile eased the lines on his face. In the dark, it was difficult to read the look in his eyes, but she'd guess that she'd stroked his ego enough to make him happy.

"Um, let's get that fire started."

"You might not find much to make a fire," she said.

"You know where we are?"

She nodded. "This is called Deadman's Bay."

He glanced around. "It doesn't look that bad."

She couldn't help but smile. "In the daylight, it's actually quite lovely with white sand and the aqua blue water."

"Then why such a dreadful name?"

"It's said that in the old days pirates would trap merchant ships in the bay and there was no other way out than past the pirates." She pointed in front of them. "The cliffs go straight up some three hundred meters or more. Climbing them without the proper equipment is a fool's mission."

"Well, then, before the pirates get us, I should search for some driftwood or anything that will burn." He headed off.

In no time, he had started a fire with the aid of a lighter from the plastic sack. She wondered what else he had stashed in that bag. Some s'mores would be great about now. Her stomach rumbled its approval. She wondered if they made s'mores in Greece.

Xander dragged a large log over near the fire and they sat down. He wrapped a hand over her shoulders and pulled her close. "Are you warm enough?"

"I'm getting there." Suddenly she felt foolish for stripping down and diving in the water. "What are people going to say when they find us sitting here in our underwear?"

"I'm thinking the guys are going to be very jealous of me being here alone with you."

"But...but nothing happened."

He leaned in close and lowered his voice. "Would you like something to happen?"

The word *yes* hovered on her lips, but she bit it back. Perhaps she'd been daring enough for one evening. "I think this is, um, good. You never know when they're going to find us."

"Really? Because I'd be willing to risk it, if you are."

She turned to look at him and realized that was a mistake. He was so close that their lips were just an inch apart. Her heart tap-tapped in her chest. She tried to tell herself that it was just the coldness but the truth was between the fire, the oversized towel and being snuggled against Xander, she wasn't cold any longer.

Her gaze lowered to his lips and then she quickly turned away before she gave in to her desires. She was marooned on this deserted beach with literally the man of her dreams, and she was holding back. Popi would tell her she was being silly. That she should go with the moment and enjoy it—enjoy him. But Lea had a baby to think about. She couldn't let herself get caught up in something that wasn't real.

"Lea, I want you to know that I can't remember the last time I enjoyed myself this much. If I were to be stuck on a deserted island, I can't think of anyone else I'd want to be with."

Her heart definitely skipped a beat. "I feel the same way." Their gazes caught and held. Maybe she shouldn't have said that. Trying to lighten the mood, she glanced away. "After all, you know how to start a fire and—"

"Lea, will you marry me?"

"What?" Surely she hadn't heard him correctly.

"You heard me, will you marry me?"

Her mouth gaped. Where in the world had that come from? And then she wondered if he felt the need to do the right thing because she was pregnant. That had to be it, because there was no other reason for them to marry. It wasn't like they were in love or anything.

She appreciated how he'd phrased the offer as a question instead of making it a demand. Her parents never stopped to ask her opinion before dictating how things should be. They'd continued to treat her as a child until the day she packed up and caught a plane to Greece—her adventure to find out about the family she never knew existed.

And Charles, had he deemed her fit to be his wife, would have told her they were getting married instead of asking her. Thank goodness that never happened.

Lea shook her head. "It won't work."

"It can if we want it to."

"I won't marry someone I don't love."

The pain reflected in his eyes had her regretting her blunt answer. She just didn't want him holding out for something that wasn't going to happen.

Lea got up and moved to the water's edge. She knew she'd hurt him and that hadn't been her intention. But in the long run, this would be less painful for both of them.

CHAPTER THIRTEEN

LAST NIGHT HADN'T gone the way he'd planned it.

Not even close.

Xander had been frowning all day today—at least that was what Joseph had accused him of. Why did Lea's rejection sting so much? It wasn't like he was madly in love with her. He was just trying to make things easier for her—for both of them.

Because the baby needed them both. And for that reason, he wasn't giving up on changing Lea's mind about marrying him. He would give Lea and the child his name—it would get them a long way in life—plus a sizeable chunk of his fortune. And when the time came, the child would inherit his empire.

Xander, along with a work crew, finished putting a new roof on one of the bungalows. And since it was nearing lunchtime, he decided to ask Lea to share a meal with him. They had barely spoken since she'd turned down his marriage proposal. And now that the sting of her rejection had worn off, he had to take emotions out of the equation and focus on the end goal—creating a family for their baby.

As he walked from the bungalow to Lea's office, he had to navigate through the throng of wedding guests. They were everywhere—there was even a line of people waiting to be seated at the Hideaway Café. That was a first. So much for his plan of a grabbing a decaf caramel latte for Lea as a peace offering.

Xander continued on to the main offices when he saw Lea step out into the sunshine, but she wasn't alone. She was with a middle-aged couple. The man carried a briefcase and the woman wore a dark skirt and jacket. They definitely weren't here for some romance in the sun and he highly doubted they were the bride and groom. So, who were they?

The smile slipped from his face. They were prospective buyers for the island. He was certain of it. Who knew so many people were interested in running a wedding island?

Suddenly it felt like all the progress he'd made with Lea was in jeopardy. The thought of at last having his own family—people he could trust—people that would always be there for him and him for them—was slipping through his fingers. And it was only then that he realized just how much he wanted this—wanted the family he hadn't known he could have.

He headed for Lea. He wasn't sure what he was going to say. He felt a little betrayed that as close as they were growing she still wouldn't consider accepting his help, but she would consider selling to strangers—people she didn't know she could trust with her beloved island.

"Please feel free to explore the island at your leisure," Lea said to the couple with her back to Xander.

"I just wouldn't take the boat tour, if I were you."

Lea immediately spun around and leveled a dark, warning stare at him. The look immediately brought him to his senses.

"And why would that be?" the man asked with a concerned look on his face.

Lea turned to the man. "It's nothing to worry about. Xander was just making a joke. It was something you had to be there to understand. But our boats are all well maintained and available should you like to see the island from the sea. Just let me know. If you'll excuse me for a moment, I need to have a quick word with Mr. Marinakos."

It was impossible to miss the anger written all over her face as she faced Xander. This time he had no one to blame but himself for taking quite a few steps back in their relationship. She led them a safe distance away from the couple she'd been talking to.

With her back turned to her guests, she said, "What do you think you're doing?"

"I was just trying to make a joke. Like you said."

Her gaze narrowed. "That was no joke. So what gives?"

She had called him out and maybe it was good to tell her the truth—all of it. After all, at this point, what could it hurt?

He swallowed. "I thought that you and I, we were growing closer."

She hesitated. "As friends."

They both knew their relationship had gone beyond friendship, but if it made her more comfortable to think of them as merely friends, he wasn't going to correct her.

He stared into her eyes. "I thought you were beginning to trust me."

"I… I am." He read confusion in her eyes. "But what does that have to do with you trying to run off prospective buyers? You know how important this is to me."

And he felt bad for letting himself act rashly. He raked his fingers through his hair. It wasn't something he ever allowed himself to do when he was conducting a business deal. In fact, he was more inclined to take his time and let the other man sweat it out. But with Lea and the baby on the line, he was the one sweating out how this was all going to work out.

"I thought by now you'd realize you could trust me— that you would consider letting me give…" He paused. This wasn't coming out right. If he didn't handle this correctly, she would dig her heels in even deeper. He sighed and lowered his head. "Never mind. I'm sorry I interrupted your meeting."

He turned to walk away when she reached out, touching his arm. "Xander, wait."

He glanced back to her, not sure what he expected her to say. He remained quiet, letting her have her say.

Her gaze searched his. "What were you hoping would happen?" She didn't give him a chance to answer as she barreled forward. "Were you hoping that if you sweet-talked me on a deserted beach I would suddenly decide to sell to you?"

"No." His voice was sterner than he'd intended it to be. He made an effort to soften his voice. "I'd hoped you'd let me loan you the money to fix up the island."

"With strings—"

"No. No strings attached." It wasn't how he normally did business, but he'd make an exception in this case. "It would be because we're friends."

She stepped closer to him, never breaking eye contact. "You're being serious, aren't you?"

He let out a breath he hadn't even realized that he'd been holding. "Yes, I am."

"After all of this time, you still don't get it."

His brows drew together. "Get what?"

"That what this baby needs from you isn't money. It needs you to let down your guard and love it. He or she needs you to be an active part of its life."

Xander took a step back. She was asking him to be a loving, devoted parent. And as much as he wanted that, too, he was afraid he'd follow the parenting examples from his past. "I'm not good with emotions."

"Is that what your sister would say? I see the way your eyes light up when you talk about her. You'd do anything for her, wouldn't you?"

"Of course, but that's different—"

"You love her, right?"

"Yes. But—"

"But you're willing to give your child less?"

His back teeth ground together. Why was she twisting

his words around on him? He was doing what was best for the child—protecting it from him.

Lea pleaded with her eyes. "You don't have to follow your father's example. Be the understanding, encouraging parent you always wanted him to be." She glanced over her shoulder at her waiting guests. "I have to go."

Xander had come here hoping to get through to her, but as she walked away, it was the other way around. Was she right? Could he be the father that he'd always longed for?

Should she trust him?

Lea's heart said yes. But her mind said no.

After all, he'd attempted to sabotage the sale with the couple today. She stood off to the side of the dock, watching the continuous arrival of guests for the royal wedding. She spotted the couple as they boarded the ferry and waved to them. As interested as they had been in the island and the wedding business, in the end they'd said that the island was more of a time commitment than they were willing to invest at this point in their lives. And so they'd passed on the chance to own Infinity Island.

They had seemed like the perfect buyers. The husband was all about numbers and spreadsheets and processes while his wife was more focused on the people and the romance and the weddings. Lea couldn't have asked for a better match for the island. And yet, it hadn't worked out. And it wasn't until now that she realized deep down she didn't want it to work out.

She loved Infinity Island. It was a part of her. And the harder she tried to sell it, the more she realized how much she wanted to keep it.

But she also had the baby to think of. Her hand covered her baby bump. She had to do what was right for her baby, no matter what she had to sacrifice. Even her pride.

And returning to Seattle, the land where she'd been born and raised, the place where she had friends and family, and knew exactly how things worked, might be best. Because as much as she loved this island, it was part of a country that she still had so much to learn about—including the language. There were so many obstacles to overcome if she were to stay here. And staying on in Athens would just be a reminder of how she'd come here and failed to live up to her extended family's expectations.

So if she were to go home, she should try to reach out to her parents. They had a right to know they were going to be grandparents. Xander's words of regret over his parents came to her. She didn't want to live with regrets like him. And if she couldn't forgive her parents, how was she going to be a good mother?

Lea picked up the phone and dialed the familiar number of her parents' home. The phone rang and rang. When the answering machine picked up, she hung up. She thought of calling her mother's cell phone but hesitated. Again, she recalled Xander encouraging her not to give up. She dialed the number. It went to voice mail. She disconnected.

She was not going to have this conversation via a message. To be honest, she wasn't sure if her mother was truly busy or if she was avoiding her call. Her mother would see the missed phone call and could call back if she wanted. Lea had made the first move, now her mother could make a move…or not.

Lea shut down her computer in order to head home a little early to prepare for the royal wedding. For the past year, she'd been spending all of her time working from first thing in the morning until late at night when she fell into bed utterly exhausted, but then again, until now she hadn't had anyone waiting at home for her. The thought of Xander had her moving faster.

"Hey, where are you headed so quickly?"

Lea stopped on the walk outside the office and turned to Popi. "I was just going home to get ready."

"The wedding is going to be the highlight of the year.

But aren't you leaving a little early to get dressed?" Popi made a big show of checking the time on her phone.

"I, um, finished everything early."

"Uh-huh." Popi nodded and sent her a knowing smile. "I bet I know what has you rushing home. Or should I say who?"

"It's not like that." The response was quick—too quick. They both knew she was lying.

"You keep telling yourself that. It's kinda like telling myself that I'm not pregnant." Popi placed a hand on her expanding midsection. "The bigger I get the more I wonder about the delivery and whether this was my wisest decision."

"It's a little late for second thoughts, don't you think?"

Popi gave a nervous laugh. "You would be right. But doesn't it scare you to think of delivering a baby?"

"I'll be honest. I try not to think about it." It probably wasn't the best approach, but she was not looking forward to the pain. "Why exactly are we talking about this anyway?"

"I think we were originally talking about Xander and your eagerness to see him. I'm glad to see that things are going better for you two." Popi got a serious look on her face. "This is a good thing, isn't it?"

Lea smiled and nodded. "It's good. This baby needs two parents that get along."

"If it changes, I'm here to talk, eat gelato and watch movies."

"Thanks. You're the best."

As they parted company, Lea realized Popi was as close to her as what she imagined a sister would be. She was going to miss her so much when she left here.

She didn't have long to think about it before Xander joined her.

He made point of checking the time. "What are you up to? It's not quitting time."

"Would you believe me if I said I was looking for you?"

"It's a little late to ask me to lunch. And it's too early for dinner."

"I had something else in mind." Her stomach felt like a swarm of butterflies had been set loose in it.

He gave her a puzzled look. "You're in a really good mood."

"I am." She didn't know why she was. It wasn't exactly a good day. The sale hadn't gone through. She hadn't gotten hold of her mother. And her email inbox was overflowing with unread messages. Not to mention all the bills that were beginning to stack up. But she refused to think of all that now.

His expression was neutral but his gaze never left her. "So your business deal, it went well?"

"Actually, it fell through."

"If I had anything to do with it—"

She shook her head. "You didn't. The island was too much of a time commitment for them."

"And still you're in a good mood, why?"

She shrugged. She refused to delve too deeply into the reason for her happiness. "It's a beautiful day. It's the end of the week. And there's about to be a royal wedding. Isn't that a good enough reason?"

He shrugged. "Works for me." They walked for a few minutes in silence. "What do you say about having dinner together? But this evening there will be no mention of marriage. Just two friends having a good time together."

"Can I ask you something?"

"Are you trying to change the subject?"

"No. I just want to know something before I give you my answer."

"Should I be worried?"

She shrugged. "Depends on how you look at it."

"What's your question?"

"Why are you still here? Why are you fixing up the island? Why do you want to have dinner with me?"

He stopped walking and turned to her. "Why do you think?"

"I think it's all about the baby." Inside she was begging him to prove her wrong.

"Is that what you want?"

No. No. No. He wasn't supposed to turn her question around on her. "That's not an answer."

He sighed and pressed his hands to his waist. "Is it so hard to believe that I want to spend time with you, not because I want to buy the island and not because you're having my baby, but because I like you? I like your company."

She couldn't hold back the smile that lifted her lips. "You do?"

"I do. I... I like you a lot and I would like to see where this thing between us is leading. So how about that dinner?"

"I'd love to, but I'm afraid there's a wedding and reception shortly. In fact, I was just heading home to change and head over to the festivities."

"Do you attend each and every wedding?"

"I must admit that I don't. My schedule doesn't always allow me. But I make a point to attend as many as I can. And this royal wedding is an all-hands-on-deck affair. Besides, there's something so rewarding about seeing two hearts joined together for infinity." She smiled. "It's something very special and lets me know that what I do here plays some small part in two people becoming one."

"That does sound very fulfilling. It isn't something I've ever experienced with my work. Deals are usually made in boardrooms and it's a matter of business. At most, there's a handshake and a smile, but there's no joy. From the sound of it, I've been missing out on some things."

What was he trying to tell her? Was he saying he wanted to change his life? Impossible. He was one of the world's most successful people. When they made those lists of the richest people, he was at the top of it, year after year. And she knew he enjoyed his work. So what was he trying to say?

"Any chance I can convince you to skip it?"

She sent him a look that said "Are you serious?". "No."

"I didn't think so." There was a noticeable pause before he asked, "How about I tag along with you?"

"You want to crash a wedding?" She didn't think it could be possible but things were getting even stranger.

He smiled. "I confess—it's something I've never done."

"And you plan to get all dressed up?"

"My suit from when I first arrived was sent to the dry cleaners and is now hanging in my closet, all set to go."

She was running out of ideas to reject this as a bad idea. And it would be fun to show Xander why she cared so much about the island. The happiness, the joy and the hope found at these celebrations was inspiring. It kept her wanting to do better and help more people have a smooth trip down the aisle.

"Let's do it." She smiled before setting off side by side with him on their wedding date.

CHAPTER FOURTEEN

WHAT IN THE world had come over him?

Xander couldn't believe he was willingly attending a wedding and reception—and it wasn't even for anyone he knew. These days he made a point of not attending weddings. In his experience, women had a way of turning the occasion into much more than a nice evening out. He always told himself that romantic commitments weren't for him.

But to have a date with Lea, to hold her in his arms—he would agree to most anything just to spend time with her, even walking over hot coals. Thankfully that was not a part of the evening's festivities. And it wasn't like Lea expected anything from him. She'd made that perfectly clear the other night.

And boy, was she a knockout tonight with that little black dress on. A silver satin sash around her waist accentuated her curves, including her baby bump. The black lace bodice teased him with glimpses of her cleavage. He definitely had the most beautiful woman at the wedding on his arm—too bad for the prince.

Not having to worry about meeting any romantic expectations, Xander found himself relaxing and enjoying Lea's company. And when she'd finally coerced him onto the dance floor, he was envisioning a slow dance where he could pull her into his arms nice and close.

Instead, after they were already on the dance floor, an upbeat song started to play. It was something he'd never heard before, but seeing as the bride was American, it didn't surprise him. Lea's face beamed with happiness. She was most definitely in her element here. And then people formed a big circle. The next thing he knew, they were all flapping their arms and wiggling their backsides.

He stood perfectly still, having no clue what was going on. Lea had nudged him and told him it was called the Chicken Dance. *Whatever that is.* Lea encouraged him to join in. He did so reluctantly.

He might be on a vacation of sorts, but he was still a businessman. He inwardly cringed, thinking of a video of this going viral. He had to watch out for his reputation and this…this dance was not the least bit sensical. But it did cause Lea to smile and laugh. That was worth his bit of discomfort.

But his efforts to make Lea happy were soon rewarded with a slow song. At last, he'd wrapped his arms around her. The soft hint of floral perfume teased his senses. As they moved around the floor, it was as if no one else existed. All he had eyes for was her. And then somewhere along the way, their gazes had locked. His heart pounded against his ribs.

There was something special about Lea. It went deeper than her carrying his baby. He'd dated many women in his life—beautiful, famous, rich women. None of them had made him reconsider the set of rules by which he lived his life. None made him want to open up and share not only his accomplishments but also his hopes, failures and deepest regrets.

But did Lea feel the same way toward him?

The memory of his rejected marriage proposal lingered in the back of his mouth with a sour taste. Maybe he'd had too much wine that evening. That had to be why he was rehashing the failed proposal. Otherwise he wouldn't even be considering further pursuit of this woman, who'd snuck past his elaborate walls, who filled his thoughts both day and night.

It was then that he had to confront the truth—he wanted more from Lea than an amicable friendship—more than a convenient marriage. He was still struggling for the words to describe his vision for their future, but in this moment, none were needed. He'd swooped in for a kiss. It was short and sweet. He didn't want to push his luck as the evening was going perfectly.

But now, as they walked home, he couldn't help recalling the softness of her lips against his. Even though the kiss had been brief, it had sparked a fire within him that continued to smolder. He ached for more of her. So much more.

Xander continued to hold Lea's hand. "Thank you for this evening. The wedding wasn't bad after all."

"Wasn't bad? As I seem to recall, you had a rather good time. You were even laughing during the Chicken Dance."

"Such a ridiculous name for something that in no way resembles a dance."

"It's a lot of fun and helps loosen up the crowd. Seemed to work just fine to get you to relax and enjoy the rest of the evening."

"I don't know if flapping my arms relaxed me, but I did enjoy the rest of the evening. We'll have to crash another wedding sometime."

He didn't say it but it wasn't the dance that had him enjoying this evening, it was her. Lea was the most amazing woman in the world. Beneath the moonlight, he stumbled upon another moment of clarity. If he let Lea get away, there would never be anyone nearly as special—as perfect—for him.

Lea's sigh drew his attention.

"What's on your mind?" He wanted to know anything and everything about her.

"I was just thinking that there won't be another time. At least not here on the island." She sounded saddened by the thought. "Not if I sell it."

It saddened him, too. But he didn't want to rehash the

subject of the island. He knew it would lead to nothing but trouble for them. And he wasn't about to ruin this evening.

He needed to change the subject. "Have you talked with your parents?"

They continued to stroll along at a leisurely pace. "Actually, I took your advice and tried."

"Tried?"

She nodded. "No one answered. And no one has called back, so I don't know what to make of it."

"Did you leave a message?"

"Um, no." She avoided his searching gaze.

"How are they supposed to know to call, if you didn't leave a message?"

"They'll see a missed call and my number."

He didn't say a word. Instead he shook his head.

"Why are you shaking your head? At least I tried. It's more than they've done."

She did have a point. "That's true. Maybe they're traveling. Or out of cell reception."

"My parents don't travel. They love their little corner of the world."

"When did you call?"

"This afternoon, before I left the office."

That would explain why she'd repeatedly checked her phone during the evening. He had started to think that he had been boring her.

Xander squeezed her hand. "Give it time. They'll call."

"Maybe." But she didn't sound convinced.

He knew what it was like to have your family let you down—except his sister. Stasia had always been there for him, even when he didn't want her to be. These days she seemed to think he needed to settle down and start a family of his own. He wondered what she'd think of him making a family with Lea.

"You have to understand," Lea said, drawing his full attention, "my relationship with them is quite strained. My mother thinks she always knows best. She's been making decisions for me my whole life. Like my college, I didn't even know about all the schools that had accepted me until it was too late. But the final straw was when she kept my extended family from me. Do you even know what that felt like?"

"I have some idea." His adoptive parents had never kept it a secret that he was adopted. When he was young, his mother would say he was the child they chose—the child of their hearts. That reassurance had faded away after his little sister came along.

Lea's eyes widened. "Of course you do. I'm sorry. I shouldn't make a big deal of this."

"Don't diminish your feelings just because of me. You have a right to those feelings."

"I just don't know how my parents could look me in the face after what they'd done. And instead of apologizing, they said they'd done the right thing and that they would do it again. That wasn't their decision to make. They acted like my relatives were a bunch of criminals. And nothing could be further from the truth."

"Maybe your parents were afraid you would leave them."

"That's still no excuse. It didn't have to be an either-or decision, but in the end they made it one. And now... now I don't know if my baby, um, our baby will know its grandparents."

"But I thought you were moving home." Was there a chance she'd changed her mind? Was she considering making her life here in Greece—close to him?

Lea stopped just outside the door to their bungalow and turned to him. "I haven't decided. Just because I return to the States doesn't mean I'll live near my parents. I could live in downtown Seattle, where I went to college. I still have friends from school there."

He reached out and gently traced his finger down the

side of her beautiful face. "Or you could stay here where you have friends that care about you. And you'll have me."

She lifted her chin until their gazes met. "Do you care about me?"

For a second, his heart stilled. She was calling him out—making him confess feelings that he hadn't even admitted to himself. But if he wanted her to stay—to make a family with him—then he was going to have to take the biggest risk of his life.

He swallowed hard. "Yes. I care about you. And I want you to stay."

She didn't turn away. Her eyes widened with surprise. Had he kept his evolving feelings so far under wraps? For him, it felt like his heart had been hanging on his sleeve. It was a new feeling—a vulnerability that he'd never allowed himself to feel until now.

She continued to stare into his eyes as though searching for the truth of his words. He leaned down and pressed a kiss to her lips. He wasn't sure how she would react.

At first, she stood unmoving, as though she were in shock by his admission. Maybe he was acting too swiftly. Perhaps he should slow this down and let her absorb what he'd said to her.

He started to pull back, but her hands moved with lightning speed. Her fingers clutched the lapels of his jacket, pulling him back to her. This time she took the lead. As her mouth opened to him, his tongue delved inside, tasting the sweetness of the champagne from the wedding reception.

But it was her kiss that was intoxicating. His hold on her waist tightened. Her curves fit so perfectly against his. As their kiss deepened, he realized he would never get enough of this—enough of Lea.

Hand in hand they stepped inside the bungalow. Not bothering with the lights, they headed straight for Lea's bedroom.

With the moonlight filtering in through the window

and illuminating them, Xander stared at Lea. She was so beautiful. He was the luckiest man in the world.

His heart raced and his need to pull her close mounted. But there was something he needed to say first. "Lea, is tonight what you want? What you really want?"

She nodded. Her gaze never strayed from his. "You are everything I've ever wanted."

His head dipped, and he claimed her lips. No one had ever said those words to him or made him feel the way she did. He was falling hard for her.

Correction: he'd already fallen head over heels.

CHAPTER FIFTEEN

"I CAN'T LEAVE NOW."

Xander gripped the phone tightly as his sister insisted he drop everything and fly to Italy. Normally he would do anything for Stasia, but after spending the night with Lea in his arms, he felt torn between his brotherly responsibility and cementing this blossoming relationship with Lea.

"I don't understand this," his sister said. "What could possibly be more important than business? I swear it's the only reason you get out of bed in the morning."

Xander raked his fingers through his hair. He had yet to tell his sister about Lea and the baby. He still felt protective of the relationship and didn't want to expose it to other peoples' criticisms.

"Maybe it's time I take some time for myself," he said, hoping she'd drop the subject.

"Hmph…" His sister didn't sound convinced. "So you're trying to tell me that you're on vacation?"

"Yes." He jumped at the answer, perhaps a little too quickly. "I've decided I need to slow down a bit."

"Uh-huh. And where would you be vacationing?"

"In the Mediterranean. On an island."

"Could you be any more obscure? I mean, what if there's an emergency and I need you."

Since their parents had passed on, there was just the two of them. "You can call my cell phone."

"Xander."

In his mind, he could imagine his sister with her hip thrown to the side with a hand resting on it while she glared at him for being difficult. She'd mastered that posture when they were kids and it still worked on him.

"Fine. I'm on Infinity Island."

His sister gasped. "You're on a wedding island? You're getting married and you didn't tell me?"

"No. No. Calm down." He couldn't believe his sister had heard of the island. Apparently it was renowned, just like Lea said.

"Well, what else would you be doing there? People only go there to get married or attend a wedding. And I know you hate going to weddings because you feel awkward attending solo and you don't want to ask any of your lady friends to be your date because they might get the wrong idea and start thinking you're open to making a commitment. So what gives?"

Xander really did want someone to bounce ideas off. And his sister might be able to lend some advice where Lea was concerned. And the truth was Stasia was going to learn of the pregnancy eventually. He'd rather it came from him.

"Initially, I came to Infinity Island to buy it."

"I take it that's not why you're there now."

He shook his head before realizing that she couldn't see him. "No. It's something more personal. Lea is pregnant."

"Who is Lea?"

He went on to explain how he'd gotten to know Lea and the fun time they'd had together.

"Pregnant? Wow," Stasia said. "I didn't see that coming. I didn't even know you wanted a family."

"I didn't know I did either, not until there was a baby. And now all I can think about is the three of us becoming a family."

"Xander, slow down. Are you even sure the baby is yours?"

"Yes." He said it without hesitation.

"How much do you know about this woman? Have you done a background check?"

"Stasia, I'm not doing that. What I need to know, I'll learn from her."

"Xander, think about this. You barely know this woman. How do you know she's not running a scam—"

"Because I know her. Stasia, I told you this because I wanted to share this information with my sister. But if you can't be happy for me, stay out of it."

Strained silence greeted him. He may love his sister, but she had to respect his relationship with Lea.

"Xander, I didn't mean to upset you. It's just that you're my brother and I love you. I don't want you to be hurt. That's all."

Xander smiled. "I know."

"Promise me you won't go rushing into anything."

"Don't worry. I've got this." He ended the conversation by promising to call soon.

Now that he was certain he could make this thing with Lea work, he knew words wouldn't be enough to prove his commitment to her. He had to back up his words with action—something that would show Lea just how serious he was about making them into a family of three.

CHAPTER SIXTEEN

AN INTERESTED BUYER...

A lot of mixed emotions came over Lea. Whereas, at one point, she'd thought that selling the island was her only option, now she wondered if she'd been too quick. And did she really want to move back to Seattle after making a life for herself here with so many people around that cared about her?

Her thoughts circled back around to her parents and how they hadn't returned her call. Sure, she hadn't left a message, but the missed call would have shown up on the cell phone. After all, she'd reached out first. That had to count for something.

But their lingering silence was unexpected. Lea didn't realize how deeply their unhappiness with her went. Right then and there she promised herself that she'd never do something like that with her child. A love fiercer than she'd ever known came over her. She wouldn't let anyone or anything come between her and her child.

"Hey. Hello." Popi waved at Lea to get her attention. "What has you so deep in thought?"

Lea gave herself a mental shake. "Sorry. What did you say?"

"I stopped by to ask if you wanted to go over the plans for the upcoming wedding."

These weddings weren't just your normal weddings. They were dreams brought to life. And in some cases, they took a lot of construction.

"Remind me of the details?"

Popi gave her a strange look. "It isn't like you to forget details."

Lea sighed and leaned back in her chair. "I've had a lot on my mind lately."

"You mean that tall, sexy guy sharing your bungalow has you distracted."

Lea frowned at her friend. "I meant the business."

Though Popi was partially right. When Lea wasn't thinking about what to do with the island, her mind was on Xander and how every time he kissed her, it felt like the first time. She lost touch with reality and her feet no longer touched the earth.

Popi nodded in understanding. "Have you eaten lunch yet?"

Lea shook her head. Ever since she'd heard there was another buyer interested in the island, she'd been utterly distracted. As much as she loved the island, if she found a buyer that loved it as much as she did and was capable of fixing it up the way it should be, Lea knew the right thing would be to turn the island over. It would be what was best for everyone. Wouldn't it?

Popi signaled for her to join her. "Come on. Our babies would probably appreciate the nourishment."

Lea arched a brow at Popi. She was worried her friend was going to get too attached to her niece or nephew and have a hard time handing it over to its parents. Popi assured her that wouldn't happen but it didn't keep Lea from worrying. Lea couldn't imagine ever parting with the little one inside her.

"Stop worrying," Popi said. "I'm not getting attached."

"Uh-huh." Lea didn't believe her and she doubted that Popi believed her own words.

"I'm serious. I know this is my niece or nephew. And... and I'm glad I won't be the one stumbling around in the middle of the night with a crying baby."

As they made their way to the nearby café, Popi changed the subject. "So, what are your plans?"

Lea's eyes lit up with interest. "Plans for what?"

"Mr. Hot & Sexy. Are you going to ride off into the sunset with him?"

"No. Of course not." Although he had asked her to marry him. But he hadn't really meant it. It had sounded more like a business proposition than anything else. Not wanting to talk about Xander and all of her mixed-up emotions where he was concerned, she said, "But I do have news."

"Spill it."

"I have an interested buyer for the island. And I think this woman has real potential to be the right fit. We talked on the phone this morning for quite some time. She had so many questions. She was interested in all aspects of the island."

Popi paused outside the café. A worried look came over her face. "After walking away from your life—from your family—to claim your heritage, are you ready to give it up so quickly?"

"I have to do what is best."

"Best for whom?"

Lea's gaze met her friend's. "Don't worry. I'll make sure whoever buys the island keeps the staff. You don't have to worry. I'll make it part of the sales agreement."

"That's not what I'm worried about, but thank you."

The meeting with the potential buyer was in the morning. After Xander had been so reckless in front of her other potential buyers, she wasn't about to tell him about this one. But she needed to make sure he was distracted.

"Would you mind if Xander helped you with some of the reception details?" Lea asked.

Popi gave her a puzzled look. "We have enough staff to handle the job."

"I know. I just need him kept busy for the morning. That prospective buyer is flying in."

"Oh. Okay. No problem."

"Thank you so much."

"Any time. I'm always here for you."

That was the truth, and another reason Lea so desperately wanted to stay on the island. But what was she willing to do to make that happen?

Something was up with Lea.

He was certain of it.

The following day, Xander was bothered by something Lea had said the previous evening. She'd tried to get him to go with Popi to the other side of the island to set up for a jungle-themed wedding reception. Normally he'd have volunteered, but after working on the island, he'd learned a lot and he knew the staging crew wasn't shorthanded. In fact, he'd more than likely get in their way rather than be of any help. So what had been Lea's purpose for the request?

She'd brought it up again that morning, but he'd told her he already had plans. And that was no lie. He was working on his surprise for her. Or was that it? Had she figured out what he was up to?

He mulled it over for much of the morning and then decided she didn't know because she would have said something. Lea was up to something—something that she didn't want him to know about. And for the life of him, he couldn't get the thought out of his mind.

With the nursery well underway, he decided to meet up with Lea just to make sure everything was all right between them. He headed toward her office where she spent a lot of her day. It seemed strange to him that living on this sunny, beautiful island she would be stuck inside much of the time. If his office was here, he'd make sure he was mobile. He'd take his laptop and spend as much time working outside as possible.

He really could imagine himself working here. This place and the people that lived and worked on the island felt more like a small, close-knit community than business associates.

As he walked toward the office, he considered inviting Lea to lunch. But it should be something more than lunch at one of the cafés. Perhaps they could get their lunch to go and have it down along the beach. The more he thought about it, the more the details came into focus.

He was almost to the office when he saw Lea exit the building, but she wasn't alone. There was a woman with her. They were talking and laughing. When the woman turned so that he could see her face, he came to a complete standstill.

Stasia?

What was she doing here?

He immediately knew the answer. His little sister was here to check out the woman who was going to have his baby. Stasia had to make sure Lea was good enough.

He shook his head in disbelief. His sister had crossed the line. He could just imagine her interrogating Lea. He was going to put a stop to it—

"Xander, there you are."

He didn't want to stop. He didn't want to talk to anyone but his sister. But he recognized the voice. It was Popi.

He paused and turned back. "Can we talk later? I was just about to—"

"It's really important. There's an emergency."

He searched her face to see if she was being serious. And by all accounts, Popi did look worried. "What's wrong?"

"There was an accident this morning. It's Joseph. I think he broke his leg."

"Is that why I heard the helicopter?"

"Not exactly. They delivered a visitor and were on standby when the accident occurred."

He didn't have to ask to know that his sister was the one to fly onto the island. Stasia wasn't wasting any time vetting the new woman in his life. But in the end, he supposed it wasn't all bad as the helicopter was already on the island, saving lots of time getting Joseph to the hospital.

"What can I do to help?"

"There's still lots of work to be done and I'm looking for any able bodies to help. We're running out of time."

He glanced over his shoulder to where he'd last seen Lea and his sister. They had moved out of sight. Confronting Stasia would have to wait.

And so would the nursery that he had just about finished. He hadn't even been sure that he'd be able to pull it off with Lea sleeping at the other end of the hallway. But by some miracle, he'd been able to get most of the sawing and hammering done while she was at the office.

And if by chance that wasn't enough to prove to her that he was serious about them—about their family—he was in the process of having plans drawn up to relocate his offices to the island. He never thought that he'd be happy living outside of the city—with his thumb on the heartbeat of commerce—but Lea had changed all of that.

Now he couldn't imagine living away from Lea and their child. And there was something about Infinity Island—something that felt like home.

CHAPTER SEVENTEEN

THERE WAS A buyer for the island.

And now she had to truly decide where her future lay.

Lea knew selling the island would be hard, but she hadn't realized it would be this hard. Even though the woman she'd met with the previous day was really nice, very interested in the island and had promised to keep it running in the same manner as Lea's ancestors had done, Lea was still hesitant to sell.

Selling Infinity Island would be giving up on her heritage—giving up on her friends that were now her family, giving up on finding out if this thing with Xander was real. It sure felt real to her, but she didn't know if Xander felt the same way.

Xander was offering her a chance to have everything she'd ever wanted. And he'd done everything to show her how invested he was in this relationship. Now it was time she met him halfway. It was time she took a chance with the island and most of all, with her heart.

As soon as she arrived at the office, she called the number the woman had left her. It went to voice mail. Lea didn't really want to leave this information in a voice mail.

She attempted to work, but her mind just wasn't into it. She was so excited about what the future held. Teaming up with Xander would be interesting. She believed that there was nothing they couldn't do together.

Just before ten o'clock in the morning, Lea gave up the pretense of working. She planned to swing by the bungalow and switch into more sensible shoes before she went to track down Xander at whatever project he'd gotten involved with this time. With Joseph laid up for a couple of months, there was more work than ever to be done.

Lea stepped through the doorway of the bungalow, surprised to find Xander at home. He was video-chatting with his back to her. She slipped off her shoes at the door and walked softly across the floor, not wanting to disturb him. But she had to pass by the table in order to get to her room.

As she neared him, she heard a woman's voice. It was a familiar voice. Wait, she knew that voice. She couldn't quite place it.

It was best to keep walking, ignoring the woman's voice. But an uneasy feeling chewed away at her insides. Was there another woman in Xander's life?

And then the woman laughed. It was a warm, jingly kind of laugh. Xander replied softly to her, making it impossible for Lea to make out the words. The feeling in her gut turned to red hot jealousy. It was unmistakable. But she refused to let Xander know how she felt. She kept walking, but she couldn't resist a quick glance at his monitor.

Gasp!

Lea stopped. That was the same woman that had been interested in purchasing the island. But how could that be? Was Xander plotting against her?

Xander turned around. Surprise was written all over his handsome face. "Lea. Wait." He turned back to the computer. "I'll call you when I'm on the plane." And with that he closed the laptop.

By then Lea had recovered enough from the shock to get her feet to move. She thought about leaving, but then realized this was her home. She wasn't going anywhere. Xander was the one who was leaving. Hadn't she heard him say something about a plane?

She headed to the kitchen. She could hear his footsteps behind her. She steeled herself, refusing to let him see just how deeply his betrayal had hurt her.

"Lea, it's not what you think. That was my sister—"

"Stop. I don't want to hear whatever you have to say." She turned on him. Her shock morphed into anger. "What I think is that you and your sister made a fool of me. And now it's time you leave the island."

"No one made a fool of you. And no one set out to hurt you." He stepped closer to her.

She held her arm straight out, blocking his progress. "Just stay away. Don't try and charm your way out of this."

"Lea, don't do this. We can work everything out. I… I just need to take care of something first."

What could possibly be more important than this? And then she realized the foolishness of her question. It had to be business. It always came back to his business, whether it was trying to sweet-talk her out of the land or sending his sister in to do his dirty work.

"Just go." She turned her back to him.

"Lea, please believe me. I would never do anything to hurt you, but if I don't go, my company will be put in jeopardy from a large lawsuit. Please say you'll wait here for me. And then we can talk."

She turned back to him. "I'll be here. I'll always be here. But you won't be welcome."

She didn't need to hear anything else he had to say. He'd been keeping things from her, just like her parents had kept information about her family and her heritage from her. And they all had their excuses, but none of them were reason enough to keep Lea in the dark.

"I'll be back. I promise."

His words fell on deaf ears because she refused to believe anything he had to say from here on out. If she needed any further proof that he wouldn't change—that he would always put business ahead of his family—this was it.

Frustration, pain and anger churned within her. After Xander left, she needed to do something, anything. But she couldn't concentrate enough to go back to the office.

Instead she started to clean out her kitchen cabinets. She'd been meaning to do it for a long time now but had put it off for one reason or another.

She'd inherited all of this stuff. Some of the dishes were in amazing condition. Others had most definitely seen better days. She kept working, pulling everything out and sorting out the keepers and those that could go.

When her phone rang, she considered ignoring it. If it was Xander, she had absolutely no interest in talking to him. And if it was Popi, she didn't want to get into this with her, not yet. But she realized that it could be island business and that was something she couldn't ignore. And she refused to think how her priorities were similar to Xander's.

She glanced at the caller ID and her heart stopped. It was her mother. After an entire year, her mother was calling her. Was she returning her call? *But it has been so long.* Or had something happened? Was her father ill? *Please say it isn't so.*

Lea knew that all she would have were unanswered questions unless she accepted the call. Not giving herself time to think of all the reasons that this was a bad idea, she pressed the answer button on her phone.

"Hello."

"Lea? Is that you?"

"Yes, Mom. It's me." Her insides shivered with nerves. "Is something wrong with Dad?"

"Um…no, he's fine. I'm returning your call. I'm so sorry we missed it. My battery died just after we left on an Alaskan cruise so we had to rely on your father's phone."

"Dad has a cell phone? I thought he was opposed to them as they are a nuisance."

Her mother sighed. "A lot has changed since you left."

"A lot has changed here, too." It wasn't until she heard her mother's voice that she realized how much she missed speaking to her.

And as much as she'd worried about how things would go when she finally spoke to her mother again, they quickly fell into a comfortable conversation. It was almost like nothing had happened. And Lea opened up about the baby, Xander and the island being in trouble.

"You have a lot on your shoulders," her mother said. "I'm sorry about adding to your worries. Neither your father nor I meant to hurt you. We honestly thought we were saving you from more pain by being rejected by my family. I know what it feels like to be turned away and told I was dead to them for marrying a man they didn't approve of."

That was more information than Lea had gotten before, but that might have been because she'd been so upset with her parents that she hadn't let them say much. Lea told her mother that she regretted leaving Seattle in such a huff and not calling. Her mother apologized, too.

"But what will you do about Xander?" her mother asked. "Will you hear him out?"

"I… I don't know. I trusted him and he hurt me. Can you imagine him asking his sister to come here pretending to be a prospective buyer?"

Her mother was quiet for a moment. "I know you don't want to hear this, especially after what happened between us, but is there a chance he had good intentions?"

"Mom…"

"Wait. Listen to me and then you can ignore everything I say." Her mother paused as though waiting to see if she had Lea's attention. "Perhaps you were expecting him to let you down because other people, especially me, have let you down in the past. Could that be part of it?"

Lea heard her mother, and as much as she wanted to disagree with her, she remained quiet. She had a lot of thinking to do because there was a baby relying on her to make the right decision—for both of them.

CHAPTER EIGHTEEN

"I'LL MEET YOU in Rome with the car and all of the documents."

Xander stood at the airport listening to Roberto, his second in charge, go over everything that needed to happen to head off the possibility of his sister losing her entire life's savings and putting his company in jeopardy—the company that he'd worked all his life to make the biggest and the best.

But as Roberto continued to speak, Xander's mind was not on business. It was on the devastated look he'd seen on Lea's face when he left. And then the truth of the matter struck him with the strength of a lightning strike, nearly knocking him off his feet and into a nearby chair. He'd done everything wrong.

His heart just wasn't in this business deal or heading off a business bully. In the past, there was nothing he'd have liked better than proving to a business opponent that they were wrong. But now, things had changed.

His heart was back on Infinity Island with Lea and their baby.

"Xander, did you hear me?"

He hadn't heard a word the man had said in the last couple of minutes. "Listen Roberto, we're going to change things."

"Change things? Now? We don't have time."

"We always have time to do the right thing."

Roberto paused as though confused. "We are doing the right thing. We're right and they are wrong. We just have to prove it and quickly."

Until this point, Xander had always taken a hands-on approach with his business. Until now, he hadn't imagined ever letting someone else be in charge of his company—

not even long enough to take a vacation. Until Lea, his life had been his work. And now all of that had changed.

As Roberto talked in his ear, Xander realized that he had a very competent and eager number two. Due to Xander's need to be in control of everything, big and small, Roberto hadn't gotten a chance to spread his wings. Until now...

"Roberto."

The man stuttered to a halt.

"I appreciate all the work you've done. Over the years and most especially on this project. You appear to know all of the details. And you understand what I hope to accomplish."

"Uh... Thank you, sir."

Xander realized he'd really held onto the reins of the office too tightly. He noticed how Lea ran the island with a much more relaxed attitude. Perhaps it was time he did the same, especially if his plans worked out.

"Call me Xander."

"Yes, sir. Erm, Xander."

Xander smiled. He could tell this transformation was going to take time for everyone to adjust to. And then Xander went on to tell Roberto that he was the one going to Italy to represent the company.

"Are you sure?" Roberto asked.

"If you'd asked me that question a year ago, even a month ago, I would have said no. But a lot has changed to open my eyes. You're ready for this—you're more than ready. You probably know the facts and figures of this project better than I do at this point."

"Where will you be?"

"I'm heading back to Infinity Island. I left some unfinished business there."

He just hoped Lea would hear him out. He should have made more of an effort to tell her about his sister. He'd never meant for her to learn the truth the way she did.

And he had no idea what he was going to do if they couldn't work their way past this.

CHAPTER NINETEEN

ONE MINUTE SHE was certain they had no future.

The next moment, she missed him with all her heart.

Lea expelled a huff as she paced back and forth in the bungalow. With each pass, the walls felt as though they were closing in on her. She needed to keep herself occupied.

And she didn't feel like going to the office. However, she did feel like some good old-fashioned hard work—like cleaning. It'd been quite a while since she gave the place a thorough spring cleaning. And with the kitchen done, she might as well keep going.

Lea started toward her bedroom to strip her bed and throw the linen in the wash, when she came to a pause outside Xander's room. Not that it was actually his room. In fact, it was as good a time as any to clean away any lingering memories of him.

She opened the door and stepped inside. Her gaze took in the pastel green and purple walls. *What in the world?*

There was a new light fixture. New windows and curtains. There were even new closet doors that worked, unlike the old ones. And inside the closet, she found shelves above the clothes rod. Plenty of room for the baby's things.

Lea's vision blurred and she quickly blinked away the tears. She turned and took in all of the baby furniture. It was the wooden cradle that called to her. She walked over and ran her hands over the smooth lines of the wood. It was beautiful. She didn't see any store tags like the ones visible on some of the other pieces in the room. As she examined it more closely, she started to suspect that it might be handmade. By Xander?

She recalled how he'd been absent a lot lately. He was

always going here or there. Could this have been what had him so preoccupied? Was he creating all of this for their baby?

The impact of his actions caused an emotional lump to swell in her throat. Tears stung the back of her eyes. If the baby meant this much to him, why had he left? Why did he leave so much unsaid between them?

As the questions crowded into her mind, she moved out of the nursery, pulling the door closed behind her. Staying here wasn't going to help her. She needed to get away.

Lea went to her room, a room where they'd made love so recently. Memories of Xander were everywhere. She had to get away.

She pulled a duffel bag from the back of her closet. She grabbed random articles of clothes from the closet and tossed them on the bed. Her movements were abrupt, causing her to almost trip over her own feet.

She couldn't get out of here fast enough. It felt like if she stayed here any longer the memories would suffocate her. That was it. Different scenery and some fresh air would hopefully give her a clear perspective. If she could get away from everything that reminded her of Xander, she'd be able to breathe easy. But she wondered if that place existed.

Knock. Knock.

Xander?

Lea's heart raced. Had he come back? What should she say to him? She had no answers.

"Lea?" The front door creaked open as Popi let herself inside.

Lea's heart slowed and she expelled a pent-up breath. "I'm back here."

It was good that her friend was here. It would save her a trip over to Popi's place. But how did she explain all of this to her?

When Popi appeared in her bedroom doorway, her gaze

landed on the clothes scattered on the bed. "Going some-where?"

"Yes."

"With Xander?" Popi glanced around as though searching for him.

"No. By myself. Xander is gone."

"Oh. Um… Do you want to talk?"

Lea shook her head. She didn't think she could speak of Xander without breaking down in tears and that was the last thing she wanted right now. If she could just get away from the place where she'd spent so much time with Xander, she'd be okay.

Without meeting her friend's gaze, she said, "I need you to handle things for a few days."

"But where are you going?"

Lea hadn't stopped to think about that. Her mind was in a tizzy. She could leave the island altogether and head for the mainland. There were plenty of places to lose herself there. But she wasn't up for sightseeing and she really didn't want to deal with people.

And then a thought came to her. When she'd first arrived on the island, she'd done a lot of exploring, even stumbling upon an abandoned cabin. In that moment, she knew where she could go. The secluded spot would give her a chance to formulate a plan. Because even though she'd spoken to her mother and they'd started the process of patching up their relationship, Lea realized this island and the people on it were now her home. There had to be a way to save it that she hadn't thought of yet—even if it came down to an internet fund-raiser. She would not lose the island.

CHAPTER TWENTY

WHERE IS SHE?

It was late when Xander returned to the island. Still, he'd only been gone for not quite twelve hours. How far could she get?

He inwardly groaned when he thought of the answer. Lea could have gone quite far. He'd searched every room in the bungalow and her office. She was nowhere to be seen. And that was when he realized the one person who would know where to locate her—Popi. They were as close as two friends could be.

He knew it was late but that didn't stop him from approaching Popi's door. Surely she would understand the urgency. The longer he let this thing linger, the further Lea slipped away from him. The thought of losing Lea forever had him urgently knocking on the door.

When the door didn't immediately swing open, he started to worry that Popi wasn't home. But where else would she be on the island? It didn't exactly have a night life unless there was a wedding. And he knew from his work on the island that there was none scheduled for the evening.

He knocked again. "Popi! It's Xander. I need your help."

The door swung open. Popi stood there with her hair mussed up as she clutched a short white robe around her and glared at him. "What's going on?"

"I'm really sorry to disturb you this late." And he was sorry, but that didn't stop him. He had a feeling that if he didn't find Lea soon, she would plan a new life that didn't include him and he wouldn't have a chance to change her mind. "I need to find Lea. She's gone."

Popi sighed. "And this couldn't have waited until morning?"

He shook his head. "I messed up real bad. And now I need to find her. I need to tell her... I need to tell her so many things."

Popi studied him for a moment and then she shook her head. "I can't help you."

When she began to close the door, he stuck out his foot, blocking the door from closing the whole way. "Listen, I know I screwed up in more than one way. I shouldn't have left her. I should have stayed and fixed things. I made a mistake. Surely you can understand. You've made mistakes, haven't you?"

"Sure, I have. But walking away from someone that you're supposed to care about after you've screwed up royally, well that's a special kind of mistake. It's the kind of mistake that makes the other person need time to sort things out in their head."

"And that's why I have to get to her."

"Leave her be. You can speak to her when she gets back—"

"It'll be too late. She'll have written me out of her life and we all know how stubborn she can be when she feels as though someone she cares about has betrayed her."

"You mean her parents?"

He nodded. "I've been trying to talk her into reconciling with them, but she's hesitant. If she does the same thing with me, I don't know how I'll ever win her back." He pleaded with Popi with his eyes. "Please help me. I love Lea and she doesn't know it. It might make a difference in what she decides to do next."

Popi let go of the door and crossed her arms above her rounded abdomen. "I don't want to, but I believe you. But you have to understand that I made a promise to my best friend not to tell anyone where she went."

He was the one to sigh this time. "And you are worried

that Lea will see this as a betrayal." He hated what he had to say next. "I can't ask you to do that, not only for your sake but also for Lea's. She needs you."

He turned to walk away. He'd just reached the stepping stones when he heard Popi call out to him. He paused and turned back.

"If you need a place to stay tonight, I know of a little secluded hut."

Was she trying to get him out of the way? Or was she trying to tell him something? He quietly waited for her to go on.

"With it being out of the way, it would be a good place for you to figure out your next step. If you're interested, I can tell you how to get there." A small smile pulled at Popi's lips.

And then he knew she was giving him directions to reach the love of his life. He agreed and she gave him the instructions. She told him he might want to wait for daybreak before heading into the rough terrain and getting lost. But he couldn't stand to live any longer with this rift between him and Lea. With every passing moment it felt like Lea was slipping away.

And so he set off down the path with a flashlight and a few supplies. He would find her and then he'd plead his case. He just prayed Lea would be willing to listen.

CHAPTER TWENTY-ONE

SLEEP ELUDED HER.

Lea stretched out on the small bed and stared into the darkness. She had never felt more alone, not even when she'd packed up and left everything that she knew and loved in Seattle. This loneliness was so much deeper and so much more painful.

But Xander had made his choice of what was most important to him when he'd left before explaining exactly what was going on with his sister. Now that she'd calmed down, she recalled a few of the words she'd overheard when she entered the bungalow while he video-chatted with his sister.

His sister had said that she was only doing what she thought was best for him. And he'd told her he didn't need her being so overprotective. He could take care of himself. It was shortly after that that he'd noticed Lea's presence.

At the time, Lea had been so upset and wallowing in the pain of betrayal that she hadn't bothered to consider what Xander might have meant. But out here, away from the drama, she could think more clearly. And she didn't like what she was thinking…

She loved Xander.

She missed Xander.

She flopped over in bed and fluffed her pillow. Thinking of Xander and missing him wasn't doing her any good. How was she supposed to get over him?

Just then she felt a kick. *The baby.* It caught her completely off guard. She rolled onto her back and placed her hand on her expanding abdomen, willing it to move again.

Each day, the baby was getting stronger. Lea wished Xander was there to share this special moment with her.

What would have happened if she'd stayed at the bungalow and waited for him? Would he return? Would he wonder what had happened to her?

He'd never find her because she'd only told one person where she'd gone. And she'd sworn Popi to secrecy. Maybe that had been overkill, but she'd been running on pure emotions at the time.

She reached for her cell phone to text Popi but there was no signal out here. With a grunt, she returned the phone to the side table. Her hand pounded the pillow into what she hoped was a more comfortable position. And then she rested on her side and closed her eyes, willing sleep to take her to dreamland, where anything was possible, including happily-ever-afters.

Knock. Knock.

Lea's eyes sprang open. The beginning signs of dawn illuminated the room. Had she at last fallen asleep? She was pretty sure that was the case. But what had awoken her?

Knock. Knock.

"Lea?"

Was that Xander? It sure sounded like him.

She sat straight up in bed. It couldn't be Xander. He wouldn't even know where to find her. But someone was definitely pounding on her door.

She jumped out of bed and rushed to the door. She swung it open and stood there speechless when she saw a very tired Xander staring back at her.

"Can I come in?" he asked.

She pulled the door wide open and moved off to the side in order for him to enter. At last finding her voice, she asked, "What are you doing here?"

Even with heavy stubble covering his jaw and his hair mussed up, he looked so amazingly handsome. "I had to find you. I had to tell you I'm sorry."

"For leaving?" She was about to tell him that she understood, but he didn't give her the chance.

"For that. And for not realizing soon enough how important you are to me. And for my sister pulling that overprotective routine and coming here to investigate you after I told her we were going to become a family." He glanced down at the floor. "I guess I got ahead of myself when I told her that last part."

"Why didn't you tell me right away about your sister?"

He'd meant to and he had legitimate reasons why he put it off, but it boiled down to... "I couldn't at first. There was that accident with Joseph and Popi asked me to help fill in. And then I kept putting it off because I knew it would spell trouble for us and we were in such a good place."

"And you were afraid I'd think you betrayed me like my parents?"

He nodded.

"What my parents never understood and what I hope you'll understand is that I don't need anyone to protect me. I need a partner who is honest with me about everything— the good and the bad."

"I can do that." His eyes reflected the truth of his words.

Lea's heart swelled with hope. This was the second chance that she'd been lying in bed all night hoping for. She couldn't mess it up. "As for being a family, is that what you still want?"

His gaze met hers. "More than anything else. I know I've messed things up more than once, but I'd like a chance to make them right."

Her heart raced. He was saying all the right things. But there was just one more thing she needed to hear. "And if you could make them right, what would you say?"

His gaze searched hers. "I would say I'm sorry I hurt you. I will do my utmost best to never do that again. And I'm sorry that I put my business ahead of our relationship. That will never happen again." When she sent him a doubtful look, he added, "I've just recently opened my eyes to the fact that I have a very capable number two. He is now on his way to Italy to handle this latest crisis."

"Really? I mean, you said it was so important. I don't want you to risk your company—"

"What I was risking was far more important than business." He reached out and took her hands in his own. "Lea, I love you. And I want to spend the rest of my life showing you just how much you mean to me."

Tears of joy spilled onto her cheeks. "I love you, too. I was just too stubborn to admit it to myself. But my mother helped me to see that I was closing myself off because I was afraid of being hurt again."

"Your mother? You spoke to her?"

Lea nodded as she squeezed his hands. And then she explained about her mother's phone dying while they were on a cruise. "And so I have you to thank for talking sense into me and welcoming my parents back into my life."

"Did you tell them about the baby?"

"I did. And I think my mother cried. Happy tears. They're even planning to fly here, which I know is a big thing for them as they were banished from the island by my grandparents."

"Maybe this baby will help bring everyone back together. After all, it worked for us. You are the only woman in the world for me."

"And you are the only man for me."

"In that case, I have a proposition for you." He dropped to one knee. "I know you've turned me down before and rightly so. But a lot has changed since then. I've learned a lot. I love you, Lea, with all my heart. And I can't imagine my life without you in it. Will you do me the honor of being my bride?"

Happy tears clouded her eyes. "I would love to be your bride."

Just then the baby kicked again. Lea took Xander's

hand and pressed it to her abdomen. And then there was another movement. This time Xander's face lit up when he felt the baby move.

"He or she likes the idea." When Lea looked at her future husband, she saw that he was a bit misty-eyed, too.

Her heart overflowed with love. The future looked so amazing. There was nothing they couldn't accomplish—together.

EPILOGUE

Infinity Island, two weeks later...

"WE'RE GETTING MARRIED."

Lea was so happy she felt as though she was going to burst. First, Xander had told her that he loved her and then he'd swept her off on a trip to Seattle. He thought the peace she'd made with her parents deserved to be followed up with an in-person visit.

The trip had been amazing. Xander had been amazing. And then he had done something most unexpected: he'd asked her parents for their approval for him to marry their daughter. It might have been done a bit backwards, but it still touched Lea's heart.

And then atop the Sky Needle, with the sun setting and casting the most glorious streaks of pinks and purples through the sky, Xander had once again got down on one knee. This time he had the biggest, most sparkling diamond ring ever.

Lea remembered how everyone around them had grown quiet. You could have heard a pin drop if it hadn't been for the loud banging of her heart. It had echoed in her ears. But above it, she had heard Xander claim his love for her.

And now that they were back on Infinity Island, she couldn't be happier. "He proposed again." Lea held out her hand for Popi to see her sparkly engagement ring. "We're really and truly going to be a family."

"It's beautiful." Popi rushed forward and gave them both a big hug. She pulled back, looking at both of them. "I always knew this was going to work out. You both deserve your happily-ever-after."

"There's more." Lea wasn't sure how Popi was going to take the other news. "Our wedding is going to be the last wedding on the island."

In a blink, Popi's expression changed from one of excitement to one of horror. "You're shutting down the island? You're giving up?"

Lea felt bad for not phrasing it better. In her excitement, she'd just let the words tumble out. But she knew this island meant almost as much to Popi as it did to her. Infinity Island was home for them. "No, I'm sorry. I didn't mean to worry you." Lea turned to Xander. "Do you want to tell her?"

He shook his head. "You're doing fine."

Lea's heart fluttered in her chest as Xander gazed into her eyes. Every time he looked at her that way, her heart swelled with love. She wondered if it would always be that way—even fifty years from now.

Lea turned back to her best friend. "The reason ours will be the last wedding is that while we're off on an extended honeymoon, the island will be undergoing renovations."

Popi's face lit up and then she clapped her hands in delight. "That's wonderful. This place could really use some help. If there's anything I can do, just let me know."

Lea's gaze dipped to her friend's expanding midsection. "I think you'll have enough to do with your little niece or nephew on the way. Your sister and brother-in-law must be so excited."

"They are. We all are." Popi's gaze lowered. "You know, in the beginning I wasn't so sure about this whole plan."

"You certainly hid it well."

"I didn't want anything to ruin this for my sister. I kept telling myself that it was nerves."

"And how do you feel now?"

"Excited. I can't wait to see my sister with the baby in her arms."

"Even though you have to go through childbirth."

"That's the part I'm trying not to think about. But enough about me. Tell me more about the renovations."

"We're relocating Xander's executive offices to the island."

"Really?" Popi's gaze moved to Xander. "And you're okay with this? Won't you feel a bit isolated out here?"

"Hey," Lea said, "are you trying to talk him out of this?"

"No." The smile slipped from Popi's face. "Never mind. I didn't mean anything by the questions."

"They're legitimate questions," Xander said. "And I'm happy to answer them. I would follow Lea wherever she led."

"You would?" Lea asked.

He turned to her. "I haven't gotten to this level of success without knowing a good thing when I see it. And so I'm not going to let you slip away. I need you in my life."

Lea moved to him and wrapped her arms around his neck. "You do say the sweetest things. And in case you didn't know, I need you, too."

His hands wrapped around her waist as she lifted up on her tiptoes to press her lips to his. Her lips had barely touched his when she heard Popi clearing her throat rather loudly. Heat rushed to Lea's cheeks. With great reluctance, she pulled away from Xander.

"Sorry." Lea couldn't believe how easy it was for this man to totally distract her. If this was love, she didn't ever want it to end.

"Not a problem." Popi grinned at her. "If I had a man as hot as him, I'd get distracted, too."

"You will," Lea said. "I bet he's just around the corner."

"Not with this baby on board. A man wouldn't even think of getting near me."

"You won't be pregnant much longer," Lea said encouragingly. "At least that's what I keep telling myself as each day my toes seem to get further and further away from me."

Popi laughed. "Just wait until your third trimester—they disappear from sight."

"Seriously," Lea said with a sigh, subduing the banter. "Will you be all right while the island is being renovated? Do you have someplace to go?"

Popi placed a protective hand over her rounded abdomen. "Now that you mention it, I was hoping to take some time off to visit with my sister and her husband. My sister wants to be with me for the birth. So this will work out perfectly."

"Wonderful." Lea smiled broadly. "We have so much to look forward to." And then she turned to the man of her dreams. "It doesn't get any better than this."

* * * * *

TEXAN SEEKS FORTUNE

MARIE FERRARELLA

To
Elliana Melgar,
The Incredibly Precocious
And Intelligent
Three-Year-Old
Who Was My Inspiration
For Ava And Axel

Prologue

Connor Fortunado was torn.

He glanced out of the window of his first-class seat. The flight was just about over.

He was almost there.

Houston.

Home.

Connor half smiled to himself. Home, better known as "The House of the Incurable Romantics." The whimsical title had recently occurred to him because every one of his five siblings was either married or going to be married.

Except for him.

And that little fact of life, he promised himself, wasn't about to change anytime soon.

Or ever.

Connor was pretty happy with his life. He was thirty-one, single, carefree and able to take off at a moment's notice without an explanation to anyone if he wanted to—the way he had just done. If he were married and had what was whimsically referred to in some circles as "a better half," right about now that "better half" would most likely be giving him hell for the double life he was leading. She would have doubtlessly not looked favorably on his giving up an executive position with a prestigious corporate search firm just so that he could follow his passion.

Everyone in the family still thought he was that highly paid executive at his old firm. His former career had been a dependable, respectable position with an excellent, if somewhat boring, future laid out in front of it. None of his relatives knew that somewhere along the line he had discovered he had a real aptitude for detective work.

It had begun innocently enough. He'd helped his boss uncover an embezzling scheme within the company. But once he'd discovered the culprit, Connor found that he was hooked on the rush that came in the wake of untangling all the twisted skeins and getting to the bottom of the mystery. After a bit of soul-searching, he'd decided to put his newly honed skills to better use. So he had turned his back on the corporate world and became a highly paid private investigator.

Career changes like that wouldn't have sat well with a wife and she would have undoubtedly had no qualms about making her displeasure known.

To everyone.

Connor frowned. The moment of reckoning was almost here. He was going to have to come clean to his family once he landed in Houston. Telling his siblings should go fine because for the most part, they were pretty open-minded. It was coming clean to his parents that was going to be the problem. His parents, especially his father, were not going to look favorably on this change in careers.

He was *not* looking forward to this. All things considered, he would have gone on keeping his secret for as long as possible.

However, fate had other plans for him and was forcing him to own up to this major change in his life. All in the name of the family good. He just hoped his parents would see it that way. Yes, he was an adult, but there was still a part of him that preferred parental approval.

But he really didn't have the luxury of keeping this to himself any longer. His family needed him. There was no other conclusion to be reached.

Someone was out there, trying to get them.

It wasn't merely a paranoid thought reserved for the rich but an honest assessment of the situation. How else could he view what had been happening to different members of his family in the last two months? Like to his father's half brother. Gerald Robinson's estate, palatial by any standards, had been the target of an arsonist, set on fire and almost burned down to the ground. The family-based technology firm, Robinson Tech, had been the victim of cybersabotage. And Fortunado Real Estate, a company his father founded and two of his sisters and one of his brothers-in-law now worked at, had been the target of sabotage, as well.

It was as if no one who was even remotely related

to the Fortune family—no matter how they spelled their last name—was safe.

Connor had a gut feeling that it was only going to get worse unless whoever was responsible for wreaking all this havoc was found and captured. As a Fortunado, he had found that he and his family were related to the Fortunes. And that meant he couldn't just sit on the sidelines and watch this little drama play out.

He had to *do* something. He had natural skills, he had connections and he had the money to fund the investigation, all of which would serve him well in his search for whoever was attempting to carry out this vendetta against the entire Fortune family.

His family.

In his mind, Connor was already getting started on the case even though he was still airborne.

All he had to do, he thought, was get past telling his parents.

"Ladies and gentlemen, we will be beginning our descent to Houston shortly. Please return your tray tables to the upright positions…"

The cheerful flight attendant continued with her instructions, her voice fading into the background for Connor.

Connor's stomach felt just the slightest bit queasy. Not because of the airplane's descent, but because of what lay ahead.

Zero hour was almost here.

Chapter One

They walked into the big, sprawling living room en masse: his sister Valene; his sister Maddie and her husband, Zach McCarter; and his parents, Kenneth and Barbara Fortunado.

Here goes nothin', Connor thought, putting on his game face.

Kenneth Fortunado, a robust giant of a man, had never been known for beating around the bush. He got right to it.

"All right, Connor, what's the big mystery?" Kenneth asked his son as he came in. "What suddenly brings you here?"

"My guess is it has to be something big to get Connor to leave that cushy, high-paying executive job of his back in Denver and bring his butt back home,"

Maddie said, making herself comfortable on one of the oversize sofas in the room.

"It's not bad news, is it, dear?" Barbara Fortunado asked, her brown eyes wide with worry as they searched her son's face. "Please don't let it be bad news. I couldn't bear to hear about anything else bad happening after all that's been going on."

"Come to think of it, you do look rather unsettled, boy," Kenneth said, looking more closely at his son's face. "Out with it. What's going on? Why are you suddenly here?"

Unable to remain quiet any longer, Connor's sister Valene spoke up. "Everybody, let Connor breathe. We're all getting way too jumpy." Valene was referring to the fact that the place where they all worked, Fortunado Real Estate, had suddenly and inexplicably seen a turn for the worse in the last two months. They'd lost a good share of their best clients.

Taking Maddie's hand in his, Zach McCarter gave Connor a sympathetic look, as if to say that he was glad he wasn't the one in his brother-in-law's shoes, although for now he wisely remained silent.

Connor looked around the room. There were members of his immediate family who were missing from the gathering although he had put the word out that he wanted to speak to all of them at the same time. He saw no sense in having to go through this little drama twice, but obviously his message hadn't registered properly.

"I was hoping to say this when everyone was here," Connor told his father.

"You're going to have to settle for half the family,"

Kenneth told him, his tone already growing impatient. "In case you haven't noticed, trying to get everyone together in one place—apart from holding a wedding—is like herding cats—"

"More like herding chickens," Valene said under her breath, then flashed a smile at her father when Kenneth shot her a look. It was obvious she hadn't thought she was going to be overheard.

"Connor, please tell us," Barbara entreated her son. "You're getting me very nervous."

Feeling guilty that he was adding to his mother's concerns, Connor stopped stalling. Half a family was better than none.

Taking a deep breath, he launched into the reason for his unexpected return home.

Connor started slowly. "It's nothing to make you nervous, Mother."

"Spit it out, Connor," Kenneth ordered. "If you beat around the bush like this at that corporate search firm of yours, it's a wonder that they haven't shown you the door yet."

This was as good an opening as any, Connor thought. "Well, that's part of what I wanted to talk to you about," he began.

Kenneth cut him off. "They fired you?" he cried, astonished despite what he'd just said.

"No," Connor replied firmly. "They didn't fire me, but I'm not working for them anymore."

His father's complexion was turning a shade of unflattering red. "What do you mean you're not working for them anymore?" Kenneth demanded.

"Kenneth, please, let him speak," Barbara pleaded,

putting her hand on her husband's arm as if she was trying to gentle a wild stallion. "I'm sure he has a good explanation for all this." She looked at her son hopefully. Waiting.

"Well?" Kenneth demanded, his eyes all but pinning Connor against the wall.

Connor took in another breath, as if that would somehow shield him from the explosion he sensed was coming. "I'm not with that firm anymore because I'm a private investigator now."

"You're a PI?" Maddie cried in awed disbelief. Suddenly, a smile bloomed on her lips. "You mean like Magnum?"

Valene looked at her sister, lost. "Who's Magnum?" she wanted to know.

"Some guy on a classic TV show," Zach volunteered. "I caught a few episodes on one of those channels that show nothing but programs from the seventies and eighties."

"No, not like Magnum," Connor corrected tolerantly. "Most of the work isn't as glamorous as TV makes it out to be. It requires a lot of patience and a great deal of attention to detail," he told his family, hoping that was enough.

Apparently, it wasn't. Exasperated, Kenneth waved his hand for everyone else in the room to be quiet. He obviously intended to go toe to toe with his son.

"You're a *private eye*?" Kenneth cried, completely stunned and grossly disappointed. There was no question of that. "What the hell were you thinking?"

"It's 'private investigator,' Dad," Connor told his father patiently. "And what I was thinking was that maybe I could help find out who's responsible for everything that's been going on around here lately."

"There are professionals for that sort of thing, dear," Barbara told her son, speaking up.

Connor turned to look at his mother. He hadn't thought this was going to be easy, he reminded himself. "I *am* a professional, Mother."

Kenneth let out an exasperated breath. "Since when?" he mocked.

Connor turned his attention to his father. He couldn't back down now. If he did, it was all over. "Since a few months ago."

Kenneth frowned, shaking his head, unable to accept the information or come to grips with it.

"I don't believe you," Kenneth countered. "You wouldn't do something that was so life-altering without telling me."

"I *am* telling you," Connor pointed out. "Now. There was no reason to say anything earlier."

It was plain to everyone that Kenneth found the explanation entirely unacceptable.

"How did this happen?" his father wanted to know. "Did you wake up one morning and just say, 'Gee, I'm tired of my high-paying executive job. Let me throw it all away and do something totally mindless, like become a private eye.' Is that what happened?" Kenneth demanded hotly.

"Private detective, dear," Barbara corrected her husband.

"Private *investigator*," Connor said calmly, correcting them both. "And no, I didn't just wake up one morning and decide to become a private investigator," he told

his father. "My boss suspected that there was someone embezzling money from the firm, but he didn't
know how to go about finding out who was behind it.
He shared his concern with me and I told him I'd do a
little snooping around. I did and as it turns out, I discovered who was stealing the firm's money in a little
less than a week."

Kenneth dourly dismissed the accounting. "You
got lucky."

"No, I didn't," Connor informed his father. "I was
persistent. And I found that I had a natural aptitude
for ferreting things out."

Kenneth snorted. "My son the Ferret. I can't wait
to tell people your new job description."

"Dad, you're missing the point here," Valene insisted,
looking at her father with a touch of annoyance as she
came to her brother's aid. "Connor said he was here to
help us get to the bottom of what's been happening to
the family lately."

She looked at her father, waiting for her words to
sink in.

"That's for the police to do," Barbara reminded her
children. No doubt she didn't like the idea of any of her
children getting involved with something that could
be dangerous.

"And how far have they gotten with their investigation?" Maddie challenged her mother.

Barbara raised her shoulders in a helpless shrug,
then offered an excuse to Maddie. "It's still early,"
Barbara said.

"Do you really want to wait until someone's killed

before we do anything, Mother?" Connor asked his mother gently.

Barbara's eyes widened, as if she hadn't thought about that possibility. "Do you really think that could happen?" she asked Connor.

His inclination was to shelter his mother, but he had to be honest. "The way things are escalating, there's no reason to believe that it couldn't."

Kenneth was still unconvinced. "Okay, hotshot, let's hear it. What's your big 'theory' about what's been going on?" the senior Fortunado asked. "Do you even have one?"

Mindful that his father was judging every word out of his mouth, Connor began slowly, speaking distinctly. "I think that these aren't just random acts the way the police initially thought." He paused for a half beat, looking at each of them before delivering his bombshell. "I think there's one person behind everything that's been happening."

Kenneth's eyes squinted as he regarded his son. "You're talking about the fire, the hacking and the sabotaging of the real estate dealings?" he wanted to know.

"Yes," Connor replied stoically.

"One person is behind all this?" Zach asked, wanting to get his facts clear.

Relieved to hear a nonjudgmental voice, Connor glanced at Maddie's husband. "Yes, that's what I'm thinking."

"That must be one very energetic person," Kenneth commented. The sarcasm was hard to miss.

"People can be hired to carry out these things. But I

believe there's one person orchestrating all these things being executed against the family," Connor told them.

As he looked around at their faces, Connor could see that his mother and sisters, as well as Zach, were more than willing to be convinced. His father, however, was still digging in his heels. Whether it was because the man didn't agree with the theory or because he was angry over the fact that Connor had suddenly switched careers, Connor didn't know.

He waited for his father to say something. He didn't have long to wait.

"And just who is this vengeful person targeting the family?" Kenneth wanted to know. "Do you know, or is this all just one big theory you're hoping to get us to buy into?"

Connor kept his eyes on his father as he answered. "I found evidence of rumormongering."

"You're going to have to explain that to me," his mother said. "What does rumormongering mean?"

Kenneth began to open his mouth, undoubtedly to define the term for his wife, but Connor was already explaining it to his mother in what he felt would be simpler terms than his father was wont to use.

"Someone has been bad-mouthing Fortunado Real Estate's dealings on the internet, Mother, causing business to drop. Because of the so-called rumors, people have withdrawn their business from the company and taken it elsewhere."

"And does this 'someone' have a name?" Kenneth asked again, his impatient tone suggesting that he sincerely doubted his son had gotten that far in his so-called "investigation."

Connor managed to surprise his father, as well as his mother, by answering, "Yes."

"Well?" Kenneth asked, waiting to hear who this person was.

"From everything I've managed to learn, I believe the person who's causing all this chaos is Charlotte Prendergast Robinson."

"Gerald's wife?" Barbara cried, astonished at the revelation.

"Uncle Gerald's *ex*-wife," Connor corrected his mother. It was being Gerald's ex that had caused the woman to launch her vendetta in the first place, he believed.

Kenneth looked at his son skeptically, although in all truthfulness, the woman's name had been mentioned in connection to all these acts once or twice before.

"I know that Charlotte's angry," his father began, rolling the idea over in his mind.

"She's way more than that, Dad," Valene interjected. "You know that line about a woman scorned," she reminded her father.

"Val's right," Maddie said, adding her voice to her sister's as well as Connor's. "Aunt Charlotte wasn't exactly a hundred percent stable before Uncle Gerald finally left her to go back with that woman he called his first love, Deborah. Think about it," Maddie stressed. "I mean, who in their right mind puts together a whole big binder devoted to her husband's illegitimate children?" She shook her head at the very thought.

"Maybe the woman just wanted to have a book devoted to her family's genealogy," Barbara said. Connor knew his mother was always ready to see the good in everyone.

"More like having a book she could use to blackmail everyone," Maddie said. "Besides, I doubt she thinks of the people in that binder as 'her' family. It's more like his family—not that Uncle Gerald even knew some of them existed until Charlotte got started collecting names."

"I wouldn't put anything past Aunt Charlotte," Connor told the others.

"I think it was finding out that Deborah was the mother of his triplets that did it," Maddie suggested. "It was the last straw, the thing that finally unhinged Charlotte."

"Why would that do it any more than knowing about the other illegitimate ones?" Kenneth asked. He frowned. It was obvious that he didn't like or welcome the fact that he was actually related to Gerald. "That man spread his seed more than anyone ever cited in the Bible," he said with disgust.

"Kenneth," Barbara chided, obviously surprised at her husband saying something like that.

"Well, it's true," Kenneth told his wife. "He didn't care who he impregnated. The man should have been neutered."

"Are you *sure* we're actually related to Gerald Robinson?" Maddie asked. "Maybe there was some mistake made."

Connor sympathized with his sister's desire to sever ties, but it wasn't that simple. "Dad and Gerald are both Grandpa Julius's sons," he pointed out.

"We're half brothers," Kenneth corrected tersely. "For what that's worth."

"That was when Gerald was still known as Jerome Fortune, before he decided to run off and assume another complete identity," Barbara explained to her children, no doubt to keep things straight in case the fact had gotten lost among the preponderance of offspring who had been discovered.

Maddie squinted as if she was trying to reconcile a few facts with ones that already existed. "Wait, my head hurts," she said as she dramatically put her hand to her forehead.

Valene laughed at her sister's theatrics as she shook her own head. "One thing I have to say about this family. We are definitely not boring."

"No, Gerald and his extended family aren't boring," Kenneth corrected with feeling. "We are just an average, run-of-the-mill family with some decent monetary holdings," he insisted. "Or we were," he said as he looked in Connor's direction, "until one of my sons decided to completely turn his life inside out and become a—" his eyes met Connor's "—PI," Kenneth concluded.

Connor wanted to put this behind them once and for all. His father had to understand that his new career would only help the family in the long run, not embarrass it. "Dad, you're getting off track here," Connor respectfully pointed out.

"And your 'track' is that this was all done by Charlotte as her way of getting even, is that it?" Kenneth asked.

"Yes," Connor answered simply.

"But why would she do all this?" Kenneth asked. "Wouldn't her vengeance be focused directly on Gerald, not the rest of the family?" He rethought his words. "Or better yet, on Deborah? After all, in Charlotte's warped mind wouldn't she think Deborah is responsible for stealing her husband away from her?" Kenneth insisted.

There was no simple, hard-and-fast answer to that. "I think we can all agree that Aunt Charlotte is a complicated person. I wouldn't begin to try to analyze exactly what's on her mind. I would be lost in that maze for days," Connor predicted.

"And yet you think she's the one behind this?" Barbara asked her son.

The two were not mutually exclusive. "Yes, I do," Connor answered.

"She might be a cold, vengeful person, but she is still family, Connor. I really don't think she'd go to such great lengths to get back at Gerald or Jerome or whatever he wants to call himself," Barbara argued.

"Well, Mother, I'm not as kindhearted as you. And according to the evidence I've found, she is definitely mixed up in this, if not the actual orchestrator—which I actually believe she is."

Connor looked around at his family in silence, allowing his words to sink in. Hoping he had finally gotten them to see the situation the way he did.

He was convinced the only hope they had was to fight this as a united front.

Chapter Two

"**O**ne question." Kenneth moved to the edge of the sofa he was sitting on, raising his hand as if he was a student in a classroom instead of the former CEO of Fortunado Real Estate.

"Only one?" Connor asked, unable to keep the amused expression off his face.

"One's enough," Kenneth responded sternly. "Charlotte Robinson seems to have done a disappearing act—"

"I know that," Connor answered, anticipating his father's question. "Which is why I'm planning on finding her."

Kenneth waved a hand at his son's declaration, for all intents and purposes dismissing it.

"And therein lies my question," Kenneth replied. "There are countless people trying to track this woman

down, from the local police to the FBI to even our il-
lustrious matriarch herself, Kate Fortune, who you
might remember, despite being in her nineties, is one
exceptionally formidable woman. With the boundless
resources that are at Kate's disposal, if she can't find
Charlotte, what in hell makes you think that you're
going to be able to do anything different?" his father
wanted to know.

"I'm not an egotist, Dad," Connor replied mildly. "I
don't think that I'm the only one who can find Charlotte. It's just that," he continued despite the cynical
look on his father's face, "sometimes I wind up getting
results by thinking outside the box. Besides, the more
people putting their heads together and working on
locating Charlotte Robinson, the greater the chances
are of actually bringing her to justice."

Kenneth blew out a breath. "I suppose I can't argue
with that."

"Give him time," Valene said to Connor with a
wink. "He'll find a way."

She went on in a louder voice, clapping her hands
together to get everyone's attention. "Okay, now that
we've all been told about Connor's new career and
all agreed that Connor should try to find that awful
woman before she does anything else, possibly even
more reprehensible, to the family, let's get back to our
favorite topic."

Connor looked at his sister quizzically. "And that
would be—?"

"An engagement party," she answered him gleefully, her eyes dancing as a broad smile slipped over
her lips, curving them.

Connor closed his eyes. Engagements and weddings. His least favorite topics of conversation in the world. "I think that's my cue to exit, stage right."

But before he could take a single step to make that happen, Maddie linked her arm through his.

"Not today, brother dear. Mother told me that you're spending the night at the old homestead," she said, gesturing around the area, which couldn't by any stretch of the imagination be referred to as "the old homestead," at least not if accuracy was a factor.

"Looks to me like you're trapped," Zach told his brother-in-law, traces of amused compassion in his voice.

"Trapped? No, no offense, Zach, but that's one thing I'm never going to be." Connor shook his head as he glanced at his sisters and thought about his missing siblings, all of whom were undoubtedly with their "significant other" at the moment. "You know, I really can't get over how domesticated everyone's gotten over this past year and a half."

"Yeah, yeah, your time'll come," Valene predicted, letting Connor know that she wasn't buying into this act of his.

However, Connor remained steadfast because he honestly believed that his status was never going to change. "Sorry, not going to happen. Not to me."

"Just because you're the last man standing, brother dear, doesn't mean you're going to stay that way," Maddie told him.

"You're right," Connor answered his sister. "I *am* the last man standing. And I intend to keep on standing for a very long, long time."

"What do you have against being happy?" Zach asked Connor as he slipped his arm around Maddie's shoulders and drew her closer to him.

"But that's just my point," Connor told the other man. "I *am* happy. I *like* being free and not accountable to anyone except for myself. And you people on occasion," he added as an afterthought, looking around at the others in the living room.

Barbara Fortunado merely smiled at her son as she reached over and patted his cheek affectionately. "Your time will come, dear," was all she said before she turned her attention to her daughters.

A moment later, she became fully immersed in finalizing plans for the wedding—which at this point was only a month away.

Connor turned to look at his father, who from what he could determine was also standing on the outskirts of this conversation, the way he was.

Yes, he thought, romance was all well and good, but when that faded and the day-to-day business of living had to be addressed, that was where it all fell apart. He liked keeping things fresh, not facing the same old stale fare day in, day out. In his opinion, marriages were about routines and he liked to mix things up.

"You understand, right, Dad?" Connor asked the man sitting across from him.

"Do I understand how you feel right at this moment? Yes, I do," Kenneth admitted freely.

Connor was glad to hear that he had his father's support. "Well, at least you can see that—"

"I also understand," Kenneth went on as if his son

hadn't said anything, "that all that'll change the moment the right woman comes into your life."

"Lots of women have come into my life, Dad," Connor pointed out. That was part of the joy of being unattached. "And I'm still free."

"I said the *right* woman," Kenneth emphasized. "And it's not something anyone can convince you of until it actually happens to you," his father said knowingly. "Until then," he counseled, "just enjoy thinking that you're happy."

Connor merely offered his father a smile. He knew he couldn't change his father's mind any more than his father could change his. But he *was* happy, Connor thought with conviction. He knew that. And he intended to remain that way no matter what anyone else might think to the contrary.

But because the upcoming wedding seemed to make his sister so happy, he remained in the room and pretended to listen to all the plans that were being made for the anticipated nuptials.

He even nodded and smiled in the right places while his thoughts were elsewhere.

"Do you need anything, Connor?" Barbara Fortunado asked her son much later that evening.

Talks regarding the wedding plans had gone on much longer than anyone had thought they would and time had just gotten away from them. To his credit, she thought, Connor had feigned interest and even contributed a word or two, which made his sisters happy. It was nice seeing her children getting along.

She paused now to look in on her son, who was spending the night in what had once been his bedroom.

"No, I'm good, Mom," Connor told her. Sitting on the edge of the bed, he looked around the room. It had been a long time since he'd been here. "Although I have to admit that it feels a little strange to be back here after all this time," he confessed.

Barbara nodded. Like all good mothers, she realized that her children had to make their own way in the world and she was proud of each and every one of them. But there were times when their very success at forging their paths out in the world made her feel just a little sad. There were times, fleeting moments actually, when she longed for the days that they had all been together, under one roof, and needed her.

She smiled at Connor now. "It's nice to have you back, even if it is for just a little while and even if the reason you're here is because this nasty business was what drew you back." Her mouth quirked a little. "No matter what the reason, you're here and that's all I care about."

Connor crossed the room to the doorway where his mother was standing. Slipping his arm around her shoulders, he pressed a kiss to her temple.

"You were—and are—the primary draw that brought me back, Mom. You always have been."

Barbara laughed softly. "You always did have a way with words. Not always a truthful way, I grant you, but always sweet," she concluded. And then she became his mother again as he crossed back to his bed. "Get some sleep, dear."

Connor couldn't help grinning at her. "I am thirty-one, you know."

Barbara nodded, as if she had heard all this before and was prepared for it. "And you'll always be my little boy no matter what age you are. Good night, Connor."

Connor inclined his head obligingly. "Good night, Mom," he replied.

He waited until his mother had closed his bedroom door behind her. Getting up off the bed, he crossed over to his desk and took out the folder he had slipped into the top drawer. Pulling out his chair, he sat down at the desk and began to go through the folder. It was filled with notes he'd made to himself regarding Charlotte Robinson's dealings, as well as her possible current whereabouts.

He reviewed his notes slowly, rereading everything as if it was the first time he was seeing it. In his compilations, he'd come across the name of a freelance researcher, a Brianna Childress, who had handled some work for Charlotte Robinson over the course of the previous year.

He looked at the papers thoughtfully. Whatever this Brianna person had been doing for Charlotte had to have been sent to some address, even if that address turned out to be a PO box. That PO box in turn had to have been paid for, which meant that there'd been a check that could be traced to a bank account.

In addition, this freelancer had to be paid for her trouble. That brought him back to the bank account again, or at least a traceable credit card. All this meant that there was a possible paper trail. One he intended to follow.

It was a start, Connor told himself.

"You don't know it yet, Brianna Childress, but you are about to be paid a visit tomorrow morning," he said aloud. He closed the folder but went on holding it in his hands a little longer, as if the act connected him to the woman he was pursuing. "You just might be instrumental in helping me find the elusive Charlotte Prendergast Robinson before she can do any more damage."

Connor doubted that it would be that easy, but at least it was a lead, and who knew—maybe he'd get lucky. At the very least, this Childress woman might be able to provide him with the name of someone else who could in turn give him some clue as to where Charlotte Robinson was currently hiding.

He'd had less to go on before, he thought as he rose from the desk and got ready for bed.

Connor was up early the following morning and got dressed quickly.

He looked at the address he'd left out on his desk. It was the address where he was going to find this Childress woman. Initially, for about a minute and a half, he considered calling her to tell her he was coming to see her today.

He decided against it.

A face-to-face meeting would be the better way to go. He needed all the help he could get and the element of surprise might very well be useful in this case. If this woman turned out to be as nefarious as Charlotte, calling her might cause her to flee. If this Childress woman was actually involved with Charlotte, the last thing he wanted to do was tip her off.

He knew nothing about Brianna Childress, which meant that there was no reason to suppose that she *wouldn't* warn Charlotte that he was looking for her. That in turn would send Charlotte into even deeper hiding.

He wouldn't put anything past Charlotte no matter how innocent his parents, especially his mother, thought she was.

Since it was rather early, Connor decided to just slip out of the house without waking anyone.

The sooner he was on the road, the closer he would be to possibly bringing all this to a satisfactory conclusion.

He had another reason to get out of the house without being noticed. He didn't want to get involved in a possible discussion with his mother about Charlotte Robinson. Barbara Fortunado seemed reluctant to think badly of the other woman, but then, his mother had a tendency to view everyone in a good light.

However, there was no doubt in his mind that Charlotte was behind everything that had gone wrong in his family lately. She was a dangerous woman. The very fact that she had either tried to burn down Gerald Robinson's estate or had hired an arsonist to do it for her said it all in his book.

The woman was evil and the sooner he found her, the sooner he would rest easy.

Connor made good his escape and got to his car without anyone seeing him. Loading the address he'd found for Brianna Childress—the location was unfamiliar to him—into his car's GPS, he got started.

He turned on his radio but hardly heard any of

the music coming out of it. He was completely focused on the encounter that was ahead of him.

Connor expected the address of the research company he was looking for to lead him to an office building somewhere in Houston. Instead, the address wound up leading him to what appeared to be a rather small, homey-looking cottage.

Puzzled, he stopped his car a few hundred feet away from the house, wondering if he had made some sort of a mistake copying the address down.

Still, he thought, he was here so he might as well check it out.

Who knew, maybe this Brianna Childress ran her business out of her house. She wouldn't have been the first person to start out that way. The names of several computer companies and software firms came to mind.

Making up his mind, Connor started his car again. He brought it up closer to the cottage, then stopped a second time and parked.

Getting out, he made his way up the front walk. He noticed that there were some sort of bushes planted in the front yard. He wasn't very good at recognizing plants, although to his credit he did know a rose from a lily, he thought with a disparaging smile.

He saw neither in the yard.

Walking up to the front door, he noted that it was in need of a fresh coat of paint. Shrugging, he rang the doorbell. In his mind, he rehearsed what he planned to say to Brianna Childress in order to get her to let him come inside her house.

His finger had no sooner pressed the doorbell than the front door flew open.

A rather frazzled young woman with reddish-brown hair and heart-melting brown eyes looked up at him as if he was her personal savior. She was wearing jeans and a T-shirt, both of which lovingly highlighted all of her curves and nearly made him permanently lose his train of thought.

He recognized the woman from her online photo. But to be honest, she could use a new head shot. That one didn't do her justice.

"Oh thank goodness you're here!" Brianna cried, a look of relief washing over her features. "It's right in there!"

She pointed toward the back of the house where "it," whatever that referred to, was.

Without waiting for a response from him, Brianna grabbed his hand and pulled him in her wake, quickly leading him toward the back of the house.

Given that she had rather a good grip for such a delicate person, Connor realized that at the moment, he had no choice but to follow her.

"I was at my wits' end," Brianna confided unabashedly. "Luckily, I saw your ad on TV the other day and remembered the phone number. Actually, I copied it down," she confessed. "I had a feeling I was going to need you sooner rather than later and I was right. If you hadn't come, I'd probably be underwater before noon."

"Um—"

At a loss, Connor got no further. He had followed the woman into a bathroom. The "it" she was obviously referring to was a toilet. The water was rising precariously high within the bowl. It looked as if any second, the water was going to overflow and go all over the floor.

The sprightly redhead was standing in front of the toilet, her hands on her hips. "Kids," she said to him by way of an explanation.

"Kids?" Connor echoed, unable to understand what she was telling him.

"Every time I turn around, one of them has decided that one of their stuffed animals or trucks or figurines is dirty and needs to be washed. I guess the toilet's like a bathtub to them." She sighed and looked at him plaintively. "So, can you fix it?" she asked, a hopeful look on her face.

It was a face, Connor realized, that he couldn't bring himself to say no to.

Chapter Three

Connor forced himself to focus on something other than Brianna Childress's very expressive eyes. He knew that he couldn't very well lie to the woman, not if he needed her help and wanted her to be truthful with him. If he lied, or omitted telling her the truth, that wouldn't exactly be starting off their relationship, however short it might turn out to be, on the right foot. Lies just begat lies.

"I'm afraid that you've made a mistake," Connor began.

Dismay washed over Brianna's face as she took in what he had just said. "You can't fix it like the commercial said?" she asked.

"It's not that, it's—"

Connor got no further in his explanation than those first four words because right at that moment there was a bloodcurdling scream followed by a wail and then the sound of things either falling or being thrown.

The jarring noise went clear down to the bone.

"Oh dear lord, now what?" Brianna cried in exasperation.

Before Connor could venture a guess, she made an abrupt about-face and dashed out of the room, heading toward the scream. That left Connor standing alone in the bathroom with a toilet that looked as if it was about to blow at any moment.

"There's obviously never a dull moment around here," he commented under his breath.

Left to his own devices, Connor looked around the small, blue-and-white-tiled bathroom. From what he had gathered, this wasn't the first time the toilet presented a problem. Judging from the tools that were scattered on the floor, Brianna had the right things to deal with the situation.

The fact that she hadn't dealt with it told him that she'd never learned how to put any of these tools to use. She'd probably just seen the plumber using them and had thought ahead—or wanted to be prepared for the next time. Next time had obviously arrived.

He gave the woman an A for observation. Too bad her execution was sorely lacking.

Connor had no desire to follow the woman into the other room, given the high-pitched screaming that was coming from another part of the house, but on the other hand, he was never much for standing around gathering dust, either.

Looking around again, he took inventory of the tools in the room. There was a long, thin metallic tool expressly made for breaking through the debris that gathered in clogged pipes. Whimsically dubbed a "snake," it was lying beside a standard plunger. There were a couple of other tools, as well, but in his opinion, they were just overkill.

Connor prided himself on being rather handy. He decided that he might as well do *something* while he waited for the woman to come back.

Assessing the problem one last time, he rolled up his sleeves and got to work.

The job turned out to be easier than he had expected. The reason for the clog was a miniature toy train that had been wedged in the bottom of the toilet's evacuation pipe. The train had been covered in what appeared to be a massive wad of sopping wet toilet paper that had wound itself around the toy. It had been a little tricky getting the train free, but in the end, he managed to get it loose—all without breaking the toy.

He looked down at the item that was now safely nestled in his hand. *Such a little thing, so much trouble*, he thought.

It was only when he finally rose back to his feet again that he realized the knees of his pants had gotten quite wet. He looked around for a mop to at least dry the floor, but it appeared to be the one thing that the woman hadn't brought out with the other equipment.

Shaking his head, Connor muttered under his breath. "It figures."

"What figures?"

The voice startled him. Swinging around to face the doorway, he saw that Brianna had finally reappeared.

She was not alone. She was carrying a squirming, very vocal preschooler on her hip. A boy.

The slightly surprised look on her face gave way to a wide, relieved smile when she saw the toy train in Connor's hand.

"You fixed it," she cried, delighted.

The little boy on her hip saw the toy at the same time that his mother did.

"Mine!" he cried, eagerly putting his hands out as if that would somehow cause the toy to levitate out of the stranger's hand and into his own.

"Then what's it doing in the toilet?" Connor asked, pretending to be serious as he presented the train to the little boy after rinsing it off in the sink.

The kid had the same wide, sunny smile that his mother had. He flashed that smile now at Connor as he grabbed the toy train and pressed it to his chest.

"Mine," he repeated.

"We've established that," Connor replied as if he was talking to someone his own age. "But why did you—?"

Brianna anticipated his question. "You're not going to get an answer," she told him. "He knows he's not supposed to throw anything down there but for some reason, the toilet just seems to really fascinate him." She looked at her son with an indulgent smile. "Axel used to have a pet hamster until one day he decided that Howard was dirty and needed a bath."

"Let me guess," Connor said to her, "Howard drowned."

She surprised him by saying, "No, actually, he

didn't. I managed to fish him out of the toilet bowl just in time."

"So you saved Howard," Connor concluded.

"No," she said with a heartfelt sigh. "I didn't." When he raised a quizzical brow, she told him the rest of the story. "As near as I can figure it, Howard died of a heart attack. After I rescued him and dried him off, I put Howard in his cage. I found him the next morning, lying on the floor of the cage, as stiff as one of the kids' figurines."

The boy had stopped making noise and now sniffled a couple of times.

"We had a funeral," Axel said solemnly.

"So he *can* talk in sentences," Connor marveled, looking at the boy. The boy seemed pretty young to him and he had no idea just what kids were able to do at any given age.

"Only when he wants to," Brianna answered. Shifting her son to her other hip, she looked contritely at the man whose pant legs she had just noticed were wet. "I'm sorry I'm going on and on here. I don't get much of a chance to talk to adults," she admitted. Setting Axel down, she looked around for her purse. "How much do I owe you?"

Smiling at the woman, Connor shook his head. "Nothing."

Brianna looked at him, confused. "But you just fixed my toilet—and got your knees wet in the process," she pointed out.

"That's okay," he told her, shrugging off her offer of payment. "This is on me. No charge."

That only managed to confuse things even further

for Brianna. "I don't think your boss is going to appreciate you doing things for free."

"On the contrary," Connor said. He thought of his father, who he was, in essence, working for at the moment while he was conducting this investigation. "I think he'd approve."

Judging by her expression, his answer made absolutely no sense to the woman. "But you're a plumber. How are you supposed to make any money if you don't accept payment for doing a job?" she asked, confused.

"Because," Connor answered cavalierly, "I'm not a plumber."

This was making less and less sense to her. She began at the beginning. "But the company I called, they said they were sending someone right out."

"They probably meant what they said, but they didn't send me," he told her.

Things were finally falling into place. Brianna looked at the man standing and dripping in her bathroom. She was horrified at her mistake. He probably thought she was an idiot.

"I'm so embarrassed," she confessed, "I don't even know where to begin."

Amused, Connor laughed off her attempt at an apology. "Don't worry about it," he told her. "It was just an honest mistake."

The fact that she had let a perfect stranger into her house and that he was still standing here suddenly registered with her.

"But if you're not the plumber," she cried, backing away from him, "who are you?"

She was doing her best not to panic or appear nervous. After all, she had no idea who this man was or what he was doing in her house.

Brianna thought of her children and a chill went shooting up her spine.

She had to protect them!

Connor offered her an easy smile as he put his hand out to her. "Connor Fortunado, at your service."

But who was Connor Fortunado and why had he come to her house? His answer just created more questions.

Before she could ask him, the doorbell rang. For a split second, she appeared torn between questioning the man in her bathroom further or going to answer the doorbell.

The doorbell won.

Making up her mind, she hurried to the front of the house.

"Does it ever let up?" Connor called after her, curious.

"Sometimes," she answered. *Just not today.*

Brianna opened the door and found herself looking at a slightly overweight man in coveralls that had seen better days.

"Somebody called for a plumber?" he asked her.

"Yes, I did, but I don't need you anymore," Brianna began, ready to close the door again.

The man looked at her skeptically, then glanced down at what was apparently a work order in his hand. "The toilet fixed itself?" he asked with a touch of sarcasm.

"No, but—"

Connor was about to intervene for her but Brianna's

son beat him to it. Or, more accurately, her son and her daughter did. The duo had decided to resume whatever battle they had been deeply embroiled in a few minutes earlier.

Connor came forward, listening. The battle was apparently over whether or not the rather scrappy-looking mutt who had come running in with them should be wearing a dress. The vote was tied. The little girl—Ava, according to the name her brother had yelled—was saying yes while Axel was very loudly proclaiming, "No! He's a boy dog!"

Their supposedly small voices were completely drowning out the plumber, who, judging by the disgruntled look on his face, was protesting being sent away without collecting a fee. The fact that he hadn't done any work didn't seem to matter.

Meanwhile Connor found himself fascinated by the dynamics of the household he had walked into. Besides the scrappy dog, by his count he had glimpsed two cats and some sort of creature—a sea turtle perhaps?—living in a tank in the far corner of the living room. All he could really make out were a pair of eyes looking in his direction.

Connor's attention was drawn back to the squabbling children, who were growing progressively louder with each passing minute. Glancing in their mother's direction, he thought that she definitely looked overwhelmed. Taking pity on the woman, Connor decided to distract the children so that she could at least clear things up with the plumber.

"Gimme that!" Axel shouted, grabbing a frayed dress from his sister.

Though small, Ava was every bit as strong as her brother.

"No!" she cried, pulling the dress back out of her brother's hands.

Connor thought of physically pulling them apart but decided that he'd get more accomplished if he treated them as short adults, not discipline problems.

"You know," he began, "my brothers and sisters and I once dressed up our horse for Halloween." He had to raise his voice above theirs in order to actually be heard.

Axel stopped trying to pull the dress away from his sister. Meanwhile Ava's eyes widened as she suddenly became aware that there was someone besides her brother in the room.

"You dressed up your horse?" the little girl questioned, looking up at the strange man in her living room. Though she appeared a year or so younger than her brother, she was more articulate than Axel was.

"We sure did," Connor told her, subtly coaxing the brother and sister away from the front of the house and the plumber. The dog decided to trot along with them, as well. "My sisters wanted to put a ballerina costume on Lightning but my brothers and I said that the ballerina costume would just embarrass him."

"Who won?" Axel wanted to know. He gave his sister a superior look. "Bet it was the boys."

"Bet it wasn't," Ava countered, ready to get into yet another argument with him. "Everybody knows that boys are dumb."

"No they're not!" Axel yelled back.

"Actually," Connor said, raising his voice as he took

each of them by the hand and brought them toward the kitchen, "Lightning won."

"The horse?" Axel questioned, scrunching up his forehead.

"How could the horse win?" Ava wanted to know. "Could he talk?" she asked in awe.

"No, he wasn't a talking horse," Connor managed to say with a straight face.

"Then how did he win?" Axel asked, crossing his arms before his small chest and waiting to be given an answer.

"Lightning won because he got to keep his dignity," Connor told his small audience.

Ava and Axel exchanged perplexed looks. "What's dig-nitee?" Axel asked.

"Being proud of yourself," Connor explained.

Intrigued, Ava asked, "How did the horse get to keep that?"

"Well, Lightning was a boy horse," Connor told them. "We put a pirate's costume on him, using some of my mother's scarves. We all agreed that he looked a lot better in that than he would have in a ballerina costume. Besides," Connor confided, lowering his voice and winking at the children, "the tutu would have really been impossible to get on Lightning."

The abbreviated reference to the ballerina costume seemed to tickle Axel and he started to laugh. He laughed so hard, he wound up rolling around on the floor. The sound was infectious and it set Ava off. In no time flat, both children were on the floor, holding their sides and laughing.

Which was how Brianna found them when she walked into the kitchen.

The sight astounded her. For once, her children were actually getting along and no longer at each other's throats. Brianna stood for a moment, drinking in the sight.

Stunned, she looked at the man who was apparently responsible for her kids' miraculous about-face. She was both amazed that this Connor Fortunado had somehow managed to calm her little hellions down and horrified that she had allowed a total stranger to come into her house.

Allowed? She'd literally dragged him in, Brianna thought, berating herself.

Okay, there'd been a mix-up, which caused her to make the mistake, but even so, she'd let a stranger into her house. The house where her children lived. The man could have been an ax murderer or a serial killer and she had just let him come waltzing in without so much as checking his credentials.

What kind of a mother did that make her?

"Did your mom yell at you for making the horse wear her scarves?" Axel asked the possible ax murderer.

Connor looked perfectly serious as he said, "No, she decided she didn't like those scarves anymore. She said she was happy to give them to Lightning."

They were lapping this up, Brianna realized. And this stranger was obviously very good with children.

She supposed she was overreacting, she thought. If this man was a possible ax murderer or a serial killer, chances were that he wouldn't be sitting cross-legged on her floor with her children, telling them this exaggerated story.

And besides, he *did* fix her toilet, she told herself. She strongly doubted that ax murderers went around fixing toilets for their victims just before they did away with them.

Brianna had just decided to exonerate the man in her kitchen when he suddenly looked in her direction with the softest brown eyes she'd ever seen.

For the briefest of moments, she felt something inside of her tighten in response.

"Everything all settled?" he asked her.

It took her a minute to focus on his words. "With the plumber?" she finally asked. When he nodded, she said, "Yes, I convinced him that it was a false alarm and that the toilet was running fine now. He wasn't happy, but he left." Coming closer, she stood over Connor and extended her hand. "We never got a chance to finish with our introductions. I'm Brianna Childress," she told him. "And those are my children, Axel and Ava."

"I know," he said. "At least, I know who you are. The kids I have to admit were a surprise." *In more ways than one*, he thought.

Brianna's suspicions returned. She shifted so that she stood directly in front of her children, as if to protect them. "Why do you know who I am?"

Chapter Four

Connor smiled at her, doing his best to assuage the wary look that had returned to her eyes. He didn't want her afraid of him. If she was, then getting any useful information out of her might be difficult.

"I know your name," he told her, "because I've done my homework."

"You have homework?" Axel cried, appalled. "But aren't you old?"

"Axel!" Brianna chided, upset at her four-year-old son's unfiltered response to the situation.

"Yeah!" Three-year-old Ava joined forces with her mother and got into her brother's face. "You don't tell old people they're old."

She couldn't have her children here while she was trying to deal with this stranger. "Axel, Ava, why don't you two go play with Scruffy?" Brianna said, herding the dog and the half-pint dynamic duo toward the bedroom that they shared. "*Quietly* this time."

It was obvious that both children wanted to stay and hear what this new person who had come into their house had to say, but one look at their mother's face told them that they needed to listen to her.

Looking miffed, Ava reluctantly walked out of the room. "This is all your fault," she accused her brother. "You got mommy upset."

"It is not!" Axel shouted back at his sister as he left the room.

"And they're off," Brianna sighed. She tried to remember a time when life was peaceful and couldn't. Collecting herself, she turned to face Connor. "Would you mind explaining just how I figure into your 'homework'?" she asked.

"That's easy." First order of business, he thought, was to assure Brianna that he meant her no harm. Taking out his wallet, he flipped it open to show her his credentials. "I'm a private investigator and I need to ask you a few questions if you don't mind."

"What kind of questions?" Brianna wanted to know. For the life of her, she had absolutely no clue what this was about or what she could possibly tell him. Regarding him warily, she asked, "Should I be worried?"

"Why?" He tucked his wallet back into his pocket. "Have you done something bad?" he asked, amused despite himself.

"No," she answered with a little bit too much feeling.

She couldn't remember a time when she had done anything even remotely "bad." She was too busy rais-

ing two overenergetic children and holding down miscellaneous part-time jobs trying to make ends meet to
do anything even remotely bad. Or fun for that matter.

"But you're here wanting to ask me questions and I
haven't got the vaguest idea why," she informed him,
still eyeing him nervously.

Connor felt a little guilty for making her feel so uneasy. He quickly began to explain the situation to her.
"I'm looking for some information about a job you did
for Charlotte Robinson last year."

Brianna blinked. She prided herself on remembering the names of the people she dealt with but this
name was definitely not familiar.

"Who?"

"Charlotte Robinson," Connor repeated a little bit
louder now.

The name still meant nothing to her. Brianna shook
her head. "Sorry, that name doesn't ring a bell. Maybe
you have me confused with someone else," she told
him.

"Maybe," he allowed, not wanting to come on too
strong. But he had done his due diligence and he knew
he wasn't wrong about this. "However, I don't think
so," he told her politely. "This is a photo of Charlotte
taken in the last six months." Connor took out his cell
phone and swiped through a few pictures until he came
to the one he was looking for. He held it up for Brianna to see. "Look carefully. Does she look familiar?"

She took the phone from him and studied the pho-
tograph for a moment. Shaking her head, she handed
the phone back to him.

"No." When he looked disappointed, she explained.

"But that really doesn't mean anything. All my business is conducted over the phone or online. I never get to meet any of my customers. But her name definitely isn't familiar," she repeated. "Sorry."

Connor put his phone in his pocket. "How about Charlotte Prendergast?" he asked. He knew that Charlotte had a number of aliases. Maybe she had been using one of them when she'd contacted Brianna.

Again Brianna shook her head. This was turning into a waste of time for both of them and she didn't have time to waste.

"Sorry," she said again. "Now I really have to—"

But Connor wasn't ready to give up just yet. "How about Charlene Pickett?" he asked, remembering yet another alias he knew that Charlotte had used at least on one other occasion.

That got Brianna's attention. While she wanted the man to leave, she had too much integrity to lie and the name he'd just said *did* sound familiar. "Say that name again, please."

"She might have used the name Charlene Pickett," he said, watching Brianna's face for the slightest sign of recognition in case she denied knowing the woman.

But she didn't.

"That does ring a bell," Brianna acknowledged. "What's with all the different names?" she couldn't help asking. "What is this woman, some kind of spy or undercover agent?" She didn't know of any other reason why anyone would be using so many aliases. Con artists were not a part of her world and she didn't do business with them.

Connor laughed dryly. "Nothing nearly that glamorous or interesting," he assured her. And then he grew more serious. He was following bread crumbs, doing his best to follow the trail left behind by the woman he felt was responsible for everything that had befallen his family. "Just what was the nature of your business with her?"

Brianna shrugged, completely at a loss as to what was going on and what it had to do with her and her family. "Charlene told me that she was putting together a genealogy chart for the Fortune family. She also asked if I could find addresses—and possible aliases—for certain people she'd uncovered in the family tree."

Connor never took his eyes off Brianna's, doing his best not to allow himself to be mesmerized by the soft brown orbs. He was onto something and couldn't afford to be distracted.

"And did you?"

"Yes, I did," she answered. "My turn," Brianna declared, catching him off guard. "Why do you want to know all this?"

Connor paused for a moment, weighing his options. He decided that sticking as close to the truth as possible would be useful in this case.

"I'm a Fortune myself, related to them," he clarified. "In all probability, one of those people she had you looking for might have been me."

Brianna's eyes widened even as she exhaled. Now it was all beginning to make sense to her.

Connor Fortunado.

Connor Fortune.

The man standing before her wasn't a potential ax

murderer. He was a man who was looking for his family, or at least parts of his family.

Brianna caught herself smiling. There was nothing sinister in that.

Reassured, Brianna relaxed. "I'm afraid I'm not going to be much help to you. I haven't heard from Charlene, or whoever she really is, in months. As a matter of fact," she said ruefully, "she still owes me money. She paid half up front and she said that she'd pay me the rest when I gave her the information.

"It took a little doing, but I managed to find some of the people she was looking for. I sent the information on to her, but…" Her voice trailed off as she looked at him, embarrassed at her naivete. "I'm still waiting for the rest of the payment."

Connor nodded. "That definitely sounds like Charlotte, all right." And then, under his breath, he murmured, "She doesn't care who she sticks it to."

He looked around the living room. There were toys, mostly very used-looking ones, scattered all over the floor. The furniture, what there was of it, was pretty threadbare.

Brianna pressed her lips together, trying not to wince as she saw him take everything in. She didn't have to be a mind reader to guess what he was thinking.

This shouldn't have happened to this woman, Connor thought. He found himself feeling guilty that she had been used like this.

"If I can track down Charlene—Charlotte—" he corrected, "maybe I can get your money for you. How much did she wind up owing you?"

Brianna didn't even have to pause to try to remember the sum. She had a good head for figures and this one was etched into her mind. "Three thousand dollars."

"Three thousand dollars," he repeated. Growing quiet for a moment, he seemed to be thinking something over. And then he said, "You said that you located those people for her?"

Where was the man going with this? she wondered. "Most of them, yes."

"Tell you what," Connor proposed. "If you can help me find Charlotte, I'll pay you that three thousand dollars she owes you—and a fee for helping me locate her on top of that. Do we have a deal?" he asked, ready to shake on it.

She wanted her money, but she was still cautious. Brianna had no intentions of entering into any agreement blindly.

"Just exactly what do you need me to do?" Brianna asked. And then, as he opened his mouth, she quickly issued her disclaimer. "Before you answer, I have to tell you right off the bat that I can't travel anywhere. I have Ava and Axel to take care of, not to mention the various furry creatures that seemed to have adopted us. And, because this job doesn't exactly provide a steady salary, I have a couple of part-time jobs to help make ends meet. I can't just abandon them."

The woman definitely came with strings, Connor thought.

"What kind of jobs?" he wanted to know, curious.

"I'm a medical transcriber and I fill in at the animal shelter reception desk a few times a week," she told him. As she said it, she was sure that any one of these things would be a deal breaker.

"Animal shelter," he repeated. "That would explain the menagerie," Connor commented.

"I've always loved animals," she told him a little defensively. She took a breath, resigning herself to the conclusion he'd undoubtedly reached. "So I guess it's a no regarding our working together."

"What makes you think that?" Connor asked, surprised. Just then, there was another crash, followed by a very plaintive "Oh-oh" coming from the room where her children had retreated. Connor couldn't help grinning. "I can come back at a more convenient time," he told her, rising to his feet.

"That would be in another fifteen years when they're both in college, provided I can keep them alive that long," Brianna commented, struggling not to be overwhelmed again. She'd lost count how many times that made in the last week.

Connor smiled at her. "I've got a feeling you can." He saw the skeptical look on her face and knew it didn't have anything to do with his last comment. She was worried about his coming back. Obviously he hadn't laid all her fears to rest. "All I want to do is pick your brain, Brianna," he told her sincerely. "I want to go over all the names that Charlotte asked you to investigate and I also want to know just what information you discovered for her."

The skeptical look was still on her flawless face. "And that's worth three thousand dollars to you?" she asked in disbelief. Something just wasn't adding up in her estimation. There had to be something more going on that she wasn't privy to.

"That is worth *everything* to me," Connor answered in all sincerity.

Brianna waited for him to elaborate, but Connor didn't say anything more on the subject.

She frowned. She didn't like getting into something without having all the cards laid out on the table, especially when she had a gut feeling that there was something more going on.

But there was no denying the fact that she could really use the money and she had a feeling that she was never going to see that money from Charlene or Charlotte or whatever the woman's real name was. This was going to be her only chance of recouping her loss.

"So, do we have a deal?" Connor asked her again, this time putting his hand out.

Common sense told her that she needed more blanks filled in, but the bills that were piling up on her desk weren't going to be paid with common sense.

Brianna put her hand into his and shook it, praying she wasn't going to regret this. "We have a deal," she told him.

"Great." A hair-raising scream came from the kids' bedroom. "You need help with that?" he asked, nodding in the direction the scream came from.

"I can handle it." Brianna looked toward the front door. "I'll just walk you out first."

He was going to tell her that he could see himself out. But there was something about this unconsciously sexy lady that told him Brianna had trust issues and he had already pushed things about as far as he thought he could for now.

So he flashed a smile at her and said, "Then I'll walk fast so you can get to your emergency."

"No emergency," she told him with just a touch of weariness as she led the way. "Just business as usual." Reaching the front door, she asked, "Is it wrong for me to hope that the next fifteen years will fly by?"

Connor laughed. "Given the situation," he answered, "there would be something wrong with you if you didn't. At least once in a while," he added, sensing that the woman really loved these two whirling dervishes that were disguised as her children. "I'll give you a call soon so we can set a time to get started," he told her.

"You have my number?" she asked, wanting to be sure he did.

"Oh yes."

The way he said that caused her stomach to tighten. She was reading into it, she silently insisted. Stiffening slightly, she said, "Goodbye."

Before Connor could respond in kind, he found himself looking at the door. She had closed it on him in one fluid motion.

He could hear her running toward the back of the house and her children. Connor shook his head. How did she manage to keep on going day after day, faced with these mini explosions? The woman definitely had her work cut out for her. Where did she find the time to get anything else done, he marveled, turning away. Her kids seemed to take up every single moment of the day as well as suck up all the oxygen in any room they were in.

Connor walked back to his car at the curb and got in. If he listened, he could still make out the sound of high voices talking over one another. This sort of thing just reinforced his feelings about the single life. The thought of coming home to that kind of chaos night after night sent a cold shiver up and down his spine.

Starting up his car, he thought of what Brianna had said about not being able to travel because of her children and their pets.

Hell, he couldn't imagine a life like that. Not being able to travel, being restricted like that because he had to be there day after day for two little warring people who had no idea of how much was being sacrificed for them.

He thought of Ava and Axel. He had to admit that he'd gotten a kick out of how they seemed to hang on his words when he told them about Lightning, but hell, he could get the same sort of attentive effect from one of his friends if he just bribed them with a couple of drinks at a restaurant.

This Brianna woman probably didn't even realize all the freedom she was missing out on, all the freedom she had given up just to put up with those two walking accidents-waiting-to-happen. He hadn't seen any evidence, such as photographs, of a husband on the scene. Nor was she wearing a wedding ring. Was the woman tackling all this by herself? She had to be a little crazy to do that.

Yes sir, Connor thought, he was really glad he wasn't in a committed relationship. Heaven forbid some cute little number started having designs on him, making wedding plans in her head.

Wedding rings reminded him much too much of
nooses and he wasn't about to slip one of those around
his neck, no way. While he could see, he supposed, his
brothers and sisters settling down into what they were
hoping were lives of domestic bliss, he had just been
exposed to a *real* picture of what happened after the
words "I do" were spoken.

In very short order "I do" turned into "I don't" as
those words applied to doing things, taking off at a
moment's notice, having fun. All of that fell by the
wayside, a casualty in the wake of deluded dreams
of happiness.

That kind of happiness was just a myth. *Real* happiness was something that the individual made happen. The individual, not the couple, Connor silently
underscored as he drove back to his parents' home.

No, if he was ever tempted to go the route that his
siblings had all opted to tread, he hoped that someone
would have the good sense to shoot him—or at least
tie him up until the moment of insanity passed and he
was back to himself again.

Connor turned up the music and tried, just for the
next half hour, to clear his brain of everything.

It was easier said than done. For some reason, images of Ava and Axel insisted on flashing through his
mind's eye.

Along with that of their mother.

He turned the music up even louder.

Chapter Five

Brianna didn't have time to think about the unsettling stranger she had just sent on his way. She had a volatile situation she needed to defuse. The shouting was getting louder.

Moving quickly, she headed toward the children's bedroom.

When she got there, she saw that Axel and Ava were at each other's throats, fighting for sole possession of a one-eared stuffed rabbit. Getting between them, she managed to separate her children—and save the rabbit.

"Okay, you two, you need a time-out," she told them sternly. Physically holding them apart, she informed her children, "I'm going to separate you so you can think about how you're supposed to behave." Brianna gave her noisy twosome a dark look. "Especially when we have company."

Axel looked up at his mother, puzzled. "What company?"

"*Any* company," Brianna emphasized. Axel was just pretending not to understand. He was brighter than that, she thought.

"She means the man," Ava told her brother in her superior voice. And then a thought seemed to occur to her. She turned toward her mother, distressed. "Is he mad at Axel?"

Judging by the look on her daughter's face, Brianna guessed that Ava was harboring a crush on Connor Fortunado. *Wonderful*, Brianna thought. Just what she needed.

"No, Ava, Mr. Fortunado is not 'mad' at Axel. I'm sure he understands that sometimes children need to be reminded how to behave around people," Brianna told the battling duo.

"Can I be around him?" Ava asked hopefully.

Brianna wasn't sure what her daughter was asking. It was hard to second-guess what was in either of her children's heads.

"What?"

"You said you were sep-per-ating us," Ava answered, carefully enunciating the word that was giving her tongue trouble. "So I want you to put me in his room. Mr. Fortu—what you said," she concluded, unable to say Connor's last name.

Not waiting for permission, Ava darted out of the room she shared with her brother and ran back to the living room.

"Ava Susan Childress, you come back here," Brianna called after her daughter. Ava's escape had caught her completely off guard.

"You're in trouble now," Axel declared gleefully, running in after his sister. "Mama called out all your names."

Ava had reached the living room. Surprised to find it empty, she looked around with a puzzled expression on her face. When she heard her mother and brother coming in behind her, she spun around to face them.

"Where is he, Mama?" Ava asked, disappointed. "Where's the man?"

Brianna tried not to focus on her daughter's disobedience. Instead, she tried to remember what it was like to be Ava's age.

"He went home, Ava," she told her daughter.

Distressed, Ava whirled around to glare at her brother. "He went away because you made his feelings hurt."

"No, I didn't!" Axel protested, growing defensive again. It seemed to be his default state.

Ava had turned her attention toward her mother, the woman who could fix anything.

"Make him come back, Mama. I liked him. He has a horse he puts clothes on," Ava said as if that was what made the man so special to her. "I wanted to see the horse."

"Come here," Brianna coaxed.

She took each of her children by the hand and led them to the sofa. Sitting down, she tugged each of their hands to get them to sit down on either side of her. Their upturned faces made her think of tulips seeking out the sun.

"Listen to me, you two. I am thrilled you have such a zest for life, I really am. But just for now, could you try to be a little less…zesty?" she asked, looking from one small upturned face to the other. "You're wearing me out."

"Wearing you out where?" Axel wanted to know, looking all over his mother. He was obviously taking what she'd said literally.

Ava frowned disdainfully at her brother. "She means she's tired, dummy."

"Oh." Axel sat up a little straighter, apparently feeling he had the solution. "Go lie down, Mommy," he urged with a smile.

There was no way she was doing that and leaving her two hellions to their own devices.

"Heaven forbid. By the time I got up again, I wouldn't have a house standing," she murmured under her breath. "Besides, I don't want to lie down," she told her children, slipping an arm around each of their shoulders. "What I want is for you two to *calm* down. Do you think you can do that for me?"

Both Axel and Ava solemnly bobbed their heads up and down.

Brianna didn't believe they meant it for a minute, but at least she had them pausing for a moment, allowing her to catch her breath.

"Is he coming back?" Ava asked in a smaller, hesitant voice.

"You mean Mr. Fortunado?" Brianna asked.

Axel giggled, then covered his mouth. The giggle only grew louder. "That's a funny name."

"Yes, it is," Brianna agreed. "And yes, Ava, he's coming back."

Ava's eyes widened and practically sparkled. "When?" she asked eagerly.

"I'm not sure yet." Brianna scrutinized her daughter's face. She had never known either of her children to take to an adult this quickly before. "You liked him, didn't you?" she asked her daughter.

Ava looked shy for a moment, and then almost blushed. "Uh-huh."

Curious why she was so taken with the man, Brianna asked her daughter, "Why?"

"'Cause he told us a story. And he smiled nice," Ava added very seriously.

She was going to have to watch this one, Brianna thought. Her daughter was obviously skipping right over the "boys are icky" stage, going straight to being a tiny, budding femme fatale.

Not to be left out, Axel added his two cents about the stranger who had been in their house. "And *he* didn't tell us to be quiet."

"Well, if you calm down a little once in a while I wouldn't have to tell you that so often, either," Brianna pointed out.

Axel hung his head as if he had suddenly become contrite and in a very small voice said to her, "Okay, Mommy."

"Okay, Mama," Ava added, not to be outdone by her brother.

Brianna sighed quietly. This docile moment had a life expectancy of about a minute and a half, but it was nice while it lasted and she intended to enjoy it until Axel and Ava returned to their natural, rambunctious behavior.

Kissing both of their heads one at a time, Brianna

rose from the sofa. "See how long you can be good," she requested.

"I can be gooder than Axel," Ava assured her boastfully.

Small light eyebrows drew together forming an annoyed, wavy line that joined together above Axel's sprinkling of freckles.

"No, you can't," he informed his sister. "I'm gooder than you."

"You're *both* equally as good," Brianna told him, raising her voice to stop the argument before it could take off.

Today was going to be a very long, long day, Brianna thought.

Leaving her pint-size warriors, she walked into the small room she used as an office. There was barely enough room there for her desk and chair. Directly in the corner she had a set of plastic drawers she'd bought at the local membership store. She kept all her files in those drawers, packed away.

She wasn't looking forward to the task ahead of her, but she needed to get started. She intended to find her notes outlining what she had sent to this person Fortunado was looking for.

She knew she had sent the last correspondence to the woman approximately three months ago. Brianna remembered that it had taken her more than a bit of searching before she tracked down a large number of the people the woman told her she was trying to find.

Brianna recalled thinking that the request was a little strange. Her client had told her it was for a genealogy chart but the people she was trying to find all seemed to be around the same age.

At the time she decided that it was none of her business. She didn't care that much *why* the woman was looking to find these people as long as the woman was willing to pay money for the results.

Apparently, though, this Charlene/Charlotte person wasn't willing to make good on her promise. When Brianna hadn't heard anything from her client, she'd tried to contact her and request payment. But the letter had been returned, stamped Unable to Deliver, Return to Sender.

At the time, she'd been too busy to try to follow up and find Charlene's whereabouts. And then both of her kids came down with really bad colds that they kept passing to each other, so she had no time to track the woman down. Stressed, she'd given up, deciding to philosophically chalk it up to just one of those things— and then Fortunado had turned up on her doorstep.

She caught herself wondering what he must have thought when she opened the door and grabbed his hand, dragging him into her bathroom and pointing to the almost-overflowing, nonfunctioning toilet.

Brianna laughed to herself as she began to look through her files. You just never knew how things were going to turn out, she mused. Maybe she'd actually see that three thousand dollars after all.

At least she had hope.

"You have a lead?" Valene asked, staring at her older brother uncertainly. The moment she had seen Connor pull up to the house, she had all but waylaid him at the door.

"What are you doing here?" he asked, surprised to see her. After all, she hadn't lived on the family estate for a while now.

She gave him a look that all but said he was being a typical male. "Wedding plans, remember?" she reminded him.

That made him a little confused. "I thought that was yesterday."

Val rolled her eyes. "Could you *be* more of a man?" she asked, referring to his cluelessness as to what it took to pull together a wedding.

"That depends. What's in it for me?" he teased her with a grin and a wink.

Valene blew out a breath. "Can the charming stuff. I'm talking about how clueless you are when it comes to planning a wedding."

He saw no point in arguing her assessment. "And I intend to blissfully remain that way for the rest of my life."

"Really?" she questioned, giving him an evil eye, unwilling to believe he was actually serious. "You actually plan on remaining alone for the rest of your life?"

A twinkle came into Connor's eyes as his grin grew wider. "I didn't say that," he pointed out.

Valene sighed mightily, exasperated. Oh well, Connor would change his mind when the right woman came along, she thought. "Getting back to what I asked before you started to give me your unwanted opinion about weddings, do you have a lead? So soon?"

"What makes you say I have a lead?" he wanted to know.

He had left early this morning in order not to say anything to anyone. He'd wanted to find out if he could get anything from the freelancer first. There was no point in raising people's hopes for no reason.

"Mom said you took off really early this morning. I assumed that meant that you might be onto something," Val explained.

"Right now what I have is a lead on a lead," Connor told his sister.

Val frowned slightly, confused. "What's that supposed to mean?"

He debated keeping his own counsel for a minute, then decided there was no harm in sharing what he'd been doing. "It means that I found someone who did some research for good old Charlotte—"

Questions immediately filled his sister's head. "What kind of research?"

"Do you remember that binder Charlotte was supposed to have compiled on all of Gerald's offspring?" he asked.

"Yes?"

Valene stretched out the word, as if afraid of where this was going. She remembered talk of a binder. She also remembered thinking that Charlotte was really strange to take the time to carefully put together all that miscellaneous information. To her it was like deliberately rubbing salt into her wounds since the names represented all of her husband's infidelities.

"Well, it now looks like she was trying to locate the whereabouts of as many of her former husband's progeny as possible," Connor said.

Valene shook her head, mystified. "Why would she go through all that trouble?"

"Well," Connor said thoughtfully, having pondered the matter on his drive home, "if I was to make a guess, I'd say she was trying to locate them so that she could hurt them."

Valene's first reaction was to dismiss what her brother had said. "Even she's not that evil."

That wasn't the way Connor saw it. "Would you like to make a bet on that?"

His sister shook her head, feeling dismayed. "No," she answered. Charlotte Robinson was the very definition of evil. "You know, Gerald is a soulless alley cat, but Charlotte's no prize, either. If you ask me, those two royally deserve each other. Someone should take both of them, lock them in a room and throw away the key. Forever."

Connor laughed dryly. "I'm certainly not arguing that, but it's way too late in my opinion. They've already done a lot of damage, both in their own way."

"So," Valene said, returning to the subject, "what are you planning on doing with this lead to a lead?"

He'd outlined that in his mind on the way home, as well. "First thing is to see if I can find out just who Charlotte had this woman—"

"It's a woman?" Valene interrupted, realizing she had no idea exactly who her brother had gone to look up.

"Yes, Brianna Childress is most definitely a woman," he answered. "I'm going to see if she can give me the names and address—"

Valene interrupted again. "A pretty woman?" she wanted to know.

She'd picked up a vibe from her brother and wondered if there was something more to his interaction with this Brianna than he was telling. His response that Brianna was "most definitely a woman" had Valene thinking.

Valene's question out of left field made him come to a skidding halt again. Connor frowned at what he considered a pointless question.

"What difference does that make?" he asked.

Val smiled at her supposedly perpetual playboy brother. She was pretty sure she saw beneath that act of his. "You tell me."

"I haven't got the slightest idea what you're talking about," he said, exasperated. "All this wedding planning that you're talking about all the time has obviously fried your brain."

Valene merely smiled at him as if she knew something that he didn't. Not about to get distracted, Connor decided to just ignore his sister.

"You were saying about getting the names and addresses...?" Her voice trailed off as she indicated to her brother that she was waiting for him to continue what he had been saying.

"Since we don't know who Charlene was looking for, getting those names and addresses might help me get in touch with these people so I can warn them that Charlotte might be out to get them."

Valene frowned. She completely agreed with her brother's intentions, but she had a feeling he was going to have some trouble convincing people he was on the level.

She looked at him dubiously. "That doesn't sound crazy at all, does it?" she asked sarcastically.

"Well, whether it sounds crazy or not, I have to try to reach these people. Now that we agree Charlotte's most likely behind some if not all of the things that have been going on, I don't want to have these people on my conscience.

"Besides," Connor continued with a grin, "you forget, little sister. I can be very convincing when I put my mind to it."

"No," Valene replied. "I haven't forgotten. I just hope, if you're right about this—" and she had a feeling he was "—that it's not too late."

Connor grew serious. "You're not the only one," he assured her.

Chapter Six

She hadn't expected to hear from Connor Fortunado so soon.

When the landline in her office rang the following morning, Brianna thought it was either someone calling to make use of her research service—or some anonymous person conducting a survey. It seemed like these days there was always someone conducting a survey and she would have loved to just let the call go to her answering machine, but because of the business she was in, she couldn't afford to miss even one potential client.

The moment she picked up the receiver and heard the deep voice on the other end, even though she'd never received a call from him before, Brianna knew who the caller was. She recognized Connor's voice the moment she heard him say, "Hello."

Even though yesterday had turned out to be an even more hectic day than usual—she had transcribing to catch up on and then she got a last-minute call to fill in at the animal shelter—images of the tall, hazel-eyed private investigator kept popping up in her head when she least expected them. For some reason that she couldn't even begin to understand, she felt like there was a connection between them, though for the life of her she couldn't explain why.

"Ms. Childress?" the baritone voice asked, rumbling against her ear. "This is Connor Fortunado. We met yesterday."

Did Fortunado think that dealing with her children had wiped out her memory? "Yes, I know who this is," she replied.

"You were expecting my call," Connor guessed, thinking that was why she was able to recognize his voice so quickly.

"Actually, I wasn't," Brianna admitted. No, she thought, that was a lie. She'd been hoping he'd call. After all, he had said he'd be in touch. "At least, not this soon," she amended.

"You're busy," he surmised, judging from the unsettled note in her voice. That, and the woman obviously had her hands full dealing with her children. He could hear their voices shouting in the background. "I got you at a bad time."

"No, no, I'm not busy," Brianna assured him quickly. Maybe a little too quickly, she realized. She tempered her answer. "I mean, no more than usual."

The next second she winced as Ava's and Axel's voices grew louder, arguing over the board game they were playing. She'd given them a classic game—Chutes and Ladders—in hopes that it would keep them busy for a while. Busy and quiet. Apparently that had been too much to hope for.

Connor chuckled. "I hear your kids," he commented. He'd meant it as an icebreaker, nothing more.

Brianna sighed. She knew that her children were going to outgrow this stage, but when? "Everyone hears my kids."

He laughed out loud. The woman apparently still had a sense of humor despite everything. Since he'd called her, he decided to ask, thinking he had nothing to lose, "Do you have any time today to get together for a couple of hours?"

"I have time," she answered with feeling. "My schedule is chaotic, but flexible. What time would you like to come over?"

He thought for a second, trying to decide what might be best for the woman. "How does one o'clock sound?"

Brianna thought for a moment. "Right after lunch and before the second wave of insanity starts," she pronounced. "Sounds fine."

"Good. Then I'll be there at one," Connor agreed, glad that was settled.

"I'll be here," she assured him. As she hung up the receiver, placing it back in the cradle, she murmured, "I'm always here."

For the most part, Brianna had made her peace with being a homebody several years ago. But she had to admit there were times when she wished that her life was about something more than juggling three jobs, two children and a varying, ever-growing number of cats and dogs.

Not that she minded all that, she quickly amended, but every once in a while, she caught herself thinking that it would be nice to have something else to look forward to. To occasionally have someone around who appreciated how she never dropped any of the proverbial balls she was perpetually juggling.

"This is no time to feel sorry for yourself," Brianna lectured herself, exasperated with this momentary lapse on her part. "You're doing just fine."

There'd been a time when she was certain that she wouldn't be. That she was just going to fall apart in little pieces. That had been just after Jonny walked out and left her.

Left *them*, she corrected because the man she had devoted herself to had walked out not just on her but on Axel and Ava, as well.

His children.

After several years of putting off taking that "big step" as he had always referred to marriage, Jonny decided that not only wasn't he cut out to be a husband, he didn't *want* to be a father, either. After years of being there for him, bending her life around the man, she'd been devastated when Jonny made it very clear that he didn't want to be there for her.

A substance abuser who had never really kicked the habit despite all his promises to "clean up his act," he wound up choosing his habit over her and left.

She and Jonny had been a dysfunctional unit, but being without him was worse.

At least at first.

But she couldn't fall to pieces, Brianna had told herself fiercely. She'd had an eighteen-month-old and three-month-old depending on her and *only* her. So she'd forced herself to put one foot in front of the other and somehow she'd got through one day, then another and another until somehow a whole month had passed. And then six months.

Somehow, she'd just kept going, setting her sights on making it through another month.

She'd had no longer-range plans than that. All she wanted to do was get to the end of the month.

Each month.

And she had. In fact, she'd made it three years.

Rousing herself, Brianna blocked out any more thoughts that fell outside of the parameters of the project she was currently working on. She just focused on that.

For once, there were no bloodcurdling screams coming from anywhere in the house to distract her. The noise level had lowered to a familiar, almost-comforting hum.

Brianna started to work, knowing this peace wouldn't last long.

It was too quiet. In the last twenty minutes she hadn't heard any crashes, any yelling or even the sound of scuffling that occasionally came from the wrestling matches that Axel and Ava sporadically engaged in.

Had they run away? Or worse, done something to each other simultaneously so that neither one was able to cry out?

Uneasy now, she knew her imagination was running

away with her. She didn't usually break for lunch until twelve but even though it was just eleven thirty, she stopped and went in search of the twosome.

Maybe they had both come down with something, she thought, trying to find a reason why she wasn't hearing *anything*. Nothing short of a sudden mutual illness could render them this quiet for this long.

Walking into the living room, Brianna was both relieved and somewhat concerned to find her children watching one of the cable channels. As she drew closer she saw that they were both sitting on the floor, mesmerized by a lion stalking his prey, in this case a helpless zebra.

She knew how this story ended and she didn't want them to see it.

Moving swiftly, Brianna got in front of the TV monitor and changed the channel. She pressed the numbers and the picture on the screen instantly changed from a stalking lion to a cartoon rabbit getting the better of a determined, if inept hunter.

That was more like it, Brianna thought with satisfaction.

"Mom!" Axel lamented indignantly, "The lion was just about to get that striped horse!"

"No, he wasn't," Ava insisted. Her arm was draped over Scruffy, trapping the dog against her. Scruffy was used to this and didn't seem to mind, Brianna noted. "The horsie was going to get away," she informed her brother with the kind of confidence reserved only for the very young and innocent.

And they're back, Brianna thought.

"You want lunch in the kitchen or in front of the TV?" she asked.

Once, in her younger, prechildren days, she had come up with all sorts of rules she was going to make her future, unborn children follow. They were going to do chores and only be allowed to watch one hour of TV programming a week.

All that had fallen by the wayside rather quickly when she was faced with the reality of actually *living* with children and making it all work. Especially as a single mother.

"In front of the TV!" both children cried out in unison.

Finally, she thought, they had found something to agree on. It didn't happen that often.

"Okay," she told them, "but you have to promise not to argue."

"I'll be good, Mom. I won't argue," Axel promised, slanting a look at Ava. The look he'd flashed implied that he thought his sister would.

Ava was quick to pick up on the implied insult. "No, *I* won't argue," she declared with feeling.

Any mother could read between the lines, especially when those lines were two feet high the way they were here. It was only a matter of time before the next argument would break out.

But she pretended, for the time being, to believe them.

"Good," Brianna said with finality, "you both won't argue. Try to remember that," she cautioned her children as she turned around and went into the kitchen to prepare their lunches.

* * *

Brianna had just collected the empty dishes and put them into the sink when she heard Ava—Ava moved with a light step, while Axel seemed to stomp whenever he hurried—rush across the room.

Since nothing had crashed or fallen, Brianna didn't think anything of her daughter's sudden mobility until she heard Ava calling out excitedly.

"He's back, Mama! He came back. I see him outside the house!"

"Who came back?" Axel wanted to know.

The next second, not to be left out, the little boy made tracks to the window so he could see whatever it was that his sister saw.

"He did. The man," Ava cried happily, pointing out the window.

Brianna realized what was going on and who her daughter was so excited about.

Grabbing a dish towel, Brianna dried her hands and hurried into the living room. Before she could reach either of her children, she saw that Ava was already at the door, just about to open it.

"Ava! What did I tell you about opening the door?" Brianna cried loud enough to freeze the little girl in her tracks.

"Not to do it?" It wasn't a statement, it was more of a guess.

"Then why are you opening it?" Brianna wanted to know. Reaching her daughter, she put her hand over the doorknob and removed Ava's hand, preventing the little girl from throwing the door open.

Ava looked up at her, totally mystified.

"'Cause it's him," she answered as if she couldn't understand why her mother was even asking her that question. "The man from yesterday. The man who put clothes on his horsie," Ava added for good measure just in case her mother still didn't know who she was talking about.

"That doesn't matter," Brianna told Ava sternly. "You don't ever, ever open the door, understand?" she warned her daughter.

Light eyebrows scrunched up, disappearing beneath dark brown bangs.

"Ever?" Ava repeated. "Not even when I'm going to school?" she asked. "How're we gonna get out of the rooms?"

"We can't get out if we can't open the door," Axel complained, chiming in. For once he actually appeared to be on Ava's side.

They were just too smart for their own good, Brianna thought wearily. They were certainly too smart for *her* own good.

"We'll talk about that when the time comes," Brianna told her daughter, doing her best not to lose her temper right now.

The doorbell rang.

Ava looked at her mother, the lecture forgotten as excitement filled her at the prospect of seeing her mother's friend again.

"It's him!" she cried. Ava tugged on her mother's arm to motivate her. "Open it, Mama. Open it before he goes away!"

Any hope Brianna had that yesterday had been a

fluke evaporated. She knew better now. Ava definitely had a crush on the private investigator.

She was going to have to address that before it got out of hand, Brianna thought.

But obviously not now.

Shooing Ava away from the door, she opened it to admit Connor, doing her best to keep her composure.

He smiled at Brianna, then immediately saw that she wasn't alone. "Hi, I see you brought your welcoming committee," he observed.

"No, no commit-tee. It's just me," Ava told him. "Ava," she said, in case he had forgotten her name. She preened a little as she said it.

"And me," Axel said.

"And they were just going out to play in the backyard," Brianna assured him, ushering her children toward the rear of the house and the sliding glass door that led into the fenced yard.

"No, we weren't," Ava protested, speaking up. She moved a little closer to Connor. "We were going to stay right here," she said, looking up at him with a big, sunny smile.

Okay, this had gone on long enough. "Axel, Ava, backyard. Now," Brianna ordered.

Long faces greeted her order. Seeing that their mother meant business, very slowly they shuffled their feet all the way to the sliding glass door, and then went out into the backyard. It was very clearly under protest.

Connor watched them go along with their mother, who kept a watchful eye on their reluctant exodus. He couldn't help grinning at the pint-size dramatics.

Satisfied that they had gone out the way they had

been told to, Brianna finally turned around to face her guest.

"Was it just my imagination, or was Ava flirting with me?" Connor asked her mother.

He was accustomed to being flirted with, but the person doing the flirting was usually at least old enough to vote. This time the person flirting with him wasn't even old enough to attend kindergarten.

"I'm going to have a problem with that girl," Brianna said, answering his question indirectly. "Ava's never done that before, although that's not saying much since she's only three," she was quick to add. Brianna shook her head, at a loss how to effectively handle this. "Before I had kids, I used to think I had all the answers. Now even my questions have questions. It seems like every day there's something new to deal with," she said with a sigh.

"What does her dad say?" Connor asked.

The question had come out automatically and the moment he said it, he found himself regretting it. He hadn't meant to get so personal.

Brianna shrugged as she led the way to her office. "Nothing as far as I know."

Connor read between the lines. Then, to make sure, he glanced at her left hand. Still no wedding ring. She hadn't forgotten it, she didn't have one, he thought. "You're doing this on your own?"

She thought that was obvious. "Can't you tell?" she asked ruefully.

His tone was serious as he answered the question. "Not really."

That surprised her. She'd gotten the impression that

the man was on top of things. "You're kidding." Reassessing the situation, she decided that Connor Fortunado was just being polite.

He looked at her and said in all seriousness, "No. I just see a couple of happy, spirited kids. Nothing to indicate that there's no dad in the picture."

"Spirited," Brianna repeated, amused at the private investigator's choice of words. "Oh, those two are spirited all right. They're spirited from sunup to sundown and longer. One thing those two don't run out of is spirit. Sometimes I really wish they had less of it."

But he had a feeling he knew better. "No, you don't," Connor said.

His comment surprised her. "Oh? Why's that?"

Connor smiled at her, stepping back so that she entered her office first. It was the kind of smile that told her he wasn't fooled by what she'd just stated.

"Because spirited kids become the people who turn their dreams into reality."

He said it with such certainty, she found herself really wanting to believe him.

Chapter Seven

Brianna's eyes met his and she smiled gratefully at the private investigator. "I think I really needed to hear that," she told Connor. "That was a very nice thing for you to say." She gave him a way out. "Even if you didn't mean it."

"Oh, but I did," he said. "I was pretty much a hellion when I was a kid. You can ask any of my sisters—they'll tell you," he added as verification. "Even so, things turned out pretty well for me. I got to follow my passion."

His disarming smile seemed to burrow right into her. Brianna blinked, rousing herself.

"You have sisters?" she asked Connor, trying to envision the tall, handsome man before her as a rebellious little boy. There was a glint in his eye, but she still couldn't see him that way.

"That I do," he assured her. There was no missing the fond note in his voice.

"How many?" she wanted to know. She couldn't deny that the idea of being part of a large family had always intrigued her. It was something that she had always wished for and never had.

"Three," he answered. Seeing that he had caught her interest and wanting to cultivate that interest so that she felt more at ease with him and more inclined to be forthcoming, he added, "I've got two brothers, as well."

Having grown up alone, she could hardly visualize being part of such a large family. She found herself envying him. "Wow, that *is* a full house."

He laughed softly. "I'm sure my mother would agree with you." Since Brianna seemed so interested in his family dynamics, he felt it only fair to return the favor. "How many siblings do you have?"

Her smile struck him as sad when she answered his question. "None."

"Oh." There was a moment of awkwardness because of the sad tone he'd detected in her voice, but then he found a way to turn the situation around. "That means you got to be the center of your parents' attention."

Her sad smile seemed to intensify. "You have a nice way of saying things," she told him, "but no, that wasn't the case." Clearing her throat, Brianna changed the subject. "I went through my files after you left and found most of my correspondence with that woman you were asking about yesterday."

"Charlotte," Connor said, supplying his step-aunt's name.

"Charlotte," Brianna repeated, confirming that was

who she'd meant. "Although she did sign all her email Charlene Pickett," she reminded him, "so don't let that confuse you." Brianna paused for a second, debating whether she should ask, then decided he could always just beg off giving her an honest answer. He'd been vague yesterday. "Why the need for different names?" she wanted to know. "Is she wanted by the law or something like that?"

"She should be." The answer came out without any thought and for now, it was all he allowed himself to say on the subject. Once he found a way to definitely prove that Charlotte was behind all the things that had been going on, he was confident that Charlotte Prendergast Robinson—or whatever she chose to call herself—was going to be languishing in a prison cell for a very long, long time.

When he didn't say anything further, Brianna continued with what she had been saying to him. "Well, I haven't finished going through everything—sometimes my filing system gets away from me," she confessed, embarrassed. "There might be a couple more names that she wanted me to look into, but I did find most of them," she told Connor.

Brianna placed a bunch of folders on the desk in front of him.

Picking them up, Connor quickly reviewed the names that were written on the side of each of the folders. Some were familiar, many weren't. "You found these people for her?" This would make finding these people easier for him.

The smile on her face was a bit rueful. "Again, I did manage to track down most of them." She paused, deciding to be more specific in her answer. "Eleven of these people, to be exact. I told her I'd get back to her when I found where the others were." She shrugged, hating that the situation had gotten away from her. She was accustomed to being more in control than this. "But since she didn't get back to me with at least another partial payment, I was forced to just let the matter drop."

"But you did manage to locate eleven of these people?" he asked, wanting to be clear.

"I recall a twelfth person," she said now, remembering another name. "But that last one isn't in these files. I checked," she told him. "It has to be somewhere in the rest of the folders."

Connor looked down at the folders she had handed him, then raised his eyes to hers. "And these aren't in your computer?" he questioned incredulously.

She'd been on the receiving end of that look more than once. She admitted that in this day and age, it was hard for people to understand why she'd choose to keep handwritten notes instead of storing everything on a laptop or a tablet.

"I prefer to hold paper in my hand," she said. Then, not giving him an opportunity to comment, she quickly said, "I know, I know, you probably think I'm incredibly old-fashioned. Well, you're right," she confessed. There was no point in pretending otherwise. "I am."

"Actually, I wasn't thinking that at all," Connor replied. "What I was thinking was that I kind of thought that was charming."

Charming. The word replayed itself in her head. She hadn't seen that coming.

"Well, that's the first time I've ever heard it referred to as that," Brianna admitted. She rather liked hearing him say that. "Most people think it means that I'm computer illiterate, which I'm not," she assured him quickly. "I just prefer to work this way."

"And you're perfectly entitled to your choices," he responded. "They obviously work for you."

Brianna wasn't used to being on the receiving end of compliments and she had absolutely no practice in how to respond. At a loss, she cleared her throat again.

"Yes, well, why don't you read what I came up with," she suggested, nodding at the folders he was still holding, "and I'll try to see if I can find the missing file—or files."

She really couldn't remember at this point just how many more names there were.

"Okay." Connor looked around the exceptionally small room. His parents' house had closets that were larger than this room she was apparently using as her office. "Where can I sit?" he wanted to know. From what he could see—and everything *was* out in plain sight—she just had the one desk, a pressed wood affair that looked as if she had put it together herself. There was a chair up against it that didn't match the desk.

"You can take the desk," Brianna told him. "I don't need to use it to go through the papers in my filing cabinet."

Connor looked around again, but he still didn't see anything that fit that description.

A monk's cell probably had more furnishings than this room, he thought.

"I don't see a file cabinet," he told her. "Is it in another room?"

"Not *file* cabinet," Brianna corrected. "*Filing* cabinet. It's what I call these," she said, gesturing toward the plastic drawers that she had piled on top of each other.

There were three see-through drawers all told, the type made to hold anything from toys to towels. But apparently in this particular case, they held the various notes and files that comprised her research projects.

Out of the corner of his eye, he saw her looking at him. He proceeded delicately. "You have a unique filing system," he finally commented.

At least he wasn't being critical, Brianna thought, relieved. "It works for me."

He didn't care how she had gone about doing it; he just cared about the results she had come up with. "That's all that counts, isn't it?"

Brianna studied the man in her office. Was he just trying to make her feel good, or was there a reason he was saying all these nice things to her, she wondered.

Was he trying to get her to lower her guard? Did that mean that there was some sort of an ulterior motive behind what he was saying?

What kind of an ulterior motive?

What happened to you? You used to trust people, Brianna upbraided herself.

But that had been a lifetime ago, before Jonny had walked out of her life. She'd always had a penchant for picking up strays, Jonny included. And for trying to fix things, from animals to people. But when Jonny had abruptly left, something had broken inside of her and she'd found herself second-guessing everything that happened, everything that she felt, from there on in.

Connor picked up on her mood shift. She'd grown quiet.

"Is something wrong?" he asked her, wondering if he'd said anything to set her down this path.

Brianna blinked, banishing the fog that had temporarily descended on her brain.

"What? No, no," she said with feeling, as if to deny anything he might be thinking, whatever it might be. "I was just trying to remember where I filed that missing folder or folders."

It was a lie, but it was better than going into a long explanation about her gnawing uncertainty. Besides, the man wouldn't want to hear about that. He just wanted to review her findings and glean whatever it was he was trying to find out. She knew he wasn't telling her everything. But as long as it didn't interfere with her work, that was his right.

She cleared her throat again, not realizing that he was beginning to think of that as her "tell."

"Did you mean what you said yesterday?" she asked Connor.

He had sat down at the desk and had just begun to look through the first folder. Looking her way, he said, "Refresh my memory. What did I say?"

She knew it. He was going to plead amnesia. "About paying me the three thousand dollars that Charlene Pickett was supposed to pay for the information I sent her."

He remembered that quite well. "Yes, but I also

said that payment was contingent on you helping me locate Charlotte."

Brianna nodded, recalling the whole exchange. "Yes, you did say that," she agreed. "I was just asking to see if *you* remembered."

Connor was *not* in the habit of paying off any of Charlotte Robinson's debts. Until it had come to light that Gerald Robinson was his father's half brother, he hadn't even given the woman so much as a second thought because he hadn't *known* about her or her bizarre behavior, nor about her connection to his own family.

But it was clear that Charlotte had obviously stiffed Brianna and had no intention of making good on her promise to pay. Beyond the fact that it was the wrong thing to do, this mother of two was clearly in need of every dime that had been promised to her for services rendered. He felt somewhat responsible that she had trusted Charlotte even though he'd had nothing to do with that.

That fact notwithstanding, Connor still felt he should cover the outstanding debt.

"Tell you what," Connor proposed. "Since you're obviously an honorable woman of her word, why don't I pay you the money for the work ahead of time?"

Pride reared its head and had her looking at him warily. "Why would you do that?"

Turning in the chair to face her, he spread his hands wide. "I'm just paying up front for services rendered— and to be rendered."

That was all well and good, Brianna thought. However, there was something else to consider here.

"But what if I can't find her?" she challenged.

She needed the money—she had yet to get ahead of all of her bills and possibly never would—but she had her pride. She wasn't a charity case and didn't want Fortunado to treat her as one.

"I have a feeling that you will," he told her easily. "But even if it turns out that we can't locate Charlotte because she's hidden herself in some cave, that's no reason why you shouldn't be paid for your efforts. It's only fair," he stressed.

Still, the situation disturbed her. Temptation warred with her sense of integrity. "I don't want to take advantage of you," she protested.

This woman had to be one in a million, Connor thought with admiration. He knew of a lot of people who would have jumped at the chance to take him up on his offer. For that matter, he knew of people who would be more than willing to take advantage of the situation if they could find a way to get away with it.

And here *she* was, definitely hurting for money— the woman was working three jobs for heaven sakes— and she was definitely *not* jumping at the chance to take advantage of his offer. She was even trying to talk him out of it. Who did that?

"You're not taking advantage of me if I'm the one trying to get you to accept the money," he pointed out.

Making up his mind, Connor pushed aside the folder he was reading and took out his checkbook. The desk space was limited and he needed a flat space in order to be able to write out the check.

"Do I make this out to you, or do you have a company name you'd rather I use?" he asked her, looking at her over his shoulder.

He was really going to do it, Brianna thought, amazed. He was just going to hand her the three thousand dollars whether or not she found the woman he was looking for. She knew she should try to talk him out of it, to tell him that she would wait until her part in this was done. But the truth of it was she really didn't have that luxury. She had children and bills and she could *definitely* use the three thousand dollars he was offering to pay her.

Suspicions were born in the wake of her amazement. There had to be something more, she thought. Didn't there? "And all you want me to do for this money is to help you locate this woman?" she asked.

He didn't answer her directly. "Trust me, there's no 'all' about it. If there was, I would have already done it myself." Charlotte had proven to be as slippery as the proverbial greased pig. "Like I said, you will definitely be earning your money."

She tended to believe him despite her newly acquired suspicious nature. "How long have you been looking for her?" she wanted to know, curious.

"A few weeks." Up until that point, he'd still been piecing things together. The link between the three attacks aimed at the family hadn't come to light before then, nor had the link blatantly pointing toward Charlotte.

"*Why* are you looking for her?" Brianna asked him, pinning him with a look.

She had a very compelling way about her, not to mention eyes that could induce any man to suddenly feel as if he wanted to make a full confession of any secret he might be harboring from the world.

But the fewer people who knew what was going on—until he could safely prove it—the better.

So Connor told her, "For now that's my business."

He waited for her to attempt to coax the information out of him. All the women he'd ever known were as curious as cats. However, she surprised him.

"I can respect that," she said quietly.

He waited for the other shoe to drop and for her to change her mind.

Neither happened.

"Okay, then," he said, regrouping. "You didn't answer my question. Shall I make this out to you, or to your company?"

"To the company," she told him.

"The company it is," Connor replied. With smooth, even strokes, he wrote out the check to the business he'd originally looked up, and then handed it to her.

Brianna glanced at the check out of habit, even though something told her it would be for the correct amount.

It was.

What she noticed more than the correct amount was the fluid letters that were on the check. "You have nice handwriting," she commented.

"That was my mother's doing," he admitted, giving credit where it was due. "She's not a strict woman, but there are certain things she always insisted on. One of those things was that we all had handwriting that was not just legible, but uniform. She maintained that people could tell a lot about a person by their handwriting and she wanted all of us to be held in high regard by everyone we dealt with."

"Sounds like you were being groomed," Brianna commented.

Now wasn't the time to talk about family money, not when he could see that Brianna had clearly come up the hard way—and was still struggling.

Connor gave her his standard go-to reply. "Only to be good people and to work hard."

Again she caught herself envying him and the up-bringing he'd had. The childhood he'd lived.

When his eyes met hers, she hid her feelings and smiled her approval. "Both very admirable qualities."

Chapter Eight

Connor had barely finished reading the notations in a quarter of the folders that Brianna had given him when his concentration was suddenly interrupted.

This time it wasn't because the sounds of a pint-size World War Three was breaking out somewhere in the house.

This particular interruption was an up close and personal one and came in the form of one Ava Susan Childress. That was how Brianna addressed her daughter in exasperation when the latter strode into her office and in a loud, intrusive voice asked her, "Are you finished with him yet?"

Startled—her children were supposed to be playing out in the yard—Brianna cried, "Ava Susan Childress, where are your manners? We don't ask questions like that," Brianna insisted.

Undaunted, her daughter actually looked rather upset over being unceremoniously called out on the carpet and admonished in this fashion. Cocking her small, silky dark brown head, she focused her bright blue eyes accusingly at her mother.

"Well, I did. I wanted to know if you were finished with him so he could tell us another story. It was for Axel, too," the little girl added, as if that should make everything all right. "He wanted to hear another story, too."

Brianna flashed an apologetic look toward the private investigator. As usual, her children had managed to embarrass her.

"I'm sorry about this," she told Connor.

Amused by the little girl's straightforward approach, he brushed off Brianna's apology.

"No need to be sorry," Connor assured her. The truth was, he was getting a kick out of all this. "I've never been in demand by members of the short person set before," he said with a grin.

Ava was trying hard to understand. "Does that mean he can go with me?" she wanted to know.

Axel appeared in the doorway. For once he was there to back up his sister instead of disputing every word she had to say.

"Mr. Fortunado doesn't take orders from me," Brianna informed her son and daughter. "He's here strictly as my client."

Connor saw the way the two children's faces fell. He looked from one to the other. They looked too young to know the meaning of the word *client*, so he asked Ava and Axel what they thought.

His eyes studied their expressions. "Do you know what the word *client* means?"

"Yeah," Ava answered. She slanted a grudging look toward her mother. "It means the person's important and we have to leave them alone." She ended with a rather dramatic sigh.

"Yeah, alone," Axel echoed, sticking out his lower lip and pouting.

"I see," Connor responded, looking at them thoughtfully. "Well, I'm not that kind of a client," he told them.

Hope instantly lit up the two small faces and they smiled.

"What kind of client are you?" Axel wanted to know.

"The kind that likes to take breaks so that he can tell two really great little people stories they want to hear," Connor answered, struggling not to laugh.

Ava's grin grew twice as large as it had when he'd first walked in today. "You mean like us?" she asked her new hero eagerly.

"Exactly like you," Connor replied.

Although it warmed Brianna's heart to see Connor being so nice to her children, it was a source of concern, as well. Ava and Axel had both taken to this man in an incredibly short amount of time, so short that it didn't even seem as if it was possible—except that they had.

Therein lay the problem. She didn't want her children getting used to having this man around because the moment he got all the information he was after, Connor would be gone, and Ava and Axel wouldn't be able to understand why he wasn't coming back anymore. They were sure to take it personally, she thought. They'd think it was because of something they had done.

She didn't want that happening.

It was one of the reasons she didn't date. The fact was, she wouldn't be dating for one, she'd actually be dating for three, and her children's feelings meant everything to her.

Looking at Connor over their heads now, Brianna's voice sounded a little strained as she told him, "You know you really don't have to do this."

He thought she was trying to ease him out of what she probably felt was an imposition by her children. He didn't see it as an imposition, though.

"That's okay, I don't mind," Connor told her. He was already trying to think of a story that he could tell the duo.

Ava and Axel somehow seemed to have surrounded him even though he was still just sitting at the desk. Their combined presence had a way of being overwhelming.

"No, *really*," Brianna emphasized, her eyes meeting his. "You don't have to do this."

Something in her tone caught Connor's attention and he tried to read between the lines, but failed. Transparency was *not* one of her strong suits, Connor thought.

So he decided to go the simple route and just ask her outright. "Are you saying that you *don't* want me to tell them a story?"

"Mama," Ava wailed in disappointment. She wanted to hear the story that Connor had to tell whatever it turned out to be.

Not to be left out, Axel joined in and cried in a loud voice, "Mom!"

With Connor clearly on their side, she knew she was outnumbered. Brianna retreated and surrendered. She was not about to be the bad guy today.

"Never mind," she told Connor, waving away the whole thing. "I just didn't want you to feel you were being guilted into anything."

He flashed another smile at Brianna as Axel climbed up onto one of his knees and Ava scaled the other. "Don't worry about me," he told their mother. "I can handle myself."

She highly doubted that, not when it came to her kids.

"Remember," she told him as she crossed the threshold out of her office, "you said it, I didn't."

Her departure took him by surprise. "You're leaving? Where are you going?" Connor wanted to know, calling after her. He had just assumed that Brianna would remain in the room along with her children.

"I've got a chicken to get into the oven," she tossed over her shoulder, never breaking stride.

Before he could say anything more, he felt two small hands on his face, turning it so that he found himself looking down into Ava's face rather than the doorway.

"Don't worry, the chicken's not alive," she assured him in a voice that very easily could have belonged to someone four times her age.

"Yeah, Mom gets them at the store and they're already dead," Axel said with authority, not to be left out of the conversation.

"Tell us about your horse," Ava prompted. "Did you put other clothes on him?"

Connor laughed. Obviously the story had left a big impression on the children. "No, my dad put an end to that pretty quick."

Ava was very quiet for a total of five seconds, and then she told him, "We don't have a dad. What's it like to have one?" she asked.

"Doesn't your dad let you play with your horse?" Axel wanted to know.

Connor thought about the annoyed look that had descended over Kenneth Fortunado's face when he told his father that he'd turned his back on the firm and decided to become a private investigator. That, he thought, had been the face of disapproval.

"Sometimes he can be difficult," Connor told his small audience, not really wanting to say anything derogatory about his father. He knew the man had been disappointed by the news, but in reality, it had been his decision to make.

Small, expressive eyebrows knitted themselves together over the bridge of Ava's nose. "What's diffy— diffy—that word you just said," Ava finally said, giving up.

"It means that sometimes my dad doesn't see things the way I do," Connor explained, wanting to leave it at that.

He hadn't reckoned on the inquisitive minds he was dealing with.

"Mama's like that all the time," Ava confided in a hushed voice that was a little louder than a stage whisper.

"Yeah," Axel cried, wiggling into the conversation, "she's always trying to get us not to do things because it makes her nervous."

"Well, being a mom for two smart kids can be pretty hard sometimes," Connor reminded them sympathetically. "I'm sure that your mother's just trying to do the best she can."

Ava apparently thought his words over before she nodded her head. "Yeah," Ava agreed. "She does. She doesn't even spank Axel when he's bad."

Rather than deny that he was bad, Axel just lumped her in with him. "You're bad, too," he insisted, looking pointedly at his sister. He was not about to take the blame alone.

The expression on Ava's face was indignant. "Am not!" she cried.

Axel did not go down without a fight. "Are, too!" he retorted.

Connor was beginning to catch on. This showed every sign of escalating. Connor quickly spoke up, raising his voice above theirs.

"Hey, hold it," he ordered. When they turned to look at him, he told them, "I don't think either one of you are bad."

Instead of their protesting his intrusion into their argument, Connor found himself looking down into two beaming faces.

"You don't?" the two cried in unison.

"No, I don't," he replied calmly.

The best way to handle the escalating feelings was to divert attention away from the cause. So he did.

"You want to talk about *bad*, you should have met

my brother Gavin when he was a kid. Now there was *bad*," he told them with feeling, although there was no judgment attached to the words. "My mom called it being mischievous." He laughed to himself. "But my dad just called it bad."

"Did Gavin get a lot of time-outs?" Axel wanted to know, no doubt thinking of the way he and his sister were punished.

"Time-outs?" Connor repeated. He decided to play along. The kids didn't need to hear every single fact that had been involved in Gavin and his upbringing. "Yeah, he got those, along with other things when he was particularly bad."

Axel rose to his knees, balancing himself on Connor's knee as he looked into his face. Small blue eyes probed his.

"What kind of things?" he wanted to know.

The boy made Connor think of someone who was afraid of horror movies but still wanted to go on watching to see what happened next.

"You don't want to talk about that," Connor told him casually. "Don't you want to hear about Manchester?"

Ava scrunched up her pretty little face, trying to understand. Axel appeared to be totally lost.

"What's a Man-chest-ta?" Ava asked.

Connor struggled to keep a straight face. "Manchester was my dog when I was growing up."

"You mean like Scruffy?" Ava asked eagerly. Like her mother, the little girl had an instant affinity for anything on four legs.

Connor glanced down at the dog that was never far away from at least one of the children if not both. A mixed breed, Scruffy looked as if he was part Chihuahua, part teacup poodle, with a little of something else thrown in.

The dog barely came up to the bottom of his shin. "Oh, a lot bigger than Scruffy," Connor told them. "Manchester was a Great Dane."

"What made him great?" Axel wanted to know, asking the question in all seriousness. "Was it something he did?"

It was harder and harder for Connor to continue maintaining a straight face. Instead of correcting the boy and possibly hurting his feelings, Connor told Axel in all solemnity, "He always came when I called."

"He doesn't do that anymore?" Ava asked, looking at her hero with sympathy.

Connor smiled at her, although the smile was a little sad around the edges. Manchester had always been his favorite dog. He had been almost inconsolable when the dog died. That had been years ago.

"I'm afraid he doesn't do anything anymore."

"Why?" Ava wanted to know.

Axel answered the question for her. "Because he's dead, stupid." He turned to look at Connor. "That's what you're trying to say, right?"

"Not in those words, no," Connor answered the little boy, then gently said, "And it's not nice to call your sister stupid."

Axel couldn't see why that was a problem. "But she is," he insisted.

"No, she isn't," Connor said kindly but firmly, "and you didn't mean that, either, did you?" he asked the boy. He smiled at the duo. "Someday you two are going to realize that you need to have each other's backs."

"Why?" Ava wanted to know, looking disdainfully at her brother. "I don't want his old back."

Again Connor had to struggle not to laugh. "Maybe not today, but you will soon," he said confidently. "That's what family does," he explained simply. "They take care of each other's backs."

From the look on her face, it still made no sense to Ava, although since Connor was her new hero, she seemed more than willing to be convinced.

"Do you have Gavin's back?" she wanted to know.

He smiled at the display of curiosity. "Yes, I do."

It was Axel's turn to ask a question. "Does he have yours?"

Turning to the boy, Connor nodded and said seriously, "He does."

Axel looked at his sister. It was obvious that he wasn't happy with this latest piece of information. "Do we have to?" he wanted to know, pained.

"You'll want to," Connor assured him. When he saw the dubious look crossing the little boy's face, he told him, "Trust me, you will."

Axel frowned but it was obvious he didn't want to oppose this new friend.

"If you say so," the little boy responded rather reluctantly.

Brianna stuck her head into the room. Part of her was surprised that Connor hadn't decided to bolt out of the house by now. The man had an amazing amount of patience and an incredible amount of staying power, she thought with admiration.

"You're still alive," she quipped, taking a step into the room.

He turned slightly to look at her. Perforce her children did, too. "You didn't expect me to be?" he asked, amused.

"Actually, at this point I expected you to be running for your life." With a smile, she nodded toward her children. "These two have been known to wear down concrete, and besides, this wasn't what you signed on for. Not in any manner," she added.

"Where did he sign, Mama?" Ava wanted to know. She wanted to know everything about this person her mother was working with.

"And what was it?" Axel asked in a louder voice, not to be outdone.

"Never mind, you two. Why don't you go outside again and play?" she suggested. "You've worn Mr. Fortunado down enough for one day."

"No, we didn't," Axel protested. "We didn't wear you down, did we?" he asked Connor, obviously regarding the man as a higher court of appeal.

Connor grinned, tickled at how seriously the boy viewed what his mother had said. "You didn't even scratch the surface," he replied.

"See?" Axel declared, looking at his mother. "We didn't even scratch anything."

Brianna felt drained. She decided to change the subject. She could tell that there was no winning this one.

"Dinner'll be ready in about forty-five minutes," she told the children. Then, looking at Connor, she added, "You're welcome to stay if you like."

"Yay!" Ava cried, clapping her hands. "Stay!"

"Yeah, stay!" Axel told him, adding his voice to his sister's.

It was hard to say no after that.

Connor turned his attention toward the woman who was sharing her research results with him. "Are you sure I won't be putting you out?"

"I wouldn't have extended the invitation if you were," she answered.

"Then I guess I'm staying," he said with a boyish grin.

Both children cheered again.

Chapter Nine

A schedule of sorts slowly emerged. Over the course of the next few days, Connor came over to her house and met with Brianna a number of times.

Admittedly, the young mother of two had given him enough information to set him on the right path. He had names and locations, not Charlotte's, but he felt that eventually, that would materialize. However, Connor still kept coming back to see her on the outside chance that there was perhaps even more that she could help him uncover.

Part of him secretly knew that what he was really doing was just coming up with excuses, giving himself reasons to continue seeing Brianna for just a little longer.

There was no question in his mind that he was attracted to her. Brianna had a rather memorable figure, even though all he had ever seen her wearing was jeans and a T-shirt. It really got to him. The amazing thing was that the woman didn't use any makeup or glamorous clothing to make herself look beautiful. Nevertheless, she just was.

Brianna was very simply a natural beauty, he thought. A natural beauty who would most likely turn him down if he asked her out, for the same reason she'd told him that they would have to work in her house—because of the children. She'd made it quite clear without actually stating it that Axel and Ava always came first.

The funny thing about it, Connor mused, here he was, a confirmed bachelor and he actually really *liked* her kids. In all honesty, he had never given much thought to kids at all, other than not wanting any. And yet, he liked hers.

Not because they were hers—if anything her children served as a reminder of the life Brianna had had with another man—but because both of them were so lively, so precocious and really amusing, the latter rather unwittingly.

"She's just the flavor of the month, that's all," he told himself. "Don't try to read anything more into it, Fortunado."

But even as he voiced what was his prevailing sentiment out loud in his car while he was driving to Brianna's house, Connor wasn't quite convincing himself that he was telling the truth.

That was because he found himself looking forward to seeing her—and those kids of hers—the way he couldn't remember looking forward to seeing *any* of the myriad of women who had passed through his life since just after his adolescence took hold.

"What the hell are you thinking?" he asked himself, annoyed. "You haven't even kissed the woman yet."

He wasn't attracted to her, Connor silently argued, he had just gotten caught up in a fantasy, that's all. All this wedding talk and planning had made him wonder what it would be like if he gave in to his family's pressure and joined the ranks of the newly married.

C'mon, Connor, get a grip. You don't want any of this. You're just curious, that's all.

He pushed all thoughts of Brianna and her children aside. Today would probably be the last time that he would be seeing any of them.

Or at least the second to last time, he amended—just in case.

Before he knew it, Connor found himself pulling up to the curb in front of Brianna's house.

How had that happened?

He had blanked out the entire way from his parents' estate to here, Connor realized. He supposed he should just be grateful that he hadn't gotten into some sort of an accident.

It was a sobering thought.

"He's here, Mama. He's here!" Ava announced excitedly, jumping up and down at the window in the living room.

Brianna automatically glanced at her watch, although there was really no need. The man had been turning up like clockwork every day.

"I'm going to let him in!" Ava declared, hurrying

from the window that faced the front of the house and running to the door.

"No, I am!" Axel announced, trying to beat his sister to the door.

"Neither one of you are opening the door," Brianna informed her children sternly. Short of putting a leash on them, how did she get this across to them? "Nothing's changed. You're still too young to open the door to anyone."

"But, Mama, it's Connor," Ava wailed, stopping— unwillingly—just short of the front door.

"It's who?" Brianna asked, looking pointedly at her daughter.

Ava sighed. It was a huge sigh for such a little girl. "Mr. Fortuna-dough," she dutifully said, correcting herself because that was what her mother was expecting to hear.

Brianna nodded. "Better."

Her eyes swept over the pint-size welcoming committee. Then, motioning both of her children aside, Brianna opened the door just as Connor was about to ring the bell.

He looked a little taken aback as he dropped his hand to his side again, then raised one quizzical eyebrow as his eyes met hers.

"My lookout told me you were coming up the front walk," Brianna explained.

"I was looking for you," Ava told him proudly, flashing a big grin.

"I was looking for you, too," Axel announced, not wanting to get lost in the shuffle. It was clear that because of his mother and his sister, he felt really out-numbered.

Before Connor could respond, Axel's eyes alighted on the big, flat box he was carrying. The boy's blue eyes all but shone with interest.

"Is that pizza?" Axel cried, not giving Connor a chance to comment on his sister's statement.

Rather than answer either of the children, Connor looked at their mother.

"I thought that I'd bring lunch with me and give you a break for a change." When she didn't say anything, he asked, "Is it okay?"

"It's a little late to ask that question, isn't it?" Brianna asked, amused that he'd think to ask her now. There was a lot to like about the man, Brianna thought.

Connor couldn't tell if he'd somehow offended her with this gesture, or if she really didn't mind. "We don't have to eat it," he told Brianna.

Axel looked as if he was about to burst into tears. "'Course we gotta eat it," he declared. "What else can you do with pizza?"

Ava took their cause to the highest authority—their mother. She looked at Brianna hopefully. "We can eat it, right, Mama?" she asked.

"Yes, you can eat it," Brianna agreed. "At lunch-time," she specified.

The last few days Connor had begun arriving at ten rather than after one, so she supposed it was only natural that one of these times he decided to bring a take-out lunch with him.

This time it was Axel who sighed mightily. "Okay,"

he agreed with something less than wholehearted enthusiasm.

"Yes, Mama," Ava's voice mimicked her brother's submissive tone.

"And only after you both say 'thank you' to Mr. Fortunado," she told them.

Both children turned toward the newcomer in their lives.

"Thank you!" Ava and Axel cried almost in unison. This time there was no mistaking the enthusiasm in their voices.

"My pleasure," Connor told the duo, pretending to bow his head in acknowledgment to their thanks.

"Now go clean up your room," Brianna told them. "Mr. Fortunado and I have work to do." The long faces were not lost on Brianna. "It's either that, or you go out and play in the backyard."

That required no prolonged debate at all. Axel made his choice instantly. "Play!"

"We'll go play," Ava told her mother with no hesitation.

Brianna waited until her children had dashed out of the room and gone out to play before she turned toward Connor holding the pizza box. She wasn't sure if he was just being generous, or if he felt that she was having trouble feeding him as well as her children.

"You didn't have to bring lunch," she told him.

"You fed me. I thought it was only fair that I return the favor, at least once." Connor realized it was a slip of the tongue the second he'd said it. He hadn't meant to say "at least once." That meant he had plans to come back for lunch again—and he didn't. He didn't want it to sound as if he was committing to anything—because he wasn't, he silently insisted.

"Well, I appreciate it," she told him crisply, trying her best to be gracious.

Brianna took the pizza into the kitchen. When he followed her, she took advantage of having him there. Still holding the box, she turned toward him.

"Would you mind putting it on that shelf?" she asked, pointing to the highest shelf in the pantry.

He looked a little bemused. "Why not just leave it on the counter?"

"Simple. I don't want Ava and Axel succumbing to temptation," she told him. Passing the box to him, Brianna caught a whiff of the pizza. "That does smell good," she commented with appreciation.

What he caught a whiff of was not the pizza but the very light fragrance that Brianna tended to wear. Something delicate and flowery. It made him think of that old line about stopping to smell the roses.

"Yes, it does," he agreed in a low, appreciative voice.

Brianna felt a wave of heat flash over her entire body.

If she didn't know better, she would have said that Connor wasn't really talking about the pizza.

But of course he had to be, she told herself the next moment. She was letting her imagination get the better of her.

"Um, you can put the box right up there," she told him, pointing up to the shelf above her.

As Connor started to do as she instructed, the corner of the pizza box accidentally hit a box of rice that was precariously perched on the edge of that shelf, knocking it down. The box of rice flipped as it fell and since it apparently had been opened, it rained grains of rice all over Brianna.

More than a little of the rice wound up in her hair.

Connor really didn't want to laugh. He had a feeling that it would either make Brianna angry or embarrass her. But he couldn't help himself. She did look rather adorable with all that rice looking as if it was woven through her hair.

"I am sorry," he apologized, losing his struggle not to laugh as he quickly brushed as much rice out of her hair as he could.

"That would sound a little more believable if you weren't laughing," she told him.

He noted with relief that Brianna didn't seem to be angry.

"Sorry," Connor apologized again, biting his lip to keep a laugh back. "I'm not laughing," he protested, although not very believably.

"Your eyes are laughing," Brianna pointed out.

"No, they're not," he protested.

Connor continued brushing the rice out of her hair, doing his best to focus on getting the grains out and not looking at her.

"I'm not very good at this," he confessed ruefully. He reached around her to get the rice at the back of her head.

Somehow, as he did so, Connor wound up getting much too close to her. That, in turn, led to something else. Something he hadn't counted on.

Before Connor could stop himself, he kissed her.

It was hard to say who that surprised more, him or her.

Connor fully expected her to pull away. But she didn't.

And he couldn't.

At that moment it occurred to him that he had been wondering all along what it would feel like to kiss Brianna. To press his lips against hers with feeling.

When it happened, he couldn't really begin to describe it. Couldn't encapsulate the sensation into words.

He just went with it, losing himself in the taste of her lips and reveling in it.

Just like that, Brianna lost all concept of time and place, feeling as if she'd suddenly fallen through the mythical rabbit hole and rather than try to pull herself out of it, she just continued to free-fall, to whirl around within the endless, bottomless cylinder.

All she could do was to draw in the delicious sensation vibrating through her and—just for the moment—allow herself to enjoy it.

Pleasure reached out to every single part of her.

What if the kids come in now?

The sudden thought flashed through her mind and was enough to startle her back to reality. Brianna pulled her head away from him.

She was breathing very hard. It took a great deal of concentration to get herself under control and not sound as if she'd just raced up three flights of stairs doing double time.

Connor looked at her as if he had never seen her before and maybe he hadn't.

Not in this light.

By doing nothing else except kissing him back, Brianna had knocked his proverbial socks off.

He had not seen that coming, and at first, he didn't know how to handle it—or himself.

"Sorry," he mumbled.

Brianna thought he was apologizing for kissing her and she didn't want him to.

"For knocking over the box and getting all that rice in your hair," he said, completing the sentence.

He *wasn't* apologizing for kissing her, she thought. She hadn't expected to be so happy and relieved that he wasn't.

Despite having a relationship in her past and two children from that relationship, this was all brand-new to her.

"That's all right," she finally replied. "I don't remember when I put that rice up there. It was probably stale anyway, being opened like that for who knows how long."

Connor looked around at the mess that had spilled out all over the floor. "You have a broom around somewhere?" he wanted to know. "I'll clean all this up."

The offer caught her off guard even more than the falling box of rice had. In all their time together, Jonny had never lifted a finger to help her around the house. He'd get up from the table leaving his dishes, and any clothes he took off wound up on the floor. It got to the point where she just accepted that as normal male behavior. Obviously, it wasn't.

"You're serious?" she asked Connor.

"I knocked it over. I should be the one who cleans it up," he told her.

"Okay." Brianna opened the door to the tall, narrow closet located opposite the pantry. Taking out the broom and dustpan, she held out both to Connor. "Take your pick," she said. When he reached for the broom, she said, "Okay, I'll hold the dustpan."

"Teamwork," he said with an approving smile. "And by the way, I'll pay for the rice," he added as an afterthought.

"I already told you, it was probably stale at this point. Besides, that was the store's own brand," she told Connor. "It didn't exactly cost me a king's ransom." She squatted down, holding the dustpan in position as he swept up the rice.

It wasn't just the cost, it was the inconvenience—and his being clumsy, Connor thought. "I still feel bad about knocking it over."

Brianna waved away his guilt as she rose to her feet and dumped the rice into the garbage. Turning, she squatted down again, holding the dustpan in place for Connor.

"You bought lunch, I absolve you. Consider us even," she said.

"Speaking of even," he said, getting the last of the rice. "Have you deposited the check yet?"

Brianna emptied the dustpan, then placed it back in the closet. She was stalling, trying to brace herself for what possibly might be coming. Was he going to tell her that he'd changed his mind about paying her? Or was he going to say that there were no funds to cover the check after all?

"I was going to do that Friday," she said. "Do you want me to hold off?"

He looked surprised that she would ask that. "No, I was just wondering why the check hadn't been accounted for yet."

Her smile was somewhat sheepish as she admitted, "I just wanted to hold on to it in case you decided that you changed your mind."

He handed her back the broom. "Cash it," he instructed. "The funds aren't going anywhere."

And neither was he, he silently added.

For now.

Chapter Ten

He caught himself watching Brianna while they all ate lunch.

Watching her and thinking.

It surprised Connor that he had mixed feelings about what had just happened between them. Normally, whenever he kissed a woman, no matter who initiated the kiss, it registered as a pleasurable experience, one that, on most occasions, led to something more physical. But then, for one reason or another, the effects would always fade and he would move on to something else.

To some*one* else.

But this time it was different. Or it *would* be different, he thought. If he was inclined to get involved with Brianna. What made it different was that she came as a package deal. There were children to consider. Children he actually found himself liking.

Children who would be hurt once he left, he thought. Because he *always* left. No matter how long or short the relationship lasted, he never committed to it, not in any sort of a permanent way. It just wasn't him.

And yet...

There was no "yet," he silently insisted. Whatever this strange feeling was, it would be over with soon enough. And he'd be home again, living the high life again.

He couldn't think about this now, Connor silently insisted. He had a dangerous woman to track down and catch and everything else had to come second—if it came at all. Which it wouldn't, he promised himself. Right now, he still had credit card activity to follow up on. The woman had to be out there somewhere.

A small, high-pitched voice broke into his thoughts, scattering them.

"Why aren't you talking?" Ava wanted to know, looking up at Connor.

To cover his temporary lapse, Connor said the first thing that came to his mind. "Because I'm busy eating."

"I can eat and talk at the same time," Axel told him. "Why can't you?"

This time it was Brianna who came to his rescue. "Because it's not polite to talk with your mouth full," she told her son.

"I don't," Axel protested, looking hurt as he looked at his mother. "I chew fast. See?" he asked, giving her a demonstration that involved chewing and then opening his mouth for his mother.

"Oooh, gross!" Ava cried, wrinkling her nose.

"Make him close his mouth!" Her request was directed toward Connor. "He'll listen to you."

This was getting out of hand, Brianna thought. First he'd thrown her for a loop by kissing her, and now her children were acting out because of him.

"Axel, behave," Brianna ordered. "You, too, Ava," she told her daughter, who had started to laugh at her brother, pointing a finger at him because he'd been called out.

"What did I do?" Ava wanted to know, pouting.

"Axel, Ava, Mr. Fortunado was nice enough to bring over pizza for the two of you. At least try to behave like little people instead of little wild animals," Brianna requested.

Grateful to have something to focus on besides his confused feelings toward Brianna, Connor looked at her two children.

"Would you two have liked me to bring something else for lunch besides pizza?" he asked.

"Oh no, we love pizza," Axel told him with feeling, stressing the word *love*.

"We'd eat it every day if Mama let us," Ava said, bobbing her head.

"But then it wouldn't be special, would it?" Connor pointed out.

"Yes it would," Axel said with conviction. "There're so many different kinds of pizza to eat," the little boy told him.

"Well, that answer's too smart for me," Connor told Axel, pretending to surrender. He glanced at Brianna. "You've got a couple of special kids here," he told her.

Axel and Ava were both beaming at the compliment.

Brianna loved seeing them like that—proud and *quiet*, she thought, suppressing a grin. She raised her eyes to Connor's. Just for a moment, she wondered what it would have been like if *he* had been their father instead of Jonny, wherever he was now.

That thought pulled her up short. She couldn't let herself go there. There was no point in fantasizing about something that didn't even have a prayer of happening. She had too much to deal with right now to let her mind wander like that.

"I guess I do at that," she agreed quietly.

The pizza disappeared in an amazingly short amount of time.

Moving slightly back from the table, Connor held his stomach as if it ached. "I think I ate too much," he groaned.

"*You* ate too much?" Brianna laughed. Despite cautioning them, Axel and Ava had wolfed down their food as if it was the last they would see for a long time. "These two ate so much I'm surprised they're not exploding."

Axel's eyes widened in fear. "Can we do that?" he asked not his mother but Connor, who seemed to be his go-to authority on everything. "Can we explode?"

Connor tried to recall if he had ever been this literal when he'd been Axel's age, but he couldn't remember. Whether or not he was, he was quick to set the boy's mind at ease without directly contradicting his mother.

"You have a long, long way to go before that ever happens," he assured Axel and his sister. "But all that food might have made you sleepy. You might want to take a nap."

"No, no naps," Axel cried with a little less vigor than he would have been inclined to display if he'd been less full.

"How about playing a quiet game, then?" Connor suggested, thinking that doing anything more strenuous right now might cause the boy to throw up.

Axel's eyes lit up. "Sure! What kind of a game you wanna play?"

"I wanna play, too!" Ava said eagerly, adding her voice to that of her brother. She made it clear that she wasn't going to be left out.

"I didn't—"

How had this happened? Connor wondered, stunned. He hadn't meant that he wanted to play a game with them, only that they should play a game with each other. He was just trying to come up with something they could do that didn't require them being physically taxed.

Brianna felt sorry for him. She knew exactly what it was like to feel outnumbered by the twosome. "I think that Mr. Fortunado meant that you two should be the ones to find a game to play," she told her children as she stacked all their dishes together.

"No, he didn't," Axel protested fiercely. And then the little boy turned to look at Connor, expecting the man to back him up. "Did you?"

Connor had never had trouble saying no to people, not even to his superiors if he felt strongly about something. He'd always been the kind of person who stuck to his guns no matter what the situation was. But to his dismay, he found that when two small, sad faces looked up at him hopefully, the word *no* was somehow emulsified, vanishing from the face of the earth.

"You're right," he told them, nodding his head. "I didn't."

Oh Lord, she didn't want to lose her heart to this man, she really didn't. It was only asking for trouble, she thought. She'd been that route and wound up having her heart handed back to her, crushed and carelessly stuffed into a plastic bag like so much confetti.

But reason just wasn't working here. She could feel her heart slipping away from her and moving toward this man who had fixed her toilet rather than tell her that she'd made a mistake. This man who gave in to her children rather than disappoint them by just shrugging them off and turning away.

Each of the children grabbed one of his hands, pulling him to his feet. "Looks like they have plans for me," Connor said as they began to drag him away.

Brianna rose, holding the stacked dishes. "Do you want to be rescued?" she asked him, ready to call off her children if he gave the word.

His grin was amused rather than martyr-like. "Not particularly."

"Okay," she said, backing off. "Just remember," she told him, smiling despite her attempts to keep a straight face, "this was your idea." She'd been saying that to him a lot lately.

"C'mon," Axel cried, tugging insistently on his hand. "No more talking to Mom. The game's in our room."

She saw Connor looking over his shoulder at her. He actually looked as if he was enjoying himself, she thought. "I'll be in their room."

"I know where that is," Brianna replied, humoring him. "I'll be working in my office," she wanted him to know. She said the words just before he disappeared around the corner.

Brianna turned to go back to her office. She could hear Ava's and Axel's gleeful laughter floating down the hall from the opposite direction.

It's just a game he's going to be playing with them. Don't overthink this and don't get carried away, she warned herself.

But it was really hard not to.

By the time Connor finally walked into her office, it was more than two hours later.

She was aware of his presence before she even turned around. Somehow, the very air felt different to her.

"I was getting ready to send out a search party for you," Brianna quipped.

He laughed, not at her but at his own part in this. "Every time I started to get up after a game was over, they talked me into playing 'just one more,'" he told her, sitting down in the extra chair she'd brought into the room. The chair had eaten up what little space was left within the office.

"Your kids can be very persuasive," Connor informed her.

Brianna laughed. "You realize that you're preaching to the choir," she told him. "It turns out that everything with them is always a negotiation, or a battle of wills. You'd think that kids so young would go along with everything I tell them to do. Ha!"

She laughed at the very notion of complete, uncomplicated obedience from her children. That would be the day, she thought. And, although it might be nice once in a while, she really did love their spirit. Just as she loved them.

"Half the time you'd think that they were the parents and I was the kid."

In his opinion, Brianna sounded as if she was being too hard on herself. "Oh, I don't know. I think you've done a pretty good job raising them."

"All smoke and mirrors," she confessed. "I'm really just hanging on by my fingertips."

"And you've raised them without any help?" he asked. She'd told him that the children's father had walked out on her, but maybe there was someone else she could turn to, someone to help her, like a relative who was there for her.

But the next moment, she shook her head, letting him know that she hadn't done absolutely *everything* by herself.

"Occasionally, I get a sitter to stay with them and there's Beth Wilson." She saw curiosity enter Connor's eyes.

"She's the mother of two kids who are about Ava and Axel's age. She watches them when I go in to my two other jobs, but I'm not at either one of those places for long periods of time," she said quickly.

"So what you're saying is that there's really no one

you can turn to for help with the kids on a long-term basis," Connor concluded.

"No, not on a long-term basis," Brianna confirmed. With a sigh she told him, "For better or worse, it's mostly me."

"Oh, I think it's for the better," Connor said with feeling. "Definitely for the better."

Brianna turned all the way around from her desk and looked at him, confused.

"I don't know why you're being so nice to me. My kids must have run you ragged these last two hours. I know what they're like when they get someone to play a game with them. I know they appreciate it, but actual war games are a lot easier to handle than playing with those two."

He laughed, amused by the comparison. "Oh, it wasn't so bad. I had fun."

The man obviously had a strange definition of *fun*, Brianna thought.

"Now you're just lying," she told him.

"No, I'm not," he assured Brianna. "Ava and Axel can be very entertaining when they want to."

She knew that she felt that way, but she had an excuse. She was their mother. Connor was someone who had absolutely no ties to her children, nothing to be gained by going easy on them or professing that he was enjoying himself.

Brianna looked at him closely, scrutinizing the man. He didn't look any different than he had before, but it really wasn't adding up.

"What did my kids do to you?" she wanted to know.

He laughed. Another woman would have taken the

easy way out and not pressed. She obviously valued honesty more.

"Nothing. They just reminded me what it was like to be their age. It's been a long time since I had such an innocent view of the world."

"Do you have any kids?" she asked, realizing that she knew nothing about this man who had invaded her children's lives and her own.

"Kids?" he repeated. "Oh God, no. They wouldn't fit into the life I have in Denver."

Denver. The man lived in Denver. And he made it sound as if he didn't want kids. Brianna felt her heart drop. Boy, she could sure pick 'em, she thought ruefully.

"Yes, well, listen," she said, rallying, "if they wore you out and you want to call it a day, I totally understand. You can come back tomorrow and we'll pick up where we left off. I'll be here—at least, in the morning," she clarified.

"Oh? Where'll you be in the afternoon?" he asked her before he thought better of it. It wasn't any of his business, he thought.

But he still wanted to know.

"I promised to fill in at the reception desk. Emily, the woman who's usually there tomorrow, has to take the afternoon off," she explained, "so they need me to come in. Unfortunately Beth isn't available so..."

"You need someone to watch the kids?"

Her kids were far too young to be left alone. Finding someone to watch them was on her to-do list today.

"Well, it's either that or not come home to a house," she told him simply.

He saw the wary look in her eyes. He didn't want to put her off. He needed her help. Connor realized that he needed to make amends, even if this wasn't his forte. "Why don't I watch the kids for you?" Connor volunteered. "That way, you won't have to pay a sitter and the kids already know me." He smiled at her. "They won't have to get used to anyone new."

Brianna looked at him, totally taken aback. "You really are a glutton for punishment, aren't you?" she marveled.

"No, I really enjoy it," he insisted. He was lying, but she didn't need to know that, he thought. He looked down and saw that Juliana, the calico cat who was the latest addition to Brianna's menagerie, was batting his pant cuff back and forth. Connor's eyes crinkled. "All of it," he added, amused. His words surprised him more than they did her.

"You say that now. Wait until Juliana misses and winds up scratching up your leg," Brianna predicted ominously.

Bending over, Brianna picked up the cat and carried her out of the room. She put the animal down and then retreated back into her office, this time closing the door behind her to keep the cat out.

"You're closing the door," Connor pointed out. Was that on purpose or by mistake? "Does that mean you want me to stay?"

Oh Lord, yes, Brianna thought, suddenly remembering the way his lips had felt against hers.

Because she found herself longing to feel that sensation again and knew how dangerous that was for her in her present state of mind, especially given that there was no future for them, Brianna said the first thing that came to mind.

"Actually, I didn't mean to close the door. It's just to discourage the cat. Just give it five minutes and then you can go. Otherwise, she might still be hanging around. Once she sees you again, she'll just exert her little feline wiles on you. Before you know it, you'll find Juliana wrapped around your leg or some other vital part you can't do without."

He laughed. "Everything about you is intriguing, Brianna. Even your pets."

"They all have unique personalities if that's what you mean. Actually, they're all strays. Or they were before I took them in." Brianna smiled ruefully.

She knew how that had to sound to someone who wasn't moved by stray animals.

"I have a penchant for attracting strays and trying to fix them," she admitted.

It had been that way all of her life, she thought. Jonny had just been another lost stray who she had tried to fix—and failed.

He had a feeling he knew where she was going with this. "I'm not a stray, Brianna," he assured her.

She looked away, pretending to look for something on her desk. "I didn't say you were."

He ignored her protest. Neither one of them believed it. "And you won't have to fix me."

She smiled then. Her eyes met his. "That's a matter of opinion."

Intrigued, he asked, "You think I need fixing?"

"I think everyone needs fixing to some extent," she said evasively. "Some more than others."

"Interesting idea," he told her. "Maybe we'll pick this up when I come back tomorrow."

Brianna merely smiled. "You're the client."

Right. Then why did he feel like she was the one in the driver's seat?

Chapter Eleven

When he came over to Brianna's house the following day, Connor went through what had by now become his usual ritual: greeting Axel and Ava and answering any of their questions.

It amazed him how two young children could come up with so many different questions to ask each and every time.

Eventually, Brianna managed to herd the two away, directing her children either to the yard, the living room or their room, and they were always prevailed upon to go play, which they did, but never without protest.

"They certainly are a handful," Connor commented, not for the first time, as he followed her into her office. "Dealing with all this every day, how do you manage to stay sane?"

She grinned at him. "Who says I'm sane?"

"Well, you seem pretty sane to me," Connor told her.

"And the illusion continues," Brianna said cryptically.

Pausing at her desk, she picked up several folders she'd been working on and handed them to Connor. "These are all the rest of the names I managed to track down for Charlene—Charlotte." Brianna corrected herself before Connor could.

Connor accepted the folders from her, folders it was now obvious that she had placed elsewhere once the project had been suspended.

He knew that she had to have unearthed them after doing some really intensive searching through the plastic drawers she referred to as her "filing cabinet."

"What's that?" he asked, nodding at a stray paper on top. At first glance it looked like a photocopied list of names.

She didn't have to look to know what he was referring to. "Those are the names I didn't get a chance to look for," Brianna explained.

Connor wasn't sure if he understood her. "Come again?"

Taking the adjacent chair, she pulled it closer to the desk and sat down facing Connor. "Well, initially, this Charlotte person sent me about ten names, all people she wanted to locate. I reported back to her regularly on my progress and, like I said, she paid half up front and promised the rest when I finished. But she kept adding names to that list and there turned out to be a great many people who weren't exactly easy to find, so I concentrated on the ones that I *could* find and did those first.

"When she didn't make good on her payment for the

next installment of reports I sent her, I stopped trying to locate people. I was waiting for her to live up to her side of the deal," she confessed. Brianna shrugged, at a loss. "She never got back to me and then I got that Return to Sender letter back in the mail. Since she'd made it clear through her actions that she wasn't going to pay any more money and that she obviously didn't want to be found herself, I didn't continue looking for any of these other people."

"Wow," he murmured under his breath as he thumbed through the remaining list of names. "But you think you can find these people?" he asked.

"Well, I can't promise anything," Brianna told him cautiously, "but I can certainly try."

He looked at the list again. It astonished him how one man could have been responsible for bringing so many people into the world. Finding them was going to be a big job, he thought.

"I'll pay you, of course," he told Brianna in case he hadn't made that clear to her.

"In addition to the three thousand dollars you've already paid?" she asked him, surprised.

"Well, sure," he told her. He didn't expect her to do this strictly out of charity. This was going to take effort. "This is additional work on your part." He saw the puzzled expression on her face. "What?"

"I have to ask," Brianna told him, concerned that maybe she was getting involved in something that had more to it than there seemed to be on the surface. She knew she'd already asked him once before without really getting an answer, but this time she felt she needed it. She didn't want to risk getting involved in something illegal. "Why are you trying to find the same people that this woman was looking for?"

Connor debated whether or not to tell her. Quite honestly, he'd been feeling rather guilty about keeping Brianna in the dark this way—not that any of this would affect her. She certainly wasn't in any danger the way some, if not all, of the people on that list were. The list, if he were to take a guess, contained the names of all the family members who were related to Gerald Robinson either directly or indirectly.

And Charlotte, he knew, hated all of them. Not in principle, but in actual fact. In his estimation, the woman was a walking psycho. Gerald leaving Charlotte to be with his "first love" had obviously pushed the woman over the edge and now she was bent on getting her revenge on the whole lot of them.

Brianna was still looking at him, waiting for an answer.

Connor made up his mind.

"To warn them," he told her.

"Warn them?" she repeated, no less confused than she had been a moment ago. "Warn them about what?" she wanted to know.

That was just it. He didn't know any of the actual particulars. Didn't know what further mayhem Charlotte was capable of.

Frustrated, he told Brianna, "That they could be in danger."

She felt as if they were taking baby steps here, trying to get to the truth. "From what?"

"From Charlotte," he said bluntly.

Ordinarily, she'd just back away and let him keep

whatever secret he was trying to preserve. But she'd come this far, she wasn't about to stop until he gave her an answer that made some sense to her.

"I don't understand."

She was an outsider, not family, but in his opinion, Brianna had earned the right to know some things. "It's my feeling that Charlotte wants to hurt as many of these people as she can."

"But why?" Brianna pressed. Why would anyone want to hurt people she didn't even know or had never met?

"It's complicated," he told her, thinking of all the stories he'd come across regarding Gerald Robinson.

She knew what that meant, Brianna thought, frowning. "So you're not going to tell me," she guessed.

He blew out a breath. The die had been cast. "No, I am. You just have to keep a very open mind," he warned. When Brianna nodded, Connor began. "In a nutshell, some of the people on this list are her husband's offspring and she's determined to track them all down."

"His offspring?" Brianna repeated, stunned. "There's got to be almost twenty-five people on that list. Maybe even more."

She wasn't saying anything that he wasn't aware of. "I know."

"And you're telling me that they're all his—his children?" she asked incredulously, still unable to wrap her mind around what Connor was saying.

He laughed dryly. There was no humor in the sound. "The man got around. But this also includes his half brothers' kids."

Brianna's eyes widened as she looked at all the names on the list again. Names of people she'd searched for and found. Names of people she hadn't gotten around to looking for. And names of people she'd looked for but hadn't found. And all these people were most likely in the dark about their family tree.

It was beginning to make a little sense to her now. "Is that why you're trying to find them first?" she asked Connor. "So you can find a way to break it to them to minimize their getting hurt?"

Connor shook his head. "If that was the only thing, I'd just let it all go and hope for the best. It's really none of my business if they know or don't know. But I honestly don't know how far Charlotte will go in order to get her revenge." He frowned, thinking of the havoc the woman had already caused. "She's already done a lot of damage."

"What's she done?" Brianna wanted to know.

She looked so innocent, for a second, he had second thoughts about exposing her to all this ugliness. But he wanted her help, so he told her.

"For openers, I'm ninety-nine point nine percent positive that she's the one who burned down Gerald Robinson's mansion."

Stunned, Brianna asked, "She's an arsonist?"

Connor nodded. "That's what I think." Since he'd opened the door on this, he continued. "And she's also behind the creative sabotage that caused Fortunado Real Estate to lose so many clients, not to mention the cyberattack on Robinson Tech," he added grimly.

They were back to this not making any sense to her. "If this Charlotte woman is behind a cyberattack, what did she need me for?" Anyone capable of launching a cyberattack was able to find people using the internet.

He'd already thought about that. "I think she approached you first. The cyberattack happened just in the last couple of months." Charlotte was either upping her game, or finding people willing to do her bidding for a price without asking any questions.

"Maybe I should be happy that she disappeared out of my life." It was clear to Brianna that she had dodged a bullet.

He put his hand over hers. "Unless you have the bad luck of being one of Gerald's multitude of kids, I don't think you have anything to worry about."

A person who was so out for revenge didn't always stay within the lines, she knew. "But you can't be sure."

"You're right, I can't," Connor agreed. "But I'd say Charlotte's too focused on hurting her ex-husband's progeny to waste her time and effort on hurting an outsider."

Brianna shook her head, still having trouble taking all this in. She hadn't had an easy time of it in her life, but she couldn't visualize the kind of anger that would make someone plot this sort of far-reaching revenge. Or any kind of revenge for that matter.

"It's hard to believe that someone can be this eaten up by hate," she told him.

Connor smiled at her as he tucked a bit of stray hair behind Brianna's ear. "You really are a good person, Brianna," he commented.

She wasn't so sure about that. Good people didn't have these sorts of feelings rushing through them in response to someone just casually brushing against their skin.

"Not all the time," she finally told him quietly.

Damn it, they were sitting here talking about Charlotte, the Dragon Lady. The very personification of evil. So why, in the middle of all this, was he suddenly wanting Brianna? And why, in the middle of all this, of discovering that there were more people he had to find, to warn, was he suddenly consumed with the desire to possess this woman?

She was the single mother of two little kids, kids she was struggling every day to provide for. He had no right to disrupt her life because he wanted her.

No right at all.

It didn't seem to matter.

Logic was not getting in his way. It was *not* keeping him from leaning into her and rediscovering just how sweet her mouth was.

And it was.

It was very, very sweet, he thought, as what had begun as just a quick kiss flowered into something a great deal more. Something that shook him down to his very toes even as it begged him to go on, to lose himself in all that Brianna had to offer.

Oh Lord, she had promised herself that this wasn't going to happen again, that she wouldn't get close enough to him physically to be tempted to relive that spectacular kiss that she had sampled the other day. And yet, here she was again, feeling her heart slamming against her chest so hard, she thought her ribs would crack. This kiss was stealing away her very breath even as it somehow managed to magically dim the very sunlight that had, until a second ago, been in the room.

Struggling, she managed to gather what little strength she had left and somehow pulled her head back.

"I can't do this," she told him, trying very hard not to sound as if she was breathless. "I can't get involved with you." Her eyes pleaded with him to understand. "It's not that I don't want to, but I have to think of the kids."

"They like me," he reminded her, his voice surrounding her. Keeping her warm.

"That's just the problem. They *like* you," she told him. "They're used to you. And you're not going to be staying." She released a shaky breath, searching for words to make him understand why she was pushing him away. "You don't even live in Houston," she cried. "When we finish finding those people on that list— when we finish our business together—you'll be gone and…they'll be devastated."

She'd almost said that she would be devastated but stopped herself at the last moment. He didn't need to know that.

"I've got to remember that and not let them sense that there's anything going on between us," Brianna told him. "Because then they'd really think that you were going to stay."

"They won't know," he argued.

Connor realized that he was pleading his case without actually saying the words—but he *was* pleading. Because that was how much he wanted her.

She shook her head, dismissing his words. "They're kids. Kids intuit things. They'll know." She willed herself to fight back tears. "I'm sorry, Connor, but I can't."

"No, I'm the one who's sorry," he told her with emotion. "For a lot of reasons." Connor raised his hands like someone who was backing off from something he desperately wanted to touch. "Don't worry, I'll back off," he promised. "You don't have anything to worry about from me, Brianna. I give you my word. Scout's honor," he added with a wink.

She sincerely doubted that the man sitting at the desk right next to her had ever been a Boy Scout, but she pretended to take him at his word.

After all, it wasn't as if she had any other choice available to her.

Any further discussion of this truce they had awkwardly struck was suddenly tabled as it became clear to them that they were not alone. And this time, it wasn't one of the pets that had come wandering into the office.

Instead, it was Ava.

Brianna forced a smile to her face as she looked at her daughter. "What are you doing here, sugarplum? I thought you were playing with Axel."

"He's in the bathroom," Ava dutifully informed her mother with a shrug just before she dropped her bombshell. Turning toward Connor, she asked, "Were you kissing Mama?"

Connor was very grateful that he hadn't just taken a sip of the coffee he had brought into the room earlier. If he had, right now he'd either be choking or spraying it all over everything like a human geyser.

It took a minute for him to clear his throat sufficiently to speak.

"I'm sorry, what?" he asked. He was trying to stall

as his mind raced around for the right way to answer Ava's question without either feeding her young imagination or lying.

"Were you kissing Mama?" she repeated, then told him guilelessly, "It looked like you were."

"How do you know about kissing?" Brianna asked her younger child.

Ava gave her mother a look that all but said: You have to be kidding. She tossed her head. "I know about kissing, Mama."

"Your mother had something in her eye," Connor spoke up out of the blue. "I had to get in close so I could get it out."

"Oh." The answer seemed to satisfy the little girl. She bobbed her head up and down. "Okay." And then she looked at Connor intently. "Are you finished in here with Mama yet?"

"No, not yet," Connor answered, hoping she was asking if he was finished working and not if he was finished kissing her mother.

Again Ava nodded. "Okay. Come find me when you are," she told him just before she made her way out of the room again. A small adult trapped in a child's body.

Brianna turned to look at him. There was no need for words. The expression on her face said it all. That what had just happened proved her point and backed up the reasons why she couldn't afford to get involved with him no matter how tempting that was.

He took his cue and got as comfortable as he could sitting at her desk. "I guess we'd better get back to work before Ava comes looking for me again."

She'd never seen her daughter like this, or her son

for that matter. Both of her children had taken to Connor almost instantly. She'd be more than happy about that if she and Connor were serious about one another.

But no matter what she might feel, she could tell that Connor was not the type to get serious about anyone, not in the true sense of the word. Not when *serious* meant everlasting commitment. Connor represented the exact opposite of that. He was the very definition of a carefree bachelor and she was certain that he intended to stay that way.

And as long as he felt that way, she was not about to let her guard down and let him in.

She couldn't.

Chapter Twelve

Right after he fulfilled his babysitting obligation, he tried to stay away, he really did.

Full of selfless, altruistic intentions, Connor's resolution to keep his distance from Brianna lasted all of one day before finally crumbling.

The so-called leads that he told himself he needed to run down turned out to be nothing more than paper trails that really led nowhere.

Just as he suspected they would.

Presently, the most useful information he had to work with was all coming out of Brianna's past efforts on behalf of Charlotte, as well as the efforts she was putting into working with the list of names that Charlotte had forwarded to her.

So, after spending what felt like a completely restless night tossing and turning in his bed and then coming up with every excuse he could think of not to turn up on her doorstep, Connor turned up on Brianna's doorstep the following afternoon.

Even so, standing before her door, he wrestled with his conscience, raising his hand and then dropping it to his side before he could ring her doorbell.

Anyone watching him from the street would have assumed he was crazy, Connor thought.

And maybe he was, he conceded as he finally made contact with her doorbell and pressed it.

The chiming sound seemed to vibrate in his chest, mocking him.

Time froze until he saw the door open.

And then there she was, Brianna, standing in the doorway. He watched as a myriad of emotions passed over her face in the space of a few seconds.

And then she recovered, clearing her throat. "Um, I was beginning to think that you had decided to pursue another route in tracking down your target."

"I was just looking into a few things that didn't wind up panning out," Connor said, telling her the first thing that came to his mind.

Since Brianna was still standing, blocking the doorway, he nodded toward the inside of her house. "Can I come in?"

"What?" Realizing that she was standing in his way like a statue, she snapped to life. "Oh sure. Of course." Painfully aware of how awkward she had to sound to Connor, Brianna turned away from him and led the way back to her office. "I've been looking into some of the other names," she told him.

"Even though I wasn't here?" he questioned. He

found himself looking at her, puzzled. What kind of a woman was she? "I mean, I didn't call you about not coming over yesterday. Given the so-called family record," he said, thinking of Charlotte, "you would have been within your rights to think I was guilty of pulling a disappearing act."

Now that he'd raised the point, she wanted it clarified. "Why didn't you call?" she wanted to know.

There was no actual good reason he could give her. "I got caught up in something," he answered evasively.

It was the shakiest of lies, but telling a woman you were trying to keep your distance from her didn't sound like the best way to go, either, especially now that he really wanted to put all that behind him.

Brianna nodded, as if accepting the flimsy excuse. "Well, I didn't have anything to work on at the moment and no one called me yesterday to fill in, so I thought I might as well just continue hunting for any information on those missing family members," she explained.

He couldn't see someone as busy as Brianna not having anything to do.

"You mean the dynamic duo didn't manage to run you ragged yesterday?" he asked. As soon as the words were out of his mouth, he glanced out to the hallway, expecting the children to appear. They didn't. "Speaking of which, where is my welcoming committee?" he asked Brianna. "I haven't seen or heard them since I walked in a whole five minutes ago." He stepped out into the hall to look around, but he didn't see either one of them. "They usually come charging out by now."

"Well, if they're charging out, it's at Joey and Debbie's house, not mine." She smiled to herself, thinking how both of her children had pleaded with her to let them go. It was starting. Her children were beginning to grow up. Before she knew it, they'd be getting married and leaving. The prospect of an empty nest was not all that far away, and she felt sad.

"Joey and Debbie?" he repeated, unfamiliar with the names Brianna had just mentioned.

"Friends from the park," she explained. "Their poor, brave mother—my babysitter, Beth—and her husband are hosting a slumber party for them at their house tonight."

He didn't care how brave the other woman was, he was concerned about Axel and Ava. "Aren't they a little young to be going to a slumber party?" he asked. The second the words were out, he realized that he was making noises like a parent, but the truth of it was he *didn't* think they were old enough to attend a slumber party. What had Brianna been thinking? "How many kids are going to be there?"

"Counting my two and her two?" Brianna asked. When he nodded, she answered, "Four. Beth thought she'd start out small and see how it goes. I'll probably have to wind up reciprocating." She could hear her children pleading for a slumber party of their own already. "But not until I finish working on your project."

Picking up a folder, she looked at him. "Any questions?"

"Yes. How can you stand it?" he asked her, gesturing around him to indicate the rest of the house. He was only half kidding. "It's so quiet."

She paused for a moment, cocking her head as if listening.

"It is, isn't it?" Brianna agreed. "I forgot what this could be like, working without having the walls shake every fifteen, twenty minutes." The awkwardness behind them and having slipped back into a comfortable groove with Connor again, she said, "Shall we get started?"

The next four hours were spent following up on the lead that Brianna had managed to find, plus discovering information on another person on the list along the way. The latter had happened almost by accident.

Verifications were made as well as plans to follow up with a phone call and eventually, hopefully, a face-to-face meeting.

It was all beginning to fall into place.

Leaning back in her chair, Brianna looked rather satisfied with their joint effort.

"All in all, I think we've had a very productive afternoon," she told Connor. She rotated her shoulders. They had begun to ache.

"Afternoon?" he echoed, glancing at his watch. "It's almost evening. I didn't realize we've been at this for so long," he admitted.

"I guess I can get a lot done when I'm not rushing out to check into screams and crashes every few minutes," she said with a smile. "Are you hungry?" she asked suddenly, turning toward him.

"You don't have to make dinner," Connor told her. She'd worked almost harder than he had today. He didn't want her going to any extra trouble now on his account.

Brianna waved away his protest. Besides, she wasn't making anything from scratch.

"How do you feel about leftovers?" she asked. "I made meat loaf yesterday and it's not exactly the kids' favorite."

Right now, he was hungry enough to eat the pan the meat loaf had been made in, although he kept that to himself.

"Meat loaf sounds great," Connor answered, then added, "But just so you know, I would have settled for peanut butter and jelly. Or just peanut butter," he told her.

She laughed, trying to picture him eating a peanut butter and jelly sandwich. She really couldn't. "You know, for a man of your background, you don't have very expensive tastes."

Connor wasn't sure he followed her. "My background?" he questioned.

Maybe she should explain, Brianna thought. "I said I had time on my hands. I spent part of that doing a little background research on you," she confessed. "Fortunado Real Estate—you're part of that, aren't you?" she asked, citing the real estate company that he'd told her had experienced a severe downturn.

What was she getting at? he wondered. "I didn't try to hide that," he pointed out.

"No, you didn't," she agreed, then explained her thinking. "But you showed me your private investigator credentials and a private investigator isn't the first thing that comes to mind when someone thinks of Fortunado Real Estate."

For a second he thought she was going to withhold any further information until he agreed to up her payment. He'd been dealing with people who were only out for themselves for too long.

But he knew better. Brianna wasn't like that.

Relaxing, he asked, "Is this your way of saying that your offer of meat loaf is off the table?"

Rather than go on explaining why she'd decided to look into his background and wind up embarrassing herself, she decided that the safest thing to do was just to feed him.

"Come with me," Brianna told him, taking hold of his hand.

"To the ends of the world," he quipped, then added, "Or the kitchen, whichever is first."

She laughed, dropping his hand. "You're crazy. You know that, don't you?"

He took no offense, knowing she didn't intend any. "I usually play with the kids to use up any excess energy I might have. They're not here so I guess you get to see this side of me. I can usually keep it hidden," he added with a straight face.

"Uh-huh."

Brianna warmed up what was left of the meat loaf in the microwave, then put the platter on the table. A serving of corn and leftover mashed potatoes accompanied the main dish.

Connor set the table for them as she warmed the meal. He'd been here often enough now to know where everything was kept and taking part in the domestic scene felt right. It made him uneasy that this came to him so effortlessly. This wasn't the self-image he had of himself. Why wasn't he running for his life?

"Much better than peanut butter and jelly," he commented, sitting down when she did.

She noted that he had set the table and smiled her thanks.

"They asked about you, you know. Yesterday, when you didn't come, the kids asked about you," Brianna explained. "They wanted to know what I'd done to chase you away."

He'd just taken a bite of the meat loaf and had to wait until he swallowed before asking, "What did you tell them?"

She thought of being confronted by the duo. Both had been deadly serious. "That you were a busy man and had other things to do besides working on a project here."

"Did that satisfy them?" he asked as he continued eating. His mind was hardly on the food. She'd stirred his curiosity with her story. And his libido with her nearness.

"No," Brianna said with a sigh. "They were convinced that I'd done something to make you stay away."

He waited for a couple of minutes before quietly saying, "Well, in a way, you could say that the two pipsqueaks were right."

Brianna looked up sharply at him. "I *did* do something to make you stay away?" she asked him, even though, in the back of her mind, a little voice had answered that very question yesterday, undermining her confidence. She'd managed to squelch the voice but here he was saying the same thing. "What?" she wanted to know. "What did I do to suddenly make you stay away?"

He paused, debating the wisdom of what he was about to say.

And then he said it.

"You were you."

Brianna frowned. "That makes no sense."

He didn't see it that way. "It does when I'm struggling to do the honorable thing, to stay away from you the way I promised."

"I didn't ask you to stay away," she denied. "I just asked you not to..." *Kiss me.* At a loss as to how to phrase it, Brianna found herself searching for words.

"Yeah, about that..." Connor reached over and cupped her cheek, trying his best to stifle feelings that were threatening to overwhelm him. "I can't. I can't stay away," he admitted. "I wasn't following up other leads yesterday," he confessed. "I was listing all the reasons why I should keep my distance from you. All the reasons why I should just go away." It had actually been a consideration. One he couldn't follow through on. "There was just one reason why I couldn't."

She nodded, guessing at the reason. "Because you wanted to find Charlotte."

"The hell with finding Charlotte," he said. Didn't Brianna understand what he was trying to tell her? "I couldn't go away because I couldn't get myself to leave you. To walk away and never see you again."

She had another theory about that. A far more common one.

"Maybe you can't leave because I turned you down. Probably no woman has ever said no to you before and it's a classic case of wanting something you can't have," she guessed.

"No," Connor insisted, "this is different." He saw the look that came into her eyes. "Don't worry, I'm not going to try to change your mind. I understand why you're telling me no and I respect your choice." Even though it was killing him, he added silently, "I just wanted you to know that despite everything that's currently going on in my life and despite trying to track down this woman who's trying to bring down my entire family, you were all I kept thinking about these last twenty-four hours. I couldn't get myself to focus on anything else."

She had what she wanted, Brianna thought. He was telling her that he wasn't going to try to get her to change her mind, wasn't going to try to seduce her, and she believed him. Once this project was completed, she could send Connor off and that would be that. She would be home free.

The hell she would be!

Getting up from the table, she stood beside Connor and pulled him up to his feet with her. Before he could ask her what she was doing or even say another word, Brianna threw her arms around his neck and brought her mouth up to his.

The kiss took him completely by surprise and totally incinerated every single word he had just said to her. All his noble intentions and promises just vanished into the night air as if they had never existed.

"Was it something I said?" he murmured against her lips even as he kissed her back.

"Shut up," was the only thing Brianna said before she utterly surrendered to what she had known since he had kissed her that first time was inevitable.

Her destiny.

Since she had dropped all the barriers she had so carefully constructed and diligently kept in place since Jonny had left her, Brianna expected Connor to lose no time in taking her, in uniting their bodies and satisfying the urges that she knew had to be consuming him.

She was completely surprised when instead of doing that, Connor took his time and made love to her instead. The experience was still fiery, but at the same time, his lovemaking was slow, deliberate, making her feel cherished and beautiful with every movement, every thrilling caress he delivered.

Instead of tearing off her clothes and throwing his own aside in a mad, overwhelming rush to consummate their union, Connor kissed her.

Slowly.

Deliberately.

He kissed her lips, her throat, her shoulders, sending shivers through her whole body with each touch of his mouth. His lips skimmed over each and every part of her that was exposed to him.

Somehow, although she wasn't totally aware of how, her clothes kept vanishing, allowing him to press his lips against more and more of her.

Claiming more and more of her.

She'd never made love like this before, never felt this mounting frenzy building within her before, turning her into this insatiable creature she didn't even recognize. She wasn't a shy, shrinking violet anymore. She was a woman possessed with a desire to give pleasure as well as receive it.

Somehow, without any conscious thought, she and

Connor made their way from the kitchen into the living room.

They never reached the bedroom.

It seemed as if it was leagues away and she felt demands vibrating through her body *now*.

But first she wanted Connor to remember tonight, to know that he made love with *her*, not just another one of the women she was certain passed through his life. Brianna suddenly wanted to leave her mark on his soul. Years from now, after another score of women had come and gone, she wanted him to remember this night.

To remember *her*.

She went with her instincts, some innate force he had woken up within her, and made love to Connor with the same verve and intensity that he had been making love with her.

Breathing heavily, their bodies gleaming with sweat, they finally began the last leg of this wondrous journey that was still before them.

With his eyes on hers and their hands laced together, Connor entered her.

Brianna used the last ounce of her energy to match him movement for movement, causing the sensation to swell and rush up, catching both of them in the last wave that pushed them all the way to the top.

Clinging to one another, they allowed the tide to come and carry them away.

Chapter Thirteen

"I guess it's a good thing the kids went to that sleepover," Brianna murmured.

She was curled up against Connor on the sofa. Euphoria was slowly settling in, taking the place of the wildly thrilling thunderbolts of desire that had all but done her in. She smiled as she ran her hand along his hair. "Otherwise, this might have been a little hard to explain."

"No, it wouldn't," Connor contradicted. "Because if Axel and Ava hadn't gone to that sleepover, this wouldn't have happened," he informed her, turning so that he could look into her face. He cradled her closer to him, their naked bodies touching, sending out renewed signals of longing. "At least, not until they were asleep and we were in your room with the door closed."

His response surprised her. It also warmed her.

"That's a very responsible approach," she told him, amazed that he would think of that. She'd just assumed that Connor would have put his own needs ahead of the children, especially since they weren't his and in all likelihood, he wouldn't be seeing them much longer.

"Why do you look so surprised?" he asked, brushing the back of his hand against her face, caressing her. "I'm not exactly a charging bull moose in heat."

Unable to hold herself in check, she started to laugh then, her body brushing up against his on the sofa. "I never thought of you as a bull moose, charging or otherwise," she confessed, tickled by the image he'd created.

He wasn't insulted by the reference he'd just made. "There's one thing to be said about a bull moose, though. It has great staying power."

Her brow furrowed as she frowned. "You're making that up."

Connor's expression gave nothing away. "Maybe," he allowed. Raising himself up on his elbow, he looked into her eyes. "Why don't we take this into your bedroom and see? Your sofa did in a pinch, but it's not all that comfortable."

"You didn't seem as if you were all that uncomfortable," she reminded him, amused.

"You'd be surprised how much more accommodating I can be with a little more space to work in," he told her, the look in his eyes pulling her in.

Exciting her.

"All right," she told him, "surprise me." Her smile was warm and inviting as Brianna started to rise to her feet.

Standing already, the first thing Connor did was literally sweep Brianna off her feet and into his arms.

She felt as if her very breath had whooshed out of her lungs. "What are you doing?" she squealed.

"Surprising you," Connor answered, satisfaction curving the corners of his mouth. Then he added, "I aim to please."

Brianna tucked her arms around his neck to secure herself.

"You've already taken care of that part," she told him, her eyes dancing as she thought of the last hour they had spent together.

"In the words of Al Jolson—" he began, only to be interrupted.

"Who?" she asked him. She had no idea who he was referring to.

"A famous old vaudeville showman," Connor explained.

"Vaudeville." Brianna shook her head. The man was turning out to be a walking font of information. "You are an endless source of surprises."

He laughed, then continued. "As I was about to say, in the words of the immortal Al Jolson, 'You ain't seen nothin' yet,'" Connor told her.

And it was a promise that he definitely intended to live up to.

This time, Brianna felt her heart pounding so hard when they finally fell back against her bed, she didn't know if it would ever be able to slow down to normal again. If the first time they made love had been wonderful, the second time absolutely defied all description.

It took several minutes for the room to stop spinning and several more for her body temperature to even begin to return to normal.

In all honesty, she was surprised that they hadn't set the bed on fire.

"I'm not sure," she murmured to Connor, "but I think I just died."

"I'll check you for a pulse once I get my oomph back," Connor promised. "You really wore me out. I guess it must have been all that stored-up, leftover energy you had because you didn't have to chase after your kids today."

Right now, Brianna wasn't sure if she would ever be able to move again. "Just trying to keep up with you."

"Funny, I was going to say the same thing," Connor told her. He stopped for a moment, listening. "And now I'm hearing bells," he said. "You've had some effect on me."

"That's the phone, silly," Brianna said, identifying the sound.

She turned her head toward the landline on her nightstand.

He raised his head to get a better look at the intrusive object. "That's right. I forgot you had a landline. *Why* do you have a landline?" he asked. Most people he knew didn't own one of those things these days.

"In case the electricity goes out and I can't charge my cell phone," she told him. "My line of work depends on my being reached."

She was tempted to let the landline go on ringing.

It couldn't be a potential client on the other end of the line, not at nine thirty at night.

But by the third ring, her concern that it could have something to do with the children overcame her. "I guess I'd better get that. Whoever it is probably won't go away until I answer."

With what she felt was her very last shred of energy, Brianna reached over and picked up the receiver. Bringing it up against her ear, she murmured an exceedingly tired "Hello?"

The next second, Connor saw her bolt upright. She was holding on to the receiver with both hands. "What?" she cried.

Connor sat up beside her. He had no idea what was going on, but whatever it was, he could see that it was distressing Brianna.

"What is it?" he asked. And then it came to him. There was only one thing that could get this sort of a reaction from her. "Is it one of the kids?" he wanted to know.

Brianna held her hand up, asking for silence as she continued listening to the voice on the other end of the line.

"All right, I'll be right there," she finally said, then hung up the phone.

"What is it?" Connor asked her the second that she ended the call.

"Axel threw up." He'd been so eager to go, even more so than his sister. And now she had to go and bring him home. She felt awful for the poor kid.

"Flu?" Connor asked, saying the first thing that occurred to him.

He tried to remember if flu season was over yet. He vaguely remembered hearing something on the radio during one of his drives here, but couldn't recall anything beyond that.

"Candy," Brianna answered. When Connor looked at her, confused, she explained. "Seems that besides dinner, my son decided to stuff himself with as much candy and as many snacks as he could get his hands on. Then they played some kind of game involving spinning and, well, you can imagine the rest."

"Poor kid," Connor commented.

"Poor kid?" she echoed as she walked into the living room where they'd both left their clothes. She knew why she felt that way, but what had prompted Connor to say that?

"Well, sure," he told her, collecting his clothing and quickly getting dressed. "This isn't the way he would have wanted to remember his first night away from home. It's kind of embarrassing for him."

She fully understood that, but as Axel's mother, she had a job to do. "That's nothing compared to the lecture he's going to get. He knows he's not supposed to stuff himself with that kind of garbage, especially not before bedtime."

"That's probably why he did it," Connor pointed out. "Because you weren't there to police him. Face it, you have a typical boy on your hands."

"Right now, I'd welcome him being a little less typical," Brianna answered, pulling on her jeans.

"This is harmless. Go easy on him," Connor advised. She detected a note of sympathy in his voice.

"Right now, the guy's pretty miserable and he feels bad about having to come home."

She relented. She hadn't been all that hell-bent to deliver that lecture anyway. "Maybe you're right," Brianna agreed.

Finding her purse, she began hunting through it for her car keys.

Connor put his hand out for the keys. "I'll drive," he offered.

It took her a moment for his words to register. "What?"

"Give me the address and I'll drive you," Connor told her. "We'll use your car because you have their car seats," he added.

He seemed to have thought this all out, Brianna realized. That he had really surprised her. "You're not going home?" she asked.

"I figure that Axel's going to need a guy in his corner. I'm sure Ava's probably filling in for you right now, reading him the riot act for doing something she no doubt considers dumb. With both of you there, the poor guy'll feel outnumbered. I just thought I'd offer him a little moral support."

Then, as if he knew what she was thinking, Connor added, "It's still early. Any other time, we might still be working on those names Charlotte had you looking for."

He knew she was worried about the way this looked, she thought. But he was right. On all counts. She was just being self-conscious. The kids were too young to think that anything was going on between them.

Don't get used to this.

If she did, it would be all too easy for her to start leaning on him. Depending on him.

And looking forward to his being there beside her in bed.

You know that's not how this is all going to play out, she silently insisted. *The man's here today. He's not making any commitments about tomorrow.*

Brianna took a breath, looking at him. "You sure you want to do this?"

Connor didn't answer her question, not directly. Instead, all he said was, "Let's go," and led the way out of her house to her car.

Brianna followed, focused on getting to her son.

"I'm really sorry about this," Brianna said, wholeheartedly apologizing to Beth Wilson, the mother who had called her.

"Don't worry about it," Beth told her, waving away the apology. She seemed to genuinely mean the words. "It's my fault. I shouldn't have put out all those snacks, but this was the first sleepover the kids have ever had and Joey kept saying that Axel and Ava liked all these different things." She smiled ruefully at her mistake. "I guess I didn't realize that he was eating so much." She looked down at Axel and it was obvious that she really was sorry. "Do you feel any better?"

Axel shook his head. He just looked really miserable, like he never wanted to see another piece of chocolate again.

Connor stooped down and scooped the boy up in his arms. Axel put his head against Connor's shoulder. "You'll feel better in the morning, big guy," Connor promised.

The woman hosting the children's slumber party looked at Connor with unabashed appreciation, her eyes traveling up and down the length of him.

"You're not their father, are you?" she asked.

Brianna felt that it was time to step in and she placed herself between Beth and Connor as he held her little boy.

"This is Connor Fortunado, a client," she told the other mother. "We were working on some files when you called about Axel's mishap."

"Working," Beth repeated, drawing the single word out with a wide smile. "I see." Then, touching Axel's arm, the woman said, "I hope you feel better, dear. We'll have you both back when you've recovered from this," she promised the little boy, looking at Ava, as well.

"Can't he stay, Mom?" Joey asked. Six months older than his friend, he was clearly unhappy to have the evening end so abruptly.

"Not tonight, I'm afraid, honey," Beth told him. She walked the foursome to the front door. Joey and his sister, Debbie, trailed after them. "It was nice meeting you, Mr. Fortunado," Beth made a point of saying to Connor.

Brianna caught the interested, friendly note in the woman's voice. She couldn't really blame her, Brianna supposed. Connor was certainly a great deal more handsome than the average man.

"Again, I'm sorry about this," Brianna apologized one last time for her son.

Beth waved her hand, although her attention was still partially divided. "Don't give it another thought. Bye." Then she added almost wistfully, "Enjoy the rest of your evening."

"You know what she's thinking," Brianna said to Connor in a low voice as they opened the car doors.

Even so, Ava managed to overhear her. "What's she thinking, Mama?" the little girl asked.

"That she's sorry the two of you had to leave so early," Connor told her, saving Brianna from having to come up with an answer.

"I didn't have to leave," Ava informed them with a pout. "*I* didn't throw up," she added almost accusingly. "Axel did."

Normally Axel would have spoken up in his own defense at this point. Most likely he would have offered up a denial or come up with something to throw back in his sister's face. But this time, all the boy did was moan.

"You still feeling sick, big guy?" Connor asked sympathetically. "Do you think you're going to throw up again?"

The miserable look on the little boy's pale, freckled face told Connor that the answer was a definite yes.

"Tell you what, why don't I sit in the back with you to make sure you don't wind up throwing up on your sister?" Connor suggested.

Both of the car seats were in the back. He figured he'd just sit between them.

Whoa, Connor thought. What was he doing? He was getting in way too deep here with these kids. As soon as Brianna got them home, he needed to put on the skids. Otherwise, there would be no getting out and he could just kiss his carefree life goodbye. Permanently.

The idea of her brother throwing up on her horrified Ava. "I don't wanna sit with Axel!" she wailed indignantly.

"You won't be," Connor assured her. "You'll be next to me. I'll be sitting between you and your brother. If he starts to throw up again, I'll turn his head away so that it'll land on this old blanket." He pointed to the blanket he'd folded up and tucked against the door next to the boy.

Ava walked over to the blanket he'd indicated. "Oh." Satisfied that she would be out of the line of fire, she nodded. "Okay," she agreed, circling back to her side of the vehicle. She waited for Connor to put her into her car seat.

"Here're your keys back." He offered them to Brianna, then heard himself saying, "I'll get the kids into their seats."

He had to stop doing that, he thought. But then, this was just for a little while longer. And then he'd be gone, right?

About to tell him that she would take care of strapping her children in, Brianna stopped and let Connor take over.

He'd be gone soon enough and she might as well enjoy this now, while it lasted.

He was right to insist on coming, Brianna thought, despite the fact that his presence had given Beth Wilson something to think about and most likely to talk about. There was really no way she could have handled

Axel in his present condition and still driven the children home. Ava would have voiced her displeasure in a high, loud voice all the way home.

This was all a lot easier with Connor, she thought, finally getting in on the driver's side.

Everything was a lot easier with Connor around.

You have to stop doing that. This is temporary. Just temporary. If she allowed herself to get used to this, it was going to be twice as hard on her when he left. And he *would* leave. She just needed to remember that.

"Everything all right, Bri?" Connor asked, breaking into her thoughts. "You haven't started the car," he pointed out.

Bri. He called her Bri. As if they were a couple. Her heart melted.

Stop that! she silently upbraided herself.

"As fine as it can be with one nauseous little boy in the backseat," she answered.

"I'm sorry, Mommy," Axel bleated.

Her heart went out to him. "You'll feel better soon. But just remember how you feel the next time you want to eat everything in sight," she told him.

"I will," Axel said meekly.

This time, Brianna started up the car.

Chapter Fourteen

The minute Brianna parked her car in her driveway, Connor got out and came around to Axel's car seat. Undoing the restraints, he was careful to gently pick the boy up and take him into his arms.

Walking behind Brianna, who had her daughter by the hand, Connor carried Axel to the room the boy shared with his sister. After helping Axel wash his face and hands and changing him into his pajamas, Connor asked him, "Which is your bed?"

"He sleeps in the top bunk," Ava announced, coming back into the bedroom once Connor walked back in with her brother.

There was a problem with that tonight, Connor thought. He exchanged looks with Brianna. "And the bottom bunk is yours?" he asked the little girl.

"Uh-huh." Ave bobbed her head up and down, confirming her response.

"How about, just for tonight, you let your brother have the bottom bunk?" Connor suggested.

"But why?" Ava wanted to know, her eyes widening.

"If he feels sick again during the night, Axel will be able to get to the bathroom faster if he's in the bottom bunk. Besides, you don't want to have him suddenly throw up while he's up there, do you? It could get pretty messy down here for you," Connor warned, eyeing her closely.

He felt he had made a winning argument, but one look at Ava's face told him that they weren't home free yet. Ava appeared to be totally distressed. "But I'm afraid of top bunks," she told Connor.

"Ava's afraid of heights," Brianna explained. "That's why I gave her the bottom bunk." She looked at her daughter. There was only one way out of this without a squabble. "Tell you what, how would you like to spend the night in my bed?"

"I won't fall out?" Ava asked uncertainly, looking up at her mother with wide eyes.

Brianna smiled. This was familiar territory. Ava was never going to be a daredevil. "No, you won't fall out, sweetheart. I won't let you," she added to reassure her.

"Okay," Ava agreed, although she still sounded rather reluctant.

"Problem solved," Connor pronounced with a wide grin, looking at Brianna.

"You're getting really good with them," Brianna

told him. She didn't bother to keep the pleased note out of her voice.

"It's simple. I just watched you," Connor said, shrugging off any credit.

Brianna turned toward her daughter. "Ava, why don't you stay with your brother for a few minutes while I walk Mr. Fortunado out? When I come back, I'll get you ready for bed," she told the little girl.

Ava brightened immediately. Brianna knew that the little girl liked the idea of being put in charge of her older brother. Ava liked being the boss.

"Okay, Mama," she replied.

Her obedient tone wasn't fooling anyone, Brianna thought fondly. First chance she got, Ava would be ordering her brother around.

Ruffling the little girl's silky hair, Brianna told her daughter, "I'll be right back."

"Good night, half-pint," Connor said to the little girl, then he turned toward the very unhappy-looking little boy lying listlessly in the bottom bunk. "Feel better, big guy."

Rather than saying anything, Axel moaned in response.

"How come I'm a half-pint and he's a big guy?" Ava wanted to know. She obviously thought that the word *big* was complimentary in this case.

Brianna patted the small, dark head. "I'll explain it all later, honey," she promised, hoping to buy herself a little time to come up with an answer. Then, turning toward Connor, she said, "Let's go."

"Yes, ma'am," he answered obediently. When they

reached the front door, Connor commented, "Some night, eh?"

"Well, you can say that again. At the very least, it's certainly been an eventful one," she agreed. And then she smiled up at him, grateful he'd been there with her. "Thanks for all your help," she told him. "It wouldn't have gone nearly as smoothly without you there."

He looked at her for a second, and then seemed to understand her meaning. "Oh, you're talking about with the kids. Sure. It wouldn't have been right just to leave you high and dry, having to cope with a sick kid and all," he told her.

"My ex-boyfriend had no qualms about doing that," Brianna recalled, addressing his last comment first. "And of course I'm talking about help with the kids. As for the other part of this evening," she said, referring to making love with Connor, "that's something that we *don't* need to talk about."

It struck him that she was highly unusual. A woman who *didn't* want to take apart and dissect the meaning behind every nuance, every action that had taken place during their lovemaking.

He looked at her for a long moment, impressed. "You are in a class by yourself, Brianna Childress," he said just before he bent over and kissed her.

In a strange, ironic sort of way, Connor thought, he had Charlotte Robinson to thank for this. For bringing Brianna into his life. Not by design, but certainly by happy accident.

He had a feeling finding this out would *not* be well received by the woman. Connor suppressed a pleased smile.

"I'll see you tomorrow," Brianna said, waiting for him to verify her statement. She would be lying if she said that she didn't live with the specter of Connor leaving permanently in the near future.

Connor nodded. "And I promise I won't bring any ice cream or cookies for Axel and Ava."

"Axel'll probably be ready to eat them by tomorrow," Brianna predicted about her son. "But don't," she cautioned just in case Connor was having any second thoughts about what he'd just promised.

A smile played on his lips as he gave Brianna a little salute, touching two fingers to his temple like a soldier.

But before he could say goodbye, Ava's voice was suddenly heard calling, sounding high-pitched and insistent. "Mama, Axel's going to be sick again."

"Go, go!" Connor told her, although the words were rather needless since he addressed them to Brianna's back. She was already hurrying to the children's bedroom. "Good luck," Connor murmured as he pulled the door closed behind him.

He heard the lock click into place. Satisfied, he walked to his car. He still had to drive home, he reminded himself, and admittedly, he was rather tired.

But thoughts of making love with Brianna kept him wide-awake all the way home.

"So, how is he?" Connor asked Brianna when he arrived at her house the following day.

It was almost noon. He would have been there earlier, but he'd actually been busy taking care of some extraneous details, all of which had kept him from driving over here first thing in the morning.

Although it hadn't kept him from thinking about making love with Brianna the entire time.

"Like it never happened," Brianna answered his question, opening the door all the way for him. The resilience of children never ceased to amaze her. "Come see for yourself," she said, inviting Connor in. "He's asking for a do-over."

"A do-over?" Connor questioned, puzzled.

"Yes, he wants to go over to Joey's house for another sleepover tonight. I told him it wasn't happening, at least not for a while. He's not happy about the news," she added. "But he'll get used to it," she said philosophically.

Connor nodded. Instead of going into the children's bedroom, he suddenly asked her a question out of the blue, "Can you get a babysitter?"

The question caught her completely off guard. Brianna looked at him quizzically, then slowly told Connor, "I guess so. For when and for how long?" she wanted to know. She couldn't make any sort of plans without that information.

"This Saturday," Connor answered. "And as for how long, that's anyone's guess."

That wasn't exactly helpful, she thought. "You're going to have to be a little more specific than that."

"I've been invited to a baby shower," he told her. Then, before she could point out the obvious, Connor added, "It's a coed baby shower. They're all the thing these days."

They might be all the "thing," she thought, but she wouldn't know anyone there and she was rather shy. "I don't think—"

He didn't want her to say no. He wasn't about to analyze why, but it was suddenly important to him that she come with him, if for no other reason than she see some of the people she had been researching.

"It's a family affair," he told her, then specified, "A *big* family affair. Some of the people I've been trying to locate may be there, along with a lot of other members who I already know." He'd met some of them a few months ago when his sister Schuyler had organized a family reunion. "I thought you might like to meet some of the names you encountered during your initial research for Charlotte."

He was tempting her.

Everything seemed different to her now that she'd made love with him. She found herself *wanting* to meet his family.

"Well, I have to admit that I am kind of curious about them," she confessed.

He couldn't have been more pleased. "Great, it's all settled," he declared happily.

It didn't quite work that way, she thought.

"Hello, mother of two," she reminded him, waving a hand before his eyes as if that helped underscore her point. "Nothing's settled until I can make arrangements to leave the kids with someone."

"You're leaving us?" Ava cried, clearly horror-stricken. Neither one of them had seen the little girl come into the doorway of the living room. "It's 'cause Axel threw up, isn't it?" she asked her mother, then whirled around on her heel, turning toward her room, where she'd left her brother. "Axel, you're making Mama go away."

Brianna sighed as she shook her head. "Never a dull moment," she said to Connor.

Axel stumbled into the living room, still somewhat unsteady after last night's episode.

Connor quickly took over. "Hey, guys, your mother's not leaving you. You know better than that. She'd never leave you. She's just going to get someone to stay with you so she can go to a party for a few hours," he explained to them.

"You're fibbing," Ava accused. "Mama doesn't go to parties," she insisted. "She just goes to work. Sometimes to the store."

"You went to a party," Connor reminded the small, judgmental audience. "Don't you think your mom should have a chance to do that, too?"

Ava looked as if she was really thinking the question over. Axel took the momentary lull as his chance to speak up. Drawing closer to Connor, he eagerly asked, "Can you be the one to babysit us?"

This was getting out of hand again, Brianna thought. So what else was new?

"Axel, Ava, stop putting Mr. Fortunado on the spot," she told them.

"I would," Connor said, interrupting Brianna and answering the little boy's question. "But I'm the one taking her to the party."

"Can you take us, too?" Ava wanted to know, looking at him hopefully.

"Okay, you two," Brianna said, her voice growing serious now. "I think you both need to stop bothering Mr. Fortunado and just be grateful for everything he's done for you so far."

"Like what?" Ava wanted to know. The little girl wasn't trying to be wise, she was really asking for an example.

"Like helping to bring you home last night," Brianna answered. "Like bringing over pizza for you to eat. Like playing games with you two," she enumerated, looking from one child to the other.

A light seemed to dawn on Axel. "Oh. Yeah. That," he remembered, hanging his head.

"Yes, 'that,'" Brianna echoed. Her annoyance spent, she said, "Now why don't you two go play with Muffin and Scruffy for a while? Mr. Fortunado and I have work to do," she told them.

But apparently Ava had more questions for her mother. "Why do you call him that?" she wanted to know, glancing toward Connor as she asked her mother.

Brianna knew her daughter. Ava wasn't stalling. She appeared to really want to know the answer to her question.

"Mr. Fortunado?" Brianna repeated. Ava's head went up and down. "Because that's his name," she told the little girl.

Ava knew that, but it apparently didn't answer her question. "Don't you like him?" she asked.

"Yes, I like him," Brianna said. She avoided looking at Connor as she said it.

"Then why don't you call him Connor?" Ava wanted to know. "That's his name." The little girl smiled at him. "He likes being called Connor."

Why was everything a struggle with these two, Brianna wondered. A struggle and a debate. "All right. If

I call him Connor, will you and your brother go back in your room and play?"

"Sure!" the two cried, united for the space of exactly a moment. Even so, the children remained where they were.

Brianna frowned. "Well? Why aren't you going to your room to play?"

Ava exchanged looks with her brother. It was clear that for now, she was the spokesman. "'Cause we're waiting for you to call him Connor," Ava answered.

Brianna tamped down her annoyance. "Let's get to work, *Connor*," she said.

And just like that, her children grinned and took off.

Connor, she noted, had been struggling to keep a straight face. Now that her children were gone, he gave up the effort.

"I think," Connor said, laughing, "if they gave out medals for mothers, I'd definitely nominate you to get one."

"Thank you," she murmured. She debated her next words, then told him, "I'm just grateful that you're not making a run for the hills. That you didn't make a run for it the first day you heard my two arguing with each other at the top of their lungs," she admitted.

She was serious, he realized. In all fairness, ordinarily he would have been that guy. But there was something about this woman that got to him from the first moment she mistook him for the plumber and grabbed his hand, pulling him into her house.

"They're entertaining," Connor told her as they went to her office.

"Their dad didn't think so," Brianna murmured, more to herself than to him.

Connor slanted a look at her as they sat down, wondering if he should say anything. He didn't want to insult Brianna and he certainly didn't want to say anything that would make her back off.

But he owed her honesty, he decided, and he did feel strongly about this point. "No offense, but their dad was an idiot."

"None taken," she assured Connor with a humorless laugh. And then she added, "And between the two of us, yes, he was."

Now that she had pushed open the door, Connor had more questions for her. "How long were the two of you together?"

Brianna was quiet for so long, he thought she was going to ignore the question. And then she said, "Five years."

Five years seemed like an awfully long time to spend with someone who was obviously so self-centered. "Why did you stay?"

Brianna debated coming up with excuses. But there really was no point in making anything up. So she was honest with him.

"I guess I'm just a sucker for strays. I kept thinking I could help him, turn him around so that he could be the father the kids deserved." She pressed her lips together, remembering. "Jonny had a substance abuse problem and I thought that if I could just say the right thing, find the right way to approach his problem, I could help him kick the habit. Help him become a better person." She laughed at herself.

It was a sad sound, Connor thought.

"You can't change anyone, Bri, no matter how good

your intentions are. They have to want to change themselves," Connor said.

"I know, you're right, but I really thought I could help," she said ruefully. "And there were the two kids we had."

"The kids he didn't want, as you said," Connor recalled.

"The kids he didn't want," Brianna repeated, confirming the truth behind those words. Brianna blew out a breath. There was no point in rehashing the past and there was work to get done. "Look, hurricanes Axel and Ava are liable to come whirling back here at any moment, so I suggest that we use this time to work on that list of names we're whittling down," she told Connor.

"Right as usual," he answered warmly. And then he paused. "But you are coming with me to the shower this Saturday, right?"

"If I can find a sitter," Brianna reminded him pointedly.

"Don't worry, you'll get a sitter even if I have to buy one for you," Connor told her.

She wasn't sure if he was kidding, but she intended to do this on her own. She didn't want him thinking of her as some helpless female. There were only so many times he could be allowed to ride to her rescue.

"Don't worry. It's not going to come to that," Brianna told him. "I have a few people who owe me favors. I'll find someone."

He nodded. "Okay. But if you don't, my offer's still open."

Connor smiled at her as he said it.

Brianna did her best not to get lost in that smile. She didn't succeed.

Chapter Fifteen

"You're not saying anything," Brianna said self-consciously.

Butterflies were madly crashing into one another in her stomach. She was already nervous that she wasn't going to fit in because the dress she'd borrowed from Beth Wilson wasn't good enough to wear to the shower that she was attending with Connor.

When she'd opened the door a minute ago to let Connor in after he'd rung her bell, he hadn't said a single word in response to her greeting.

Not even *hello*.

He was still just standing there in total silence, just looking at her.

Brianna drew the only conclusion she could from his silence. "You don't like it."

Connor finally forced himself to snap out of his trancelike state.

"Like it?" he echoed. "I *love* it. It's gorgeous. *You're* gorgeous," Connor corrected himself. For the first time in his life he felt like he was tripping over his own tongue. "I'm just trying to get used to seeing you like this. I've never seen you wearing anything but jeans and a T-shirt before."

Brianna still wasn't convinced. "So it's okay?" she asked hesitantly.

He had to laugh. "If it was any more 'okay' I wouldn't let you leave the house. I know guys aren't supposed to say things like that these days, but—wow. Just *wow.*"

"*Wow* is fine." She pushed back her uncertainty and her nerves. "*Wow* is good," Brianna amended.

Connor took in a deep breath. The light scent she was wearing almost made him dizzy. *She* made him dizzy, he thought.

"Are you ready?" he asked her.

Brianna nodded as she grabbed her purse. "Just let me tell the sitter we're leaving."

At the last minute, she'd managed to get Beth Wilson's younger sister, Meredith, to stay with Ava and Axel. Meredith was getting her teaching license and wanted to be a kindergarten teacher, so she was more than happy to watch the children. She saw this as perfect training for her future vocation.

Connor stood patiently by, waiting for Brianna to say goodbye to her clinging children. He found himself reassuring them, that yes, he'd bring their mother back to them tonight.

And then finally, they were off.

"I'm really glad you're coming with me," Connor said once they were in his car and on their way to the baby shower. Admittedly, a baby shower was *not* his thing, but attending the event would allow him to get together with members of the Fortune clan he hadn't met yet. "I've never been to one of these things before and I don't want to make a fool of myself."

"A coed shower's probably different from a regular shower," Brianna told him. "I doubt if there'll be any silly games or anything like that," she told him. "So you can relax. I'm the one who's going to be out of her element." She saw him turning toward her quizzically. "I won't know anyone."

"Don't worry about it," he counseled. "I probably won't know half the people there, either. The whole idea of my going to the shower is to meet relatives I haven't met yet and to spread the word about Charlotte. To warn them about Charlotte," Connor amended.

"So they don't know that she's done all those things you told me about? The hacking and burning down your—half uncle, is it?" she asked. Connor nodded in response. "Burning down his mansion," Brianna continued. "They don't know she's the one behind it?"

It hadn't been as obvious as she thought. "I've just put the pieces together recently myself," Connor explained. "So in all likelihood, a lot of these people might not have figured it out yet. And others probably don't even know about Charlotte."

Brianna sat back in the passenger seat, thinking over what he'd just said. "This is going to be an interesting baby shower," she commented.

* * *

Truer words were never spoken, Connor thought less than half an hour later.

When they arrived at the party, most of the guests were already there. The baby shower was being thrown for a very pregnant Billie Fortune Pemberton and her husband, rodeo champion Grayson Fortune. Since this was his family's company as well as the company that had suffered recent setbacks thanks to Charlotte's devious machinations, Connor felt they were all connected to one another in a number of ways besides just by blood.

"I'm really looking forward to meeting Grayson, Nathan and Jayden Fortune," Connor confided to the woman at his side as they made their way through the room where the party was being held. The triplet brothers hadn't made it to the reunion.

Brianna found herself wishing that she had brought the notes she'd been working on for Connor. Maybe then she could keep people's names and faces straight, she thought.

"My Lord, those three look like carbon copies of each other," she whispered to Connor, spotting Grayson and his brothers.

Connor grinned. "They're triplets," he told Brianna. All three had dark brown hair and brown eyes and stood over six feet tall.

"How do their wives tell them apart?" Brianna marveled.

"I'm sure they have their ways," he answered with a wink. "Those are the sons that Gerald didn't know he fathered until recently," Connor said. "They were raised by their single mother, Deborah."

Right now, he didn't remember how much Brianna knew and how much of this information he'd discovered for himself before he'd come to her. Repeating the information drove it home for him.

"Once Gerald finally found out about them, that's when he finally left Charlotte. He was furious that she knew of the triplets' existence and had been keeping it from him all this time. I think she secretly knew that unlike all the other women Gerald had slept with, both as Gerald Robinson and under his first identity as Jerome Fortune, Deborah was the one woman he had always really loved. Once he found out that Deborah had given birth to his sons, he tracked her down and begged for her forgiveness."

Brianna supposed maybe there was hope for the man, after all—if he survived Charlotte's wrath, she thought. "Well, if that's the case and Charlotte is as vindictive as you said she is, why hasn't she tried to seek revenge against Deborah yet?"

She was certain they would have heard about any attempts by now. She was beginning to realize that Connor had his finger on the pulse of everything connected to the family.

"Because the woman is nothing if not crafty. She might be evil personified, but she is definitely patient when it comes to exacting her revenge," Jayden Fortune said, answering Brianna's question. The triplet had walked up behind them just in time to overhear the conversation.

After formally introducing himself and his wife,

Ariana, to both Connor and Brianna, he told them that he and his two brothers were as surprised as anyone to have Gerald suddenly show up in their lives after all these years.

"We'd never met him until then and it wasn't exactly a *warm* reunion as far as my brothers and I were concerned," Jayden told them.

"That's putting it mildly," Grayson said with a harsh laugh.

"As a matter of fact, we were ready to ride the man out on a rail," Jayden continued, "'father' or no 'father.' We all thought that he had deserted Mom as soon as he knew she was pregnant. But he swore up and down that he never knew. We all had our suspicions that his wife knew—the woman's a viper that knows *everything*," Jayden maintained, "but Charlotte would have never told him about us because she was probably afraid that Gerald would have tried to do right by our mother."

"She turned out to be right," Nathan said, joining the conversation. "And Mom," he said as he exchanged looks with his two brothers, "well, our mom has this kind, forgiving heart," he told Connor and Brianna. "And she believed Gerald when he said he never knew that she was pregnant when he left."

"She seems genuinely happy with Jerome or Gerald or whatever the hell he calls himself these days," Grayson told Connor and Brianna. "My brothers and I haven't really taken to him yet," he said honestly. "But as long as Mom's happy and he's good to her, well, that's all that really counts."

"Your wife was writing a series of articles on Gerald Robinson, wasn't she?" Connor recalled, addressing the question to Jayden.

"Yes, she was." He looked around for Ariana, who had wandered off to talk to someone else at the party. "That's how Ariana and I initially met," Jayden explained.

"I'd love to pick her brain and ask her a few questions sometime if I could," Connor told the man.

Jayden saw no reason to wait. "Now's as good a time as any." Turning toward an attractive woman who was talking to Billie, the next mother-to-be, Jayden put out his hand. "Honey, I've got someone here who wants to talk to my wife, the reporter," he told her. "Do you have a few minutes to talk shop?"

Ariana's smile was warm and relaxed. "Always," she told him. Turning toward Connor and Brianna, she asked, "What would you like to know?"

Connor didn't hesitate. "Everything."

Ariana looked mildly surprised.

"Connor here thinks that Charlotte is bent on getting revenge against the family," her husband explained.

Ariana automatically shivered at the mention of the other woman's name.

"It certainly wouldn't surprise me," the reporter told the small gathering. "I think Charlotte could probably trace her lineage back to Lucrezia Borgia."

"She hasn't poisoned anyone," Nathan's wife, Bianca, pointed out.

"Yet," Jayden said.

The others laughed, but it was an uncomfortable laugh that had an element of truth in it.

"Personally, I don't know what Mother sees in Gerald," Grayson told them. "The man cheated on Charlotte so many times he's probably lost count. I don't know how many illegitimate offspring he has. In fact, I don't think *he* knows."

"I bet Charlotte does," Jayden told the others.

This was his cue to speak up, Connor thought. "Brianna and I are trying to locate as many of those offspring as we can." He saw Bianca and Ariana look at him quizzically. "I want all of them to know that Charlotte potentially might have them in her sights. They need to be warned so she doesn't catch them off guard and wind up doing something awful to them," Connor said.

"You do know that Julius Fortune, Jerome's father, had four illegitimate sons himself," Ariana asked.

Jayden's wife seemed uncomfortable telling him that, perhaps because she didn't know how much Connor knew about the so-called family patriarch and she didn't want to be the one telling family secrets.

"Oh, I know," Connor replied, effectively negating her concern. "I even know their names." He proceeded to recite them. "There's my dad, Kenneth. There's also Miles, Gary and David," he told the small gathering. "I met Miles and his family at the family reunion in January. I haven't made contact with Gary or David or any of their families yet," he confessed, "but I'm going to see if I can get in contact with them next. Provided no other major disasters take place," he added, thinking of the estate fire that had set everything off.

"Hey, everybody," Bianca cut in, calling their attention to the front of the room. "They're bringing out the cake."

The present conversation regarding the devious Charlotte Robinson was tabled until after the gifts were opened and everyone had gotten at least one slice of the multi-tiered cake.

"So, did my family manage to overwhelm you?" Connor asked Brianna when they left the party and were finally on their way home.

"I'm not sure if *overwhelm* is the correct word here, but there certainly are a lot of them," Brianna replied with a quiet laugh.

"And there's even more." Connor smiled. He was a little overwhelmed himself. "It's kind of hard to tell all the players without a scorecard," he admitted, then sighed. "It's not exactly a Norman Rockwell painting come to life."

"Families can be messy," Brianna agreed. She tried to be kind in her assessment. "I guess parents don't always realize the kind of damage they can do to their children by their actions."

"No argument there," Connor agreed. "I didn't realize it at the time, but I'm really lucky to have grown up in a happy home with two parents who loved each other and still do."

The words were no sooner out of his mouth than Connor realized his mistake. He shouldn't have drawn attention to that. He saw Brianna wince and he knew she was thinking of her own children, who had never really had a father on the scene.

"I'm sorry. I didn't mean that the way it came out," Connor apologized.

But she waved off his guilty reaction. "There's no need to apologize," she told him. "You're right. Parenthood is a heavy responsibility and it's definitely not for everyone," Brianna said, thinking of Jonny again. He just hadn't been cut out to take care of a family.

To him they had been a burden, not a blessing.

She'd finally come to terms with that.

Connor was silent for a moment. "Do you ever regret having Ava and Axel?"

She didn't hesitate. "Not for one second of one day," Brianna told him. "Those kids are everything to me. I love them more than life itself and I'll always put them first."

They had reached her house. Connor pulled up into her driveway and turned off the ignition. Rather than get out, he shifted to face her.

"And who puts you first?" Connor asked.

Brianna had no answer for that. She'd been so busy giving and taking care of people and animals, she hadn't thought of herself. It felt that she hadn't had any alone time until Connor had showed up.

Shrugging, she looked away because the answer to his question was no one.

Connor crooked his finger beneath her chin, turning her head so that she faced him and he could look into her eyes.

"Let me be the one, Bri," he told her softly. "Let me be the one who puts you first."

It wasn't a proposal, she knew that. But it was a sign. A sign of hope.

She knew she was setting herself up, that she was as likely to be disappointed as she was to be elated, but she refused to dwell on the downside, to think that this wouldn't lead anywhere.

She had lived so long without being in love, without any hope that the future was going to turn out the way that she wanted it to, that Brianna found herself grasping not at straws, but at the mere *promise* of a straw.

For now, that was enough, and who knew? Maybe that promise, that *hope* would swell and take root, becoming something that would flower into the happiness she so desperately craved.

Craved not just for herself, but for her children, as well.

Because her children deserved to be happy and to grow up feeling loved not just by one parent but by two parents.

"You're crying," Connor realized. About to open his own door to get out, he stopped and looked at her. "Did I say something wrong?"

"No," Brianna answered, shaking her head. "No, you said something right."

He rubbed his thumb along her cheek, brushing away traces of her tears. He brought his thumb up to his lips and tasted it.

"Salty," he commented. "I need something sweet to counterbalance it." Connor leaned in closer to her, lightly taking hold of her shoulders. "I know just the thing," he whispered.

The next moment, his lips met hers. Instantly he could feel passion taking hold of him. There were no regrets over what he had said to her moments ago. He'd meant it. He wanted to take care of her. This was the woman he wanted to have in his life. The woman he felt he'd been looking for. He realized that he had done a one-eighty from the man he had been such a short while ago—and he liked it.

"Definitely sweet," he whispered just before he kissed her again.

And then, after a beat, Connor drew his head back. "We'd better go in before I get carried away," he told her. There was a twinkle in his eyes as he asked, "By the way, when are the kids going to go on another one of those sleepovers?"

The sound of her laughter returned everything to normal.

Chapter Sixteen

She was in love.

Brianna had to be honest with herself and admit the truth. Although she had tried to resist this, she had definitely fallen in love with Connor Fortunado.

Connor was spending more and more time with her and he was no longer hiding behind an excuse. He wasn't coming over because she was working for him or with him. He was coming over for the simple reason that he wanted to spend time with her, as well as with her kids. That, for her, was the cherry on the sundae.

Although Brianna told herself she needed to put the skids on, to go into this relationship slowly, she knew it was too late for that. She'd opened up her heart to this man. Connor didn't shut out her kids or pretend to put up with them when he actually secretly wanted them to be elsewhere. On the contrary, he included them. He took them along on their dinners out and let himself be pulled into the games that Ava and Axel wanted to play at home.

She knew it was still early and she shouldn't get too far ahead of herself, but it was so hard not to. So hard not to just love this man who her children adored.

"He seems like a really nice guy," Beth Wilson said to her one afternoon while their kids were playing together in the backyard. "But if you don't mind my butting in, I'd proceed slowly with him if I were you," her friend cautioned.

"Because I have an awful track record," Brianna said, guessing at the reason why Beth was attempting to warn her.

"No, because Connor might not be as committed to this relationship as you are," Beth explained. The older woman smiled at Brianna. "I just don't want to see you get hurt."

She appreciated the concern, but she wasn't going to change anything. "Until he came along, I was convinced I couldn't feel anything at all anymore. Connor woke up my heart—and it's really wonderful to be able to feel again," Brianna said with enthusiasm.

"Well, then go for it," Beth told her. "And I'll keep my fingers crossed for you—and maybe my toes, too," she added with a smile.

"Just not while you're walking," Brianna advised with a grin.

"Mama, I don't feel so good," Ava complained a couple of days later. She presented herself listlessly in front of her mother. "My hair hurts."

Brianna immediately thought of Ava's brother. Things could get physical very quickly between the siblings. "Axel, did you pull your sister's hair?" she wanted to know.

The little boy was sitting on the sofa. "No, I didn't," Axel denied indignantly. He pointed to the TV. "I was playing the video game. The dragon keeps trying to eat me," he complained.

Ordinarily, Brianna tried to limit the amount of time Axel played video games every day. But right now, her mind wasn't on video games. She was concerned about her daughter.

She turned to look at Ava. The little girl looked very pale and there was sweat pasting her hair to her forehead.

"What do you feel, baby?" she asked Ava.

The normal enthusiasm she always heard in Ava's voice was missing.

"Hot," the little girl told her in a quiet voice. "I'm hot."

"Come here, let me see." Brianna beckoned her over closer. Rather than going to get a thermometer, she decided to rely on the tried and true, old-fashioned method. She lightly pressed a kiss to the little girl's forehead. "You *are* hot," Brianna confirmed. "Stay right here."

She went to get a thermometer out of the medicine cabinet and brought it over to where Ava was slumped against the sofa. She pressed the button, bringing the thermometer to life. The word *low* flashed across the tiny screen where the numbers usually registered.

"Okay, you know how the drill goes," she told her daughter, trying to sound cheerful and turning this into a game. "Put this under your tongue," Brianna said. "Can you do that for me?"

"I can do that for you, Mom," Axel volunteered, raising his hand and waving it at her while still holding his video controller in his other hand.

"Next time, Axel," she told her son. "Right now I need to see how high Ava's fever is."

"Is it high?" Axel asked before she had even taken Ava's temperature. "Is she going to die?"

The question was jarring, but she tried to remember that he didn't really mean it the way it sounded.

"No, she's not going to die, Axel," Brianna said, doing her best to sound patient. Ava still hadn't opened up her mouth. "C'mon, baby, I need to see what your temperature is." After some more coaxing, she finally got the thermometer under Ava's tongue.

When the noise went off, she took thermometer out again.

"What is it? What is it?" Axel wanted to know, coming over and trying to see over his mother's shoulder.

Brianna knew that Ava had to be sick because she wasn't even asking what the temperature was.

"Well, you definitely have a temperature, but it's not *too* high," Brianna emphasized. A hundred wasn't too high when it came to children under seven. She'd heard that somewhere. "But I am putting you to bed, young lady."

Ava didn't protest. That *definitely* worried her.

When evening came, Brianna transferred the little girl to her bed. She didn't want Axel catching the cold she figured her daughter had.

Axel looked overjoyed to finally have his own room. "Cool. I get the whole room all to myself," the boy crowed happily.

His elated mood lasted all of half an hour before he came into Brianna's bedroom, a sheepish look on his face as he peered in.

"Mom, can I sleep here, too?"

"What about having the whole room to yourself?" Brianna asked him, surprised that he wanted to give up the temporary arrangement.

"It's too big," he finally said after a few minutes. "And it makes noises. I can hear it," he complained.

"That's just your imagination, honey." She knew that both of her kids had exceptionally vivid ones.

"My imagination makes noises, too," Axel told her solemnly.

She started to tell Axel that he needed to be brave and return to his room when Ava's breathing suddenly became labored.

Axel's head instantly whirled in his sister's direction. "Why's she breathing so funny, Mommy?" he wanted to know. For all of his blasé attitude, the little boy looked worried.

That makes two of us, Brianna thought, still trying to maintain a brave front for her children's benefit.

This time Brianna didn't bother with the thermometer again. She had already taken Ava's temperature over half a dozen times since she had brought the little girl into her room and put her to bed there.

Putting her hand against her daughter's forehead, Brianna pulled it back almost immediately. Ava's forehead felt as if it was on fire.

"Go get dressed, Axel. I'm dropping you off at Mrs. Wilson's house," Brianna told her son as she reached for the phone.

"For a sleepover?" Axel asked eagerly.

There was no point in alarming him and telling Axel the truth. "Yes. For a sleepover," she answered instead.

"Ava, too?" Axel wanted to know.

The fact that he was including his sister squeezed her heart. The phone on the other end was ringing and she was waiting for Beth to answer. "No, I'm taking Ava to the hospital."

Rather than run happily off to get ready for the sleepover, Axel stood where he was, looking at his sister. He had a sad expression on his face. "She's really sick, isn't she, Mommy?"

Rather than say yes, Brianna told her son, "The doctors'll get her well." She heard Beth pick up. "Now hurry and get dressed!"

Axel hurried out of the room.

"Don't worry about a thing," Beth told her twenty minutes later as the woman met her at the car. As she spoke, Beth took hold of Axel's hand. "Just get Ava to the emergency room. I'd come with you, but Harry's not home," she said, referring to her husband. "He's working the late shift tonight and there's no one to stay with the kids. Meredith's not answering her phone," she added, mentioning her younger sister.

"I really appreciate you letting me leave Axel with you," Brianna said, getting back into her car.

She had barely heard half of what Beth was saying to her. Her attention was entirely focused on Ava. Ava was her baby and she looked so small right now, almost curled up in her car seat,

She should have brought Ava to the emergency room earlier, Brianna upbraided herself angrily. Had she waited too long? Had she been too cavalier about her daughter's condition, mistakenly chalking it up to just a cold?

Or had she hesitated bringing Ava in because the health coverage she had wouldn't pay for an ER visit? Since she was self-employed, she had bought the only policy she could afford. The ER fee would go toward her very large deductible and she would have to pay the bill out of her own pocket.

A pocket that was *very* limited, Brianna thought ruefully.

How could she have even thought about money at a time like this? she silently demanded, recriminating tears beginning to fall.

Ava was moaning. It was making her feel even guiltier.

"It's going to be all right, baby. It's going to be all right," Brianna promised. "Mama's going to get you to the hospital and they'll make you all better."

Ava merely moaned again.

She wished that Connor was here. If he was, he could reassure her that everything was going to be all right. She needed to hear his calm, soothing voice, Brianna thought, fighting back the ever-growing feeling of desperation.

But Connor had gone to New Orleans to look up

some more of his extended family. She hadn't been able to reach him the one time she did try.

She hadn't bothered to leave a message. There was no time.

She was on her own, Brianna thought. Just the way she always had been.

"We're going to get through this, honey," she promised her daughter, just as much to bolster Ava as to bolster herself. "And you're going to be better than ever. You'll see."

Brianna prayed she was right.

"Pneumonia?" Brianna repeated the diagnosis numbly. "She has pneumonia?" she asked the weary-looking ER physician. The latter had returned to her with the news once all the results of the tests that had been taken had come in.

The diagnosis still hadn't penetrated. It just didn't make any sense. Ava was just so little. How could she have gotten pneumonia?

"Are you sure?" Brianna asked, her voice all but breaking.

"Very sure," Dr. Valdez replied solemnly. "We're going to have to keep your daughter here at least overnight. She's having trouble breathing," he continued matter-of-factly, "so for now we'll be putting her on oxygen."

"On oxygen?" Brianna echoed. She knew that would frighten Ava. "Is that really necessary?"

"Hopefully, this is just a precautionary measure. But her breathing *is* labored, so before it gets any worse, we need to do this."

Brianna nodded numbly. "Of course. I understand." The words were coming out almost mechanically. She could feel fear all but freezing her vocal cords. "Ava's not—she's not in any danger, is she?" Brianna couldn't get herself to phrase it any differently, afraid to say anything more specific, as if saying the words would make something awful come true.

The doctor's expression softened slightly, as if realizing just how scared she really was.

"There's always a risk in these cases," he told her, "but I think you came here just in time. Is there anyone I can call for you?" he asked. "To come stay with you, or to take you home?" he said gently.

She looked at him blankly for a moment, a mixture of numbness and fear playing tug-of-war with her emotional state. Then, as the doctor's question registered, she shook her head. "No, there's no one," she answered quietly.

Accepting Brianna's answer, the doctor changed the subject. "As soon as we have Ava set up in her room, I'll have a nurse come get you and you can stay with your daughter."

Her room.

She hated saying this, it seemed so crass and petty, especially at a time like this. But she needed to have the doctor aware of her circumstances.

"Doctor, I can't afford to pay for a private room for my daughter."

"Don't worry, the hospital only has single care units for patients. However, the insurance companies process them as if they're semiprivate rooms," he explained.

Brianna wasn't really sure what that meant. Everything seemed to be running together in her head. But she nodded anyway. The important thing was to have her daughter taken care of, and this hospital had the best reputation in the area.

"Thank you, Doctor," she murmured.

She found a chair in the waiting area and sat down.

"Bri, what happened?" Connor cried as he rushed into the room. He looked beside himself with concern.

Exhausted, sleep-deprived—she'd been here for close to twenty-four hours—she looked up at Connor. She didn't even know where to begin, so she just let him go on talking.

"When I didn't find you or the kids at home, I called Beth and she told me that you had taken Ava to the hospital."

Even as he said the words, Connor looked at the sleeping, pale little figure in the hospital bed. They had run out of beds in her size and had put Ava into an adult-size bed for now. She looked even smaller and more helpless in it than she would have appeared in the children's bed.

"What's wrong with her?" he wanted to know, almost afraid of the answer. "Why does she have those tubes running through her?"

He had come back from New Orleans ready to celebrate. The trip to find his newly discovered relatives had gone particularly well. The first thing he'd done once he'd landed was hurry over to see Brianna to share the news with her. When he couldn't find anyone there, he'd grown progressively more worried.

But nothing could have prepared him for this.

Connor felt as if he'd been kicked in the stomach and all the air had been knocked out of him.

"Bri?" he asked when she hadn't answered him yet. "Why is she here?"

"Ava has pneumonia," Brianna began shakily.

"Pneumonia?" Connor echoed. There was an edge in his voice. An edge because fear had seized his gut. He turned to look at Brianna. "Just like that? You didn't see it coming? There was no warning?"

It sounded as if he was accusing her, she thought. She was already taking herself to task over that. She didn't need him making it worse.

"She said she felt achy," Brianna answered. "I thought she had a cold." With each word, she felt guiltier and guiltier that she'd allowed her daughter's condition to get to this stage.

The guilt coupled with anger. She was sleep-deprived and half out of her mind with concern and worry. Brianna felt as if she was backed into a corner.

"There's a difference between a cold and pneumonia," Connor pointed out. All sorts of thoughts began popping up in his head. What if something awful had happened? What if Ava had wound up dying?

The thought suddenly materialized, seizing his heart and haunting him.

Brianna felt as if he was attacking her. Something snapped inside of her. Everything she'd been feeling these last few hours suddenly came pouring out.

"I know that, Einstein," she retorted sarcastically. What right did he have to talk to her this way? Connor hadn't even been here to support her when she needed him the most.

The sight of the little girl, looking so ill, sent a panicky feeling through him. He couldn't take it, couldn't take the thoughts he was struggling to tamp down.

"I'm going out. I need some air," he suddenly said to Brianna.

"Go ahead. Go get your air," she snapped at him. "And while you're at it, just keep on going."

Connor turned to look at her, stunned at the anger he heard in her voice. Stunned at what it sounded like she was telling him. He had to be wrong.

"What are you saying?"

The more she spoke, the angrier she got. She'd been wrong about him. He was bailing at the first sign of a problem. Well, she wasn't going to placidly stand for it. "I'm saying I want you to get out of here. Now!"

"You don't mean that. I just need to get out for a minute," he told her. "Brianna, calm down."

"Calm down?" she shot back, incensed. "Look, you weren't here. I had no one to talk to, no one to turn to and my little girl was sick. I don't have money to run to the doctor every time one of them has a cold. So I gambled and nearly lost my daughter." Angry tears glistened in her eyes.

"Bri—" He reached for her but she pulled away.

"You have no right to criticize me. Now get out of here!"

"Bri—"

"Now!" she insisted.

He looked at Brianna, and then at Ava. All sorts of scenarios filled his head. Scenarios he couldn't deal with. Scenarios that threatened to bring him to his knees.

All he wanted to do right now was get away so he could pull himself together.

"All right," he told Brianna.

And he left.

Chapter Seventeen

When his heart finally stopped racing ninety miles an hour, and the cold, clammy feeling he was experiencing throughout every inch of his body finally receded, Connor was at last able to think more clearly.

He understood now why fear had seized him in such a viselike, death grip.

For several awful minutes, all he could think of was what if Ava had died. He hadn't been here to help Brianna, to give her his support, his money, whatever it took to prevent this from happening, or at least to lessen its impact on Brianna.

If Ava had been taken to see a doctor when all this had started, he felt that it definitely wouldn't have evolved to this degree.

Guilt ate away at him out there in the darkened parking lot.

Seeing a doctor took money, he realized. Picking up and going to see a doctor was something he took for granted. He'd always taken it for granted, he thought ruefully. He hadn't stopped to think what it was like for people in Brianna's circumstances. He'd never had to budget money out of necessity the way he knew Brianna always had.

Damn it, why hadn't he given Brianna money just in case something unforeseen came up while he was gone? He shook his head, annoyed with himself. But he had never had to think that way, so he hadn't.

She wouldn't have taken it anyway, he thought now. Connor felt guilty, helpless and afraid as he got into his car.

At a complete loss what to do with himself, he knew he needed to clear his head as well as calm down before he could approach Brianna again.

Turning on the ignition, he slowly pulled away from the hospital and began to drive home.

The guilt wouldn't leave him alone, threatening to all but consume him.

He should have been here for her. He shouldn't have allowed his obsession to play such a big part in his life, pushing him to meet more and more of his extended family so he could warn them about Charlotte. Who did he think he was, Paul Revere?

The only thing he *had* to do was be here for Brianna and her kids.

The road before him was empty and desolate.

The look on her face haunted him as the sound of her voice ordering him to go away echoed over and over again in his head. He continued driving.

Connor desperately wanted to turn his car around to drive back to the hospital, to apologize to Brianna again for not being there when she needed him. But he knew she needed time. She needed to calm down first. She had been through a crisis—if he felt this awful about almost losing Ava, how much worse was this for Brianna?—and she needed to regain her mental equilibrium before he approached her again.

He wanted her to forgive him, not permanently cut him out of her life. He needed to be patient when patient was the last thing he was.

Blowing out a huge breath, Connor forced himself to continue driving to his parents' house. Things needed to have a chance to settle down.

Everything, he told himself, would be better in the morning.

But it wasn't.

Morning arrived and it was pure agony for him to wait until a decent hour before calling Brianna. As anxious as he was to talk to her, he didn't want to wake her. When he saw her in the hospital room, she had looked really wiped out. She needed her rest.

As for him, Connor had hardly slept all night. He finally gave up trying and got up by five. He was dressed within five minutes, then paced around until eight.

At eight o'clock on the dot, he called Brianna.

His heart sank when he got her voice mail instead of her.

Tempted to hang up, he left a message instead. "Hi, it's me. How is she?" he asked tensely. When he'd left, the prognosis had been positive, but he was taking nothing for granted. "Brianna, I can't tell you how sorry I am that I wasn't here for you. And that I fell apart in the hospital room. You have to understand that—"

A metallic *beep* went off, telling him that his time was up. He was cut off.

Connor dialed again. The same recording came on, telling him to leave a message.

"Bri, I need to talk to you. I have to explain what happened. You need to know that I—"

Another beep. He was cut off again. Apparently only very short messages were to be left.

Frustrated, fearing the worst even as he tried not to jump to conclusions, Connor called the hospital this time, requesting the nurses' station on the pediatric floor.

"Can I speak to the nurse taking care of Ava Childress?" he asked the person who had picked up.

"Just a minute."

Placed on hold, he found himself listening to some song he couldn't identify. It played all the way through, and then started again from the beginning. He was almost all the way through it again when he heard the receiver finally being picked up.

"Hello?"

He talked fast, afraid of being cut off. "I'm calling to find out Ava Childress's condition. She was brought in over a day ago with pneumonia."

"Are you a relative?" the young voice asked him.

Connor hesitated, then was forced to say no, he wasn't.

"Look, I know it's against the rules, but...could you just tell me how she's doing? I'm really worried."

The woman on the other end paused, as if debating what to do. "What did you say your name was?"

"Connor—Connor Fortunado. I'm a good friend of the family." He wasn't used to lying and his heart was pounding. "Please, I really need to know. How's Ava doing?"

The woman looked around to see if anyone was listening. Her expression softened. "She's doing better. I'm sorry, I can't tell you any more than that, though."

Connor closed his eyes. Relief flooded through him like a river swollen with rainwater, making him almost weak.

"Thank you," he told the nurse. "Thank you so much. I can't begin to tell you how grateful I am to hear this news."

The young woman nodded. "If you'll excuse me, I really have to go."

Before Connor had a chance to say another word, the nurse was gone and he found himself listening to a dial tone.

He sighed, drained. At least he knew that Ava was recovering. That she was going to be all right.

Now all he had to do was get her mother to return his calls.

She didn't.

Over the course of the next few days, Connor must have called Brianna at least a dozen times. She never picked up.

Each time he called, he left her a message. She

never returned a single one. He would have gone to see her at the hospital, but he didn't want to cause a scene. Connor was afraid that might upset Ava, and right now, the little girl needed to get well more than he needed to get Brianna to listen to him and forgive him.

To keep from thinking about Brianna, as well as making himself crazy counting the minutes as they dragged by, Connor focused his attention on something else.

Something positive.

It felt as if she'd been gone for an entire month instead of just a few days, Brianna thought when she finally drove up to her home again.

The doctor had pronounced Ava recovered and he had released the little girl from the hospital that morning right after nine.

Parking her car, Brianna got out and came over to the rear passenger side. She was all set to carry Ava from the car into the house, but the little girl pushed her hands away.

"I'm all better, Mama. I can walk," Ava insisted.

Brianna had her doubts, but she didn't want to argue on her daughter's first day back.

"Okay, I'll let you walk into the house, but then you're going straight to bed, young lady. You still need to rest," Brianna told her.

Ava pouted. "But I'm better. The doctor said so," her daughter reminded her.

Apparently things were getting back to normal, Brianna thought. "I know, baby," she said with a smile, "but humor me."

"What's that?" Ava wanted to know, puzzled.

Both of her kids were so precocious, there were times that she forgot she was talking to children, not adults. "It means do as I say, please." They walked up to the front door slowly. Brianna unlocked the door, then paused to look at her daughter. "You gave me quite a scare, baby."

Ava looked up at her, confused. "I'm not scary, Mama."

Brianna laughed and shook her head. "No, not anymore," she agreed. "But you were, baby, you were."

They'd walked in and Ava cocked her head now, listening. "Axel's laughing," she said, recognizing her brother's voice. "Did you tell him I was home?"

"No, not yet," she answered. "We just got in." Brianna paused and listened herself.

There was someone else with her son, she realized. She heard a deep, male voice laughing with Axel.

Beth came out of the kitchen just then. Brianna had told her friend that she was bringing Ava home from the hospital today and asked Beth to come to the house with Axel.

She looked at her friend quizzically now.

Before she could ask, Beth said, "He's been over to my house every day to see Axel while you were in the hospital with Ava. He told me that he didn't want the boy to worry about his sister or to feel like he was being left behind. When I told him you were coming home with Ava today, he said he wanted to come with the boy in case you needed help."

Beth smiled at her. "I think you finally have yourself a keeper, Brianna, but that's just me. I left Harry with the kids," she went on, "so I'd better get going. The kids tend to overwhelm him after an hour." She squeezed Brianna's hand, then looked at the little girl. "I'm glad to see you home, Ava."

Ava smiled. "I'm glad to see me home, too," she said to her mother's friend. Turning toward her mother, Ava complained, "They're having fun without me."

"Well, we'll just see about that," Brianna answered. "But you have to promise you're going to lie down very soon."

Ava nodded. "Promise," she answered.

When Brianna walked into the living room with Ava, both Connor and Axel stopped what they were doing.

Axel scrambled up to his feet. "You're back!" he cried. And then, because he didn't want Ava to think he was happy to see her, he said, "I gotta finish playing with Connor."

"Hold on a minute," Connor told the boy. Getting up, he crossed over to Brianna and her daughter. But instead of saying anything to the woman, he first stooped down to Ava's level and pretended to scowl. "What are you doing out of bed, young lady?"

Ava raised her chin. "Doctor said I'm all better."

"Oh, he did, did he? I bet he also said he wanted you to get some rest when you came home," Connor told her. "Am I right?"

Reluctantly, Ava nodded her head and said in a small voice, "Yes."

"I thought so," he said. "Let's get you in bed." He picked Ava up in his arms. And that was when he finally looked at Brianna. "Right, Mama?" he asked her with a smile.

Oh Lord, she'd missed that smile. Missed the sound of his voice, too, Brianna thought. She felt guilty now for the way she'd treated him at the hospital. She'd been so afraid of losing Ava that she had just lashed out at the first target she could find, which in this case turned out to be Connor.

"Right," Brianna answered. She followed Connor to the kids' bedroom.

Ava was asleep before they finished tucking her in.

"I'll stay with her to make sure she doesn't wake up and need something," Axel volunteered, totally surprising his mother.

"You're a real big help, Axel," she told her son, kissing the top of his head.

It was obvious that he was pleased to have his efforts recognized, but Axel pretended to shrug off her words. He dragged over his chair and sat down beside the bottom bunk, a silent sentry watching over his sister.

Connor waited until he and Brianna were both out of the room before he suddenly took her aside and said, "I can't tell you how scared I was when I saw Ava looking so sick that day. I didn't know how to act," he admitted, "and I was afraid to think."

Brianna nodded. She understood that now. "I could see that from your reaction at the hospital," she confessed, "but I thought you felt it was too much for you to handle and that you just wanted to bail."

Connor took her hands in his, grateful beyond words for a second chance.

"I just wanted to catch my breath," he said. "I didn't realize just how much I loved all of you until I saw Ava lying in that hospital bed, looking so tiny and helpless. I'd never been so scared about anything in my life. Scared of losing her. Scared of losing all of you," he emphasized. "That's when I realized that I already thought of us as a family. I'm so sorry I didn't make that clear to you. I had my doubts in the beginning," he admitted, "but not anymore."

This one time in her life, Brianna told herself that she wasn't going to jump to conclusions. "What are you saying exactly?"

His eyes met hers. "What I'm saying is that I love you and I want you to marry me."

"Are you sure?" she asked him. She didn't want to say yes and then have her heart broken again. She couldn't bear it. "I'll understand if you just got swept up in the moment and you want to back out—"

Putting his hand in his pocket, Connor took something out. And as Brianna watched in utter amazement, he got down on one knee, opened the box he'd taken out and offered her what was inside it.

The diamond ring caught the light, winking at her like a flirtatious young girl. Brianna stared at it, her breath caught in her throat.

"Does this look like I want to back out?" Because she was still utterly speechless, Connor went on to tell her, "I'm moving back to Houston for good—and in with you if you'll have me. So what do you say, Bri? Will you marry me?"

"Say yes, Mama! Say yes!"

They turned to see Axel standing in the doorway

with Ava right beside him, eagerly adding her voice to his. Axel had woken her up when he heard Connor talking to his mom.

"I guess it's unanimous," Brianna told Connor with a laugh.

"Good answer," Connor replied. Then he turned toward the children and told them, "I'm going to kiss your mom now, so, Axel, take your sister back to her bed, will you, son?"

Axel giggled in response to being called *son*, and Ava did, too. Taking his sister's hand, he led her back into their bedroom.

"This is as alone as we're going to get," Brianna told Connor.

"Fine with me," he said just before he lowered his lips to hers.

And it really was fine.

For all of them.

* * * * *

MILLS & BOON

Coming next month

HONEYMOONING WITH HER
BRAZILIAN BOSS
Jessica Gilmore

It was time.

Deangelo pushed himself to his feet and held out a hand. 'Come along.'

Harriet clutched her glass. 'What do you mean?'

'You wanted to learn how to be a Brazilian? Right there,' he nodded at the dance floor. 'That's where you'll find out.'

She clutched the glass harder. 'I can't go out there!'

'Why not? If he can…' he nodded at a rotund tourist, furiously jiggling away, his face serious as he tried to remember the steps his partner was teaching him. 'You definitely can.'

'But…' he didn't wait for her to finish the sentence, removing the glass from her hand and drawing her to her feet.

'The thing to remember about samba,' he said. 'Is you have to find the rhythm. It's three steps to two beats, the middle step is the quick one. Once you have that, then add bounce, keep your knees soft. So it's back, feet together, forward…' they were on the dancefloor and Deangelo swept her into his arms, murmuring the steps to her. 'That's it, back, together, forward, knees bent,